CRY OF THE PEACOCK

GINA BARKHORDAR NAHAI

CROWN PUBLISHERS INC., NEW YORK

Published by Crown Publishers, Inc.,
201 East 50th Street,
New York, New York 10022.
Member of the Crown Publishing Group.

CROWN is a trademark of Crown Publishers, Inc.

Manufactured in the United States of America

Library of Congress Cataloging-in-Publication Data
Barkhordar Nahai, Gina.
Cry of the peacock / Gina Barkhordar Nahai.
     p.   cm.
1. Jews—Iran—History—Fiction.   I. Title.
     PS3552.A6713C79   1991
813'.54—dc20   90-20311
                                                    CIP

ISBN 0-517-57479-9

Book Design by Shari de Miskey

10 9 8 7 6 5 4 3 2 1

First Edition

For my parents,
who gave me courage

My husband,
who said I should write

My children,
who have not seen the Persian sky

For the memory of my grandmother,
Heshmat Nik~Fahm Meraj,
Who died in America dreaming of Iran

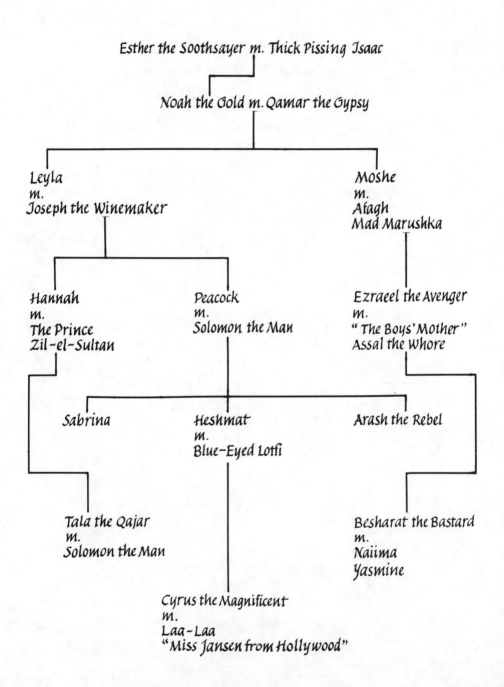

Prologue
1982

In the women's prison where the Guards had taken Peacock, six people slept in a cell designed for one. They sat on the floor, occupying every rat-infested inch, blindfolded and handcuffed for weeks in a row until they developed an infection and were executed or released. They ate twice a day—bread and walnuts thrown before them on the floor that was soiled with feces. Every morning the Guards took a number of prisoners outside before a firing squad. They removed the prisoners' blindfolds and lined them up against a concrete wall thickened with blood. They shot them—sometimes with real bullets, sometimes with blanks.

The mullahs used fake executions to extract a confession, or raise the amount of bribe each prisoner would offer for his release. The regime of God was avaricious and without mercy. It often arrested people not for any crimes they may have committed in the past, but for the single purpose of forcing them to pay the money they had hidden away or invested abroad. When all the money had been paid and all the confessions were made, the guns would be loaded and the prisoner would fall.

Blindfolded and bound in her cell, Peacock could hear the executions and count the number of prisoners who came back alive. She had been in jail for three weeks, and still no one had decided her fate. She had arrived one summer afternoon surrounded by Guards, sitting in the back of a military jeep with her face unveiled and her hair uncovered. She had sat there in her clothes that shocked the eye and defied all Islamic codes, in layers of bright chiffon and fiery silk, yellow scarves and sequined shirts and a gold-embroidered belt above a crushed velvet skirt.

She wore white schoolgirl stockings and satin shoes decorated with rhinestones and beads, a dozen gold bracelets, countless strands of pearls, rings on every finger. Her pockets were stuffed with gold and precious stones. In her shoes she had thousand-rial bills. Still, it was not her clothes that so shocked the mullahs, it was her age. Peacock the Jew was so old, they said, she remembered God when he was a child.

The mullahs had prisoners as young as six, and as old as ninety. They arrested women who had tried to stage a counterrevolution, and those who had worn nail polish and makeup. They imprisoned communists and nationalists, Jews and Baha'is, and, most of all, Muslims who refused to abide by the mullahs' rules. But they had never arrested someone as old as Peacock, and they were at a loss as to what to do with her.

The Guards took her into a detention cell. A woman in a full-length dress with long sleeves, and wearing a scarf to hide her hair, strip-searched Peacock and took all her jewels and money. She sent Peacock for interrogation.

"How old are you?" a young mullah asked Peacock without looking at her.

She stared at him.

"Answer!" he commanded.

He still had not looked at her.

"How old are you?"

"I was born the year of the Plague."

He looked up.

"*What* plague?"

He knew nothing of the past.

"*What* plague?" He stood up, breathing on her.

"Answer." He smelled of sweat and American whiskey.

I was born the year of the Plague, Peacock wanted to say, *and raised in a cave underground, with lice crawling the*

4

walls and scorpions in the dark and worms in every gulp of water I drank.

"*What* plague?"

The Guards took her into a cell. Weeks went by. She listened to executions every day. Her cellmates asked her the same questions.

"How *old* are you?"

The woman to Peacock's right was a Communist who said she believed in genocide. The one to her left was a housewife who never knew why she was arrested. Mehr-Allah the Guard, who stood in the corridor outside, was a father who had sent his children to war only because he believed they would die and go to heaven.

"Peacock!" he cried one morning as bullets exploded in the courtyard. He had come for her. They had decided her fate.

"Peacock!" he cried again, and she stumbled to her feet. The door opened. Mehr-Allah the Guard removed Peacock's blindfold. Light burned through to the back of her head. She stood up, dizzy, and held on to the wall for balance. When she could see through the light, she realized that Mehr-Allah was scrutinizing her.

"So how old *were* you?" he asked as if her life were over.

Peacock let go of the wall.

"I am a hundred and sixteen years old," she said, "and still, I intend to live."

Inside the cell on the floor, the Communist who said she believed in genocide wet her pants with laughter.

1796

Esther the Soothsayer was tall and wide-shouldered, her skin dark and shiny as the oil she rubbed on her stomach and hands to make them soft. Her eyes, black as the waters of the Gulf, were always dusted with a glossy powder made of silver nitrate. Her lips were thick, and red like the heart of a young bird. Her hair was long and wild and as dark as her eyes, her voice deep and throbbing and filled with mystery.

She had been born in the south, in the port city of Bandar 'Abbas, on the Persian Gulf. Like many Jewish women in the area, she had grown up working as a harem maid to the wives of wealthy Arab and Persian men. She sewed the women's clothes, braided their hair, delivered them of their children. And she practiced sorcery and witchcraft.

She said that she could look in the palm of a newborn child and tell of its destiny, make potions and write spells that made barren women pregnant, kept fear out of the hearts of old men, returned husbands gone astray. She went around collecting tools—pieces of cloth, skeletons of animals, lizards' and cats' tails, and strands of hair from dead virgins. She kept them all together in a locked chest for the day when one of her ladies came to her asking to poison a rival wife, or rot an in-law with smallpox.

"I bring you magic and good fortune and the knowledge of the dead," she whispered to the ladies of the harem in the Muslim accent she had learned to substitute for her own ghetto language.

"I can reach into your past, unveil the secrets of your sorrow. I know your sins and your longings. I can make your wishes come true."

Esther the Soothsayer could see the future in her dreams. Long ago, when she was still a child, she had foretold the death of sailors lost in the furious waters of the Persian Gulf. Later, before the first British ships had ever docked at Bandar 'Abbas, she had spent entire nights describing them to the women of the harem.

"They will come floating across the Gulf—giant mountains of wood—and aboard them will be men with eyes the color of the sea and skin that glistens like the moon."

Breathless, the women had listened to her tales of the future.

"The men will leave the ships and come into the city. They will seek our women, give them children with mist in their eyes and faraway mountains in their dreams. They will rob the rich of their wealth and the poor of their honor. But in return they will leave us with a gift far more precious than what they took: the knowledge," her voice had throbbed inside the harem walls, "of the world beyond."

She knew more than she said—tales so strange and unlikely that no one would have believed them, secrets so dark and frightening she held them to herself. She knew how to read people's eyes, walk into their dreams when they were asleep, and probe their minds.

But with all of her powers, Esther the Soothsayer was trapped in a life of loneliness and bondage. She was a Jew, born of a mother who had worked and died in the service of the Sheikh's family, inherited by him and doomed to spend her youth and desire as a slave without a face, until she was too old to work and they sent her back to die in the ghetto outside Bandar 'Abbas. She could never marry: no one but a Jew would marry her; no Jew would marry a girl who had been raised in a harem. She could have no children, no home of her own, no freedom.

Every night in the harem, she watched the wives paint their faces and color their lips, perfume their skin, wait for their husband to come and choose from among them. Afterward she lay in bed and imagined the wife in the folds of the Sheikh's arms, their bodies clinging like snakes, the sound of their breath marking the passage of time. She thought of the world outside the harem, outside Bandar 'Abbas. She thought of places she had seen in her dreams. She was fifteen years old and her flesh burned with the call of desire.

She began to leave the harem at night. She would wait till the wives had sunk into their beds and the eunuchs were asleep. Then she crept out across the vast, dry gardens of the Sheikh's house into the streets of Bandar 'Abbas. She wore a thin white veil reserved for Muslim women, took off the patch of yellow cloth that all Jews sewed on their clothes. She went to the harbor, breathing the air that smelled of burnt wood and the cries of fishermen lost in the waves, and watched the shadows of fishing boats and palm trees, as transparent as ghosts, reflected on the dark waters. She waited, her body moist with the unrelenting heat of the south, her hair damp and salty, her ears scratching with the sound of rats' feet running up and down trees. Sometimes a man would approach her.

"Take me away." She would smile at him with eyes darker than the night. "Love me till I'm old."

He would take her to his wooden shack by the sea and lay her naked on his rug. Esther the Soothsayer would close her eyes and pray for love. She smelled the vodka in her lover's sweat, the fear of the sea on his breath. At dawn she walked back with him to the harbor and watched him row slowly toward the sharks.

She went back every night, waiting, hoping for the man who would open his heart and feel her warmth, hold her in the morning and ask that she stay. She used all of her powers to convince the men, wrote spells and hid them in their hair, hung talismans above their beds. She walked into their dreams when they slept, conjured up the love they would never feel for her on their own. But all of the spells failed and all of her powers came short and still, Esther the Soothsayer was alone.

For three years she looked in Bandar 'Abbas. In the end, she came back empty-handed and more alone. One night she cried and prayed to the darkness for escape: "Save me," she asked the ghosts she knew so well. "Help me change my fate."

She fell asleep and dreamt of a land she had never before seen or heard of: a world of calm and plenty, a place where men loomed bigger than God, and gold blossomed in every field. She saw a palace, a structure built entirely of glass, where a king slept unafraid of the daggers of assassins. She saw men who commanded the power of God; women who walked the earth with pride; money and jewels and beauty such as she had never dared imagine.

"I will go there," she swore to the darkness. "I will walk there and never stop till I die."

The next day she took all her money and bought a place on a caravan bound for the north. For three weeks they traveled—the men riding in front, sitting cross-legged in wooden boxes that hung from the backs of camels and mules, the women walking behind the animals. At night they camped on the road, or in caravansaries along the way. Esther the Soothsayer kept to herself and pretended to be Muslim. When they reached Esfahan, she left the caravan and went to find the Jews' ghetto. She had come far enough, she thought. Destiny had lost track of her.

 The Jewish ghetto of Esfahan was called Juyy Bar. It was a collection of houses and shops, an old square, four synagogues, three public baths. It stood on barren ground—the earth beneath it composed of an impenetrable layer of clay that served as a good foundation for homes, but created shallow wells that soon dried. The wells were infested with worms—long, milky white creatures that crawled in staggering numbers from a never-ending source in the earth. They slid down the walls and into the water where they laid their eggs. Across the ghetto in Esfahan, the river Zayandeh-Rud—Life-giver—irrigated hundreds of acres of land and returned some of the best crops in the country. But water was controlled by the mullahs, and they denied it to the Jews.

In Juyy Bar, the Jews lived like ants trapped inside an underground hole. Their houses were all one-story high, built of mud and clay. The rooms were small and dark and without windows, separated from the courtyard by columns of red mud that were cracked and lopsided and on the verge of crumbling. In the courtyard there was a pool of stagnant water where women washed the day's clothes and dirty dishes, children bathed in the summer, and frogs screamed through the night. In one corner was the only toilet—an open hole in the ground. Next to the toilet was an underground oven that all the tenant families shared.

The Jews, as anywhere else in Persia, were considered impure and untouchable. They were not allowed to live and work outside their ghetto, to plant their own food or drink from public waters. The men wore red or yellow patches on their clothes, the women covered their faces with thicker veils than those reserved for Muslims. Anything a Jew touched became soiled forever. If accused of a crime, a Jew could not testify in his own defense. He could not even step out of the ghetto on a rainy day for fear that the rain may wash the impurity off his body and onto a Muslim's. Esther the Sooth-sayer looked at the ghetto and went cold. She had escaped the harem, she realized, but not her bondage.

She tried to find a place to live, and was met with re-fusing eyes and probing questions. The Jews had been talk-ing about her since she arrived. They said that she was a whore because she had traveled without a man, that she was godless because she claimed to know the future. They were suspicious because she spoke a different dialect, ate different food. They insisted on knowing why she had left Bandar 'Abbas.

"I have come to change my destiny," Esther the Sooth-sayer told them as if she were God. "I have come to leave my fate and find a new life."

No one understood.

She must have been *driven* out, they decided—punished by her own people and banned for a crime she had come here to hide. She must have been a thief, an adulteress, a whore. She must leave Juyy Bar and take away her corruption.

"Go!" Rabbi Yehuda the Just screamed at Esther in his Sabbath sermon. "Leave, and take your talismans and your spells."

Esther the Soothsayer could not fight the ghetto. But she had come to Esfahan for a reason, and for that she wanted to stay: out in the heart of the city that had once been the capital of Persia, she had been told, there was a palace built entirely of glass. She thought her dream had called her here.

She knew that if she were married, the Jews would not chase her out. She looked around and found Thick Pissing Isaac: a big man with a bald head and a shyness that made him look away every time she passed by. He owned the teahouse at the far end of the ghetto and lived alone. As a child, he had once sat with his friends to eat a bowl of soup. There was not enough for everyone, and the boys had started to fight. Desperate to eat and too shy to fight, Isaac had stood up in the midst of the quarrel and urinated in the soup. Then he had sat down, crying, and finished the food.

Esther the Soothsayer liked the story of Isaac's childhood. She liked his eyes that never dared look at her, his loneliness that reminded her of herself.

So she went to call on him—in his dreams at first, where she appeared every night and spoke his name—and by the time she knocked on his door late one night when all of Juyy Bar was asleep, she knew he would not refuse her warmth.

Thick Pissing Isaac lay terrified in his bed. He was awake, hours after midnight, listening to Esther call him. For many nights now he had been dreaming of her—a tall creature he thought he had seen before but could not place. In his sleep he had tried to remember who she was, strained his mind until it was dark. She stood so close to him he could smell her skin. Now at last she had spoken, and her voice had forced him awake.

So he went to her, drawn by her call and the need to feel her. He found her standing by his door, a shadow in the night, and even before he had touched her he knew that she was naked under the black chador, that her hair was unbraided and long and dark as her eyes, that her skin was soft, and her tongue blistering red.

She walked in and slipped into Isaac's bed—under the old comforter that smelled of tobacco and dust—and taught him what she had learned of love in the long and murky nights of Bandar 'Abbas. She went back to him every night, hiding in the darkness as she traveled the distance between his teahouse and the rubble where she stayed by day. Afraid his neighbors would see her come in, Isaac waited for her in the light of a candle, then closed the door and prayed that no one heard their whispers. He offered her tea and dates and all the food in the house. He was startled by her passion, filled with a thousand questions he dared not ask. He waited for her to speak first.

"Marry me," she told him, "and I will give you a son. I will stay in your house forever and you will never know pain."

Isaac lay beside her—cold, silent. He had been expecting the question, wondering what he would say when it came. If he married Esther he would be shamed forever, unable to look into the eyes of other men, ridiculed and ostracized by all his friends. No one married a woman he knew was not a virgin.

"She is old," he reasoned with himself, "perhaps eighteen, perhaps more. Her womb is tired, and infected with the seeds of other men. She may never give me a child, and if she does, I won't know that it is mine."

In the long silence that spread between them, Esther the Soothsayer read Isaac's doubts and became furious. She made love to him again, this time with anger, and all the while Isaac did not dare look in her eyes. Then she left his house and said she would never return.

Thick Pissing Isaac dreamt of her through nights of agony and anticipation. He saw himself lying beside her and woke up to find that he was alone. He stood by the teahouse all day in the hope that she might walk by his door. He could not stop wanting her; his flesh burned where she had touched him last. He went to look for her.

"Come back," he cried.

The next day they were married.

 The night of her wedding, Esther the Soothsayer became pregnant. She dreamt of a bird with blind eyes and silver wings—a giant who flew toward her out of the red desert sky and sent rats and scorpions digging the earth in their fury to hide. It came closer, its wings shimmering against the light, and just as the sun was about to rise, the bird landed in Esther's hands. It had a woman's breasts.

Esther the Soothsayer woke up and touched herself. Her face and neck were covered with moisture. Her hair had clung to her throat as if to choke her. She felt her stomach, her groin. She closed her eyes. It was dark. She saw her child.

She told Isaac that she carried a boy, that it would look nothing like anyone he had ever seen. She told him that he would be wise, that he would bring honor to their name, that he would walk in the sun one day with his arms full of glory and his eyes full of pride. Isaac wanted to believe her, but all of Juyy Bar was laughing.

The child, they said, would come before its time. It would look like an Arab, or a stranger, but nothing like Isaac himself. It must have been conceived out of wedlock—from Isaac, or perhaps another man. Esther must have come to Esfahan pregnant, run away from her own town to hide her shame and find a man simple enough to marry her.

"Watch yourselves," Rabbi Yehuda the Just warned the women of Juyy Bar in his sermons. "A child conceived in sin will bear the mark of his mother's dishonor."

Thick Pissing Isaac began to doubt and could not stop himself. He loved Esther, loved her smell, the echo of her voice. He wanted her and wanted the son she had promised him and he would have been content if only the ghetto had let him. But after a few weeks he could not help looking at Esther differently. He went to see Yehuda the Just.

"You must wait before you judge," the rabbi advised. He was trying to appear calm, but his eyes, Isaac would remember later, gleamed with excitement. "Count the weeks of your wife's pregnancy and mark the day she delivers. If she comes short of nine months and nine days, she is carrying a bastard. Then come see me and we will return just punishment."

A month went by, then another. Every night when he lay down, Thick Pissing Isaac put his hands on his wife's stomach and prayed that the child she carried was his. Then he went to sleep, leaving Esther terrified, awake, trapped. She knew the rumors about herself and the child. She knew the fate of adulterous wives. She had named her son Noah. She begged him to wait a full nine months before he claimed his place in the world.

But in the seventh month of their marriage, Esther the Soothsayer woke up one night to find her bed full of blood. She ran to the basement and locked the door.

She endured the labor alone, without a whisper, and for three days she did not leave the basement. She sat crouched above a tray full of ashes, dug her nails into the hard ground, and vomited with the force of every contraction until all the darkness had been jolted out of her and all her fears were purged and she felt nothing but the warmth of the child sliding out between her thighs.

Esther the Soothsayer wrapped her son in her chador, then buried the placenta. Outside, Yehuda the Just waited. She opened the basement door and walked toward her fate.

They had come since dawn, standing in huddles around the main square, in the doorways of houses and shops along the street, on top of the roofs overlooking the square. An hour before noon the heat became nauseating. Sweating under their black chadors and thick veils, women pressed their children against themselves and sighed expectantly. Men stood together, spitting on the ground every once in a while as they talked to one another about unrelated things. Their attention was elsewhere, their minds preoccupied with the anticipation of the event they had come to watch. Not since the death of Sabyah the Adulteress fifty years ago had a woman been punished in Juyy Bar.

At noon the wailing sound of the Muslim *namaz* rose from the minarets of Esfahan. Minutes later they brought Esther the Soothsayer—her face unveiled, her body uncovered, her legs bare. A woman who had lost her honor, Rabbi Yehuda the Just had ordained, must not appear in honest garb.

She walked to the center of the square and sat on the ground, crossing her legs under her skirt so as to cover them. She was still pale from the birth, bleeding so hard she had to keep herself wrapped in layers of cloth. Her breasts secreted a clear liquid that was bitter and tangy and without nutrition. The child she had borne—Noah the Gold—had to be nursed by strangers. Esther the Soothsayer had lost the will to fight, lost even the memory of what she had come to

Esfahan to seek. Her eyes were devoid of fire, her voice was no longer full of echoes.

Yehuda the Just allowed for an appropriate interval, then made his own entrance. In spite of the heat, he wore a long black coat, a white shirt buttoned to the top, a black hat. His red hair glowed in the sun and made his freckled skin look even more jaundiced. He stopped next to Esther the Soothsayer, looked at the audience, drew a breath. This was, he knew, his greatest moment.

He began his sermon.

"It is said in the Torah that an evil woman is like a snake," he started calmly, then turned away from the audience to face Esther herself. "She poisons the lives of her husband and children, and casts her seeds for generations after she is gone—so that the fruit of damnation will blossom in her house till eternity."

He saw Esther tremble, and was pleased. He had dreamt of this day, prayed for it over a lifetime of longing and anticipation. For twenty years he had been chief rabbi of his ghetto. He had spoken every sermon, observed every holiday, performed every wedding and every burial, and all the time he had prayed for the chance—the moment when he would be called to judge, to control the fate of another, set down the law.

"A *woman's* crimes go beyond individual harm," he screamed.

"Sins against family and honor reap nothing but blasphemy and the harvest of all things damned. A single act will corrupt society to its roots. One person's betrayal will cause the downfall of an entire community."

He paused. Sitting there before him, Esther the Soothsayer looked small—smaller than a child, smaller than the fairies that were born, in the tales of mad poets, of old women's sighs and the tears of virgin brides.

He could have come out in Esther's defense, he knew. He could have asked Isaac for proof of Esther's infidelity, considered the possibility that the child was born prematurely. He could have done what the Book really preached—asked for indulgence, demanded forgiveness, forbidden vengeance. He could have saved Esther and her child. But to do this, he would have to forgo his one chance at immortality.

"So the fate of one must be made into a lesson for all," he delivered the verdict.

"The *whore*"—he pointed at Esther—"must not be put to death, for revenge is not the message of the Torah. She must be shamed instead, in public, so that all who know her will bear witness to her crime and learn the consequences of her betrayal. So that—" he stopped. The silence was deafening. "So that she may go on living, shamed and without honor, never daring to show her face, never able to hide it."

Far away in his teahouse where he still saw Esther's shadow, Thick Pissing Isaac pressed his hands over his ears and cried like a child.

When the rabbi had finished his sermon, David the Butcher's son came forward with his blade. He grabbed Esther's hair in his left hand, pulled it back so that her chin pointed upward and he could see the rapid pulse of the vein that ran up the side of her neck. He began to shave her hair.

David the Butcher's son wished he had never accepted this task. He was a good butcher, quick and honest and cleaner than most. In his shop he could pluck five chickens at one time: He held their legs in between his fingers and slit their throats, plucked them so fast they would dash across the shop with their skin bare and their heads hanging over the side of their necks until the last drop of blood had rushed out of them and they fell to the ground. He could skin sheep faster than any man in the ghetto, clean out the intestines and the stomach before the water for the stew had begun to boil. But a woman's head he had never shaved before. As soon as he put the blade to Esther's head it became entangled, and he had to force it out, pulling her hair and in the process cutting her scalp. Blood dripped from every patch of skin he had managed to lay bare.

He took an hour to shave Esther's head. Hair piled high on the ground around her feet. Blood licked her scalp, her face, her neck. With her hair gone, her eyes looked larger than usual. Her face was pale, thin—like a series of lines etched together into reality. David the Butcher's son looked at her then and knew he had sinned. For weeks after the punishment, every animal he slaughtered in his shop would have empty veins. He would bury them in the ground and take a loss: Kosher laws barred the Jews from eating an animal with no blood. Muslims would not buy meat from a Jew. David the Butcher stuffed the earth under his shop full of dead roosters and lamb, and he knew all along he was paying for his crime against the Soothsayer.

He tied Esther's hands behind her back and raised her on her legs. He reached into a bag on the ground and took out a lamb's stomach—white, slithery, glistening with moisture. He pulled the stomach over Esther's shaved head. Then he lifted her by the waist and placed her on the back of a mule.

He guided the mule out of the square. The crowd stepped back reluctantly. At the end of the street that led away from the square, Parvaneh the Professional Mourner made her way toward them. For thirty-seven years she had been married to a man who dragged himself on two stumps that had never grown into legs. She came forward, looking into Esther's face, the corners of her mouth twitching with disdain, and spat at Esther.

"I remained chaste."

All of that day, David the Butcher's son paraded Esther in Juyy Bar. He banged a wooden stick on the outside of a tin can and sang as he walked.

"Come one, come all, and see the whore of Juyy Bar."

His voice became hoarse and his arms ached and his feet grew blistered, but still he went on. Long into the night, the punishment completed, he stopped. He untied Esther's hands and gave her back her chador.

"Go," he said without looking at her.

For a long time after she had left Juyy Bar, Esther the Soothsayer had the sensation of traveling through the familiar. Once or twice she even turned around to look back at the ghetto. Behind her, Juyy Bar shrank under the sun, its gates and many arched roofs getting smaller as Esther walked away from them into the city that had been the pride of Persia for so many centuries.

But here, too, the houses were dirty and crowded and half-ruined. The streets were narrow and dark, the children hungry and haggard. The old men who sat smoking opium on their doorsteps were yellow-skinned and toothless, their eyes eaten by trachoma, their faces marked by the smallpox that had plagued their childhoods.

She came to a long and very narrow street with quiet houses where the doors were closed and the air was heavy with an uneasy silence. There were no people here, no one walking on the street, no children playing. The doors were all painted the same faded gray. From behind some of them Esther thought she heard the hushed whispers of women and the muffled cries of infants. She stopped, overcome by the fear she had carried from Juyy Bar, the instinctive warning of a danger she could not identify: beyond the veil of silence that spread over the street and its houses, she heard the rhythmic, metallic sound of camel bells approaching.

Suddenly she realized there were eyes staring at her, peering through the doors on both sides of the alley. She imagined faces watching her, imagined she heard the sound of breathing and whispers. She had come to the Castle.

This was the street where all of Esfahan's prostitutes

22

lived with their "keepers" and their many bastard children. They stayed inside most of the time, waiting, with their faces veiled and their bodies covered, for night to fall and Muslim men hiding in the darkness to call on them. The men would slip through unmarked doors and into small rooms where they waited, along with a dozen others, for their turn. One by one they would crawl into beds that smelled of sweat and dirt and the bodies of other men. They took from the women's bodies their many diseases and left in them the seeds of children who would grow up fatherless, doomed to watch their mothers lie with strangers every night until the boys were old enough to leave home, and the girls ripe enough to be sold as virgins.

But the Castle was forbidden to Jewish men. The prostitute who held a Jew's body with her own would forever become soiled, and in turn contaminate the Muslims who came to her afterward. Thick Pissing Isaac had told Esther about the Castle. Years ago a Jewish man had taken off the yellow patch on his robe and slept with a prostitute here. His body had not betrayed him, for Muslims, like Jews, circumcised their boys. But in the euphoria of his first experience with love he had forgotten himself, and dared to speak to the woman. She had known his way of speaking, the garbled language of Esfahani Jews that was a mixture of ancient Farsi, Arabic, and incorrect Hebrew. She had called her keeper, who had come with three others, tied the Jew to a tree, and cut off his penis.

Esther heard footsteps and turned around. Behind her in the alley, under an opening in the arched roof where sunlight shone in the shape of a perfect cylinder, she thought she saw Yehuda the Just.

She began to walk again, away from Yehuda the Just, toward the distant music of the bells. She rushed down the alley, past the houses that stretched on either side of her, toward the mouth of a tunnel that opened where the Castle ended. When she had got closer she realized that the tunnel was three steps underground and pitch dark. She went in.

The stale air froze the beads of perspiration on her face. She walked down a dirt track that sloped first deeper into the earth and then slowly rose, up seven steps that took her out of the tunnel and into the abandoned cobblers' bazaar, past the small shops all boarded up and forgotten, toward an opening at the end of the corridor where she could see daylight. Her eyes were fixed on the light, her body overtaken by its own momentum. One more step and she was out.

She stopped. She peeled off the lamb's stomach from her head, threw away her chador. It was dawn in Persia. Esther the Soothsayer was at last free.

 All around her was endless, open space. The street was wide and long, paved with cobblestones and lined with old willow trees that shivered lightly in the late afternoon breeze. The air, pale blue and sweet, smelled of jasmine and apples. Water flowed in the gutters, like streams of liquid glass. Farther behind the trees and the gutters, brick walls reached to the end of the street.

Above her the sky was calm, not oppressive, an infinity of light and colors that stretched over the roofs of houses—red brick and marble and tiles. The horizon was dotted by brown minarets and the blue domes of mosques. Far away, she could see the green jade columns of the Shah's Square: the sun was red, sinking into the glass walls of the Palace of Forty Pillars.

Esther the Soothsayer stood, belittled. She heard the sound of trumpets and drums, of women's cries and men's cheers. A crowd had appeared at the end of the street, an excited congregation of people and colors and sounds. Esther raised herself on the small platform alongside a wall and looked: Agha Muhammad Shah had come to Esfahan. His cavalcade was passing through Char Bagh Street.

Esther the Soothsayer saw a two-humped camel in front, covered with purple embroideries, ridden by the Supreme

Marshal of the Imperial Camel Drivers. Behind it was a train of Arabian camels loaded with trunks, two bells hanging from heavy silver chains on each of their flanks. They were followed by the Royal Mule—cloaked in ornaments and draperies, ridden by the High Chief of the Shah's Mule Drivers. Three hundred other mules followed, charged with tents and equipment, carrying bells of different shapes and sizes.

There was a pause. Then came a procession of riflemen. They were dressed in black tunics and riding boots, rifles slung over their shoulders, each wearing two belts of cartridges. Behind them rode the "Shah's Warriors," carrying no weapons except ornamental swords.

A multicolored parade of high officials and royal attendants, of courtiers and pages, of seers and astrologers and spies followed. The men all wore elaborate outfits of embroidered silk and velvet, rode Arabian horses with tails painted red to show the purity of their stock.

Then came the eunuchs—beautiful young boys with pale faces and arched eyebrows, dressed in bejeweled gowns, looking forlorn and nostalgic.

Esther the Soothsayer left her corner and approached the procession. The crowd was fighting to get closer to the cavalcade. Bodies pressed forward, hands grabbed blindly. He had come to their town, Agha Muhammad Shah, the King of Kings, the Shadow of God. He had come, and the people's lives would never be the same for having seen him.

There was another procession of the Shah's Warriors, then a string of children—boys and girls with lucky faces, whose very presence, the Shah believed, guarded him against evil. A single horseman galloped at full speed:

"HIS IMPERIAL MAJESTY!" he cried. "THE SHADOW OF ALLAH!"

A shower of gold poured on Esther. She looked up. The sun had burst into a million particles—tiny circles of shimmering gold that danced in the fluorescent air as two dozen riders threw coins at the crowd.

The Shah's carriage rolled slowly—a giant construction

of enameled walls and gold-trimmed doors, decorated with jewels. Around it walked young women with white lace chadors and gold veils. They threw fistfuls of offerings at the carriage—cherry and apple blossoms, almond candies, mint leaves and cinnamon, pomegranate seeds the color of the rubies on the eunuchs' robes, violets and roses and jasmine— mounds and mounds of white jasmine.

The carriage slowed, then stopped. A pale hand moved the velvet curtain shielding the glass portal and revealed the face of His Majesty. Fire moved up from Esther's legs, into her thighs, her stomach, her chest. She knew Agha Muhammad Shah. She had seen him in the quiet of her dreams.

 Darkness was fast seeping into the air. The crowd was moving behind the Shah's caravan into the square outside the Palace of Forty Pillars. Esther the Soothsayer walked with them—to find the eunuch Shah.

She knew Agha Muhammad Khan's future. She had seen his death. Long ago, when she was still in the harem and he was not yet king, she had heard tales of his battles and of his quest for the throne. One night she was caring for the Sheikh's blind daughter—rubbing gold dust into her eyes to make her regain her sight. She had put the child to sleep, and gone to wash her own hands. She had looked into her palm, all shimmery and golden, and seen the Shah die.

Esther the Soothsayer had been frightened by the knowledge, aware that if she revealed it, she would be sought by the King and put to death. For years she had kept the secret to herself, but tonight she had no more fears, and she would speak.

In the year 1789 a new dynasty had come to Persia. For years before that the country had been at war, torn among rival tribes and warriors and heirs to old and defunct dynasties who commanded regional power, but could not unite the entire nation. Then Agha Muhammad Khan had prevailed.

He was a young man, heir to the throne of one faction of the Turkic Qajar tribe that ruled in the northwestern part of Persia. He was ugly and cruel and unforgiving, driven by a rage that came from deep within and that painted his throne in blood. As a child he had been taken prisoner by the leader of the Zand tribe and held hostage in their court at Shiraz. He had been castrated—to ensure he would not father a son that may someday avenge him—but raised with all the esteem due a royal prisoner. Still, every day as he grew older, Agha Muhammad Khan found himself more engulfed by hatred.

In 1789 Agha Muhammad Khan escaped the Zand court, rode back to his tribal lands, and declared himself leader of the Qajars. He waited for the Zand king to die. Then he led an army into Shiraz, blinded the heir apparent, and killed him by torture. From there he rode to conquer Persia.

He fought regional kings and warrior tribes, rebels and thieves and ordinary men he suspected of treason. In Kerman he had his troops rape all the women, blind twenty thousand men, and build a pyramid with the skulls of the victims. In Tiflis he killed the sick and the old, carried everyone else into slavery. In Tehran he promised his brother the governorship of Esfahan, lured him in this way into the palace, then ordered his death. He imprisoned destitute peasants, threatened death, and released them for a ransom. All of Persia trembled at the mention of Agha Muhammad Khan's name.

From a distance, Esther the Soothsayer could distinguish the Shah's Square, surrounded by rows of two-story brick shops with small balconies made of green marble. Night was falling and the square faded in darkness. Moments later a tiny light appeared where the square had been. The light flickered for an instant, then asserted itself. Another flame was ignited, and another. From every corner of the square, light bloomed until the entire structure lit up—shone—glared in the dark.

Five thousand oil lamps were burning in a space no larger than 450 by 60 feet—five thousand tiny lamps with shades of fine crystal that Shah Abbas the Great had commissioned in Esfahan two hundred years ago. They were everywhere, hanging from the walls, the pillars, the balconies, all of them hand-painted in soft pink and red colors—the soul of Shah Abbas still alive.

As the Shah's cavalcade approached the square, rows of well-dressed young men made deep bows before His Majesty: they had been chosen for their good looks, and put on parade at the sides of the street for the Shah to observe. Once in a while the royal carriage would stop, and the Shah would call forth one of the boys, who ran to him, terrified and honored at once, and presented himself before His Majesty.

Past the rows of young men, the Shah was received by a group of Pishnamaz—mullahs who chanted with all their might, praying for His Majesty's health. As they sang, they sacrificed dozens of oxen and sheep, and threw the animals' bleeding heads under the feet of the Shah's horses. Dervishes also sang in prayer for the Shah. They had glass vases, filled with sugar, which they threw to the ground and broke before his carriage.

Inside the square, street vendors and artists had spread their merchandise on display. Poets with trained voices and grand gestures recited verses from the Book of Kings. Acrobats danced among the crowd; actors re-created the Battle of Karbala, where the prophet Muhammad's third disciple, Hussein, had become a martyr:

In mid-battle, his forces on the retreat, Hussein was trying to carry water to his wounded soldiers. He was a young man with innocent eyes and the face of an angel. His archenemy and opposing general, Yazid, was tall and large and ugly, his face painted with deep black lines that made him look evil.

"Stop!" Yazid roared, intercepting Hussein's path. "May water never reach the lips of your dying men."

Hussein defied Yazid and continued on his way.

"Stop, I command thee!" Yazid raised his sword and pretended to cut off Hussein's right arm. Water spilled on the ground, mixing with blood.

Hussein let out a scream. Then he picked up the pouch of water with his left hand and continued to walk toward his thirsty soldiers.

Yazid's sword tore through the air again. When it came down, it took Hussein's left arm.

This time there was no cry of pain. Hussein bent down and took the pouch between his teeth.

The women in the audience were sobbing. The men had started flagellating themselves.

Shocked by Hussein's courage, Yazid hesitated for a moment. Then he raised his sword a last time and in one blow beheaded the third Imam. Hussein became the first martyr in Shiite Islam: he died for belief, sacrificed his life to fight injustice.

On the verge of the battleground, peasants sold sheep and horses, chiropractors advertised cures for rheumatism and old age, doctors sat on the ground, cross-legged on small rugs, and waited for patients. On one side of the square, women were displayed in front of tents, their keepers ready to negotiate a price. Shiite Islam allowed a man to take three lifelong wives and as many "temporary" ones as he liked. He could marry them for five minutes, or ninety-nine years.

Someone grabbed at Esther. It was a beggar—a young woman with a child asleep at her breast. Her bare nipple was covered with bleeding scabs and hungry flies.

On the northern corner of the square was the Shah's Mosque—tall and mighty and as vain as God himself. Directly opposite the Mosque was the Ali Ghapoo—the entrance to the Palace of Forty Pillars, a threshold considered so holy that no one, not even the Shah, would ever cross it on horseback. It was here that convicted criminals and petty thieves had taken refuge in the time of Shah Abbas the Great. No one but the Shah himself could have touched them here. They stayed, waiting for royal pardon. Even if denied, they would not be driven away from Ali Ghapoo. They would only be refused access to food or water, faced with the choice of starving in royal refuge or dying at the hands of pursuers outside.

On either side of the Ali Ghapoo were platforms, three feet high and built entirely of green jade. Here sat the best of the country's jewelers and silk merchants. Lured by tales of Agha Muhammad Shah's obsession with wealth, they had spread their wares on black velvet in the hope he would inspect them on his way to the palace.

Agha Muhammad Shah had not planned a stop. He was eager to reach the palace and rid himself of the royal clothes and the entourage. But he saw the jewels, his avarice got the best of him, and he called his caravan to a halt; he could show an interest in any or all of the precious stones, and the vendors would beg that he take them as gifts. Other kings would accept the gift and reward the vendor with gold ten times the value of his stone. Agha Muhammad Shah took what he had been offered and gave nothing in return.

So he stopped, and his caravan dismounted. Ministers bowed and the vendors prostrated themselves and soldiers formed a ring around His Majesty's carriage to protect him from the crowd. Then at last the carriage door opened and out stepped a small man with a shriveled face and tiny eyes full of suspicion. His skin was pale, smooth, hairless. His lips were thin, rigid. He wore soldiers' clothes—a long coat, dark boots. Around his waist he had a jewel-studded belt and a royal dagger. His buttons were diamonds.

A gasp went through the crowd. Agha Muhammad Shah acknowledged only Fath Ali Mirza—his nephew and crown prince who had accompanied him on this trip. Together they walked toward the platform full of jewels and admired each display.

"May I be your sacrifice?" An old man with a white beard approached the Shah. It was Shaaban, once Esfahan's greatest jewelers, now bankrupt because of his opium habit. Trembling, he offered the Shah an enormous ruby that he claimed was priceless.

"This is the greatest stone I have ever possessed," he said. "It is not worthy of your meanest servants, but I would be eternally grateful, Your Majesty, if you were to accept it as a small gift." His voice broke at every word.

Agha Muhammad Shah saw the glow of the ruby, and his face blossomed with pleasure. He was about to accept the gift when he heard a scuffle behind him and turned.

"Step back." A woman's cry echoed through the square. "Move, or I will damn your soul to hell."

Esther the Soothsayer had pushed through the crowd and intercepted the ring of soldiers around the Shah. She was bald and unveiled, her scalp covered with wounds, her face streaked with blood.

She came up to Agha Muhammad Shah, raised a finger, and told him his death:

"Beware," she said, "of the avenging hands of slaves."

Agha Muhammad Shah drew his sword, but it did not frighten Esther.

"Hands shall reach across the night," she said, "into your bed cool and calm and unafraid, and when you close your eyes to dream of conquest, they shall take your life to save their own."

Agha Muhammad Shah let out a demonic scream, and attacked Esther. He struck only a soldier, who fell, beheaded, on the ground. Where Esther the Soothsayer had stood a moment before, there was only darkness.

For months after the incident in the Shah's Square, Agha Muhammad Shah had his soldiers search Esfahan for the bald soothsayer with the thrashing tongue. They looked in every neighborhood and every house, even came to Juyy Bar and searched in the basements and on the roofs. They described the vision the Shah had seen.

"It's Esther the Soothsayer," said Rabbi Yehuda the Just, proudly identifying his victim. "Don't look for her in this ghetto. She has been banned, and will never return."

Determined to find Esther, the soldiers divided their forces and traveled to every province and town within a twenty-league radius of Juyy Bar. They looked in the caves of the Zagros Mountains, in the wineries of Shiraz. They searched the ruins of Persepolis, and the dwellings of nomadic tribes scattered across the Great Persian Desert. Everywhere, they told the story of Esther the Soothsayer and spread her name like a tale. In the end, they went trembling back to the Shah, and admitted failure. The woman in the square, they swore, was not alive. She was a ghost, an evil spirit sent by the Jews to bring the Shah bad fortune. The Crown Prince, Fath Ali Mirza, had conducted his own search for Esther the Soothsayer and met no results. Still, Agha Muhammad Shah was not satisfied. He ordered the death of all those who had failed him, then left Esfahan.

"Until you find the soothsayer," he told Esfahan's governor, "I will deprive your city of my attention and benevolence."

He rode to Khorasan in search of an old enemy: Sharukh, who was sixty years old and heir to the throne of a defunct dynasty. Though he had no political power, Sharukh had inherited a great treasure of jewels, which he had hidden in case of an enemy attack. Agha Muhammad Shah captured Sharukh and asked for his treasure. Sharukh denied it had ever existed. The Shah ordered torture. One by one, Sharukh surrendered the stones.

"No more," he pleaded as hot oil was poured into his eyes. "There is no more."

Agha Muhammad Shah was not content. He wanted the greatest jewel of them all, the famous Aurangzeb ruby, which Sharukh defended with his life.

The Shah had Sharukh stand on his feet, placed a circle of paste around his head, and, onto the paste, poured molten lead. Sharukh gave up the ruby, then died.

A year had passed since Esfahan. In 1797, Agha Muhammad Shah rode to Georgia, to attack his longtime enemy, Erekle. On his way one night, he was awakened by the sound of two servants quarreling. Irritated by the disturbance, he ordered that the men be hanged in the morning. Then he went back to sleep, and left the men unguarded to complete their tasks before the hour of execution.

They crept into his tent and killed him.

 War broke out in Tehran. In the aftermath of Agha Muhammad Khan's assassination, rival cousins and heirs to the Shah each contested the vacant throne and refused to submit to the authority of the crown prince, Fath Ali Mirza. A year later, in 1798, Fath Ali Shah was at last crowned.

He was young and handsome and vain, interested more in wealth and women than in diplomacy. He had four permanent wives, eighty-four temporaries. He had three thousand eunuchs, a hundred tailors, dozens of jewelers and biographers. He did not like the Palace of Qajars. He built another—the Palace of Roses—and filled its harem with a thousand temporary wives. He spent his days posing for portraits, listening to odes he had commissioned, designing new clothes for himself and his courtiers. He sat on his throne, surrounded by five of his favorite eunuchs, and watched the procession of virgins he had sent for across the country.

Still, with every day that went by, Fath Ali Shah found himself more startled by the reality of his uncle's assassination, and the accuracy of the soothsayer's prophecy. Agha Muhammad Shah, Fath Ali believed, could have escaped his fate, tricked time and place, and hidden away from the Angel of Death. He had only to bring faith, but he had been too vain.

Fath Ali Shah, by contrast, had such faith in the power of seers that he consulted astrologers about the smallest details of his life. The day was divided into opportune and evil moments, and the astrologers warned the Shah about each one. He had a watch that he carried everywhere: every entry and exit, every act and every word, had to take place at the exact time determined by the astrologers.

The Crown Prince, Abbas Mirza, and his Vizir, Qa'im Maqam, recognized Fath Ali's obsession with the matter, and tried in vain to explain to him the absurdity of his belief. They warned him of the danger of placing his trust in the words of seers and soothsayers, but Fath Ali Shah had the last word: Abbas Mirza died before the king. His Vizir learned to bite his lips and contain his outrage. Fath Ali Shah, meanwhile, informed his advisers that the greatest question of all, the issue of His Majesty's life and death, had yet to be resolved: no one dared chance the Shah's wrath by predicting the manner and time of his end. Faced with the impotence of his own servants, Fath Ali Shah once again ordered a search for Esther the Soothsayer.

Across Persia, messengers and troops cried her name and heard only silence. Convinced that she was a ghost, they called on every magician and sorcerer and mullah, and met no results.

"Speak our death," Fath Ali Shah beseeched, but though she heard his voice and recognized his plea, Esther the Soothsayer did not respond.

Esther the Soothsayer traveled north, through Persia and beyond, and discovered with her eyes what she had already known in her dreams. She grew old, grew wise, and although she never found a home or a man, in the end she found peace: she had rebelled against her destiny and cast the lines of her dreams into the hearts of her children, and for this alone, she knew she had triumphed.

She never wore a chador after Juyy Bar, never grew her hair. She stayed bald, silent. Her eyes were dark, her skin unctuous, and she looked so striking and so strange that no one dared stop her to ask her name. They saw her arrive and stood back in awe; the earth trembled where she stepped.

It was this tremor—the sound of Esther the Soothsayer walking in freedom—that would drive Thick Pissing Isaac to madness. He heard it first a week after her punishment and thought it was real:

"*Earthquake!*" he screamed, and ran out of the teahouse, but no one followed him.

"*Earthquake!*" he screamed again. "*Come out or you'll be buried!*"

On the street, people were calm, staring at him in surprise. Thick Pissing Isaac was confused and embarrassed.

"I *felt* something," he tried to explain, but already the ground was trembling under his feet again. "There. There. It's shaking." He was alone.

He told himself it was a temporary state, a result of the upheaval of the last months, and that he would recover once his nerves had calmed and he had managed to forget Esther the Soothsayer. He closed the teahouse and confined himself to his room, where he tried to rest. But inside the house, the tremor became stronger and the sound of the world falling apart drove him to even greater fear and he became terrified of walls. He longed for the comfort of Esther the Soothsayer's bed.

She had disappeared so fast after the punishment that

people in Juyy Bar believed she had died. She had killed herself, they said—dug a hole in the desert and buried her face until she stopped breathing and her body was devoured by beasts. Or she had been taken by bandits who raped her and left her to die. Perhaps she had gone home, to Bandar 'Abbas, and thrown herself in the Gulf to drown.

Thick Pissing Isaac wanted to find her now and inhale her breath. He wanted to close his eyes, lie in the dark, and listen to her speak of the past and the future. He wanted to smell her skin and cry at her breast and ask her—ask her until the doubts had faded and his friends' laughter had subsided, and he could believe. He wanted her now, but she was gone. Thick Pissing Isaac had betrayed her, he realized, and he would find no peace or happiness until he had calmed her rage.

He went to call on Mama the Midwife, who had been assigned the task of caring for Esther's child. Isaac had heard stories about Noah—people filing into Mama the Midwife's house every day, asking to see the boy, leaving stunned and amazed only to return the next day, and the day after. He had never seen the boy before. He asked to see him now.

"Why?" Mama the Midwife protested.

"Bring him."

Mama the Midwife went into the back room, and returned with Noah still wrapped in Esther the Soothsayer's chador. She pulled back the cover from Noah's face and watched Isaac go pale.

Noah the Gold was a shining star. He had lustrous skin, golden hair, eyes the color of yellow agates. He had long limbs, strong features, a captivating smile. When they had first brought him to her on the day of his birth, Mama the Midwife had thought he was an angel. She had taken him up on her roof and left him there under a straw basket for God to take. For three days she had stood watch. Every time there was a wind or a change of the weather, she thought that Noah's soul had been whisked away. But when at last she lifted the basket, she found him still alive. She thought God had sent him to change her life.

"Leave him to me," she now asked Thick Pissing Isaac. "Let me raise him."

Thick Pissing Isaac was choked with anguish. He shook his head in refusal.

"It will be *my* penance," he said, "to raise this child I have made motherless."

And so Noah the Gold grew up in Isaac's home and learned to accept his pain. In the years that followed, he watched Isaac preoccupied only with his guilt—the vision of the world coming apart, of the house crumbling and the sky falling every time Esther the Soothsayer walked another step. He learned the story of his birth, the fate of his mother. He knew Esther; every night when he slept, she came walking into his eyes.

 "In the beginning, there was a dream," Esther the Soothsayer whispered to her son in the warmth of the light she had brought to his darkness. She took his hand and led him through a path glistening with sunlight—a long, warm tunnel of white—and at the end of it she stopped and painted a tale onto the sky.

"Astyages, king of the Medes, dreamt that a vine grew out of his daughter's side and consumed Asia. He called his seers to interpret the dream.

"'The gods are warning you,' his seers told the king. 'Your daughter will one day have a son who will drive you from the throne and conquer Asia.'

"Astyages believed them.

"He married his daughter off and sent her to live in a neighboring kingdom. She bore a son. Astyages stole the child and ordered him killed, but a servant saved the boy.

He took the child into the mountains, and gave him to a shepherd to raise. The king's shepherd named the boy Cyrus.

"Cyrus became a soldier, rebelled against Astyages, conquered Babylon. There he came upon a tribe of Jews—descendants of slaves brought by Nebuchadnezzar when he destroyed the Second Temple. Cyrus freed the Jews. He commanded the entire Persian tribe, became the founder of the Persian Empire.

"'I am Cyrus,' he said, 'King of the World.'"

Noah the Gold was three years old when he first heard the story of Cyrus. He was tall and exuberant, filled with the smell of life, undaunted by fear or pain. He went out all day and played with the other boys, pursued them on the street and invited them with his eyes and his smile until their mothers tired of warning them against the bastard son of Esther the Soothsayer. He sat with Isaac's customers in the winery and engaged them in conversation until they forgot that Noah had been the cause of Isaac's downfall. He even went to temple—Yehuda the Just's temple—and after every Sabbath sermon, he stood in the courtyard until the rabbi came to drive him away: "That child is evil," Yehuda warned, but after a while the Jews stopped listening. Noah the Gold became the ghetto's adopted son.

"The children of Cyrus had a God." Esther the Soothsayer brought with her a breath of light and laughter, a cool breeze of a flame that burned the night open and flooded his darkness with blue sky.

"Ahura Mazda, God of Persians, fathered twin sons. He gave each the will to choose. The one, Ohrmazd, opted for light and life and benevolence. The other, Ahriman, chose death and darkness and evil. Ahura Mazda divided the world between his sons. Ohrmazd created the heavens and the earth. Ahriman created demons and death.

" 'It is not,' Ahriman said to his father, 'that I am *incapable* of good. It is that I *choose* evil.'

"To prove to the world his ability for greatness, Ahriman created the Peacock."

In the teahouse, Thick Pissing Isaac became paralyzed with fear. His world had trembled for so long that after a few years he began to shake with it. His step became unsure and his hands were unsteady and he jumped and jolted so often he could barely hold a cup of tea for fear it would spill and burn him. Noah the Gold offered to work. He was six years old but capable, and though Thick Pissing Isaac had resented him all his life, he had no choice but to accept.

"On the heels of the Great Emperor came the great invaders." Far in the distance, where Esther the Soothsayer had raised her arm, Noah the Gold saw the armies of Alexander the Greek march on Persia.

"In Persepolis, the capital of Cyrus, Alexander married a Persian princess—Roxana—and took a thousand Persian wives for a thousand of his own soldiers. Soon after, one night he became drunk on the wine of Shiraz and burned Persepolis to ruin.

"Behind him came the Turks, then the Muslims.

"A man rose in the Arabian Peninsula, a prophet and warrior called Muhammad. He spoke of a new God, created a new empire."

By the age of ten, Noah the Gold ran the teahouse alone. He supported himself and Thick Pissing Isaac, who did nothing now but tremble like a dog and whisper—for he had neither scream nor conviction left in him—"*Earthquake. Earthquake. Earthquake.*"

To stop the trembling, Isaac drank chamomile brew and cowslip tea, which calmed his nerves and made him sleepy, so that he walked around all the time in a daze, numb from sleep but still trembling like an old opium addict. Then slowly he began to smoke opium. It created a temporary state of calm, and allowed him to sleep without feeling that his bed was about to gape open and swallow him every few minutes. To keep the calm, he smoked larger doses, more frequently, until he became so dependent he refused to move from the side of the brazier where he heated and smoked the opium.

"For seven hundred years the Arabs ruled Persia, governing through the caliphs in Baghdad.

"Islam brought an age of enlightenment, a revival of the arts and sciences, a tolerance of other religions.

"But in the fourteenth century, Ismael I became king of Persia, and declared his independence from the Arab Empire. The Arabs were mostly Sunni Muslims. To mark the break, Ismael I made Persia Shiite.

"Shiism ruled through its mullahs—God's messengers who spoke to him directly, and conveyed his word to the believers.

"The mullahs declared the followers of all other religions, even Sunni Muslims, impure and untouchable. The world, they said, should be ruled only by Shiite priests. Everyone else, most of all the Shahs, were usurpers of God's name and undeserving of their wealth and power."

Thick Pissing Isaac could no longer feel the effects of opium. He resorted to smoking *shireh*—a much more potent creation that was made from the burned residue of opium, which he boiled into a paste and smoked. But after a few years, even the *shireh* failed him.

"Call your mother," he begged Noah in the days before his death. "Tell her to forgive."

Mullah Mirza was Juyy Bar's oldest and most feared doctor. He was called Mullah—really the title of Muslim priests, but which the Jews used to refer to anyone with special knowledge—and Mirza, which meant doctor, designating anyone who could read. He was small and bony, his thin face fringed with a stringy beard that grew down to his navel. Long ago it had been black, then gray, white, silver—until it had finally turned yellow and stayed that color. His eyebrows, thick and bushy and long, had refused to follow the pattern of the beard. They had stayed dark, creating a shocking contrast with the rest of his face. Underneath them his eyes were cunning and sharp, full of boundless greed and the ambition that had been the Mirza's driving force in life and that became more furious the closer he felt himself to the grave. He had three yellow teeth in his mouth—two on top and one on the bottom—rheumatism in his legs, and a bad twitch that made his head and neck jerk to the right whenever he got excited. His fingers, gnarled with age and yellow from the tobacco he smoked incessantly, were nevertheless strong and steady. He was always feeling the objects around him restlessly, as if driven by a compulsion to discover their secrets, or to possess them.

People said that in his youth Mullah Mirza had set out to become a scientist. His father, a small-time doctor in Juyy Bar, had one day brought home an enormous volume written partly in Persian and partly in Arabic. He attributed the book to the great Persian scientist Zakarayah Razi.

"In it," he had told his son, "beyond the reach of ordinary men, lies the secret of infinite wealth and everlasting power."

Poet, philosopher, mathematician, and chemist at once, Razi had devoted his life to the pursuit of alchemy and in the process discovered alcohol instead. Never satisfied with his discovery, he had always felt himself one step away from the formula that would turn any ordinary metal into gold. He had died blinded and impoverished, leaving behind vol-

41

ume after volume made of deerskin, in which he had registered the results of his experiments.

Mullah Mirza was fascinated by Razi's story. He had opened the book and run his hand over the symbols he could not decipher.

"My God," he had whispered, "to possess all that gold."

The next day he had announced that he was going to become literate in Persian and Arabic. His father had laughed.

"Jews don't learn anything but Hebrew," he had said. "Arabic is the language of the Qoran. The mullahs say that if we study it, we will defile their holy book. Persian is the language of Persians. They say we are not Persians unless we become Muslim. If you want to learn how to read, you have to go to the Rabbi's Torah class."

Mullah Mirza had no interest in the Torah. He wanted to discover Razi's secrets.

"I want to be a scientist," he had declared, "become rich, respected, immortal."

For a while he had entertained the idea of converting to Islam so he would be allowed to study Persian. Then he found a better way.

He went to the Muslim scribe who sat on a broken stool outside the Shah's caravansary in Esfahan. In return for a small fee, the scribe wrote letters that people dictated to him. At the end of each day he collected his pay and went to Juyy Bar to buy wine.

The Jews of Persia had a monopoly on the manufacturing of wine. Islam forbade its followers to drink alcoholic beverages. Muslims who could not resist the temptation of drunkenness, therefore, went to the ghetto to buy wine. The sin, they consoled themselves, lay with the person who manufactured the evil brew—not with the one who drank it. In times of hardship, the mullahs often called their people to cleanse the world of "winemaking infidels," and sent mobs to the ghetto to break into every home and burn every basement where Jews had stored wine.

"I will bring you a jug of five-year-old wine every week if you teach me how to read," Mullah Mirza offered the scribe.

"I will never tell of our agreement. If anyone finds out I know how to read, I will accuse another scribe of having taught me. If you take my wine and then betray me, I will poison you."

The scribe did not refuse.

Three years after he had first seen Razi's book, Mullah Mirza had learned to read Persian and Arabic. He moved out of his father's home, rented the basement of David the Butcher's shop on credit, and launched his career as a scientist.

From that time on, Juyy Bar had watched Mullah Mirza become slowly consumed by his obsession. He locked himself forever in the basement, poring over steaming pots, studying Razi's book until he had learned every line by memory, repeating every failed experiment until he had run out of metals and fuel and acid. Then suddenly he would resurface again. David the Butcher would approach him and ask for his rent: Mullah Mirza had not paid a penny since the day he first occupied the basement.

"Get away from me," he would attack David with unbeatable righteousness. "How dare you—*how Dare you*—speak of money when I am about to re-create the world!"

For a while he would rummage through the antique shops of Esfahan in search of books by other alchemists. He intimidated shopkeepers and housewives into "donating" the ingredients he needed for his experiments, traveled to distant cities and villages where he had heard other scientists were engaged in similar pursuits. Then he rushed back to the basement—armed, he thought, with decisive knowledge—and started again.

Over time his body began to exhibit signs of exhaustion. His hands became covered with warts and lesions and scars. The mud walls of his basement laboratory baked with the heat and were permeated with the smell of his potions, and the metal safe he had built became stuffed with tiny pieces of paper on which he furiously scribbled his findings. He guarded the safe jealously, always fearing that a rival scientist would try to steal his secrets, accusing people who could not read of spying on him while he wrote notes to himself. Once, when the roof of the basement crumbled under David the Butcher's feet, bringing him down with a pile of rubble into the laboratory, Mullah Mirza greeted him with a sharp skewer aimed at his eyes.

"Thief!" he screamed. "I will drive this metal through your eyeballs and feed them to the dogs before I let you take my safe."

From then on, Mullah Mirza slept with one hand chained to the safe.

He was so engrossed in his quest for gold that he missed the time he should have married. He worked through his adolescence, his youth, his parents' death. He never paid the butcher any rent. He never bought himself a new pair of canvas shoes or a new shirt. People went to him for advice and medical treatment, trusting that he had access to cures unknown to ordinary doctors, intrigued by his extravagant ways, his grand designs, the confidence with which he pronounced himself "master of my environment, conqueror of earthly ills."

The Mirza in turn had never disappointed an audience. He charged exorbitant sums and delivered exotic, spectacular cures designed more to display his knowledge than to relieve the patient of his suffering. When he made a house call, people in the neighborhood dropped what they had to do and came to watch the old master at work. He spent all his income on books and metal, and yet he was not content. In all the years of his suffering, Mullah Mirza knew, he had come no closer to creating gold than when he first started.

As he grew older and more frustrated in his quest, Mullah Mirza's treatments became increasingly unorthodox. He no longer limited himself to harmless displays of extravagance—to curing diarrhea with bubbling potions that resulted in terminal constipation, or inserting a long metal rod through the patient's throat into his stomach so as to "rearrange his insides." Now he tested new formulas that he had conceived during torturous nights of experimentation, proposed cruel and unheard-of operations that had left at least three of his patients permanently handicapped, or simply gave himself to displays of such burning rage while treating a simple fracture that his hand became shaky, his mind fogged, and his patient temporarily frightened out of his pain.

Still, though he would never accept it openly, Mullah Mirza realized that greatness and wealth would forever evade him.

"It is not my mind that fails me," he raged in the loneliness of his laboratory late at night when he faced yet another unyielding formula, "it is my fortune. I am not blessed enough."

At first he prayed to God.

"Give me a clue, a single hint," he would plead. "Show me one answer for everything that you have denied me."

Then he cursed all that was holy, and declared war on the heavens and the earth.

"I damn your pettiness," he screamed. "I spit on your stinginess. I curse your jealousy that keeps you from giving to me that which would make me greater than yourself."

He noticed that people were avoiding him in favor of more ignorant but less threatening doctors. He was enraged—that anyone dared doubt his work or question his methods; that they would allow their fears and their ignorance to stand in the way of "science," and revert to old and useless ways of other doctors for fear of Mullah Mirza's progressive—and therefore, he admitted, risky—methods; that they would desert him *now*—now that he was on the brink of failure and about to lose hope.

One morning he climbed upstairs into the butcher's shop and called David's customers to attention. He stood there in his long black robe and his torn canvas shoes—the customers staring at him—fixed his eyes on the bloody knife that David held in his hand, and made a simple announcement:

"Let it be known that Mullah Mirza is the master physician of this damned ghetto," he said. "From now on anyone who seeks the advice of a doctor other than me will be cursed straight into his grave."

No one said a word. Mullah Mirza had betrayed his weakness. He was desperate, at last aware of his limitations.

Years went by, and Mullah Mirza did not recover from that moment in David the Butcher's shop. Slowly he abandoned his experiments and stopped reading his books. After a while he even found himself preoccupied with the same concerns as ordinary people. He suffered his rheumatism, his ulcers. His eyes failed him. He was lonely, disappointed, poor. He had believed he could make a miracle—he could not live with the truth of his failure. He was about to give up hope, when Thick Pissing Isaac died and Yehuda the Just sealed the teahouse shut; since Noah was not Isaac's child, the rabbi said, he could not inherit the property. Fifteen years old and alone, Noah the Gold went looking for work.

One early morning in the summer of 1811, he knocked on Mullah Mirza's door and offered his services to the "Great Master." He had come to work, he said, in return for food.

Mullah Mirza stared at the boy on his doorstep that day, and, like Mama the Midwife a decade and a half earlier, thought he had been sent an angel. He dragged Noah into the lab, put him before a pot of his most advanced formula, and gave him a piece of rusted metal.

"Make gold," he commanded like God. "Turn the world into gold."

In Mullah Mirza's laboratory the walls shone. The floor was paved with gold. The chests were stuffed, the ceiling was about to drop from the weight of the treasure that hung from it. Every day Mullah Mirza brought in new loads of tin and metal for Noah to make gold. Every day he laughed like a madman and embraced Noah in gratitude.

"At *last*," he cried. "At *last*."

Noah the Gold looked at the piles of junk about him and gasped at the Mirza's madness.

"But it's just like before," he insisted in vain. Afraid that the Jews would come to steal his wealth, Mullah Mirza had put eleven locks on the basement door, and refused to let Noah out even for an hour. He wanted to keep the discovery a secret, to duplicate the formula, learn Noah's method.

"You work for *me*," he warned Noah every day. "You make gold only for *me*."

He bought out all the tinsmiths, emptied his neighbor's basements. He raided strangers' kitchens, fought the owners, took away cooking utensils and gardening tools. The Jews had never seen Mullah Mirza so excited. When he put the locks on the door, they wondered if he had come upon an important discovery. When he carted the metal home and threw away nothing, they gathered outside his laboratory and asked him about his experiments. Mullah Mirza fortified the door with more bars, and remained secretive. At some point, he realized with complete lucidity, he would have to kill Noah to safeguard the secret of the formula. Once or twice he even had the vision of forcing the boy into the pot of elixir, turning him—this radiant child of God's mercy—into a statue of gold that would preserve his beauty forever. But before he could do so, Mullah Mirza needed to take charge of the formula himself. One late afternoon he gathered all his courage and took Noah's place before the transforming liquid.

"In the name of God . . ." he began.

He was trembling—so moved by the greatness of the

moment he could not stop the rush of tears, so pleased to have his dream realized that he dared not proceed until Noah urged him to.

He immersed a steel dagger into the pot, held it for a moment, and pulled it out with a cry of glory that changed instantly into a wail of desperation.

Something was wrong.

Mullah Mirza attacked Noah with inhuman strength:

"You changed the formula."

Noah the Gold swore innocence.

"Try again," he pleaded with his master, but again the metal remained unchanged. He gave the dagger to Noah. This time it turned to gold.

A thousand times that day, Mullah Mirza repeated the experiment. At dawn the next morning he was exhausted and insane, sobbing with disappointment and rage, begging Noah for the answer.

"But there *is* no gold," Noah pleaded with him a last time. "There never was any gold."

It was then, standing before the boy who had refused him his miracle, faced with the certainty of his life's failure and the mountain of junk metal he had believed was gold, the Mullah Mirza understood:

"By God," he whispered. "I dreamt it all."

And he laughed—so hard that his body bent forward until his beard touched his feet, so long that his face became streaked with tears, and he remained there, a small, crumpled figure devoid of all bitterness, no longer frightening, a tiny old man doubled over in the middle of the floor, laughing away at the absurdity of his life, at the years of seeking and the nights of prayer all in pursuit of the impossible, laughing with such innocence and such abandon that he even made Noah smile until his limbs were stiff and his breath shut down and he fell forward on his head, rolled over, and died.

In the year 1801, Russia had claimed hegemony over the Persian province of Georgia. Four years later the Czar had annexed the provinces of Baku and Derbent. Contemplating resistance, Fath Ali Shah asked about the state of his army and discovered he had none: he had not paid his troops for years. Those who had not formally abandoned their posts were mostly opium addicts, or peasants who had never received military training. They had no uniforms, no weapons, no generals. In the arsenal at Tabriz—a strategically vital region because of its proximity to Russia—the Shah's emissaries found a few cannonballs, but even those did not fit the guns. They tried to buy lead locally, and discovered that the Shah had spent all the money in the national treasury. They asked His Majesty for money to acquire new weapons, but were refused. Fath Ali Shah would not waste his money fighting Russians over a few provinces, he said. If he had to retrieve the territories, he could easily *scare* the Czar into giving them back.

He announced a formal audience, and summoned a thousand nobles to the Garden of the Marble Throne at the newly completed Palace of Roses.

They came in resplendent garb, each gentleman surrounded by his own troupe of soldiers and guards and pages, their horses—tails painted red—clad in embroidered silks and golden bridles. Next to each nobleman walked his Guardian of the Bridles, who carried, folded neatly on his shoulder, the saddle's covering of embroidered purple and black. Two guards rode in front of the nobleman. A third and most trusted guard rode behind.

Outside the Square of the Cannons before the Palace of Roses, royal pages in bright red uniforms with elaborate headgear awaited the guests. They led the gentlemen through the palace gates into a narrow strip of garden, under an elaborate archway, and into the Garden of the Marble Throne. The nobles began to whisper: the Terrace, usually cloistered by an immense curtain, was open to view. On it was a gigantic throne, carved of green marble, its legs life-sized statues of jinns and fairies.

When all the nobles had assembled in the garden, Fath Ali Shah's favorite eunuchs stepped onto the Terrace. They were five, all white, dressed in long coats tight at the waist and with long, flared skirts. One eunuch stood beside each pillar of the throne. The fifth and most beautiful took his place in front. In his hands he held a jewel-studded cushion on which rested the Holy Sword.

The royal page appeared.

"Make way!" he cried.

"His Imperial Majesty! The King of Kings! The Standard Bearer of Islam! The Shadow of Allah! The Shah of Persia!"

Trumpets blew. Drums roared. Fath Ali Shah appeared, wearing his Robes of Wrath.

He had on a long coat made of red velvet covered entirely with rubies. He wore a three-tiered crown of rubies, a ruby-studded dagger, shoes embroidered with rubies, necklaces and rings and bracelets of rubies.

In the Garden of the Terrace of the Marble Throne, the nobles trembled: Fath Ali Shah wore his Robes of Wrath only to pronounce a sentence of death upon an esteemed enemy. In these robes, and on this same throne, he had ordered the blinding and execution of his own brother. Another time he had watched his Prime Minister boiled alive in a pot of oil.

He climbed the three steps, then reclined on the Marble Throne.

"The ill-omened Russians," he spoke, "have violated the sacred soil of Our country. We have no doubt that our unequalled army at Sari is capable of destroying the fiercest of the Czar's troops. But what would happen, do you imagine, if We were to send Our *household cavalry* to attack them?"

The household cavalry, everyone knew, merely performed the task of protecting the person of the Shah. It would be destroyed in a matter of hours by the Czar's soldiers. Still, to please His Majesty, the nobles cried and groveled at the woes the cavalry would bring upon the Russians.

"May I be Thy sacrifice," one man said, stepping forth. "Your cavalry would drive the invaders back to Moscow!"

The Shah agreed.

"And what if," he went further, "*We* were to go to the front Ourself?"

It was too much to imagine—the torture Fath Ali Shah could personally inflict upon the Czar.

"So it is settled," he concluded, already pleased with his triumph. "Spread the word and let the Russians be forewarned!"

The war in Azerbaijan lasted thirteen years and ended in defeat. The Czar had not been shaken by Fath Ali Shah's wrath. The Persian army never did manage a real fight. What resistance the Czar faced came from patriotic men and women who fought without conventional weapons, and refused to accept Russian hegemony. But at last, in 1813, Fath Ali Shah conceded to the Czar the provinces already under occupation. To further appease his neighbor, he also agreed to pay to Russia enormous sums by way of reparations. Across Persia, everyone mourned. Mullahs and clergymen called the Shah a traitor and asked for his throne. They said he was weak and corrupt, that he had squandered Persia's wealth and fallen before the strength of infidels. Trembling in his throne, afraid that the mullahs would call Jihad—holy war—against the Crown, Fath Ali Shah called once again for the Jewish soothsayer from Esfahan, and this time she answered.

 She appeared one day at the Square of the Cannons, standing by the side of the famous Pearl Cannon where thieves and murderers took refuge from the law, where old maids sat until Fate sent them a man, and lovers chained themselves together in the hope of achieving eternal union. Through the mist of opium and *arrack* that permanently clouded their visions, members of the Shah's household cavalry saw Esther approach, and immediately recognized the soothsayer in Fath Ali Shah's dreams. She was bald and unveiled, her skin was the color of oil, the air around her smelling of long distances and unknown ways.

"*Allahuo Akbar!*" the soldiers fell to their knees. They were certain Esther was a ghost. "*Allahuo Akbar!* God is great."

They took her into the palace, and sent for the Chief Eunuch. He rushed to Esther with a hundred other eunuchs, avoiding her eyes to guard against her evil, and took her into the Hall of Mirrors: the walls and the ceiling here were composed of a mosaic of small mirrors reflecting the light that poured in from arched portals around the room. Mirrors, everyone knew, protected against demons.

The Chief Eunuch went to call the Shah. All the way from the Hall of Mirrors to the Royal Quarters, he prayed aloud for his own life: Fath Ali Shah was ruthless to those who interrupted his sleep. The night before, he had spent furious hours trying to gain access to his own harem. He had wanted to sleep with his newest acquisition—a woman called Miriam, who was suspected widely of being a Jew. Early in the day, the Shah had sent the Chief Eunuch to prepare the girl for his arrival. Miriam had bathed in goat's milk and rubbed herself with rosewater, lined her eyes with antimony, and reddened her cheeks with a paste made by crushing the dried insect called *shan-djarf*. She had waited for the Shah in a bed of roses and chiffon, but the moment His Majesty had tried to touch her someone in the next room had sneezed.

The Shah left immediately. A sneeze, everyone knew, was a sign from God to refrain from the act one was about to engage in. Back in his quarters, Fath Ali Shah had waited an hour, entered the harem again, and again heard a sneeze.

He waited another hour. There was another sneeze. The

Shah realized then that one of his wives must have hired a "professional sneezer"—a woman disguised as a harem maid and hired by a jealous wife to keep His Majesty from sleeping with new virgins. The punishment for a false sneeze, everyone knew, was death. Fath Ali Shah ordered the execution of all the maids, and divorced all the wives in rooms within ear's reach of Miriam's. But he did not dare defy the sneeze: he resolved to wait another hour, in the course of which he fell asleep without ever having satisfied himself with Miriam.

Outside His Majesty's chambers, three soldiers greeted the Chief Eunuch. He went through the eunuchs' room, into a first bedroom where the commander of the palace guards slept every night in uniform, a naked sword by his side. From there he entered Fath Ali Shah's bedroom.

"May I be thy sacrifice," he said, trying to awaken His Majesty, who did not respond. The Chief Eunuch bit his lip and summoned courage.

"May I be thy sacrifice," he said again. "It seems the demon of your fate has come to call."

Fath Ali Shah turned as white as the pillow he rested on. He remained motionless, his eyes still closed, then sat up and gripped the sheets under him. In another time he would have rejoiced at Esther's arrival. Now, with the Czar at his doorstep and the mullahs calling for his ouster, the Shah feared Esther had come to predict his downfall. He looked up at the eunuch, who saw his wrath and fell immediately to his knees.

"Forgive me, Your Majesty. It was my misfortune to carry the news to you. If you grant me permission, I will have the woman flogged, cut up, and thrown to your most voracious dogs."

Fath Ali Shah descended the bed. His hands trembled visibly. He motioned for his dressers to approach.

"Keep her under guard," he told the eunuch. "Give Us time to prepare for her."

An hour after noon, the King of Kings arrived at the Hall of Mirrors. He wore a long tiara of three elevations, composed entirely of oversized diamonds. He had on a long jacket made of gold tissue covered with diamonds and decorated with two strings of pearls, each larger than a walnut, that crossed the shoulders. His belt and bracelet were composed of rows of diamonds. His dagger's hilt was covered with diamonds. He summoned the soothsayer, and the moment she turned to face him, he knew by the strength of her eyes that she was indeed a ghost.

"Speak!" he commanded, and all the eunuchs guarding Esther ran to hide. If he was not pleased with her prediction, they knew, Fath Ali Shah would order torturous death for all those who had heard her prophecy.

"Tell Us Our fate."

Esther the Soothsayer smiled at the Shah with blackened lips, and spoke to him with the voice of an angel:

"You will die old," she said, "at peace in your throne, twenty years and a thousand children from today."

 Esther the Soothsayer slept, and out of her dreams carved a woman, a creature of light like Noah, with a strange beauty and the voice of a muse. She gave the woman to Noah, her last gift, and then left him, sinking so deep into the world of hallucinations that nothing of her remained with him but a fading voice and dreams full of sunsets. Without her, Noah was lost. His days and nights blended into one until sleep and waking were indistinguishable, and dreams cast shadows on the walls.

He had buried Mullah Mirza, but never overcome his legacy. For years after the Mirza's death, everyone in Juyy Bar had come to Noah, demanding the truth about the gold. What was it, they asked, that had so driven Mullah Mirza to ecstasy? Had he found the formula? Had he shared his secret with Noah?

Even Yehuda the Just came to call.

"I am the keeper of all souls," he told Noah. "I must know all secrets."

To convince Noah of his good intentions and gain his trust, Yehuda the Just had even unsealed the teahouse and allowed the boy back into Thick Pissing Isaac's home. Still, every time he inquired about the elixir, Noah the Gold shook his head in denial.

He opened the teahouse again and tried to gather back his old customers. They came only to ask about the elixir. When he disappointed them, they denied him their friendship.

Twenty years passed after the death of Mullah Mirza. In Juyy Bar, Noah the Gold ached from loneliness and remained poor. One night in the spring of 1831, he called Esther the Soothsayer:

"I must have a wife," he told her. "I must guard against the demon of time."

In 1831 a Muslim child had disappeared in Tabriz. His parents had looked for him in vain, and concluded that he had been stolen by gypsies, or eaten by wolves. Then a young man from the bazaar had brought news.

"Shokr-Allah the Jew murdered your son," he had told the boy's parents.

"He stole the child and took him home to draw his blood for Passover. His corpse is still in Shokr-Allah's basement."

The parents had gone to the Jews' ghetto and searched Shokr-Allah's house. In the basement they had found their son's body—already half-decomposed.

Shokr-Allah the Jew swore innocence. He had never seen the body until the boy's parents had discovered it. He only drank wine on Passover. The young man who had accused him owed him money, and he must have wished to avoid paying his debt by having the mullahs kill Shokr-Allah.

No one believed him. The mullahs ordered punishment not only for Shokr-Allah, but for all of his people: all Jews were held responsible for the crimes of one. The mullahs ordered a massacre.

This time, they said, they would not offer Jews the choice to convert to Islam and escape death. This time they sought revenge—the blood of Jewish children in return for that of the Muslim boy, the pain of their parents in payment for the grief Shokr-Allah had caused the Muslims. They sent a mob to the ghetto to gather all the Jewish children. In the main square they planted a hundred daggers into the earth, blades upward, and threw the children onto them to skewer their bodies like beasts. Then they slaughtered the older people. Those who had hidden in their basements were locked in and their houses were set on fire. Those who wore gold around their wrists and necks had it carved out of their bodies. Those who begged for mercy had their tongues cut off. For days the mob returned, searching every house and every temple, looting the shops, beating the men, raping the women.

In Qamar's house, the mob had killed everyone else. She threw herself on the ground and feigned death. Twice the mob came back to search the house for survivors. Qamar pulled her sister's corpse over herself and held her breath until they were gone. One night, when she thought the pogrom had ended, she escaped. In the streets, corpses lay frozen in the winter air. In the main square, the last of the surviving children died in the field of daggers. In the gutters, rainwater would forever run the color of blood. Never again in the history of Persia would even a single Jew live among the people of Tabriz.

Qamar the Gypsy had traveled east, toward Rasht, on the Caspian Coast. She crossed the mountains around Tabriz, climbing high on treacherous roads where only bandits dared travel, across valleys so deep they swallowed entire caravans. Around Rasht the jungles were lush and dense, alive with the smell of sweet rain, roaring with the cries of panthers and leopards. Beyond them, in the flatland bordering the Caspian Sea, were the rice fields—light green and gold and silver at dawn. She stopped. She had heard the voice of Esther the Soothsayer.

"There is a boy in Juyy Bar with agate eyes," Esther said. "Find him. Give him children of light and laughter."

Qamar the Gypsy found her way to Tehran, and then to the holy city of Qom, where the greatest of mullahs received religious training. There she met a caravan of pilgrims and followed them south. The pilgrims were mostly poor men, traveling on foot or riding emaciated camels and donkeys. On their backs they each carried a large canvas bag with the remains of a relative or friend who had asked to be buried in the holy Muslim cities of Najaf and Karbala. There were shrines in those cities—consecrated places where for centuries the dead had been buried. They were placed tier on tier upon each other—to wait for the day when Allah would descend to earth and carry them all to heaven.

Qamar the Gypsy followed the pilgrims from a great distance. They were men on a holy mission and would not allow the presence of a Jew to spoil the purity of their vows. They walked in the early morning and late afternoon, resting at midday when the sun was too hot, and at night when the desert froze. Afraid to be seen by them, Qamar hid all day, and followed their trail in moonlight, guided by the sound of camel bells and the voice of Esther the Soothsayer. Even then she could smell the corpses that the pilgrims carried in their sacks. The laws of Persia and the Ottoman Empire required that bodies be buried for a year before being transported, to reduce the danger of spreading plague. But in the land of Islam, only the law of God was observed. The men carried the corpses fresh. To keep them clean, the pilgrims washed them in streams and rivers where others drank. To contain the smell of rot, they placed green apples in the sacks. They stopped in every village to buy new apples, and gave the old ones to beggar children who bit into them gratefully.

 Noah the Gold whistled in the dark. He stood outside the teahouse late at night after his customers were gone, and whistled a tune he heard inside his head. The neighbors were terrified.

"Stop that sound," they screamed. "The ghosts of darkness will hear your tune and come to strangle us all."

Noah the Gold knew about the demons who responded to whistles in the dark. Still, the tune in his head was clear and compelling, and he whistled it until he had summoned Qamar the Gypsy.

She was small and thin, with a tiny waist and the feet of a porcelain doll. She had dark skin, tear-shaped eyes, and a halo of reddish-brown hair that flew about her like a wild sunset. She came to Juyy Bar without money or a friend— running, she claimed, from a massacre in the Tabriz ghetto, at the heart of the province of Azerbaijan. She spoke a language that was a mixture of Persian and Turkish, and understood little of the dialect in Juyy Bar. She arrived when the weather was gentle, and on her footsteps she brought the cold air of Tabriz—turning the summer in Esfahan into a winter of blizzards and frozen snow.

"I have run before the Plague," she told Noah with her voice that was as cool and soothing as the wind she had brought, "from beyond the mountains of Elburz, and on my way I have seen a world of wonders."

Noah the Gold took Qamar into his room and did not let her go. He kept her in his own light, clung to her as if for every breath. He touched her skin, inhaled the smell of pine trees and rain in her hair. Qamar's hands were calm and undemanding, her eyes never probed, her tongue—patient and calm—left a cool trace everyplace it touched. Weeks later, enraged at the scandal of a man and woman sleeping together without being married, Yehuda the Just forced his way into Noah's house and performed the rites of marriage between him and Qamar. Even then, they would not stop holding each other. They made love at noon, in a darkened room with the wind howling at their doorstep. At night, when the house was calm, they sat in the moonlight and talked with their faces close to each other. Against the columns of red mud that surrounded the courtyard, their shadows moved softly—like two figures dancing to a silent tune that only they could hear—and all those who saw them then believed they were creatures of a charmed life.

 In the summer of 1834, Fath Ali Shah went to Esfahan. One night in the palace, he stood surrounded by his Royal Dressers, donning a bejeweled gown that he would wear at dinner. Suddenly he dropped to the ground.

Twenty years after he had faced Esther the Soothsayer in the Hall of Mirrors of the Palace of Roses, Fath Ali Shah died. He left behind three hundred sons, and more than a thousand grandchildren.

Immediately upon the Shah's death, war broke out in Tehran: the Shah's three hundred sons all claimed a right to the throne. Each contender was backed by a different segment of the aristocracy, or another foreign power. Fath Ali Shah's Crown Prince, Abbas Mirza, had predeceased his father. Abbas's son, Muhammad Khan, was at last pushed at the throne with the intervention of the British military mission in Azerbaijan. The Russians, too, gave the King their blessing; he was a feeble man—in body and spirit alike—and he promised not to resist the foreigners in their endeavors in Persia.

Muhammad Shah's Prime Minister, Hajji Mirza Aghassi, recognized that the King had inherited his grandfather's belief in mystical powers, and immediately set out to use them for his own advantage: instead of ordering a new search for Esther the Soothsayer, Aghassi indoctrinated the Shah in the principles of Sufism, and from then on spent most of his time performing spiritual exercises with the King. The late Abbas Mirza's Vizir, Qa'im Maqam, recognized the danger of a ruler who had lost touch with reality and the world, and tried to warn the King against the ruse of his minister. He wrote letters to Muhammad Shah, lecturing at him as if he were still a schoolchild, enumerating all of the nation's ills without adding even a flavoring of pleasant lies. He told the Shah that he was making a fool of himself before the entire nation, that the two men at the head of the nation—the Shah and his Prime Minister—were being called "the two dervishes of Persia." He claimed that Aghassi had indoctrinated the Shah in the path of asceticism only to render him powerless. Muhammad Shah was annoyed and angered by the letters: Qa'im Maqam, he believed, must understand a king's prerogative to see nothing but beauty, and hear nothing but pleasantries; Maqam had written the letters to torture the Shah and take away his peace of mind.

Muhammad Shah summoned his father's Vizir to a garden in Tehran, and had him strangled. Freed of the only voice of reason that had disturbed his peace, Muhammad Shah then continued his practice of Sufism till he died over a decade later, in the summer of 1848.

In 1836, Qamar the Gypsy became pregnant. She gave birth on a cold night, in the midst of a snowstorm that killed dozens. The winter she had brought with her from Tabriz had lingered indefinitely and became more fierce with time. Every day, children froze at their mothers' nipples and young men left home never to return. Someone found them late at night—corpses shrouded in ice.

All that time, Qamar had never felt the cold. When she was ready to give birth, she walked into the courtyard, and the warmth of her feet melted the snow. She went to the basement where years ago Esther the Soothsayer had borne Noah, and took out the large copper tray that all women used. She filled the tray with ashes from the bottom of the coal stove, then placed it on the ground next to the pool. The water was frozen, the frogs trapped inside. She sat above the tray, one knee planted on either side, and suffered her pain in silence.

It was night, but Qamar the Gypsy had sun in her eyes. At dawn, the birth occurred. From between her legs Qamar pulled an infant—a boy with white skin and golden hair and the eyes of the sailors, long ago in the nights of Bandar 'Abbas, who had first thrown the seeds of life into Esther the Soothsayer. A moment later another head appeared—a girl's this time, with the same features, but who neither cried nor trembled like her brother. They lay on the ashes, glowing as snow fell on their naked skin.

Spring arrived in Juyy Bar. Qamar the Gypsy had named her son Moshe, and her daughter Leyla. She bathed them in the sun every day and combed their hair with her fingers wet from the morning dew. She let them sleep on the porch, where all the neighbors came to see them. She told them stories about the world outside the ghetto. When they could walk, she held their hands and took them to the edge of Juyy Bar, there at the gates where the desert lay unconquered, and gave them the yearning to leave:

"You must walk someday," she told them, "a thousand miles, a thousand days. You must walk and never stop until you have found your freedom."

They grew up. When they were eight years old, Moshe ran home one day from the neighbor's yard and called his father:

"Is it true," he asked, "you can make gold?"

Noah the Gold went pale. He understood that the days of his son's contentment had come to an end. In Moshe's eyes, he could see the same longing that had ruined Mullah Mirza.

He denied the story. Moshe would not believe him. He took the boy outside Mullah Mirza's basement.

"Look," Noah told him. "There's no trace of gold anywhere."

Still, every day as he watched his son grow, Noah the Gold saw Moshe tortured by disbelief.

Moshe became obsessed with the desire for wealth, suddenly conscious of his poverty, aware of his lowly predicament as a Jew. He realized that most Jews were ugly—small and unformed for lack of proper nutrition, carrying the scars and ills of their fathers as they intermarried and perpetuated their unhappiness. He realized that they were dirtier than Muslims, that their homes were more crowded, that they showed little mercy to one another. He felt humiliated by the restrictions imposed on him by Shiite law, but instead of blaming the mullahs, he blamed the Jews for claiming him as one of them. He understood that as long as he was a Jew, he would never have respect or money or peace, but instead of accepting his predicament, he dreamt about converting to Islam. When he was twelve years old, he learned the story of Esther the Soothsayer: the same children who had told him of Mullah Mirza now swore that Noah the Gold's mother had been unveiled and punished for adultery. For weeks after that, Moshe refused to leave the house.

He stayed at home, and slowly, as if to avenge himself against Noah the Gold, he slipped into a fever so deep his skin blistered from the heat. One morning Noah the Gold saw Moshe wiping his eyes and looking around as if to escape a bright light. He touched the boy's forehead, and drew his hand away in shock.

"Quick," he yelled at Qamar. "Help me."

They put Moshe on Noah's back, and carried him all the way to the house of Yehuda the Just, where there was a water-storage tank. They tied a rope around Moshe's waist and lowered him into the water, right through the hatch where years ago the rabbi's only son had slipped and drowned. Moshe stayed there all day, shivering. The water was dark and stale, full of dirt and the carcasses of animals that had lain in the dry gutters of the ghetto, decomposing in the sun until twice a week the mullahs opened the dams and allowed Esfahan's river into Juyy Bar. Then everyone ran to the gutters and filled their buckets and gourds. Those who had storage tanks channeled the gutter into their home and filled the tanks. In times of hardship, when the mullahs refused the river to the Jews, they sold the water in the tank for the price of gold.

Moshe sat still, and listened to the ghosts that inhabited the tank—demons, he had heard when he was younger, one-eyed giants who ate children. He was not afraid of them. He sat on the narrow platform under the hatch and let water cover him up to his chin. Away from his home and his torment, he was safe. He could pull his knees into his chest, gather up the darkness around him, and sleep.

The demons woke him.

"You have the fever of madness," they said with voices that were deep and slow and threatening. "When the light returns, the rabbi will come for you. He will take you to a doctor and leech your blood."

They were all around him, their shapes changing with every movement of the water.

"You must run away. Leave before he arrives."

Moshe stood up. The demons disappeared. There was only darkness, and the smell of rotting cats.

"Call a leecher." Moshe recognized the voice of Yehuda the Just.

The sun burst in Moshe's eyes. He was lying on the ground, outside the tank. People stood around him—tall, threatening. The rabbi's wife bent over to look at him. She had an air of decay about her, as if age had eaten away at her bones. For years now she had not moved from the courtyard of her house. She sat there day and night—guarding, she said, against death, which had come once when she was not looking and taken her son.

"He has the fever of madness," Yehuda the Just was telling his wife. "He must be leeched, drained of the evil blood that has flooded and impaired his brain and caused the fever."

Moshe panicked. He pushed himself up against the light, blinded by the white spots that glared at him in every corner. He stood up and began to run. The rabbi reached for him, but too late. Moshe went through the courtyard and out the door. As he ran, the water from his clothes evaporated in the sun and rose around him like fog.

He went through the alley, Yehuda chasing him, and tried to find his way home. Still blind, he pushed against people on the street, trampled the vendors' merchandise.

"Mama!" he cried as he ran.

Yehuda the Just was behind him and getting closer.

"Stop the child!" he screamed, and Moshe realized he was about to be caught. He ran faster, but he had lost his way. There were others chasing him now—children, their faces distorted by the light, their teeth gleaming.

"Mama!" He ran faster. The children surrounded him. They were singing a riddle.

"Mad, mad, Moshe has gone mad."

"Mama." The light was unbearable.

He tripped over something, almost fell, caught himself.

"Mad, mad, Moshe has gone mad."

He peered though the white spots. He saw the children—their faces monstrous, their eyes protruding, their fingers long, almost touching him. Yehuda the Just caught up.

The circle turned and turned until it became a single whirlwind of light and consumed Moshe.

Moshe woke up in the dark. There were noises in the room, the soft murmur of a woman, the smell of wild rue burning. He pulled his body up a short distance, enough to lean his head against the wall and look. At eye level, on the ground, there was coal burning in the small brazier that served as a heater during the winter. Qamar the Gypsy stood next to the box, chanting in a monotone. Yehuda the Just had brought Moshe back, and he was a prisoner in his parents' room.

"It's the fever of madness," he had claimed, pleased to find Moshe ill, vindicated in his prediction—made the day he and Leyla were born—that Esther the Soothsayer's grandchildren would meet nothing but disaster and disease. "You must call a leecher."

Qamar and Noah had resisted at first. But Moshe's fever had only burned stronger, and they realized they were about to lose him. They sent for the leecher, but now, in a last attempt to save her son from the torture of the cure, Qamar was performing the rites of "beating the evil eye."

She bent over the brazier, and threw a fistful of wild rue on the coal.

"Damn the Devil," she said, and in the instant when the seeds popped in the heat, the orange glow of the fire licked her face, leaving dark only the shadows under her eyes and her cheekbones, and the black hole inside her mouth where her teeth shone white.

She knelt on the floor, holding a raw egg in one hand, and reached into the coal box. With her bare fingers she drew tiny circles on the shell—to represent eyes. When she had covered the entire surface, she put the egg in the fire: if it burst, she would have managed to rid her son of the evil eye. She waited. The evil was stronger that Qamar's prayer. The egg remained intact.

She tried again, with another egg. She sang louder, drew more circles on the shell, almost threw the egg into the fire. Still, nothing happened.

Just then someone knocked on the door—softly, as if in warning—and walked away. Moshe sat up, alarmed. Qamar the Gypsy touched his forehead to check the fever. Her fingers were ice-cold against his skin.

"The leecher is coming," she said. "Don't be afraid."

Moshe looked across the room, searching for help, finding no one. He heard footsteps in the courtyard.

One.

Two.

Three, and there was a pause—a split second in which Moshe realized the magnitude of the danger approaching.

One. Two. The leecher went by the pool.

He came closer to the door.

Up the steps.

He stopped.

Moshe grabbed his mother's hand. "Don't let him in."

His face was drenched in sweat. His eyes were pale, his skin gray. Crying, Qamar the Gypsy pulled her hand away—Moshe would never forgive her for this—and went to the door.

Lotf-Allah the Leecher stood in the frame. In one hand he held a whip. In the other he had a jar full of black leeches.

"Tie him," Lotf-Allah the Leecher ordered, pointing to Moshe on the floor. Two men came in from the courtyard to help. Under Lotf-Allah's command, they tied Moshe's wrists and ankles together, and stripped him of all his clothes. Moshe did not fight. He only cried—large tears of terror and anger that fell onto the bed and burned holes into

Qamar the Gypsy's heart. The room had filled with specta-tors. Lotf-Allah the Leecher began.

He picked up his whip and inhaled.

"Evil and foul spirits, beware. The master of souls has come to drive you to annihilation."

He struck the whip against the bare sole of Moshe's foot. He hit slowly at first, counting every stroke. Then he hit faster, faster, like the violent ticking of a furious clock. He screamed when he brought the whip down—a cry of fury and triumph that shook the house and robbed Moshe of his every defense.

"Oh, you misled and possessed spirits! Get ready to be driven out of this child's body! Leave *now!*" He hit one last time. Blood splattered his face and shirt. Then all was silent.

Lotf-Allah the Leecher waited until his heart had calmed. Then he picked up the jar of leeches. He had kept them hungry for weeks.

He brought the jar around and showed the leeches to Moshe.

"They will purify your blood," he explained. He took the leeches out one by one and placed them on Moshe's bare back. They dug into Moshe's skin and sucked out his blood. He screamed, and began to vomit in his bed. Then he fainted.

When the leeches had grown to six times their original size, they pulled out of Moshe's flesh to digest their meal. Lotf-Allah the Leecher collected them back into their jar.

"I will return tomorrow."

Every night for two weeks in the summer of 1848, the leecher came back to the house of Noah the Gold. He fed Moshe potions, tortured him by beating the soles of his feet. But he alternated the leeching with what he called an "air-suck."

He heated five glass cups until they were red, then let them cool just enough to prevent the flesh from burning deeply. He held the bottom of each cup with a cloth and reversed them on Moshe's bare and blistered back. He left them there as the skin turned amber, then suddenly pulled them up—sucking, he claimed, the fever and the "foul air" out of Moshe's soul. In the morning he would leave, drained of energy, weakened by the rage that consumed him as he battled with the devil in Moshe's spirit. By the end of the second week, the fever stopped. Lotf-Allah the the Leecher pronounced Moshe cured, collected his pay, and left.

Calm returned to the house of Noah the Gold. Moshe lay in bed cold and still, his lips white, his eyes so pallid they looked almost transparent. He never spoke to his father again. He never stopped yearning for wealth. He stayed at home for two months, recovering from the cure, and all the time he planned his escape: he would go to Esfahan, he knew, and become Muslim. He would change his name, deny he had ever been a Jew. He would become rich, respected, powerful, and someday he would come back to show Juyy Bar that he had triumphed. He rose from his bed and left the house.

He was twelve years old. He went through the ghetto, asking for a job. He knocked on every door and offered his services in return for a day's meal. Almost everyone refused him; he was the mad son of Noah the Gold, the grandson of Esther the Soothsayer, and no one could trust him to do good. He received one offer—to work as a gutter man, digging up human excrement that poured from the toilets of every house into the open gutters on the street— but he turned it down. Moshe knew where he wanted to work: in Honest the Antiquarian's shop, where a treasure was hidden. In order to get the job, he had to hide his ambition.

In the summer of 1848, Muhammad Shah the Dervish died. His Crown Prince, the sixteen-year-old Nasser-ed-Din, was then far away from the capital in Tabriz. In his absence, riots broke out in Tehran and Esfahan for the succession to the throne. Once again, British and Russian missions in Tehran helped the Crown Prince reach the capital and take over the reign. Nasser-ed-Din Shah ruled for half a century. He never forgot the kindness of his friends.

He was a tall man with a wide mustache and a face that revealed no weakness. He had a strong will, an ambitious vision, a keen sense of diplomacy. He was concerned with history—with his own image in the eyes of posterity. He believed in decorum, in greatness, in wealth.

In Tehran he hired artists and sculptors to beautify his palace, spent entire days posing for portraits where he would appear in royal garb, adorned with jewels and silks. Later, when he imported from Europe the art of photography, he kept a photographer on hand at the palace, and did not miss an opportunity to pose for the camera.

Nasser-ed-Din Shah paid biographers and historians to keep records of his reign, maintained a correspondence with other heads of state to make sure no one would forget him. He held court for foreign emissaries and other kings that he invited to Tehran, made certain they were impressed, that they wanted to come back. He spent an entire fortune financing extravagant trips to Europe, taking every time nearly a hundred of his entourage, staying away for so long that when he returned, he had become a stranger to his own kingdom. The trips, he believed, were worthwhile and indispensable. Persia needed to modernize with the help of the West. The Shah went abroad to represent his nation, and speak on its behalf.

But all the time he pursued the goals of modernization, Nasser-ed-Din Shah based his actions on the prophecies of his seers. For a while he contemplated a search for Esther the Soothsayer. Then he was told, by an able minister who sought to divert the Shah's attention from matters of the other world, that his quest was most certainly doomed to failure; the woman in the Shah's Square at Esfahan, the minister explained, had been a ghost—this much was attested to by none other than Fath Ali Shah himself, who had seen Esther up close, and even exchanged words with her. Ghosts did not always appear in a single form. Rather than conduct a worldwide search for the Jewess from Esfahan—thus alerting foreign powers to his taste for the supernatural—the Shah was better off heeding the advice of his own court astrologers.

Nasser-ed-Din Shah agreed, but on one condition: the person who told his death, he insisted, must be a woman—for even a female *ghost* did not have the power to become a man—and she must be a Jew, for Jews had abilities unknown to believers.

The minister brought the Shah a Jewess, promised her immunity from royal wrath, and ordered that she foretell His Majesty's future:

"You will be poisoned by one of your wives," the woman predicted, and soon met an untimely death. Content that he was now in control of his own fate, Nasser-ed-Din Shah hired three hundred food tasters to try every morsel of food destined for the royal palate. He doubled the staff of spies and eunuchs watching the women in his harem, and, once and for all, gave up the search for Esther the Soothsayer.

 Honest the Antiquarian was Esfahan's leading archaeologist and the richest man in Juyy Bar. He worked out of a tiny shop all the way at the end of the ghetto's narrowest street. He had been there for forty-seven years, married and raised his family in the back of the shop, and in all that time never once cleaned the place. The dust, he believed, gave his merchandise a look of authenticity. It also projected the image of poverty, and thus discouraged Muslims from looting him. He had piled so much junk in the shop that it was impossible to tell the real antiques from the fake. He bought cheap and sold dear, and what he sold was often not antique. In 1796, Honest the Antiquarian had sold the skull of Alexander the Great three times to three different Englishmen in the same travel company. With the money, the Jews believed, he had acquired a single precious stone—the ruby that Shaban the jeweler had offered to Agha Muhammad Shah. Everyone had heard of the sale, but no one had ever seen the ruby. Honest the Antiquarian swore on the grave of his mother he had never laid eyes on anything so precious.

He spent his life sitting on a chair in the back of the shop, watching customers come and go and bargaining over the smallest differences in price. He had stayed there so long he had developed asthma from the dust and rheumatism from lack of exposure to light. When he became older his sons offered to help him run the business, but he refused.

"You will rob me blind," he had told them, "and I won't be able to go after you because you are my own blood."

In time the legend of the hidden ruby had lost its original attraction for the people of Juyy Bar. Still, for many years Honest the Antiquarian resisted the idea of hiring help or letting his sons into the business. But as he approached the age of eighty, he became all but incapacitated. His asthma was so severe that breathing was an all-consuming task. His joints swelled so large he could barely move at all. He was desperate for help, and when Moshe asked for a job, he remembered that the boy was mad, and thought this an advantage for himself—an imbecile would not have the wits to rob him—and hired him.

Moshe worked for Honest the Antiquarian for five years, and every day planned to steal the ruby. He tried to learn Honest's way of thinking, to guess the most likely place the old man would have hidden the stone. He wanted to take the stone, run to Esfahan, and become Muslim. He felt no guilt toward Noah or Qamar the Gypsy. He had no love in him—not even for his twin, Leyla. They had abandoned him in the leecher's hands, and now Moshe would abandon them to their poverty.

He decided early on that the stone was hidden in the shop. It was here that Honest the Antiquarian spent all his time, here—on his chair—that he slept even at night when his joints were too stiff to carry him into his room in the back. He never even left to go to the synagogue anymore—not on Sabbath, not on Yom Kippur. He claimed he could not walk, but Moshe believed differently; ever since the stories of the ruby had first begun to circulate in the ghetto, Honest the Antiquarian had sat in the same spot with his chair against the same wall.

The year Moshe turned seventeen, Honest the Antiquarian let his secret slip out of his hand.

It was summer, and for three weeks no customers had walked into the store. Friday night, Honest the Antiquarian closed the shop early and pulled the shutters, leaving only a tiny crack for air through which Moshe could peek in. He sat in his chair and ate the dinner his wife had brought him. When she was gone, he remained in his chair, his eyes closed and his legs dried in place, coughing violently and cursing God. The heat exacerbated his asthma. He got up and paced the shop, making his way painfully through the clutter and the dust, hoping to shake the cough, numb the pain in his joints, and invite sleep. Then all at once he stopped before the back wall—against the stack of silver goblets he claimed had been used only once—at the wedding of Alexander the Great to Princess Roxana. He stared before him without a move or a gesture, then sat down and fell asleep.

Moshe entered the shop through the back, took an antique dagger, and thrust it in the wall where Honest the Antiquarian had stared earlier. The mud crumbled—revealing a tiny nest into which Honest the Antiquarian had placed his treasure.

*　*　*

72

Honest the Antiquarian woke up to find the wall broken and his ruby gone. He stumbled from his chair and tried to scream, but his lungs were choked, and his legs would not move.

"Thief!" he cried, but Moshe was already gone—out of the shop, through the ghetto, and into Esfahan, which embraced him, he thought, with the warmth of a thousand suns.

 Moshe sent the massacre to Juyy Bar—on the third day of Ashura, when the Muslims mourned the death of the Third Disciple, on a Sabbath morning when Honest the Antiquarian still sobbed for his beloved stone and Noah the Gold had stopped looking for his son—he sent hundreds of men armed with daggers and clubs and burning torches to destroy what he had already left behind.

He had gone into Esfahan and changed his name, become Muslim. He had found the Friday Imam and told him a story: of the Jews conspiring secretly to get rich, of Mullah Mirza learning to read Persian and Arabic, of Noah the Gold having made a pact with the devil through which he could create gold. The Imam did not wish to verify Moshe's claims. He ordered a pogrom.

So they came, and for three days in the summer of 1853 they tore through Juyy Bar and burned the temples and the shops and houses. They dragged Noah the Gold out of his teahouse, and set his hair on fire. They found Yehuda the Just's wife still sitting in her courtyard, and took her out into the street, where she withered and died. They took eleven converts on the first day and many more later, and every day they came back until they had gone through all the houses and harmed everyone, but still they were not satisfied; they wanted Yehuda the Just—the leader of the Jews—and he was nowhere to be found.

73

He had dug a hole for himself and stayed there—abandoning his family and his people—and he withstood hunger and thirst until he was certain he would die, and then suddenly he gave himself up. The day he walked to his death, Yehuda the Just was ninety years old and alone. He had lived for close to a century, and never risen above the moment—long ago, before he knew the fear of dying—when he had condemned Esther the Soothsayer. He had judged her unfairly, and elevated his own rank in the eyes of his people, but in the end he was still a rabbi in a damned ghetto long since forgotten by God. He would die, and no one would remember his name.

So he walked to the ghetto square, and stood before his executioners. His eyes were entirely white, his skin yellow with fear. They showed him the blade that would cut him open, and he began to cry, but still he refused to close his eyes. They brought him a Torah and commanded that he spit on it. Yehuda the Just looked up at the men in front of him, and for the first time in his life committed an act of greatness: he spat at his killers instead.

Someone raised a blade and cut Yehuda the Just from the side of his neck down into his stomach, so that his insides boiled out like a fountain, and his head screamed even after it was severed from his body.

They hung each half of his corpse from one side of Juyy Bar's gates. He stayed there for seven days, rotting in the sun. At night the dogs barked at him before they ate his flesh.

 Mad Marushka had wanted to be rich. In her youth she had dreamt of marrying a man who would take her away from her house in Baku—to Moscow and St. Petersburg and Europe. She had imagined herself riding alongside her lover across open roads, standing on board steamships and trains as she journeyed with him toward a new world. She had wanted passion and adventure and everlasting love.

At sixteen she had married a merchant who sold antiques and studied them as art. He was a good man, kind and gentle and undemanding, but he never understood Marushka's passions. He had white skin, pale lips that moved in a soft whisper even when he was not speaking, and a wooden leg that he hung by the side of the bed every night and tied to his knee in the morning. For twenty-three years, Mad Marushka had lain in bed every night and felt the coldness of her husband's fingers against her flesh. She had thought of the world she would never see, and imagined her skin turning white where he touched her. Every night she had prayed he would die in his sleep.

She was a small woman with dark skin, curly black hair, and bones that stood in sharp angles and made her look evil. She had the body of a boy, her mother had always said when she was younger, and lust that only men were capable of. Raised on the Persian-Russian border, she spoke both languages. She was a Jew, like her husband, but she cared nothing for God or his prophets. Mad Marushka bore allegiance only to her own passions.

She had three sons, conceived in anger, who always felt, deep in their bones where the chill of Baku never thawed, the indifference of the woman who should have loved them. At forty, with the boys all grown up and married, Mad Marushka opened her door one day and found love.

It was Moshe—now Muhammad—traveling through Baku on his way into Russia. He sought a place to spend the night. He was eighteen years old, tired and hungry, and still radiant with beauty. Mad Marushka recognized in his face the same longing for escape that had robbed her of every moment of peace in her own life. She took him in.

Against her husband's objections, she let Muhammad eat at their table, then put him to sleep in her sons' old bedroom. That night, as he lay in bed, she stood naked in his doorway.

She was dark, and she made love to him standing, the door still open. By the light of the candle she clung to Muhammad in the room where she had spent her youth, where she had come to see her children every night and prayed that they would vanish—like shadows forced away by light—so she could run into the world and chase her dreams. Afterward she took him outside, in the freezing cold, and with her tongue drew circles up and down his chest and his stomach and his penis until he dragged her back into the house and up the stairs into her sons' bedroom and made love to her again while her husband listened from the next room.

For weeks they kept at each other, shameless and wild, until Marushka's sons could no longer stand the shame of her dishonor and came home to kill their mother's lover. Mad Marushka shielded Muhammad with her own body.

"Touch him," she told her sons, "and I swear I will kill you all myself." Her cruelty frightened Muhammad. He realized he should leave her, but the next day her husband died and Muhammad became trapped.

The husband died quietly, suffocating in his sleep without a sound or a whimper, so that when Marushka found him in the morning, she would not have known that he was dead but for his joints that were chalk-white and stiff. She did not call her sons. She called an undertaker and buried her husband immediately, without observing the rites or even holding a wake. Then she sold off their properties.

She sold everything—the house, the shop, the antiques, even her children's inheritance. She converted all to cash, bought a horse and a carriage, and told Muhammad she would take him to Russia.

She waited until they were out of Baku before asking questions.

She knew Muhammad had a secret, that he was running away. She knew he was a Jew—knew it from his accent and

76

his manners and even his taste in food. She knew of the stone he kept wrapped in a cloth around his leg.

"Let me see it," she demanded, and he was afraid to refuse. She gasped at its beauty.

"It will make us rich," she said.

Muhammad the Jew felt his stomach turn with anguish: Mad Marushka, he realized, wanted him for life.

She was old, he suddenly noticed, and her skin was dry. When she kissed him, he remembered how she had been prepared to kill her sons to defend her lover. When she rolled over to make love to him, he remembered how she had rushed to bury her husband; the undertaker had had no time to stuff the corpse with cotton. At the burial, the man's intestines had erupted and stained the shroud. Still, Mad Marushka had refused to unwrap her husband and clean him before he was laid to rest.

Mad Marushka felt the change in Muhammad and understood he was thinking of escape. She sensed his reluctance when they made love, tasted his bitterness when she talked with him of the future. Yet she commanded his love and claimed his body and rode with him across frozen roads into once-glorious cities of the Czar's falling empire. She drove the horses herself, sitting in front of the carriage with her face unveiled and her hair flowing in the wind, and at every ruined town and avalanche-covered passage they crossed, she stopped and called Muhammad to make love to her till she trembled with exhaustion.

"If you leave me," she told him once and only once, "I will follow you to the end of the world and turn your tears into blood."

From Moscow she took him to St. Petersburg, and from there back into Persia. For a year they traveled, spending her money, aimless and wild and never concerned with the future. At every stop, Muhammad the Jew promised himself he would leave Marushka in the next town. In every city he was held by his greed, and the fear of Marushka's vengeance.

In 1855, Mad Marushka announced she had run out of money.

"We must sell the ruby," she said, and Muhammad the Jew realized the end had come. They were in the province of Khorasan on Persia's northeastern frontier. Mad Marushka had come here looking for an abandoned "undertakers' village."

Ancient Zoroastrians celebrated life and believed death evil. Anyone who touched the dead—all undertakers—were considered impure and outcast. They lived apart, inherited their positions from their fathers, and married only among themselves. They did not bury the dead, for the earth was holy and burial would defile it. They built mortuary towers where the dead were left exposed to the sun—which purified them—and to vultures.

Upon the mortuary tower of the Khorasan village, Mad Marushka summoned Muhammad the Jew and made love to him in the rabid wind.

He lay beneath her that day, his hands repulsed by the coldness of her skin, and despised her breath. He repeated the motions he had practiced for three years, and when it was all over she fell asleep in his arms. Muhammad the Jew stood up and dressed himself. He burned Marushka's clothes, took the pouch full of her husband's money. He took his own ruby, their horses, their food and water. He rode away, and left Marushka to die.

 Joseph the Winemaker was thirty years old and searching for a wife.

He had been married once before, to the daughter of Five-Headed Moses, whom he had taken away with the promise of two gold coins and twelve gold bangles. He was eighteen years old then, she seven. The night of the wedding, he had tortured her to death.

Her name was Khatoun. She was small and frail and so

innocent she had not known what it meant to be married until it was too late. She had black eyes, black hair, and skin the color of white tulips. The night of her wedding she had gone to Joseph's house dressed in new clothes and a white chador. Excited by all the attention she was receiving, she had played with the other children, then fallen asleep in her mother's lap. When the guests started to leave, Khatoun had woken up and asked to go home with her mother.

They explained to her that she was now married to Joseph the Winemaker, that she would have to stay in her new home and sleep "under" her husband. They carried her into Joseph's bedroom above the winery, told her to take her clothes off and wait for him to come calling on her. Khatoun had sobbed—terrified—and begged to leave.

Joseph the Winemaker had never slept with a woman before. He came into the room that night to see his wife, and found a child crying in his bed. Behind the door, a dozen people had gathered to see the marriage consummated. They were the bride and groom's parents, the rabbi who had married them, the elders who commanded authority solely by their age and their years of suffering. They would wait there until Joseph had conquered his bride and proven his manhood and her chastity. If he took too long to perform his task, they would accuse him of weakness. If he failed, they would know that he was impotent.

He tried to calm Khatoun and persuade her to give in to him peacefully. He took her hand, caressed her hair, promised not to hurt her if she did not resist him. He felt no desire for her—he remembered later—only fear that he would fail and be ridiculed by the ghetto. But he was running out of time, the people outside were becoming impatient, and little Khatoun screamed harder and cried more fiercely for her mother with every passing moment.

Joseph the Winemaker began to sweat. He forced Khatoun to the ground and lay on top of her. He would push himself in, he thought, and break the wall of her virginity. When the audience outside had left, he would deal with her fear.

But underneath him Khatoun struggled and gagged and kicked for life. Joseph the Winemaker became furious. He could hear people whispering, imagine their faces as they told one another that Joseph could not handle his wife, that he must be weak and unmanly and impotent. He felt his knees quiver, his penis become limp and useless in his fight to keep Khatoun quiet. He hit her across the face, making her bite her lip and cut it. She screamed, freed herself from under him, and ran to the door. Before the terrified eyes of Joseph the Winemaker she opened the door and threw herself into the arms of her mother outside.

It was all over. Joseph the Winemaker saw his name trampled and lost control. He took Khatoun from her mother and brought her in. He tore her white chador into strips, and with them tied her wrists behind her back. Then he took a longer strip of cloth and tied her knees up around her neck—so that she was folded in half, with her vagina exposed. And he entered her.

Afterward he wiped the blood of her virginity onto a white handkerchief and took it outside for everyone to examine. Assured of the bride's chastity and the groom's strength, the audience dispersed. Joseph the Winemaker decided to teach his wife a lesson. He left her tied all night, shut the door against her pleas, and in the morning he found her dead, with her spine broken and her veins dry.

He spent the next ten years trying to overcome Khatoun's memory. He told people that he had acted out of ignorance and not malice, that Khatoun's death had been accidental, that all Joseph had wanted in the world was to be master of his house and respected by his wife. He was not the first man ever to have caused his wife's death, he reminded everyone. Ruh-Allah the Cobbler had killed two wives by kicking them in the stomach when they were pregnant. Naiim the Blind had yelled at his wife so loudly her heart had stopped beating. But among all the men who had tortured their wives, Joseph the Winemaker was singled out as a criminal. His own family distanced themselves from him, his friends never came to call, and the winery was always empty but for the Muslims who took wine away to Esfahan. It was, more than anything, Khatoun's innocence that no one could forget.

Even after Muhammad the Jew's massacre, those who had survived would not forgive Joseph's past. In time, Joseph the Winemaker came to accept his predicament. He could live with the world's hatred, he decided, but he would not be cheated out of his future. Having lived through the pogrom, he set out to remarry.

He went to see all the matchmakers in the ghetto and promised them money if they brought him offers of marriage. He spread the word that he was not looking for a dowry, that he would pay his life's savings to the girl's parents as "the price of her mother's milk." He even inquired among travelers who came to Esfahan from other ghettos.

"Find me a girl in your town," he asked them, "and I will go there to take her away."

He would settle for an older girl, he decided, or even an ugly one. He would tolerate a small handicap, a bad name. He might even take a girl who was not a virgin—provided she was fertile and honorable. Three years after he had begun his quest, Joseph the Winemaker was still alone.

In 1854 he was thirty-three years old by his own estimation, and desperate for marriage. Having despaired of all the matchmakers he knew, he went to see Taraneh the Tulip, and threatened her for the last time:

"Find me a woman," he asked, "or I swear I will become Muslim and raise my children as Jew-haters."

Taraneh the Tulip smiled, and from the mischief in her eyes Joseph understood that she knew a girl.

"There *is* someone," she said. "The twin sister of Moshe, who sent the massacre. She will marry you because she is alone, eighteen years old, and because no one else will touch her."

On the night of his wedding, Joseph the Winemaker sat in the winery drinking as he waited for his bride to come to his house. An hour after dark he heard Raab Yahya speak to the neighbors in the courtyard. The rabbi had brought Leyla. He took her into Joseph's room—into the bedroom where years ago Khatoun had died—and left her to wait. Descending the steps into the winery, he opened the door and saw Joseph—face glowing in the half-darkness, eyes slightly protruded, filled with doubt. Raab Yahya inhaled the smell of acid wine and closed the door.

When the rabbi had left, Joseph the Winemaker swallowed a final cup of wine and climbed out of the basement. In the courtyard, his head throbbing from the wine, he knelt by the pool and washed his face. The neighbors were watching him. He stopped outside the bedroom. The house was so quiet he could hear the rats move in the far corners of the yard.

He opened the door. He saw a woman standing up against the wall. Behind her on a shelf, an oil lamp burned a pale flame. In front of her on the floor, Joseph's old comforter was spread out and waiting. Joseph the Winemaker prayed to his bed for mercy.

"Well!" he said, forcing himself to walk in. Words escaped him. He saw Leyla shiver once, and prayed he would not frighten her. He wanted her to understand about Khatoun, wanted her—this stranger who was suddenly his wife—to forgive his past, overlook his mistake: "I was young then," he wanted to say, "and no one had taught me the ways of tenderness."

Joseph the Winemaker waited for Leyla to unveil herself. To encourage her, he began to undress himself.

He took off the canvas shoes that he wore like sandals, their backs pressed under his soles. He took off his robe, untied the prayer shawl from around his waist. Sweat ran down the sides of his neck.

He imagined Leyla pale and lifeless, aged beyond her years, reluctant. He imagined himself lying next to her, suffocating in her silence as he tried to make love.

He dropped his pants, then opened the strings on his underwear. He was naked, and she was still in her chador.

Joseph the Winemaker took the oil lamp from the shelf, and brought it up to Leyla's face.

"If you don't undress right now," he told her, "I will not harm you. But I *will* call Raab Yahya, say you were not a virgin, and annul the marriage."

She took off her veil: her eyes were the color of young pine.

She took off her chador: her skin was white, her hair long and shiny and as if dipped in the sun.

She took off her dress: her neck was long and smooth, her body perfect, her flesh glowing.

Joseph the Winemaker felt the lamp tremble in his hand, sending waves of yellow light up and down Leyla's body.

 Muhammad the Jew rode west, away from Mad Marushka, and when he reached Persia's opposite frontier, there on the border of the Ottoman Empire, he still did not dare stop. He went to Baghdad, found Prince Kazim the Boy-Lover, and presented himself for inspection. He would be the prince's lover, he had told himself, sleep with him for a year, and at the end of it, collect the customary reward of cash and jewels that would help him set up a trade. It was the only way he knew to become rich: he could never have sold the ruby. He needed it to remind him he had left Juyy Bar.

Prince Kazim the Boy-Lover was enthralled at the sight of Muhammad. He reached over and fingered the boy as if to taste his flesh. He asked if Muhammad was a virgin. Muhammad the Jew shivered in disgust and said yes.

He became the prince's lover, his most treasured companion, his greatest passion. He immersed himself in a new life, learned Arabic from the prince, English from the prince's doctors and advisers. He even tried to forget Mad Marushka, but every day and every night of his life, he heard her call his name.

He told himself that he must beat the fear, overcome it as he had overcome, he thought, the memory of Juyy Bar. He told himself that Marushka had died, that no one could have survived in the desert as he had left her. He tried to believe that even if she was alive, she had gone her own way, that she had forgotten him by now, cursed him and left his memory to oblivion. He kept his past a secret and lived without friends and never confided even in his lover. Still, every time he rode into the street, Muhammad the Jew expected to find Marushka among the crowd, and every time he heard his name, he thought Marushka was calling.

At the end of the first year of his friendship with the prince, Muhammad the Jew asked permission to leave. Kazim the Boy-Lover begged for more time. He offered Muhammad money and land, jewels and horses, and all the slaves in Baghdad. Muhammad the Jew stayed, and every year he became wealthier and more imprisoned. Slowly he watched the old prince dismiss his other lovers: he gave them to friends, released them, or had them poisoned by his eunuchs. He spent all his time with Muhammad, refused to eat unless Muhammad sat with him, could not sleep unless Muhammad stayed up for him. Afraid that Muhammad the Jew would escape, he assigned guards to watch him at all times, bought women to sleep with him lest he get bored with homosexuality. Then at last he promised his entire fortune if Muhammad would stay till Kazim's death.

Ten years after he had first touched Muhammad the Jew, Prince Kazim the Boy-Lover wrote a will and named Muhammad as his sole inheritor. One morning he lay in his tub of honey-sweetened goat's milk, and asked Muhammad for his daily dose of bull's sperm, consumed orally to ensure longevity. Then he closed his eyes, reclined in the tub, and never even felt the blade that slashed his throat.

Muhammad the Jew buried the Boy-Lover, collected his inheritance, and rushed out of Baghdad. He was thirty-four years old and rich. He went back to Esfahan.

 In the year 1866, tragedy came to Juyy Bar. The winter of 1865 had been short and dry. The earth had become sterile. One by one, Joseph the Wine-maker began to count the signs of disaster. Infants died in their mothers' wombs. Fear invaded the dreams of young children. The land grew poison, and cattle lay on their backs to die in fields and open roads. Then the Plague arrived.

It was summer, and every day stories of death and devastation reached Esfahan. In the north, where the Plague had first struck, the death toll rose so quickly that mass graves could not be dug in time to bury everyone. In Tehran, Nasser-ed-Din Shah escaped his palace and left his wives behind. He quarantined the area around his summer home in the mountains, and ordered that his soldiers banish anyone who ran to him for help.

Among the mullahs, many followed the Shah and left the cities. Those who stayed behind preached that the Plague had been caused by Jews and foreigners. On the anniversary of the battle of Karbala, in which the Third Disciple, Hussein, had died at the hands of Yazid, the streets of every town and village in Persia throbbed with more than usual grief. Traditional processions of men and boys flagellating themselves to mourn a thousand-year-old death were conducted with additional fervor. Symbolic wakes at which women wept and pulled out their hair by fistfuls rang with greater sadness. But all the while the Plague spread farther, and God's ears remained deaf.

In Esfahan, wealthy Muslims packed their belongings and left the city. The Plague had appeared in the north—they moved southward. Others stayed, listening to the growing quiet, watching the shadow of death approach.

In Juyy Bar, Leyla prepared herself for the Plague. In 1865 she had had her first child—a girl, Hannah, with yellow hair, golden eyes, and hands like white butterflies. She was pregnant again, and she knew the Jews had nowhere to run: the laws of Shiism confined them to their own ghettos. She stored food in the house and waited.

In the north and the east, entire villages were emptied, their populations ravaged so suddenly by the Plague that there had been no time, or survivors, to bury the dead. Cities sank into throbbing boils of blood. The earth became pregnant with bodies.

Every day, caravans of refugees crossed the gates of Esfahan—people running one step before the Plague, leaving behind their families, their homes, their land, casting the smell of death around, carrying the germ of the Plague farther. They brought with them the corpses of those who had died along the way, strapped onto their backs, decomposing in the canvas sacks where the heat and the worms of the desert ravaged what the illness had left intact. In the bazaars they crossed, they stopped and sold the clothes of the dead for a penny that they saved for the burial. By the rivers they passed, they camped and washed the corpses, hoping to cast away the infection. Then the Plague reached Esfahan.

There was a mad run. Everyone from Esfahan's governor to the only doctor in the city—an Englishman who had come years ago from the south—took to the desert. Women and children, priests and soldiers and old, old men traveled along dusty roads of panic, pushing forward as the Plague drew closer to them every day, praying, always praying to stay ahead until finally they were caught—away from their homes, there amid the snakes and the scorpions, under a sun that knew no mercy.

To save herself and her children, Leyla went to hide in an underground cave outside the ghetto. Hundreds of years ago, other Jews had dug these caves to hide from the mullahs. Joseph the Winemaker refused to go. He stayed in the winery to guard his pitchers and his old samovar. He barred the door from inside and sat alone, his hands pressed over his ears to block out the sound of children screaming with pain, his heart beating with fear, whispering in his head, a thousand times a day:

"The next time you take a breath . . ."

In the cave, Leyla grew with the infant in her womb. She drank the water she had saved, ate the food she had scavenged in the early days of the Plague. At night she saw Esther the Soothsayer in her dreams.

She emerged out of the silence of Leyla's womb as she had come years ago into the darkness of Noah's nights. She came closer every night—watching, always watching the child in Leyla until the child was born, and then Esther the Soothsayer smiled.

Joseph the Winemaker came to see his second daughter.

"Just as well she won't live through the Plague," he said with a cold sadness. "I couldn't feed another female anyway."

Leyla believed him. The child was small, weak, undernourished. She would be the first to fall prey to the infection, the first to succumb to the darkness of the cave. She held her in her arms and waited for her to die.

She waited a day, a week, a month. She did not name the girl, because it would be harder to bury a child she had believed would live. But every day she heard the sound of her cries, watched the movement of her tiny fists as they grabbed for every faint ray of light. By the time the fever caught the child, Leyla had lost the war.

"I have held her for too long," she pleaded with God. "She belongs to me."

For a week she sat up, nursing the infant. On the eighth day she fell asleep and dreamt of Death. She woke up and went to the mouth of the cave; it was light in the desert. Esther the Soothsayer was walking toward her.

 Esther the Soothsayer arrived in the light of early morning. She walked through the desert like a vision in the sun, a woman with the feet of a mare, and appeared in Juyy Bar one step behind the Plague.

"It is Death," Leyla whispered to Hannah when she saw Esther. "She has come to take the baby from me."

She prayed that Esther would not stop by her door, that she would go on, claim another child from her mother. Her eyes were fixed on the wooden hatch at the top of the stairs, and she listened.

Esther the Soothsayer came closer, closer. She stopped by the cave. Leyla could hear the desert come alive around her, the air move with her breath. She could see the contours of Esther's body—shadowless and pale, like pieces of a dream seeping through the cracks in the hatch. Suddenly, Esther flung the door open.

"I have come to name your child."

She stood shimmering in the gray light of dawn. Her voice, soft and distant, was like the aching memory of a pain long forgotten. Leyla saw her and pressed her child closer to her chest.

It must be a vision, she thought, come to haunt me so I will lose track of time and let Death creep in.

Esther the Soothsayer was staring at the child. Behind her the sky had become silver blue, and the air trembled with the sound of the morning prayer rising from the minarets of Esfahan.

"Leave us," Leyla told her. She could feel the fever raging higher in her child's body. She could see life fluttering in her hands.

Esther the Soothsayer laughed, and the sand around her moved in waves—the desert an ocean of blue light. She reached into the cave—her hands like the branches of an ancient tree—and took the child.

"In the dawn of time there shall be a passage," she said. "A light shall beam through this child's eyes, and she shall see through it into the world of counterparts where every infant is old, and every commencement has ended."

In Esther's hand the infant was calm, as if suddenly rid of the fever.

"A man shall come, riding from the north, with blood on his hands and the anger of God in his eyes.

"He shall sit on the Throne of the Sun, and with a sweep of his hand he shall reach across this empire to free our people.

"His son shall call himself the King of Kings, heir to the Empire of Cyrus. He shall raise this child from the ashes and give her pride.

"But beware! For the King of Kings shall fall, and his throne shall crumble, and the men of God shall paint the skies of this nation with blood."

She held the child up, against the light, and gave her a name:

"Peacock."

 Taraneh the Tulip performed the local dances of twenty-two Persian tribes. She was a master at the *santour*, learned music by ear, wrote her own songs. She worked with two men—a *tar* player and a *donbaki*. They entertained at weddings and circumcisions, on new year's day and on the night of the feast of Yalda. Always at the end of the show, Taraneh the Tulip painted her face, donned a costume, and acted in a one-woman play.

She had been born in Shiraz, a rabbi's daughter, and she never knew what she looked liked until she was married. Her father did not allow mirrors in the house: a woman who saw her own reflection, he believed, might become vain, admire beauty, contemplate sin. Taraneh the Tulip had only imagined the shape of her body by staring at her older sister when she undressed. Her sister was twenty years old, but unmarried. She lived in a separate room, never ate with her family, never—never—spoke with her father.

"Your sister has sinned," their mother told Taraneh every time she questioned her sister's predicament. Her mother would not explain any more. Taraneh the Tulip always wondered if her sister's beauty had caused her to sin. She wondered if she, too, was beautiful. Once, when she was six years old, she sat in the winter sun and tried to find her likeness in a block of melting ice. The rabbi caught her. To teach her obedience, he shaved her head.

Taraneh the Tulip locked herself in the basement of their house and swore never to leave. She thought she would remain bald forever, sobbed against the wall and repented from sin. But as her hair began to grow and the memory of her punishment faded, she gave in to childish curiosity, and began to explore the basement for the first time. She dug through the junk stored around her, and imagined a purpose for everything she found. She discovered her mother's wedding dress, her father's first prayer shawl. She found the Torah where her great-grandfather had written all of his children's birthdays, the "tear jar" into which her grandmother had wept upon the passing of her husband. At the bottom of the pile, hidden in an alcove in the wall, Taraneh the Tulip found a dowry chest.

"Don't *touch* that," her mother screamed when she found Taraneh at the chest. She had brought Taraneh's dinner. She threw the food on the ground, hoisted her daughter away from the chest, and shoved the chest back with her foot. Her eyes were terrified.

"This damned thing is *jinxed*."

Afterward, Taraneh the Tulip heard her mother whispering the tale to another woman, sobbing into her chador as she spoke, interrupting herself every time Taraneh approached. There had been a wedding. The next morning the groom's mother had come to inspect the dowry. She had opened the chest, then immediately awakened the bride and sent her home to her father.

"It was the *chest*," Taraneh's mother insisted. "The chest is jinxed."

Taraneh the Tulip suddenly realized that the bride in the tale was her own sister.

For ten days in the month of her penance, Taraneh the Tulip fought to conquer her curiosity. She paced the basement from morning to night—her arms crossed as if to avoid sin—and stared at the chest that had released evil into her sister's life. Then at last she resigned herself to hell, forced the lock, and searched through the dowry: there was a pair of silver candlesticks, a few embroidered sheets, a tablecloth. There was a comforter, a small rug. Buried deep in the shroud, wrapped in canvas and rope, Taraneh the Tulip found a *santour*.

She put the *santour* on the ground before her, picked up the pair of thin metal sticks used to play the strings, held them each between her thumb and forefinger, and took them to the instrument. She heard the *santour* sigh, and knew she was lost.

She played secretly for ten years—in her father's house, where her sister taught her, then in her husband's. She married another rabbi—her father's brother—and as she hid the *santour* in her dowry chest, Taraneh the Tulip realized she was inviting doom. Two years later, her husband discovered the *santour*. Before he could send her back to her father's home, where she would suffer a fate equal to that of her sister, Taraneh the Tulip ran away from Shiraz and never returned.

* * *

She traveled across Persia, chased from one ghetto and into another, and in every place she learned the people's music and dances. When she arrived in Juyy Bar she was twenty-six years old and resolved to stay. The first time Raab Yahya attacked her at his Sabbath sermon, warning the people against "the stranger with the wicked instrument," Taraneh the Tulip realized she must fight. That night she appeared in the ghetto square, dressed in a scarlet gown, her hands and face painted crimson, her hair glowing red. She waited for an audience to gather, took a bow, and then began to dance—a slow, graceful performance that lasted twelve minutes, and in the course of which she managed to re-create a tulip's life from inception to end. No one ever called Taraneh "whore" again.

So she stayed and, to earn extra income, worked as a matchmaker, a cook, a maid. She adopted a child—Salman the Coal Seller—who had been orphaned at the age of three, and had no relatives to raise him. After a while she was invited to play in Esfahan. In 1869 she was called to perform at the wedding of the governor's son to the daughter of Esfahan's Friday Imam. Taraneh the Tulip spoiled the wedding and stole the groom.

It was an unprecedented event, the greatest wedding in a hundred years, and every person of rank and reputation was invited. The groom was twenty years old, educated in Baghdad, and so rich he had waived his right to a dowry. The bride's family were so eager to form the union, they had insisted on a wedding only two weeks after the courtship had begun. The night of the celebrations, they were outraged to find a Jew among the performers. Still, not wishing to spoil the festivities, they had allowed Taraneh to make her appearance. Halfway through her Tulip act, the governor's son annulled the wedding. He had fallen in love, he said, with the Jew in the scarlet gown.

For a year, Esfahan roared in calumny. Then at last Taraneh the Tulip married the governor's son, left Juyy Bar, and went to live in a house with rooms full of music.

When he first returned to Esfahan, Muhammad the Jew built himself a house on Char Bagh Street and hired servants and maids and gardeners. He rented five connecting shops in the Shah's bazaar and filled them with antiques and Persian carpets and silverwork. Dressed in silks and velvet, he rode around town on an Arabian horse, and wore a long top hat embroidered with gold threads and a ruby so stunning that people stopped on the street to stare at him long after he had stormed by.

He had come from nowhere—a stranger with a legendary fortune, with a face as beautiful as a dream, and eyes so bitter few were those who dared engage them. He traveled alone most of the year, traded in antiques and rugs and precious stones. And he lived alone, surrounded by the tall brick walls of his house and the ancient trees that shielded it from sunlight. He never received anyone, never spoke with his neighbors in the bazaar. At night, the maids swore, he never slept.

They heard him pace up and down his room from dark until dawn, looking out the window into the garden that was filled with shadows and the spirits of the evil dead, falling asleep at last with the morning breeze on his face, only to awaken in the twilight to the sound of peddlers screaming their trade. During the day he was watchful and alert and suspicious, always ready to question a servant or an employee about his intentions on any one matter, forever about to engage in an argument with clients or neighbors or even visitors. Muhammad the Jew, everyone said, was a man on the run.

In 1871, Muhammad the Jew traveled to Kurdistan to meet with a tribal chief—Firooz Khan—who had sent for him a year earlier, asking for jewels. Muhammad the Jew rode through bare mountains scorched by the unrelenting sun, across steep valleys strewn with dust and carved with the beds of dried streams and waterways. He found a desolate plain spotted with the black tents of the nomads, made his way through thirsty flocks of sheep and camels searching vainly for a grassy patch. Around the campground, dogs barked at him and blocked his way. A young woman sat unveiled by her tent, weaving a canvas rug as her father slept close by. Kurdish women did not wear chadors. She saw Muhammad the Jew and understood he was the guest her chief had been expecting. She called the dogs away.

Firooz Khan received Muhammad with disappointment. He had wanted to buy jewels, he said, but only weeks before, locusts had ravaged the plain where the tribe camped every year, and now the Khan's cattle were starving in the heat. He had no cash for the stones, no cattle to offer in exchange.

Muhammad the Jew dined with the chief, then went into his own tent to sleep. After midnight he stepped out, compelled as always by a sense of danger, and walked to a clearing behind the campgrounds. He saw a girl with dark skin and black hair, riding naked on a horse. She galloped up and down the foot of the mountain, her horse panting, her own skin covered with moisture. A long time later she felt Muhammad's glare, turned around and saw him, then rode off. Muhammad the Jew recognized the girl who had greeted him that morning.

"Give me *her*," he asked Firooz Khan the next day. "She will be payment enough for all the jewels you want."

Her name was Afagh. She was fourteen years old and filled with such kindness she charmed even the most hostile of her enemies. Muhammad the Jew loved her so much, people said, that he became kind and accepting and even friendly toward the world. He hired seven maids to serve Afagh, decorated her bedroom with silk curtains and pearl-studded cushions, planted a garden of jasmine on the balcony outside her window. He brought her French perfume smuggled into Bandar 'Abbas aboard European ships, paid artists from Tehran to come and draw her portrait. He threw feasts and invited all the dignitaries in Esfahan, served them wine in golden cups and lamb on jewel-studded plates, then

94

sat back and watched them admire the girl he had found in the mountains of Kurdistan.

Then she became pregnant.

Muhammad the Jew went pale at the news, and begged Afagh to kill the fetus.

"I want no heirs," he pleaded with her. "I want no trace of me left behind."

For months they fought. In the end she bore a son. Muhammad the Jew saw the boy and damned him publicly.

Afagh asked that he name his child. He chose the name Ezraeel—Angel of Death—and never touched the boy in his life.

 In 1871 famine came to Persia. It lasted longer than anyone could count, and by the time it was over, one-third of the country's population had perished. At first the people ate the carcasses of animals. They hunted for snakes, they fried grasshoppers and flies, even scorpions. They ate the leaves and roots and dried branches of trees. Children stuffed mud down their throats to choke the constant hunger. Pregnant women dug the walls with their nails and chewed on clay. When there was nothing else to eat, they ate the dead.

Decades would go by before anyone who had survived the Great Famine of 1871 dared admit to cannibalism. In ordinary times, Muslims had eaten neither pork nor anything that had been touched by an infidel. Armenians had had only fish on Fridays, and Jews had gone completely without meat unless it was kosher. Now they all fried thin strips of human flesh and swallowed it in order to live.

They waited every day in the cemeteries—scavengers hiding behind gravestones to watch people bury their relatives dead from hunger. When the burial was over, they would dig up the bodies and carve out the cheeks, the biceps, and the buttocks. If the body was too thin and had no flesh on the outside, they would open its stomach and take out the intestines and the liver. Most buried the bodies again, but many left them exposed for the vultures to attack.

In the second year of the famine, the Jews of the Tehran ghetto wrote a letter, composed in Hebrew, in which they asked the Jewish leaders of Europe for help.

"In some way or another, if possible," they prayed, "bring us forth out of this burning furnace of Persia to the Holy Land, or place us under your protective wings, or help us emigrate to other countries."

A year passed before the letter, entrusted to a messenger traveling out of Persia, reached its destination. In time, European and American Jewry would collect nineteen thousand British pounds to send to Persia, "to be distributed among Jews and non-Jews alike." The government of Nasser-ed-Din Shah, seeking to finance his next trip to Europe, fought hard to tax the money, and relented only under great pressure from Europe.

In Esfahan, news of the money brought hope. Food would arrive in caravans, people thought—enough food to save everyone. The mullahs who had always warned against infidels now found themselves hard-pressed to explain Europe's generosity. They said that the food was sent by God— at the direct request of His Holiness the Friday Imam of Esfahan—and that Europeans had taken credit for it unjustly. Members of the royal family who had done nothing to help their own subjects were also embarrassed. They claimed that the food was sent from the Shah's own kitchens, and the funds released from His Majesty's personal treasury. The Jews, who knew the truth, only believed that their suffering had come to an end.

But months went by, many more starved, and the caravan of food never appeared in Esfahan. Slowly the Jews realized that there was no food left in Persia to buy, that what little was imported remained in the hands of the very rich, that the money sent from Europe had circulated among Persian officials and corrupt mullahs until it disappeared into their pockets. Still, they did not dare give up hope. For years after they had discovered the futility of their belief, mothers in Juyy Bar put their children to sleep with the promise that when morning came a caravan of food would arrive at the gates of their city.

In the house of Joseph the Winemaker, little Peacock had waited for the caravan so long she woke up every morning insisting that they go look for it.

"It has lost its way," she would cry to Leyla with such conviction that nothing would have made her believe otherwise.

"If we don't find it soon, it will turn back and go to Tehran and we will never see it until we die."

She was seven years old, small and thin and so bony Leyla was always amazed that she could walk. Her skin was dark and aged from lack of nutrition. Her teeth had decayed before they had ever grown. Her body was small and undeveloped. But she had Leyla's eyes—those green eyes that brought a tremor to the hearts of men—and her spirit was hard and raw and unconquered. Sometimes, when they were alone together and Peacock had fallen asleep in her arms, Leyla would look at her child and believe that she was meant to have been beautiful—that in another day and age she would have grown to resemble Leyla herself, that she would have been strong and confident—that destiny, as Esther the Soothsayer had said, would have elevated her to a place of happiness and pride.

Joseph the Winemaker took Peacock begging in Esfahan. He walked into the city, carrying her most of the way because she was weak from hunger and could not walk a great distance. She was eight years old. All the way there, she fought and screamed and swore she would not go.

"They won't feed us," she said. "They don't feed Jews."

Joseph the Winemaker swallowed his bile and prayed for luck. Ever since Muhammad the Jew had returned to Esfahan, rumors had circulated in Juyy Bar that he was the son of Noah the Gold, Leyla's twin brother who had sent the massacre of 1853. People had even traveled into the city, lurked outside Muhammad's home and his shop in the bazaar, waiting to steal a glance at him, and then they had all returned to say Yes, Muhammad the Jew was indeed the son of Noah the Gold. In all that time, Muhammad never sent word to the ghetto for his sister. When the famine started, he bought food from abroad, hired armed men to fight bandits and thieves who raided the caravans, and gave away what he and his servants did not eat. For two years his kitchen fed dozens of people every day—Muslims only, for Muhammad the Jew had left strict orders to reject Jews. Still, Joseph the Winemaker insisted that Leyla go to him for help.

"You are his *sister*," he would scream. "You were born of the same seed, raised in the same womb. A man cannot despise his own blood."

Leyla never went. Muhammad the Jew never sent for her.

They survived the first two years of the famine only through the kindness of Taraneh the Tulip. She came to Juyy Bar once a month, dressed in fine clothes, riding an Arabian mare with its tail painted red. She brought Leyla a bag of rice, a keg of oil, a gourd of water. She sang to the children. She played the *santour* in Joseph's winery. But in 1873, Taraneh the Tulip left Esfahan; her husband's father had lost the governorship of the city. He moved to Tehran, and summoned all his children to live with him in the capital. Taraneh the Tulip came to Juyy Bar to say farewell. Joseph the Wine-maker cried when he saw her leave. He knew that without her they would all starve. Once again he thought of Mu-hammad the Jew.

Outside the house of Muhammad the Jew in Esfahan, Joseph saw a crowd waiting, and joined them. It was the middle of the morning, and Muhammad's kitchen had not yet opened to beggars. He found a place near the main gates and put Peacock down.

"When the gates open," he told her slowly so she would remember, "push your way in and don't stop until you find the kitchen."

He gave her an empty canvas bag.

"Give this bag to a servant and ask that they fill it. Tell them you are Muhammad the Jew's niece, Leyla's daughter, and that you will *die* if they don't feed you."

Around noon the gates swung open and all the beggars rushed inside. Joseph nudged Peacock forward.

"Go," he said, but his voice almost broke. "Come back with food."

Peacock held the bag against the yellow patch on her chest and walked quickly. She followed the other beggars through a barren garden and into a courtyard as large as the main square in Juyy Bar. She saw the kitchen; the beggars had already lined up outside. She took a place and waited. She did not look up until her turn had come. Just as she opened her bag to the maid who handed out the rations, someone pushed her:

"No Jews."

It was a boy, Ezraeel, Muhammad the Jew's son. He was younger than Peacock, but she was weak and hungry and trapped, and he terrified her.

"I said no Jews."

He pushed her again and she fell. He dragged her bag out of her fist and threw it on the ground. Peacock wanted to reach for it, but he blocked her way. "Go away." He kicked her. She looked up at him. His eyes were yellow. She saw them, and all at once she knew he was sad and afraid and unwanted.

She got up and charged the boy, hit him so hard across the chest he gasped for air and fell to the ground. The servants ran toward them, but she grabbed her chador and was about to escape when someone caught her.

"She hit me," the boy moped. "That Jew-girl *hit* me."

A woman knelt down and looked in Peacock's face.

"This child is hungry," she said, and Peacock felt her rage dissipate. "We must feed her before Muhammad comes home."

The boy began to protest. The woman took Peacock's hand and led her around the kitchen, away from the envious stares of the other beggars and the threatening glares of the maids.

The boy ran behind them. "But Father said no Jews."

They went into a house full of sunlight and the smell of life, through rooms filled with silk and lace and velvet, Persian rugs and locked oak closets into which, Peacock imagined, someone had packed all the treasures of the world. They stopped in a storage room.

The woman bent down and eased the bag out of Peacock's hand.

"Come back whenever you want," she whispered as she opened a door in the wall.

There were sacks full of rice and flour, trays of almonds and sweetbreads and dates, baskets of dried vegetables and fruit. The woman was filling Peacock's bag. She took a date from a tray and offered it to Peacock.

"There," she said. "Eat this now."

Peacock felt the sugar on her tongue and tried to swallow, but the sweetness was overpowering and she threw up.

"She's sick," the boy cried in disgust as bile flew into Peacock's chador and onto her shoes. Afagh bent down to help her, but Peacock let go of the bag and began to run.

"Wait!" Afagh cried, but Peacock went out the door and

through the house, out the gates and into the street full of dust and hunger, where Joseph the Winemaker received her with cold dismay.

All her life, Peacock would grieve for the food she had left behind.

 Taraneh the Tulip came from Tehran to see Leyla. She brought food, and the smell of hope, and the optimism that had always guarded her against life's destruction. She sat in the courtyard of Joseph the Winemaker's house, above the steps leading into the basement winery, and took Peacock in her lap. Hannah, nine years old, slept in the shade of one of the columns surrounding the porch. She was thin and frail, trembling in her sleep, but still beautiful. Taraneh the Tulip realized Hannah would die soon of starvation.

"Marry your daughters off," she told Leyla. "If you can't feed them yourself, give them to someone who can."

Leyla smiled in bitterness and shook her head. Even without the famine, she said, few men would have married Joseph the Winemaker's girls—or the great-grandchildren of Esther the Soothsayer, who was punished for adultery.

Taraneh the Tulip was not swayed.

"Give them to a Muslim, then," she insisted. "Find a rich Muslim and pray they will be loved."

She told Leyla about Zil-el-Sultan: he was the most influential of Nasser-ed-Din Shah's children, more popular than the crown prince, and the Shah had placed him in charge of the entire southern half of Persia. His title, Zil-el-Sultan, meant "The King's Shadow," and evoked an authority second only to the Shah's. He came to the Palace of Forty Pillars, replacing Taraneh's father-in-law in his capacity as Esfahan's governor, and he had brought with him a ray of hope for the Jews. In proximity to the Shah or his children, the mullahs commanded less power; in Tehran, where the Shah lived, and in other cities where his sons were governor, the incidence of massacres and persecution decreased remarkably.

Still, Zil-el-Sultan was a feared man. He was generous but cruel, strong but impetuous. His four permanent wives were all from noble blood, but he had married them only to secure his position with the powerful families of Tehran. He treated the permanent wives with indifference, spending most of his time with the hundreds of temporary ones he married on limited contract, and whom he discarded as soon as their time expired.

"Take Hannah to Zil-el-Sultan," Taraneh the Tulip urged Leyla. "Don't tell them she's a Jew, because if they find out, the harem eunuchs will poison her. Give her to the prince and pray he will like her."

Leyla understood she had no choice—that her daughters would die soon of malnutrition, that she herself would soon starve and leave the girls without hope. One night when Joseph the Winemaker was asleep, she dug into the floor of the winery, and took out the small treasure he had buried in case of a pogrom: there were twelve gold bangles and two gold coins—gifts he had made to Khatoun's parents, and which he had reclaimed after the young bride's death. Leyla filled the hole with earth, then covered it with a canvas rug. The next day she told Joseph the Winemaker she was going to Esfahan to beg for food. She went instead to the bazaar.

She sold the bangles, and with the money she bought lace. She ordered silk satin and rhinestones and a pair of white slippers embroidered with silk paisley flowers. She smuggled the material into the house and every day worked in secret. She stitched together strips of lace and satin, made a five-layered skirt, a short jacket, a long veil that she covered with rhinestones till it glittered from end to end. With the bigger stones she made a small tiara. She finished just as Joseph the Winemaker discovered that his bangles were gone.

"Thief!" he screamed one night, and turned to Leyla for answers. Leyla grabbed Hannah in her arms, threw the bundle of clothes on her shoulder, and ran out the door.

It was dark. Hannah was afraid. They walked to Esfahan, hiding in the shadow of walls and stopping at every corner: no one, least of all a Jew, was allowed to walk the streets of Esfahan at night. The Shah and his heirs suspected the world of plotting against them, and so imposed a permanent curfew to prevent conspirators from meeting under the cover of dark.

On Char Bagh Street in Esfahan, a night watchman strolled with a lantern hanging from the tip of a wooden pole. His job was to arrest anyone who did not know that night's password—kept secret among the most trusted of the Zil's friends. But he was drunk, and as he walked past Leyla, his eyes clouded by arrack, he did not see her.

"All is safe in the King's shadow," he cried as he faded down the street.

They reached the Shah's Square. Leyla waited for dawn, and the sound of the morning *namaz*—the Muslim prayer performed publicly five times a day—to rise from the minaret of the Shah's Mosque. Then she showed Hannah the wedding gown.

"Am I to be married?" the child gasped.

Leyla held her daughter's face in her hands. She knelt down and kissed Hannah's eyes.

"You are to try," she said.

She watched Hannah wear the gown. She gave her the shoes, put the tiara on her head, hung the veil around her. Then she put her hand on Hannah's head and blessed her.

"Open your hands," she said, and into each one of Hannah's palms she put a gold coin.

"Keep them in your fists. Don't show them to anyone except your husband."

They walked into the crowded street, a woman in a faded chador leading a girl in a wedding gown. They went down

Char Bagh Street to the Shah's Square, through the square and toward the Ali Ghapoo, where thieves and murderers took refuge. Eyes stared at them. Heads turned. Men left their shops and followed them. Women dragged their children and came up to watch.

Inside the Ali Ghapoo, Leyla stopped and faced Hannah.

"Stay here," she commanded, her heart full of pain. "Don't leave until they come for you from the palace."

She turned away. She never saw her daughter again.

And so it was that Hannah stood in the blazing sun of noon, on the first day of the first month of summer in the year 1875, and stared ahead into the garden of the Palace of Forty Pillars without knowing why she was there or what she was to expect. She stood there shining like a diamond in the light, her dress soft and white and beautiful, her veil reflecting the sun, blaring in the eyes of even the most indifferent of passersby until they stopped and stared at her, asking questions she could not answer, examining her without daring to touch her. She stood surrounded by an ever-thickening crowd and waited as her mother had told her to—waited until the day stretched into evening and the sun set into the shady corners of the Palace of Forty Pillars, and at last Zil-el-Sultan heard news of the child bride in the rhinestone tiara waiting in the Ali Ghapoo.

"Bring her to me," he demanded.

The guards took Hannah into the inner courts of the palace and unveiled her before Zil-el-Sultan. He smiled at her beauty. He thought she had a lucky face.

"Who left you?" he asked, but Hannah was afraid to answer.

"What is your name?"

"Where did you come from?"

She said nothing. She stood before him, lost and afraid and speechless, and, trembling, stretched out her arms and opened her hands to reveal the gold in each palm. Zil-el-Sultan was startled.

He sent her to his harem favorite, who looked her over and was pleased. She called a mullah who declared Hannah Muslim and married her off to Zil-el-Sultan. They gave her a new name: Taj-Banoo—the Crown Lady. They never asked about her family; she had come into his harem, and from then on she had no other life. The doors closed and the past faded and Hannah knew, without ever being told, that she could never look back.

Inside the harem, the wives undressed Hannah and inspected her hair and body. They rubbed her skin with cleansing plants and scrubbed her with healing stones. They put oil on her stomach, perfumed her hair, and lowered her into a shallow pool made of dark blue tiles and filled with spring water warmed by a constant flame. They washed her and dried her skin, rubbed her this time with jasmine. They painted her eyes with silver nitrate, painted her lips and her cheeks with rose petals, braided pearls into her hair, hung diamonds around her neck. They taught her how to walk before the prince, how to speak. Then they took her into his bedroom. She was nine years old, and as he kissed her that night, Zil-el-Sultan felt a tooth loose in her mouth.

 Muhammad the Jew became a stranger in his own house. The birth of his son had created a distance between him and Afagh he could not overcome. When he saw her with Ezraeel, all he could think of was Noah the Gold and Qamar the Gypsy and the dark room in the ghetto where worms crawled into the water he drank. He could not tell Afagh of his pain, but he expected her to understand him, and when she did not, he became cold and as severe with her as he was with strangers. He left her with the child and went on one journey after another, came back every time for a shorter interval and with greater anguish. He slept with her only once more, and again she became pregnant. In 1875 he left Esfahan and threatened never to return. By then he was already lost: Mad Marushka had found him and was coming to call.

She slammed her fists against the door of his house one early morning and woke up the household. It was still dark, but the servants opened the door. They saw an old woman, her hair long and knotted, her skin scarred and scabbed and so covered with grime they coughed from the stench of her dirt and infections.

"Call your mistress," she barked at them. She knew Muhammad was gone. She kissed Afagh's knees.

"Please," she begged, "I need a job."

Afagh needed no maids. She was not allowed to hire anyone without her husband's approval. But she was moved by Marushka's poverty, by her age and the revolting smell of her skin. She let her stay.

"I will carry out your every command," Mad Marushka wept gratefully on Afagh's hand. "I will even deliver your child."

She treated her mistress with a mother's kindness. She waited on Afagh day and night, became her friend, gained her trust. When Afagh went into labor, Marushka took her into the bedroom and spread a bed of sheets and pillows on the floor. She made Afagh crouch on the sheets, locked the door from inside, and forbade the servants to call a midwife.

The labor lasted all day and into the night. The contractions were long and frequent, but Afagh's progress was slow, and her womb reluctant. Mad Marushka sat next to Afagh and rubbed her back, washed her face with cold water, and held her up from under the arms when she had no more strength to crouch. At dawn the next morning, she put her hand inside Afagh and announced that the time had come.

"Push," she commanded. "It's here."

Afagh gathered her strength and pressed. Blood gushed out around Marushka's wrist. The child's head appeared. Mad Marushka gripped the skull and forced it back.

"Push," she cried again. "Push harder."

She felt the head bend in her fingers.

"Push."

She twisted the neck.

There was a single moment of terror: Afagh realized she was about to be murdered with her child. She struggled, then gave in to the force of another contraction. Drenched in the sweat of victory, Mad Marushka looked up and saw Ezraeel—hands outstretched on the glass window, face distorted in a deaf scream—standing on the balcony outside Afagh's bedroom. Distracted, she eased the pressure on Afagh long enough to allow for a last push.

Afagh delivered her child, then leaned back, closed her eyes, and died.

 The first time she heard Solomon the Man sing, late at night when all of Juyy Bar was asleep and even the stray cats were silent, Peacock sat up in bed, trembling, and thought about running from her father's house.

It was the night of the feast of Yalda, the longest night of the year, which ancient Persians had celebrated with music and song and old tales recounted to children around the fire. Long ago, before the Plague of 1866, Joseph the Winemaker had kept the winery open on this night. He had brought out his fiddle and sung to his customers in a voice that was crude and raspy, until someone had asked him to stop.

"It isn't much," he would admit to the customers, "but it would be pretty—the music—if I knew how to play it right."

But the sounds of music had long since died in Juyy Bar. In all the years since Peacock was born, Joseph the Winemaker had never played his fiddle. Music, like rain, was only a whimper in everyone's dreams.

And so, on this night when she heard the sound of Solomon's song, Peacock thought that she was dreaming and closed her eyes again to sleep. Feeling the sour bile of hunger rise to her throat, she drew her legs into her chest and felt in the darkness for the warmth of Hannah's body next to her. She felt only a bare sheet, remembered again that her sister was gone, vanished and unheard from, as if she had never been. She tried to sleep again, but the music would not fade. It was a man's voice—one she had never heard before. It emerged from among the soft notes of a flute, deep and velvety and filled with the pain of a thousand hearts. It sang a tale of sorrow, of love gone astray, of nights cold and empty but for the wine and the music of loneliness.

Between the verses he played the flute. One by one the notes of a melody drifted into the air—like pollen that turned the wasteland of Peacock's sleep into a field of violets. Next to her, Leyla had also awakened. Intrigued by the music, the voice that had erupted from the silence of a dozen years, she rose from her bed and went to the door. Through the cracks in the wood she looked into the courtyard and saw the doors of the other rooms opening as people came out to listen.

Peacock followed her mother to the door. A moment later, Joseph awakened.

"Stand back," he growled at them. "Women have no business peeking out in the middle of the night."

He pulled his pants up around his waist and slipped his feet into his canvas shoes. He was going out, he mumbled, to find the source of the disturbance and stop it. Peacock watched him. His body, like a collection of bones on which hung the skin of a much larger man, moved painfully through the darkness. She found herself praying that he would not discover the intruder, that he would not manage to quiet the voice and drive it away. When he was gone, she went back to the door again and peered out.

In the courtyard, people stood listening—men and women and dreamy-eyed children with large heads and bloated stomachs. For years now, sleep had evaded Juyy Bar. Hunger ate away at the strength of the living, disease drew them to suffering. They wandered through the night, ghosts who nevertheless felt pain, who had memories, sleeping here and there when the life had run out of them, finding no reason to return to their homes where their loved ones had died in their arms, where there was no fire, no food, no calm.

"It is coming from the top of the alley," one of the men said to the others. "It must be a traveler who's lost his way."

The music stopped. Then they heard the laughter—sudden and spontaneous and almost unreal, one man's burst of uninhibited pleasure as striking and fantastic as the music that had sung Juyy Bar awake.

Peacock opened the door and stepped out. Leaning against a column in the courtyard, she drew her chador around her and closed her eyes. She listened, hoping to draw out of the darkness the last echoes of the music and keep them in her heart forever. But the music had faded. There was another sound—a soft, rhythmic hum that she remembered from the past but could not place. She opened her eyes. The air smelled of wet dust—the sweet, sweet smell of life. A drop fell on her cheek.

He had sung—the stranger with the flute—and brought rain to Juyy Bar.

 Mad Marushka had arrived. Her crimes had paid off.

She moved into Afagh's bedroom, into her clothes and her bed. She took over Muhammad the Jew's house, invited guests, threw lavish feasts, hired men to sleep in her bed and eat in her kitchen. She placed orders with tailors and jewelers and merchants, spent hours every day in front of the mirror. She painted her cheeks and her eyelids, combed her hair and ran strings of Afagh's pearls through her braids. She tried to capture in her own image the beauty she had never known, the youth she had long since lost. Never once in all that time did she find herself disturbed by guilt, or haunted by Afagh's memory, or even

109

bothered by the fear and hatred that she saw in Ezraeel's face.

Months after his daughter's birth, Muhammad the Jew returned to Esfahan. He rode through the city on his Arabian horse, the stolen ruby still shining above his forehead, a caravan of donkeys with loads of antiques following him from a distance. He reached Esfahan at noon. The streets were silent but for the echo of the midday *namaz* against the arched roofs of the alleys that led away from the mosques. Muhammad the Jew did not stop to pray. He rode toward his house, through its iron gates and the rose gardens and the fruit orchards that were destroyed by the drought.

He left his horse at the stable and walked up to the main building. The door was ajar. The corridor that led from the garden into the courtyard smelled of horses and other men's sweat. On the balcony, two maids stood with their heads only half-covered, laughing with a young man whom Muhammad did not recognize. When they saw him, the maids tightened their chadors around their faces and ran away. The man remained in place, staring at Muhammad with insolent eyes.

Muhammad the Jew entered the women's side of the house and climbed the steps. The doors of all the rooms were open; the furniture, once immaculate, was in disarray. Here and there the sound of women's laughter rose toward the staircase. Someone came to the door, unveiled, and peeked at him as he went by.

He climbed to the third floor and toward Afagh's bedroom. He pushed the door open and walked in. Drenched in sunlight, the bed was unmade, surrounded by an open mosquito net that rose above it like a pyramid of lace. It was hot. The room, Muhammad the Jew knew instantly, smelled of Mad Marushka.

She stood on the balcony outside the bedroom. She was dressed in Afagh's clothes. She wore her shoes, her jewels, the pearl-studded combs in her hair. She saw Muhammad and came inside.

"Your wife died," she said. "I killed her myself."

Muhammad the Jew never imagined he could rid himself of Marushka now that she had found him. He left everything to her, and abandoned himself to mourning—drowned in the guilt of having left Afagh alone and unwarned. He named his daughter Sanam, and took her to live with him in a separate part of the house. He did not take Ezraeel. He never even answered his calls.

But Sanam was born deformed and retarded. Her head was misshapen, her neck twisted, her eyes terrified. As an infant she cried so hard that the nursemaids smoked opium, hoping the drugged milk would calm her. Later, before she could even walk, she was given to fits of temper so violent they would have to hold her to the ground and force her jaws open so she could breathe. She never learned to speak. She only uttered sounds—shrill, violent cries that sent a tremor up her nurses' spines and kept them from loving her. She never recognized anyone—not even Muhammad the Jew—and no one could touch her. She would scream at the first contact, tear off her clothes, and run naked through the house. The maids would chase her into the garden, where she would climb a tree and hide in the branches like a cat.

Muhammad the Jew called doctors from Tehran and Baghdad and Russia. He wrote to an Englishman he had known in India, sent for advice and opinion from as far away as Europe. Everyone said the same thing: Sanam would never improve. She was better off put to death.

"Give her rat poison," Marushka suggested joyfully every time she saw the maids chasing Sanam. "Put her in a canvas bag and throw her into the river."

By the age of four, Sanam had become dangerous to herself and others. She attacked Muhammad, hit her own head against the wall so hard she fractured her forehead. She dug her bare hands into the hot coals at the bottom of the stove until her fingers had melted together. She dragged boiling pots of water from the fire and threw them on the servants. Once she sat on the flames from a cookfire and never felt herself burn until it was too late. After that, Muhammad the Jew kept her tied to her bed. One by one her doctors stopped calling and her nurses would not come to work no matter what Muhammad paid them, and the maids, unable to stand the child's pain, avoided her at all cost.

"Kill her," they told Muhammad every year as Sanam grew older and more tortured. "Relieve her of her suffering."

He knew he should—that it would be the most merciful of all acts—and yet he refused. He watched her sometimes after an outbreak of madness—when she was restrained and calmed and bandaged in bed. She would lie still for hours, and slowly her face would be freed of its anguish. She would no longer be threatening then, not even ugly. Her skin would glow and her eyes would tear and then she would smile, close her eyes, and fall asleep.

Muhammad the Jew could have killed anyone, he knew, but he could not kill the angel who lay dreaming in chains.

 Solomon the Man was the great-grandson of Elias the Beauty, lover to Shah Abbas II, in whose pursuit the Shah had promised, long ago in the seventeenth century, to demolish the entire city of Kashan. The Shah had come to Kashan on his cavalcade of lions and elephants, and at the gates of the city he had been greeted by a congregation of young, handsome men, handpicked by the governor, to please His Majesty. As he inspected the men, mullahs had prayed aloud for the Shah's health, Armenian priests had recited passages from the New Testament, and the grand rabbi of Kashan had sung Hebrew verses, but Shah Abbas II noticed only one thing:

"A Jew," he later described Elias to his soldiers, "with a face as beautiful as the moon, and a tiny mole on the side of his lip. Bring him to me or I will never sleep again."

But in the Kashan ghetto, Elias had hidden from the

Shah's soldiers; he was a married man, recently a father, and he had no wish to become the King's lover.

"Surrender now," Shah Abbas II had said as he sent his troops to the ghetto. "Come to me, or I will destroy Kashan and bury all its children alive."

Solomon the Man was tall and slim, his body muscular, his skin resilient to both age and decay. He had shiny black hair, dark skin, sparkling onyx eyes. There was an air of ease and innocence about him, a way of talking to strangers as if they were old friends, of smiling with his eyes even in the face of pain. Luck, it seemed, followed Solomon around. Providence was kind to him, God smiled upon him.

He arrived in Esfahan in 1875—alone, penniless, with only the flute he had taught himself to play. He had come to seek a fortune, he said, to find the prince Zil-el-Sultan, governor of Esfahan, and display for him his talents. The Jews were disturbed by his presence. They had been in mourning for so long they found no cause for jubilation. Through centuries of life in Persia, they had adopted the mullahs' belief that music and song were the works of the Devil—worthy only of people as low as the Winemaker.

"You must stop this singing," Raab Yahya told Solomon on the third night of his stay in Juyy Bar. "Singing is for whores. Music is for jesters. Find yourself a trade and live like a decent man."

Solomon the Man smiled at Raab Yahya and offered him a cup of wine. The next day he went into the city, found the palace of Zil-el-Sultan, and knocked at the gates.

The guards asked him to leave. His Highness the prince Zil-el-Sultan did not receive Jews, they said. Solomon the Man stayed at the gates and charmed the guards with his good looks and his smile. Then he took out his flute and sang for them. He had sung three verses before his voice carried into the inner chambers of the palace, where Zil-el-Sultan heard him and came out. From then on, Solomon the Man sat with the prince.

He abandoned himself to a life of pleasure and excess. He charmed everyone—king and jester, Muslim and Jew. He never hid the fact that he was a Jew, but the people he befriended did not think him impure. Whores slept with him for free, ladies of class and character paid for his love, and men of lineage and wealth swore on his name.

Once a month in Esfahan, Solomon the Man filled a room with a dozen naked whores and played with them a game of love: he lay on his back, surrounded by the women, and placed a gold coin at the tip of his erect penis. One by one the whores came up to him and tried to lift the coin with their tongues, without using their hands or letting the coin fall. The one who succeeded would keep the coin. If they failed, Solomon the Man gave them another chance.

He had a quality that charmed everyone: an untamed lust for things fair and beautiful, an obsession with love, a willingness to sacrifice everything for immediate pleasure. He had been raised poor, and yet he spent his money as if he had always been king. He sang all night in the palace, and in the morning spent his entire pay on a mule's load of food, which he brought to Juyy Bar and fed to the children. He received gifts from his rich lovers and gave them away to others. He got a bag full of gold from the prince and spent it in one night at the Castle.

"I have a curse about me," he would laugh with Raab Yahya who came to warn him against the sin of excess. "I was born to live well."

He became rich so fast he never knew what to do with his money. He would build a house, he decided, a white structure with windows and a garden, and a kitchen large enough to feed a hundred people in one day. He wanted to buy land, but there was nothing left in the ghetto: the mullahs did not allow Jews to build higher than a single story. Non-believers, they said, must never be placed in a position superior to Shiites. A Jew could not live on the second floor of a home in the same city where Muslims walked on the street.

Solomon the Man knew this, but he bought the best house in the ghetto and demolished it. In its place he built another, two stories high with windows.

Raab Yahya was terrified. "Take it down *tonight!*" he screamed at Solomon when he saw the skeleton of the house being erected. "Tear it down before they see it and come to drag you through the mud."

Solomon the Man kept his house, and the mullahs' complaints never bothered him. Zil-el-Sultan himself issued an order approving the building. He came to the ghetto when it was completed, and brought Solomon gifts of gold and a dozen whores. They sat together, drinking Joseph the Winemaker's oldest wine until they had fallen asleep.

"It's the end of the world," Raab Yahya declared as he watched Zil-el-Sultan leave Solomon's house in the morning. "Lamb and lion have lain down in the same den."

Solomon the Man would live in Juyy Bar for many years. For those who knew him, his arrival marked the beginning of a new time in the ghetto. From the moment he came, rain began to fall and it did not stop until years later, when the famine had ended and the rivers were filled with life. Days revolved around tales of Solomon's excesses, and nights fluttered with the sound of his music, and every time he laughed, the ghetto was stunned and silenced, as if in the wake of a moment of greatness, when memories are created and history begins.

 Taraneh the Tulip brought Leyla news of her daughter. She came to Esfahan once a year and, on that occasion, called at the harem to pay her respects to Zil-el-Sultan's wives. She called on the harem favorite, extended gifts to her and the other wives, then sat chatting with them for the better part of an afternoon. She never spoke with Hannah. She was afraid to look at her for too long, show a sign of recognition, make a gesture that would reveal Hannah's origins to the hundreds of harem spies. After each visit, Taraneh the Tulip went to see Leyla.

"Your daughter has grown," she reported the first year. "Her eyes are full of longing, but she will forget soon enough, and then she will be content."

Leyla did not believe her. She had left Hannah in the Ali Ghapoo and seen her disappear into the palace grounds, and from that moment on she was overcome with the feeling that she had pushed Hannah to her doom—that Hannah would be destroyed by the Zil, or poisoned by his other wives; that when the term of her contract was over, she would be cast out of the palace with no money or protection, unable to return among the Jews, who did not welcome converts, and persecuted by Muslims, who considered concubines prostitutes.

"You must be proud," Taraneh the Tulip told her, but in vain. "Your daughter is the prince's wife. If she learns to protect herself from the other wives, there is no telling how long she will last. The Shah may renew her contract. He may even marry her permanently."

Even Joseph the Winemaker, who had first sworn to kill Leyla for stealing the bangles, now praised her act.

"*My* daughter," he boasted to the Jews, "*Joseph's* daughter, is the wife of Zil-el-Sultan."

Still, years after she had last seen Hannah, Leyla woke up nights to go check on her daughter in bed, and waited for her to come home at the end of each day. Then all at once she would remember Zil-el-Sultan, ache for her child, and cry herself to sleep. A ghost came to curse her in her sleep: "You forced Hannah to convert," it accused Leyla. "When she dies, neither Jew nor Muslim will bury her."

Hannah grew up in the harem. She learned to smile, to defend herself against the other wives. She lost her Jewish accent, the frightened expression of her early days. When she reached puberty, the harem favorite rewarded her with a bag full of diamonds. When she had her first child—a girl with Leyla's hair and the eyes of Noah the Gold—Zil-el-Sultan offered her a palace of her own. He let her leave the harem—a sign of respectability for a wife—then immediately sent for her.

"I missed you," he said, and for many nights after, he kept Hannah in his bedroom.

The last time Taraneh the Tulip went to call, Hannah never even engaged her eyes; she had forgotten the past, Taraneh realized. She had come to think of herself as royalty.

 "There will come a time when you will be a woman, and your body will be impure. You will bleed for days, from the place between your legs where you now piss. You will bleed every month, and from the day you start until fifteen days later, you will be impure. If you touch anything that your husband touches, or if you cook anything that anyone may eat, they too will be contaminated. If you lie with your husband you will have sinned. If you conceive a child he will refuse to give it his name. Everyone will curse you, and God will turn his back on you."

Leyla stood in the middle of the room—her tall, slender figure a shadow in the unreal halo of the oil lamp. She was teaching Peacock about the rites of purity.

"When you have counted fifteen days, you will go to bathe in the well. You will submerge your body in the cold water, and become pure again. Then you can touch anything, lie in your husband's bed, and bear children."

Leyla's voice trembled at the mention of the well. She turned her face away from Peacock, looked down a moment, then walked away.

All of that night she stood by the door, staring into the empty courtyard like a child waiting for an angel. Peacock watched her, full of questions, afraid to ask. Near midnight, Joseph the Winemaker left the empty winery and climbed the steps into the room. He slept, and the air filled with the bitterness of his dreams.

"Women have died in the well," Leyla said after she knew that Joseph was asleep.

"Sometimes one of them goes down there and doesn't come back until the well spits her up hours and hours later. Sometimes she doesn't come back at all." Peacock sat up. The night was still but for the sound of Joseph's breathing. She listened again. Demons screeched in his throat. She went toward Leyla and touched her hand.

They left before dawn. On the street, the doors of some houses creaked slowly open and other women, dressed in black, slipped out to travel along the same route as Leyla and Peacock. In the moonlight, under the thousand stars, they looked like dancing shadows come alive to perform an ancient and mysterious rite that only they knew.

Peddlers carried their junk in small heaps on their shoulders, bound for nearby villages where they knew they would find no customers. Young boys with shaved heads and dreamy eyes swept the fronts of shops where they had been left to sleep—to scare off thieves. Old men with toothless mouths and insomnia-ridden bodies sat by dried gutters on the side of the streets, waiting for morning, or death, to come.

They went past the abandoned basement where Mullah Mirza had once tortured himself in search of gold, past the underground temple where the Jews had gathered to pray in the years when they had been forced to convert to Islam but still practiced Judaism in secret. Near the gates of Juyy Bar they saw the large brick building with lopsided walls and a wooden door painted in luminous blue that shone in the dark and that led to the bath.

Peacock wanted to turn back, run away into the darkness, under the satin cold of night. But her hand was caught, her feet were powerless, her voice choked.

She heard Leyla knock, heard a hand lift the wooden pole that barred the door from inside. She saw the vertical lines in the wood where the paint was chipped move away from them as the door opened. She saw an old woman—pale, bony, carved with horizontal lines, eyes gleaming, hair silver blue and hanging down the sides of her face in uneven lengths.

"*You* again," the old woman snarled at Leyla. "You still owe me from last time."

It was Mama the Midwife. Her husband was keeper of the bath.

Leyla walked in, sidestepping the old woman, whispering that she would pay soon, dragging Peacock behind her.

They went into a large room with brick walls, a high ceiling, and a pool of water in the center where women came to wash after visiting the well. The room was dark and bare now, but in two hours it would be filled with naked female bodies and the echo of all their voices. Every morning, Mama's husband filled the pool with water from the well that was cold but clean. The women rushed to get into the tub early, before too many others had bathed in it. They climbed down a ladder and sat on a narrow platform to wash the dirt of two weeks off their bodies. By the time the bath closed and Mama's husband drained the pool, the water would be black.

Leyla led Peacock toward a small door at the end of the room, went through it and into the bare backyard of the well. She walked up to the well, then stopped. The midwife came up to her. In one hand she held a lantern that cast a misty yellow light around her and made the lines in her face look even deeper. She placed her other hand on Leyla's forehead.

"That you shall be pure and innocent," she said, "and all your sins shall be washed away, and your body shall be as clean as that of a newborn child."

She pointed with her head toward Peacock.

"Is she going with you?" she asked Leyla.

"Just to watch."

* * *

The well was dark and damp. The water level was some forty steps below the surface of the earth. The packed-mud stairs were narrow and unsteady, and gave way because the mud had softened.

At the bottom of the stairs, on a small platform at water level, Leyla stopped to undress. Peacock watched her as one by one she lifted the layers of darkness from her body, her shape emerging slowly out of the shroud of fabric that had forever surrounded her. Peacock was stunned; Leyla glowed in the moonlight like a vision, her hair a stream of gold, her skin the color of warm milk, her body soft, sacred, perfect. She stared at her mother and, before Leyla ever touched the water, saw her drown in the well.

Peacock closed her eyes, terrified, and tried to chase away the vision. Watching Leyla again, she longed to reach across the night, back into the moment of conception, back when she had been formed of her mother's body—back to where there was calm and beauty.

She pressed her lips together and let the tears run down her face. Leyla put her feet into the water. The circles that she made widened until they had reached the contours of the well and then came back, closing in around her legs, her hips, her waist. Holding on with both hands to the edge of the platform, she let the water rise to her breasts, then fill the cavity above them. It went over her shoulders, around her neck.

She stopped. For one fleeting moment the green of her eyes pierced the darkness. Then she was gone.

Gone to the tips of her golden hair. Gone to the extremity of her fingers that only a moment ago had held on to the platform so fiercely. Peacock saw the circles dancing back to the edge of the wall.

Claimed by the ghosts of the drowned women. Claimed by the well.

Peacock ran forward and thrust her arms into the water. Her eyes searched frantically, her arms moved vainly in the water, reaching deeper and deeper until suddenly it felt the cold grip of death as a white hand with long fingers grabbed it. She screamed and pulled back.

Leyla pulled her head out, gasping for air. Her lips were purple, her eyes like glass. A moment later she found the platform with her other hand and freed Peacock.

Peacock stood up, moved back against the wall, and as she saw her mother breathe, she felt the warm sting of urine run down her legs to gather in a small puddle on the ground.

That night Leyla lay on the floor, face up, and waited for her husband to come and claim her. Through the make-shift curtain that separated her side of the room from her parents', Peacock heard Joseph the Winemaker roll over Leyla, whispering greedily, "Let's see if you were worth the wait."

Peacock knew that her mother's hands and feet would be cold as ice as she lay under her husband. She knew that the sound of Joseph's breathing as he satisfied himself would be the same as the night before, when he had slept.

And she knew that all her life she would suffer alone the knowledge of her mother's death.

 Taraneh the Tulip returned to live in Juyy Bar.

She had been married thirty-five years when her husband drank a glass of poisoned tea and died in his sleep. A snake had fallen into the teapot; a maid had inadvertently boiled the reptile, and served her master.

Taraneh the Tulip held a year-long wake in Tehran. She hired two dozen professional mourners to weep at the funeral, paid a mullah to live in her house and pray constantly for her husband's soul. She wore black clothes, hung black drapes and tablecloths in her house, covered her furniture and bed with black. For forty days she held open house to friends and relatives. Every month after that, she served lunch and prayers to a hundred women.

When the year of mourning had ended, Taraneh the Tulip packed her black clothes and fired her servants. Alone in the house, she burned every musical instrument she had ever played. She sent for her husband's family; she was leaving Tehran, she told them. She was going back to die in Juyy Bar.

She became ill in mourning. She was old, suffering from rheumatism, always in pain. Her joints were swollen, her hands and feet deformed, her spine curved. She walked with the aid of a cane—this woman who had danced across an empire—and every few steps she had to stop and take a rest. The Jews watched her decay and lamented her loss. Taraneh the Tulip, they said, had willed herself to die.

She bought a room in the ghetto, in a house across the street from Solomon the Man's mansion, and imprisoned herself. She spoke with no one, rejected invitations even to her neighbors' rooms, refused visitors. She went out twice a month, to the bath, and on her way home she stopped at the ghetto square to buy a bowl of lentil stew. The rest of the time she sat in her room, or on the steps above the courtyard, and listened to the sounds of the ghetto.

Every night in his house, Solomon the Man threw a feast and invited a hundred guests. He hired whores from Esfahan, invited dancers and musicians from neighboring cities, called Jews and Muslims to come and drink his wine. He brought a blind *donbaki* from Ahvaz who sounded a storm better than God himself, introduced a woman violinist from Shiraz who played only in the nude. He brought an old *tar* player who died from excitement in the middle of a performance with the nude violinist, a Russian piano player, a guest of Nasser-ed-Din Shah in Tehran, who came to Juyy Bar only to find that his piano did not fit through the alley leading up to Solomon's house. He had an Indian dancer who was chased out of town by the wives of the men she seduced, an Egyptian singer whose voice dragged turtles out

122

of hibernation. And then, in his greatest feat ever, Solomon the Man brought a *santour* player—a young man with yellow skin and Mongol eyes, descendant of Tamerlane the Lame, famous across Asia for his talent with the instrument.

The *santour* player had come to Esfahan at the invitation of Zil-el-Sultan, played for eleven nights, and, at the end of each performance, demanded a camel's load of gold. When Solomon the Man invited him to his house in Juyy Bar, he asked for another load of gold.

"Take heed, son of Tamerlane," Zil-el-Sultan warned in anger. "Greed will destroy your talent. Play for my friend, and I will spare your hands. Ask for gold, and I will have them boiled in oil."

Solomon the Man invited the entire ghetto to watch the Son of Tamerlane play at his house. The day of the Mongol's appearance, men closed their shops early and rushed to Solomon's house to reserve their place in his courtyard. Women grabbed their children and climbed onto the roofs of Solomon's neighbors. By sundown every alley leading to Solomon's house was packed with spectators. At ten o'clock, Zil-el-Sultan arrived. An hour later, twelve Mongols—part of the *santour* player's entourage—marched through the doors of Solomon's house, beating their drums:

> *"Make way for the Celestial and the Sublime,*
> *The Son of Tamerlane,*
> *The greatest* santour *player of our time."*

Dressed in a bejeweled gown, the Son of Tamerlane rode on a black horse and remained oblivious of the crowd that awaited him, or of his host who welcomed him. He sat cross-legged on a silk rug, unpacked a *santour* cast in gold and decorated with rubies, and played for exactly one hour. When he had finished, Zil-el-Sultan praised him and Solomon the Man thanked him, but the Mongol was impatient to leave. He was about to pack his *santour* when he felt a sudden silence and looked up. Taraneh the Tulip stood above

him—her back curved, her hands dried and deformed—
ready for war. She reached over and took the Mongol's sticks,
held them in her clawed fingers, and smiled with her old
optimism.

"You think *you* can play," she challenged, and put the
sticks to the *santour*.

She played for ten minutes, a quick and dazzling tune
that was at once electrifying and unforgettable, and by the
time she finished, she had destroyed the Mongol's reputation
and altered every man's memory of music.

 In the spring of 1876, Zil-el-Sultan ordered a week-
long celebration in Esfahan. They had had months
of rain. The famine, Zil-el-Sultan liked to believe,
would soon come to an end. So he decorated the
Palace of Forty Pillars and lit up the Shah's Square, invited
musicians and poets and artists into the palace, and for seven
days and nights poured wine into jeweled cups and broiled
sheep over open flames. In all that time he never let Solomon
the Man move from his side.

On the sixth night of the celebrations, Zil-el-Sultan called
his harem into the main chambers and allowed the wives to
join in the festivities. They came dressed in jeweled veils and
embroidered chadors—three dozen women with their maids
and children and eunuchs—and marched through the receiving hall, giggling and mischievous like schoolgirls at re-
cess. Zil-el-Sultan watched proudly as they filed into the
honeycomb of smaller rooms flanking the hall: the size of a
man's harem was an indication of his wealth and power.

He drank more that night and talked to Solomon about
his wives. He showed him his latest bride—the princess
Samira, with the arched eyebrows and the tiny black mole
on the back of her neck, halfway between her head and torso,
that sent a shiver up Zil-el-Sultan's body every time he kissed
it; or his own cousin, the ugly one he had married when she

was already old, nearly twenty, as an offering of peace to her belligerent father. Zil-el-Sultan had not slept with her—he could not bring himself to—until his uncle had promised war.

He showed Solomon the Arab woman with the black skin and the golden hair that he swore knew more about love than any of the Shah's whores, the Turk whom the eunuchs believed had drowned two rival wives in the harem pool.

"But *there*"—he pointed to yet another woman—"*that* one came to me already dressed as a bride."

Solomon the Man followed the direction of Zil-el-Sultan's attention and saw a woman sitting in the room farthest from the hall. She had on an emerald chador and veil, and she sat with her knees crossed, surrounded by three maids who stood behind her, ready to serve. She did not speak to anyone. She did not smoke a water pipe.

For the first time in six days, Solomon the Man found himself captivated.

"Where did she come from?" he asked Zil-el-Sultan, his eyes still fixed on Hannah.

The prince laughed.

"I don't know," he said. "The eunuchs say she was a Jew."

Solomon the Man inhaled a lungful of opium to conceal his agitation. He was thinking of a story he had heard in Juyy Bar and never believed: the winemaker's daughter marrying a prince and vanishing from the ghetto as if she had never existed, his wife taking the girl into Esfahan one day and returning alone, claiming she had left him for Zil-el-Sultan to marry. Like everyone else who had ever heard the tale, Solomon the Man thought Leyla had sold her daughter to a Muslim and kept the money from Joseph.

"Why did you keep her?" he asked Zil-el-Sultan when he could no longer contain his curiosity. "Was she so beautiful?"

Zil-el-Sultan began to answer, then stopped. He wanted

to remember the day he had first seen Hannah, relive the moment of encounter, understand his own motivation for marrying her.

"She *was* beautiful." He saw the glimmer of two gold coins against tiny palms. His heart warmed.

"She was like an orphan," he tried to explain, "like an offering. I could not refuse."

He missed Hannah. He called a eunuch, who ran forward and prostrated himself.

"Call Taj-Banoo." He had chosen the name himself: it had a lucky sound, a charmed ring.

Solomon the Man watched the eunuch go up to the woman in the far room. He whispered a word to her and she stood up, walked through the crowded receiving hall of the Palace of Forty Pillars without looking in any direction but that of the prince, and approached him through the fog of tobacco and opium and the wave of music and laughter that brushed against her without ever moving her. She stood before Zil-el-Sultan and kissed his hand. The prince introduced her to Solomon the Man.

"My wife," he said, and she looked up. Beneath the veil her eyes were like yellow sapphires. Solomon the Man looked closer, but he could see no more until she had turned around to leave. Then he realized, from the shape of her body under the chador, that she was pregnant. He watched her go and knew he was lost.

 Solomon the Man became obsessed with Hannah—to the point of distraction, to the limit of wisdom. He thought only about Hannah, longed for no other woman, wanted nothing but to see her unveiled—to undo the mystery of her presence, see for himself the bride of Zil-el-Sultan's good fortune. He imagined her as a child, standing in the Ali Ghapoo, dressed in a wedding gown at noon, looking in every direction with her throat full of tears, crying under her veil as she prayed for her mother to save her. He imagined her lying in Zil-el-Sultan's bed with her eyes pale and her teeth loose, imagined her—this daughter of Joseph the Winemaker—living in the Palace of Forty Pillars, close to home but never allowed to go back, close to her parents but never allowed to see them or even speak their name.

He looked for Hannah at the palace, questioned the eunuchs so directly about Taj-Banoo that they were offended at his shamelessness and stopped answering. In Juyy Bar he went to the winery and met Joseph, asked his friends about Leyla. He learned all their stories—from the tale of Esther the Soothsayer to that of Noah the Gold and Qamar the Gypsy, and even Leyla's Muslim brother. When he had heard every tale and asked every question, Solomon the Man was still consumed with the need to know. For forty days and nights he did nothing but brood over Hannah. Then at last he thought through a whole night of sobriety, and in the morning went to see Joseph the Winemaker. Hannah, he accepted, was out of reach. Solomon the Man asked to marry her sister.

 News of Solomon the Man's engagement to the daughter of Joseph the Winemaker spread faster and incited more animosity in Esfahan and Juyy Bar than any other incident in recent memory. In the ghetto, mothers of eligible young women dug their nails into their cheeks and mourned. Matchmakers ran to each other in a fury as they tried to discover which one of them had made the deal. Young men despaired at the thought of having Solomon removed from the circle of womanizing and debauchery that had become the object of all their fantasies.

In Esfahan, whores cursed their bad luck and spat. Ladies of nobility felt betrayed and swore in the most wounded tones never to allow Solomon in their midst again. Even Zil-el-Sultan, unaware of Solomon's motivations in marriage, made a royal frown and asked his friend what merit he could possibly find in a monogamous life. Solomon the Man smiled in the face of all adversity and proceeded with the wedding plans as if the whole world were on his side.

He sent to Kashan for his mother to come and take charge of the festivities. She arrived a week later, a big woman with light skin and nothing of the good looks that had blessed her son. She sat in the carriage she had hired with Solomon's money, complaining of the heat and the dust of the desert, and when she arrived at the city's gates and was forced to disembark—for no Jew could ride through a town—she was so large she struggled for ten minutes before she could free herself. She had come with her daughters, all eleven of them, and with another, darker than the rest and even uglier, whom she claimed was an orphan she had raised from childhood. Solomon the Man swore the girl was his sister. His mother, he mused, had disowned her because she could not stand having yet another ugly girl.

Ghadereh Khanum—the Able One—stayed in Solomon's house for a week and held court. She sat with her daughters around the receiving room, their backs against silk cushions and their hands caressing the necks of enameled water pipes that they forced themselves to smoke; it was the habit of ladies of gentry, which they believed they had become, owing to Solomon's wealth. In Kashan they had been rug weavers. They had lived in a hovel and worked from the age of three, sitting cross-legged in front of wooden frames onto which they tied minuscule knots of wool and silk. And they would have worked till their eyes were blind and their lungs rotted from inhaling wool, except Solomon the Man had made them rich. Now they sat in his house and snubbed the visitors who came to offer their welcome.

At the end of the week of greeting, the Able One and her daughters paid a surprise visit to Peacock's house. As was customary, they arrived early in the morning, before Peacock could have a chance to comb her hair or hide her faults in deceiving clothes. They entered the courtyard without knocking, acknowledged the neighbors with a distant and haughty nod of their heads, and invaded Leyla and Joseph's room with militant urgency.

"Welcome." Leyla stood up before them, unveiled. The Able One frowned at her beauty. She put her fat hands into Leyla's hair and pulled hard to make certain it was real. She ran her fingers over Leyla's skin, felt her arms and thighs, dug into her blouse to check the firmness of her breasts. Disgusted by the perfection she had found, she turned to her daughters and pronounced the first verdict:

"God forbid," she said. "No woman like her could stay on the path of righteousness."

She looked around the room and complained of its dinginess.

"Bring the girl outside," she ordered as she stepped into the courtyard. "I can't breathe in this hole."

When they were gone, Peacock still refused to come out from under her comforter.

"Send them away," she begged Leyla. "Make them leave."

Ever since Joseph the Winemaker had announced her engagement to Solomon the Man, Peacock had cried and begged and sworn she would not marry. It was preposterous—that *Peacock* should refuse the man everyone wanted. Even Leyla could not understand the child's behavior. She held Peacock's hands and made a plea:

"For *my* sake," she said. "Come outside and don't shame me."

The Able One and her daughters stayed all morning. They inspected Peacock, commented on the thickness of her skin and the darkness of her gums, remarked that her hips were so narrow no child could ever come through them alive. They made Peacock walk from one side of the courtyard to the other so they could see her stride, examined her knees and complained that she was too thin—not fed by her parents—gave her a tray full of fresh radishes, mint, and spring onions.

"We brought our own," said the Able One, not missing the chance to point out the poverty of Peacock's home. They watched as Peacock took the traditional test: if she threw away too much of the greens while cleaning them, they would know that she was a spendthrift. If she threw away too little, she was stingy. If she worked too fast, she had no patience. If she worked slowly, she was lazy. Peacock failed in all categories. Then the Able One called her daughters and left the house.

"Stay for lunch," Leyla offered, but the Able One scoffed. She knew there was nothing to eat.

The next day the Able One and her daughters began to make the invitations. They called on each household personally—all twelve of them—and stayed half a day, drinking tea and chatting until it was time to leave and the Able One extended an invitation for Solomon the Man's wedding. Then the hostess would stand up most excitedly and run into the back of the room where she had stored dried goods. She would bring a handkerchief full of raisins and nuts and offer it to the women, who promised to serve it at the reception. House by house and room by room they made the invitations. They worked till the night before the wedding, and sent messages for those they had not had a chance to visit personally. Solomon the Man, they promised, was going to throw the feast of a lifetime.

 To the people of Juyy Bar, Peacock's wedding to Solomon the Man marked the end of the Great Famine of 1871. For although the earth did not yield a healthy crop for another decade, and although their poverty would become worse in the years to come, the three days and nights of celebration at Solomon's home managed to create in the minds of even the harshest of skeptics a lasting illusion of comfort, and a collective memory of never-ending wealth.

It began at dawn on a Monday, and did not end until after midnight on Wednesday. In between, the men gathered in Solomon's house and ate and drank and danced to the music of seven groups of entertainers he had imported from as far as Tehran and Rasht. They ate eggs and honey and sweetbread and halva for breakfast, drank cool essence of cherries and snacked on apples stewed in rosewater until noon, then feasted on roasted lamb, bread, rice, and golden cookies for lunch. In the afternoon, bands of musicians played, acrobats danced in the courtyard, and old storytellers recited verses from the book of kings while poets repeated the verses of Omar Khayyam. Before sunset, Joseph the Winemaker walked from room to room and poured Persian wine and Russian vodka into everyone's cup. By the time Homa the Ricemaker served dinner, the men were all drunk.

On the women's side, the celebrations were more solemn but just as extravagant. As tradition dictated, they gathered at the house of Joseph the Winemaker, where Solomon the Man had paid all expenses. The Able One and her eleven daughters hosted the affair. On the first of the three days of celebration, they took Peacock for a marriage bath.

They left in the dark, equipped with food, nuts and candy, jugs of cool drinks, and, most important, chunks of henna. In the bath, the Able One took Peacock into the well and watched as she performed the rites of purity. Then everyone came inside, around the pool, and undressed. A band of female musicians, courtesy of Solomon the Man, performed in the nude. Pari the Henna came forward, clicking her tongue to sound a cheer that echoed through the bath until it became deafening. She gave Peacock a dimpled smile and a reassuring pat, admired her beauty and remarked on her youth, then set about "turning her into a woman."

She tied the ends of two long threads around her thumb and forefinger, put the threads to Peacock's eyebrows, catching each hair and plucking them, until she had created two arched lines. Then she plucked Peacock's legs and thighs, the hair on her vulva and armpits. Finally she prepared a mold of henna, which she placed on the bride's fingernails and toenails, and on her hair. The other women, cheering, began to dye their own hair.

On Tuesday the women gathered at the winemaker's house to bless the bride. They brought Peacock into the courtyard and put her in a translucent chador made of gold thread. Grudgingly, while her daughters shed tears of envy, the Able One extended to Peacock the gifts Solomon had sent for her: a dozen gold chains, a sapphire necklace, turquoise earrings, and a diamond bracelet. Everyone gasped in awe. The Able One took out a bag of gold coins and placed a crystal bowl into Peacock's lap. One by one she pressed the coins against Peacock's forehead, letting each one stick momentarily—for luck, so that from now on the bride's forehead would be marked with joy and prosperity. Then Peacock bent her head and dropped the coin into the bowl as coal stoves burned wild rue seeds and smoke filled the air.

On the third day a delegation of women visited Solomon's house to arrange the bridal room. They spread the bed toward Jerusalem—ensuring that a son would be conceived of the first intercourse. Inside the sheets they sprayed rosewater, spread jasmine and rose petals. Above the pillows they put a white handkerchief that Solomon the Man would have to rub in Peacock's blood and present after the intercourse.

In the afternoon, Raab Yahya called at Solomon's house to perform the first half of the ceremony. Solomon the Man was bathed and shaved, dressed in a Western suit and top hat. He repeated the vows and then raised his cup in celebration.

"Bring her to me," he toasted.

Then Pari the Henna left Solomon the Man's house to carry the bridal gown to the bride.

But in the house of Joseph the Winemaker, Leyla was

running from room to room, flushed and frantic; the other women were searching every corner, and rumors had begun to circulate that the bride was missing; she had disappeared sometime before noon, and no one could imagine where to look for her.

 Joseph the Winemaker paced every inch of the ghetto and at last found his daughter in Mullah Mirza's basement which had been empty and abandoned since Muhammad the Jew's Massacre. Peacock sat there terrified by her own defiance, terrified also by the walls that reeked of poison and the smell of Mullah Mirza's dismay. Still, when Joseph grabbed her, she held his hand and begged that he call off the marriage.

"Solomon the Man," she cried, "will leave me."

Joseph the Winemaker took his daughter home and dressed her in a pearl-embroidered gown, and in a veil—a gift from Zil-el-Sultan's harem—made entirely of silver and gold threads. He saw her wear the jewels Solomon had given her, and fought back his own tears of joy.

"Believe in luck," he whispered to Peacock as he took her before Raab Yahya.

When the wedding ceremony was over, a caravan of women walked from the winemaker's house to that of Solomon the Man. Peacock rode in front, mounted on Solomon's black horse. At the top of the alley leading to the house, she stopped and waited for messengers to announce her arrival to the groom.

"What if they know she ran away?" Leyla asked Joseph, who trembled at the possibility.

But in Solomon's house the sound of music and laughter had never ceased, and the matter of the bride's disappearance was quickly forgotten. When they heard that the bride was about to arrive, the men cheered and all seven bands of musicians played at once as women burned wild rue seeds and threw sugar-laced almonds on the bride's path. Peacock was led into the house and straight to the bridal room, where she would wait for the end of the reception. Leyla took her inside and kissed her good-bye, and then, suddenly, Peacock was alone.

She stood erect, looking ahead, and tried to gather the courage she had lost along the way. She told herself she was not going to stay, that no one could force her to stay. She reminded herself of the dream she had had: an old woman, alone and brokenhearted, walking the streets of an unfamiliar town and crying Solomon's name. In the dream, Peacock knew that she was the old woman.

She looked around the room. The walls were plastered white, the ceiling decorated with hand-painted moldings. There was a window in this room. Peacock remembered the house of Muhammad the Jew.

"But I won't stay," she reminded herself.

She could smell food from outside.

"When he comes in, I will tell him he has to send me back. 'You keep *whores*,' I will say. 'I don't want a man who keeps *whores*.'"

She waited, but hours passed and her legs became numb from standing, and still the sound of laughter had not ceased in the house. She sat on the floor, her chador around her, and found herself admiring the softness of her dress, the shine of her jewels, the beauty of her veil. She put her head on a cushion away from the bed and fell asleep.

She dreamt that the door opened and a man came into the room. He was tall, with long arms, and the smell of rain on his clothes. He brought with him a piece of the moonlit sky.

She dreamt that he stood above her, looking, then bent down and lifted her from the ground to place her on the bed. She thought he was about to unveil her, that she should stop him, but he touched her and she was not afraid anymore. He took her off her veil.

He stared at her—his eyes submerged in the blue light of dawn—and then he reached to the bottom of the bed and pulled a white sheet, as cool as the wind that came before every rain, over her body. He left. Without him the room was vast and empty.

Peacock sat up, jolted by the sound of the morning *namaz*, and looked about. She was in a strange bed, alone but unveiled, and her eyes still burned from last night's anger. She remembered her dream. She saw the white sheet that covered her. Solomon the Man, she realized, had seen her.

She stood up on the mattress and searched her clothes for blood. She looked on the sheets. There was no stain. She breathed with relief; he had not touched her. Then she realized why: he had seen her face, and decided she was too ugly to touch. She picked up her chador and walked out.

"Good morning," a voice greeted her on the porch. Solomon's eyes were full of sleep. His face was unshaven. He sat on the steps, smoking his water pipe and watching the sunrise.

"You wake up early," he said.

Peacock froze. She was disarmed by his casual manner, his smile. She thought his eyes played with her.

"I sent everyone home last night," he said. "I told them, 'My wife is asleep and I will wait for her.' Your father insisted I do the job. He's afraid I will change my mind about the marriage."

Peacock took a step back.

"No need for that," she answered. "I will go myself."

He raised an eyebrow and smiled.

"Where to?"

"Anywhere." But she had already lost her conviction. "Somewhere. I can't stay here. You keep *whores*."

Solomon the Man laughed and reached for her. She thought she should pull away, but she could not.

"You have *married* me." He picked her up off the ground. "You can't just *leave* someone you married."

He opened the door and walked in. She wanted to fight

135

him, but he put her down and slowly opened the braids of her hair, undoing the string of pearls and letting each one fall into the bed of withering roses and dying jasmine, and then he took off her shoes and her gown, and lay her naked on the sheets and made love to her as if she were indeed a woman—as if he had chosen her knowingly, as if she were pretty, and desired, and worthy of his touch. Afterward he lay next to her and watched her cry—from the shock of encounter, perhaps, or the relief of being accepted, and then he kissed her and pulled the sheets back over her and told her to sleep.

"You *are* beautiful."

She heard his voice and wondered if he had lied and prayed she would never know. She saw him leave and missed his smell and his touch and the sound of his laughter. She fell asleep and dreamt of his eyes and loved him all her life.

 Solomon the Man stayed home for a hundred days after his wedding. He slept with Peacock till the sun was out and all over his bed, bathed with her in donkey's milk and rosewater, then sat her down in the courtyard of his house and, with a brush dipped in henna, painted miniature figures on the soles of her feet. He dressed her in clothes he had chosen for her, braided her hair, and took her out in the afternoon to see Esfahan. He showed her Char Bagh, the Shah's Square, the Ali Ghapoo. He showed her the homes of his friends, took her into the mosques where no Jew was allowed. He took her to the bazaar and bought handmade dolls with satin skin and charcoal eyes, then led her into the palace of Zil-el-Sultan and introduced her to the prince. To mark the occasion, Zil-el-Sultan called the photographer, and posed for a picture with Solomon and Peacock.

At the end of the first three months of his marriage,

Solomon the Man returned to Esfahan and sang at the palace. But for a while yet he did not go to the Castle, and he rejected all invitations from his lady friends. Even later, when his resolve weakened and he succumbed to the temptation of the flesh, Solomon the Man believed himself faithful to Peacock. He treated her well and fulfilled her every wish and never once let her doubt that she was queen in her own house. When she reached puberty, he refused to let her lock herself in the "impurity room." He arranged a bedroom for her on the main floor, and insisted he would eat only food that Peacock had prepared. When the Able One objected to the new order, Solomon the Man hired a coach and sent her back to Kashan with her daughters.

Still, two years after he had married Peacock, Solomon the Man woke up every morning from dreams of Zil-el-Sultan's wife, and slept every night thinking of the woman with the sapphire eyes and shimmering palms.

He took Peacock for her first purity bath, then brought her home and into his bed, where he prayed aloud that she would conceive a child. He named his first daughter Sabrina—after a Russian he had once adored—and celebrated her birth as if she were a boy. He named his second daughter Heshmat, and never once asked Peacock for a son, but by then, Joseph the Winemaker was already panicked.

"This is *wrong!*" he yelled at Peacock every time a daughter was born. "You can't keep having girls like your mother. No man worth his penis will keep a wife with 'girl-bearing disease.'"

As if to prove Joseph right, Solomon the Man forgot Peacock in the wake of Heshmat's birth. In 1882 he met the wife of the Turkish ambassador in Esfahan, and began with her a year-long relationship that ended in disrepute. He left the Turk under pressure from Zil-el-Sultan, came home for only a month, then found an Armenian virgin who had run from her father's house with a chastity belt still tied around her crotch. In 1884 he entered into a temporary marriage contract with a woman distantly related to the prince of Egypt, and

137

then all at once he left for India—to see for himself the woman many swore was the most beautiful in the continent.

"Have a *boy*," Joseph the Winemaker screamed at Peacock every time Solomon the Man found a new passion. "Have a boy or you will lose your man for good."

In 1885 Leyla died. She went to take a purity bath alone one morning, and she never emerged from the well. Alarmed by the long absence, Mama the Midwife descended into the well and spent hours searching the water with a long oar that she used on the occasion of a woman's disappearance. In the end she climbed up angry and exhausted.

"No one that pretty was ever meant to live," she declared to Peacock, who had gone to claim the body. Leyla died without leaving a corpse, without a burial or a week of mourning for her.

"Have a *boy*," Joseph the Winemaker told Peacock, who cried like a child for her mother. "Have a boy or you too will die someday without leaving a corpse."

Peacock was twenty years old. She went to see all the midwives in the ghetto and came back with potions designed to make boys. She ate dates and raisins and halva, gorged herself on walnuts and saffron. She went to every circumcision and swallowed the severed foreskin. She even drank wine—old wine that Joseph brought to her in secret and that she consumed without pleasure. When Solomon the Man returned from India, she crawled into his bed and asked that he make love to her. He opened his arms as if he had always wanted her.

Afterward, Peacock stayed awake and watched Solomon in his sleep: his profile was sacred, his skin holy, and she told herself then she would stay with him—through weeks and years of loneliness, through her youth and her pride and passion—that she would stay with him till he had loved every woman in the world and become tired and dejected, till he came back to her, too old to run, and she would keep him then and he would be hers and hers alone for always.

Mad Marushka was trapped in fire. She was in bed, fast asleep, and the window was closed. From underneath the door, flames rushed in and caught the rug. The drapes began to burn, sending columns of smoke toward the ceiling. Fire climbed the bedposts and caught the mosquito net. Mad Marushka awoke with a scream and stood.

"Fire!" someone called outside. Mad Marushka jumped through the burning net, ran to the door, and pulled the handle. It singed her hand.

"Fire!" someone called again. "Help me!"

Mad Marushka coughed black smoke. Her skin was blistered from the flames. She wiped her palms against her gown and pulled on the handle again. The door, she realized, was locked from outside.

She ran to the window—also locked. She reached on top of her dresser, picked up a hand mirror, and threw it at the glass. She thrust her face out and breathed.

Fire had engulfed the entire house. It had crossed the courtyard and was burning the room where Muhammad the Jew slept with his daughter chained to the bed. It had already silenced the maids in the corridor. Mad Marushka was alone, and about to die.

She tore off the bottom of her nightgown and wrapped it around her face. She climbed onto the balcony, through the burning jasmines, and grabbed the railing. The metal branded her palm.

She lowered herself from the balcony, reached for the metal drain that ran down the side of the wall, and descended. She could see the trees burning in the courtyard.

She could hear the panic of the horses trapped in the stable. When she reached the ground, she covered her face with her hands and ran.

She ran through the smoke and the flames until she knew she was safe. She fell on the street and began to vomit. Neighbors stared at her—embarrassed by her nudity, revolted by her palms, where raw flesh hung from the bones. A woman covered her with a chador. A child gave her water.

Mad Marushka felt a gaze scorch through her and looked up. She saw Ezraeel, his clothes intact, his face unsmeared by smoke, staring at her with the eyes of an executioner.

The next morning the sky was the color of sand. Mad Marushka walked through the desolate garden and into the charred skeleton of Muhammad the Jew's house. She found his corpse in Sanam's room. Their bones had melted together, their skulls had burst in the fire. Mad Marushka searched the house for her chest of jewels—for the antiques, the rugs, the wealth she had once come to conquer.

"My *jewels!*" she screamed. "I want my *jewels!*"

She hired dozens of men to search the rubble. Crews of workers went through the house with mathematical precision. Young men camped in the garden at night and spent the day hunting for treasure. Children, amused by Marushka's quest, played at salvaging the lost fortune.

"*Find* my jewels."

When the prospectors quit, she hired ordinary workers. When the workers gave up, she went to Zil-el-Sultan's palace and demanded that royal troops be dispatched to her aid. When no one else would help, she scratched through the ashes with her own disfigured hands.

"I was robbed," she concluded. "Ezraeel took my jewels and burned the house to kill me."

His father's sole inheritor, Ezraeel the Avenger was quickly selling off all of Muhammad's properties, and planned to move to Tehran as soon as possible.

"Catch him!" Mad Marushka cried every time she saw Ezraeel's shadow approach. "Catch him before he kills me."

She became convinced that Ezraeel was hunting her, certain he would not rest until he had avenged his mother's death. She saw him in dark corners, woke up nights feeling him lurk above her. She was afraid to stay by herself anymore. She walked the streets all day, wandering, and spent the night with a friend. Even then, she remained awake to guard against Ezraeel.

People whispered that Marushka was old and grief-stricken and losing her mind. They stopped inviting her to their homes, looked away when she called them on the street. They did not have room for her anymore. They did not have time to listen to her talk of her lost jewels. Mad Marushka realized it was time to go, and so she left Esfahan.

She had nowhere to go, no money, no plans. She told herself she would manage, that she could start again. But even in the desert, Ezraeel the Avenger haunted her. She had walked only a day when she stopped and understood the game: he was torturing her, she realized, with her own fear.

She turned around and faced him. It was dusk in the desert. Ezraeel the Avenger held a gun.

"Do it, then," Mad Marushka challenged. "Do it if you're a man."

He shot her twice—once in each ankle—and left.

"The hell with you!" Marushka screamed as she fell in pain. "I *lived*."

 In Zil-el-Sultan's palace, Tala reigned supreme. She was his daughter, Hannah's daughter, and he loved her more than all his children and even more than his sons. As a child, she had spent all of her time with the Zil. She had sat with him as he received the highest of dignitaries, run barefoot in the audience hall as he consulted his most important advisers. She had come calling to his room late at night, and Zil-el-Sultan had gladly sent away his women just to perch Tala on the bed and watch her laugh.

She had golden hair—hence the name Tala, which meant gold. She had green eyes, white skin, a body that was curved and long and destined to bring doom to the lives of men. She could read and write, paint and play polo, speak English and French and Russian. She had grown up believing that the world was kind, that nothing was out of reach, that every wish would be fulfilled. When she was eight years old, she told her father she wanted music lessons.

Zil-el-Sultan was reluctant, but he could not refuse Tala, and so he hired Solomon the Man to teach her. Once a week for three years, Tala sat across from Solomon the Man in the Hall of Emeralds at the Palace of Forty Pillars, and practiced the *tar*. She was veiled all the time, guarded by two eunuchs who stood on either side of her and refused to leave even for a moment as long as Solomon was in the room. She worked hard and tried to impress, but Solomon the Man never looked at her for more than a moment at a time, and she knew he never thought of her when he left their lessons. Then all at once he disappeared; he had gone to India, she was told, to find beauty.

Tala was maddened at the news, so enraged by Solomon's absence that she scalded her servant-girl's feet with a hot skewer, then gave her enough gold to buy new legs. Afterward, sobbing in her bed, Tala understood the cause of her anger: she wanted Solomon the Man, and if she could not have him, she would destroy herself and all around her.

She waited for him to return from India. She was twelve years old when he came. She called him to the palace and dismissed her eunuchs.

"Look at me." She unveiled herself. "Tell me I am not the one you seek."

Solomon the Man found eternal passion. The day he saw Tala, he went to Zil-el-Sultan and asked for her hand in marriage.

The prince turned white with anger. "Damn your insolent soul!" he cried, full of hatred. He put a trembling hand on the dagger tucked into the corner of his belt.

"Move away," he commanded. "Escape, or I will blind

your eyes that have soiled my daughter and raped her honor."

He banned Solomon from the palace. He would have killed anyone else who unveiled Tala. With Solomon, he swore eternal rancor and forbade the mention of his name. Then he called Hannah, his Taj-Banoo, and accused her of raising an indecent child.

"*Your* daughter," he raged at his favored queen. "*Your* daughter has shamed my house."

He divorced Hannah, and sent her to his darkest prison. He ordered Tala's eunuchs to keep her confined at the harem, commanded his guards to sever her head if she ever tried to escape. He sent word to all of Esfahan's nobility, making it known that Solomon the Man was the Zil's enemy. Tala sobbed at his knees and begged permission to see Solomon the Man. Hannah sent letters every day, written by the warden in ink softened by her tears, in which she pleaded leniency. Through it all, Zil-el-Sultan remained vengeful and unbending.

In Juyy Bar, Solomon the Man locked himself in the house for an entire year, and never left his room even to receive guests. He stopped singing, stopped laughing. He watched Peacock move about him, her face full of anguish, her body deformed—Solomon the Man recalled at last—with the weight of a child.

"Pray it's a boy," Joseph the Winemaker told Peacock as the tale of Solomon's love for Tala became public. When the child came, Peacock heard the midwife cry in jubilation and knew she had produced Solomon's heir. But then she took the boy in her arms, watched him search for her breast, and all at once felt the sorrow of death creep into her bones.

"He won't be mine," she told the midwife. "I will lose this child with his father."

She named him Arash, after the Persian hero who had been his people's savior. For a year after the birth, she tried to deny the overwhelming certainty that she would never see Arash grow. Then one night she heard Tala at her door.

The night Tala came to Juyy Bar, Peacock was awake, listening to the darkness for the sound of her own fate. After midnight she heard the rustle of a woman's skirt and rushed to the door. She looked out. She saw nothing. She thought she had imagined the sound.

But a moment later she heard Solomon's laugh—that same unmistakable laugh she had heard the night he sang Juyy Bar awake, the sound that had risen into the hearts of God and his angels and brought rain for the first time in a decade. Peacock opened the door and went outside.

She saw them on the stairs outside Solomon's bedroom. There was a girl, her back turned to Peacock, her long hair reaching to her hips, her dress—green satin—reflecting the moonlight every time she moved. She stood close to Solomon and whispered a word Peacock could not hear. Then she put her hands around his neck and pulled herself up against his chest. Peacock saw the gold bangles on the girl's wrists. She saw Solomon the Man pick her up and carry her inside. The door closed. All night long Peacock heard the bangles clanking in the dark.

She went to her room and cried into a tear jar. Sabrina came to her. Heshmat awoke with frightened eyes. Asleep in his cradle, Arash—the boy who should have returned Solomon to Peacock—lay calm and unaware. Peacock did not see them. She looked into the night and thought only of Hannah, her sister, who had abandoned her—Peacock had always resented her for this—to marry the Shah's son. She thought of Hannah as she had known her in their childhood: Hannah, who had slept with Peacock in the same bed, their heads resting on one pillow, who had eaten from the same bowl and washed in the same water, Hannah whose daughter had now come to claim Peacock's life. She wondered if Hannah knew that Solomon was Peacock's husband, that Tala was stealing her aunt's life.

"She *must* know," Peacock concluded for the hundredth time. "Everyone knows. She knows, but she's become like the people around her—thinking she's better than the rest, that she's entitled to everything she wishes."

She resented Hannah, but even as she cursed her, Peacock ached for her sister's warmth, the memory of Hannah's hands reaching for Peacock in the dark of night, whispering through the famine that they suffered together: "When morning comes, there will be a caravan of food."

Near dawn Peacock fell asleep, and dreamt she had walked into Solomon's bedroom. The room was large, full of light. It smelled of tobacco and wine, of Solomon's skin, the scent of a woman's perfume. Large pillows leaned against the walls. Clothes trailed on the floor. A water pipe had been left burning till all the tobacco had turned to ash. In a corner, opposite the glass doors that led onto the balcony, the bed glared at her like a shameless whore: the sheets were white, the pillows still marked by the weight of those who had slept on them. Solomon the Man was gone. Peacock searched the mirror for her own reflection, and found only the girl with the satin dress.

"Look in your palms," a voice called from behind her. Startled, Peacock turned around. There was a bald woman with amber lips and burning eyes. She took Peacock's hands and raised her palms—reflective, like glass—to her face.

"Your hands are the true mirrors of your fate."

Sabrina was screaming at her. Peacock opened her eyes. It was light out.

"They're still up there," Sabrina yelled. She was eight years old. She understood that Tala was different from the other women Solomon received at the house.

"I asked to go into the room, but they wouldn't let me."

Peacock sat up. Reaching past Sabrina, she took the tear jar into which she had cried the night before. She drank all her own tears.

She picked up Arash, took the girls by the hand. She walked out of the house of Solomon the Man.

The winter of 1888 lasted so long that by the time it was over, no one could recall when the earth had been warm. Snow piled knee-deep on the ground and then froze. The wind blew so cold it turned the water into ice as it flowed in the gutters. Children slept in their mothers' arms and woke up with blue hands. Gravediggers' shovels could not break the ground, so corpses were left in the open air, wrapped only in canvas shrouds.

In Juyy Bar, Peacock and her children struggled to survive. They left Solomon's house and went to the only place they could: Mullah Mirza's basement, where Peacock had run to hide a decade earlier, on the day of her wedding. She had known then that Solomon the Man would leave her. She had known it and tried to spare herself the pain of a lost love, but now, twenty-two years old and a mother, she sat once again on the same basement floor and, this time, prayed that Solomon the Man would come back.

A day went by, then another. Peacock held Arash to her chest, sat the girls next to herself, and, for three days, fixed her eyes on the door. Her children cried for home. Joseph the Winemaker banged his fists on the door, demanding in vain to be let in, but Peacock could not move. She was waiting for Solomon the Man, for the sound of his footsteps, the chime of his voice, the light of his eyes as he walked in through the door—Peacock imagined—to say that Tala was gone, that he had sent her away, back to her father's palace, back to Hannah, who had left the ghetto and betrayed her own blood. He had sent Tala away, Solomon would tell Peacock, and he had chosen Peacock forever.

On the fourth day, Joseph the Winemaker broke down the basement door.

"You damned fool," he screamed. "He *married* Tala this morning."

Then the light went out and all the colors turned to gray, and for years the world filled with the sound of a deaf scream that only Peacock could hear.

* * *

Sabrina was inconsolable. Arash became ill from the cold and lack of food. Heshmat sat against the wall, her face hidden by her chador, and uttered no sound.

"It's *your* fault," Joseph the Winemaker accused Peacock. "You *lost* him."

He came back every day, looking more depressed and desperate, forcing himself in and bringing food for Peacock and the children. He looked gaunt and exhausted, his bones protruding, his breath short. For eighteen years now, ever since the famine of 1871, he had been thin and getting thinner. Before that he had been an enormous man, his stomach always hanging over his pants, the fat so thick under his skin that he perspired from the mere task of breathing. But the years of the famine had melted the fat, and afterward, Joseph the Winemaker could never eat another full meal; every time he put a morsel in his mouth, he thought he was chewing human flesh.

He sat down to talk about Peacock's future.

"It's all over for you," he started every day, and his words sent Sabrina into a shiver. "Solomon the Man is going to divorce you—there is no question about that. What baffles me is why the man is still alive, why Zil-el-Sultan hasn't killed him yet. But that's Solomon for you. Things just don't *happen* to him as they do to others."

Peacock barely heard his voice. She ate the food Joseph brought, rocked Arash—crying and feverish—till her arms were numb and her legs had caved in.

"There's no *question* he'll divorce you."

Three weeks went by. Joseph the Winemaker went to Solomon's house to beg that he take back Peacock and the children. He wanted to remind Solomon of his oath of marriage, of his duty as a father. He wanted to explain to Tala her relationship with Peacock, send a word for Hannah and plead on Peacock's behalf. But every time Joseph the Winemaker knocked at Solomon's door, no one came to answer, and as much as he stood guard, no one ever left the house.

He imagined that Solomon was dead—buried in his bedroom by Zil-el-Sultan's soldiers just as he was embracing Tala. In the end, Joseph the Winemaker forced the lock on the door, and entered the house.

He stood in the courtyard, overwhelmed by the quiet, then walked to the stairs that led up to Solomon's bedroom.

"Solomon Khan," he called, but his voice was barely audible.

"Solomon Khan," he tried again, without success. He grasped the wooden railing and climbed a few steps. He called again, waited for an answer, then climbed closer to the bedroom.

He knocked on the door. "Solomon Khan, it is I, your servant."

The handle was cold in his hand. He pushed it down and walked in.

Solomon the Man stood in his bed, naked to the waist, circling with the tip of his tongue the nipples of a girl with golden hair and white skin. When Joseph the Winemaker walked in, he turned around, surprised, but his eyes were clouded and he looked as if he did not recognize Joseph at all.

"Solomon Khan," Joseph the Winemaker stuttered. Then the girl with the golden hair came up, still naked, and forced Joseph out.

 Zil-el-Sultan had lost his luck.

Tala had defied him, Solomon the Man had betrayed him, and Zil-el-Sultan avenged himself by divorcing Hannah. But the moment he sent her away to jail, he ran out of luck, and lost a kingdom.

He was the most capable of Nasser-ed-Din Shah's sons, by far the most popular among the people and inside the ruling circles. He had ruled southern Persia with success, proven his ability to reign. But his very popularity had made the Shah resent him. When the time came to name a successor, Nasser-ed-Din Shah bypassed Zil-el-Sultan and named his brother, Muzaffar-ed-Din Khan, Crown Prince. Wounded, the Zil plotted against Muzaffar-ed-Din's life. But his plan was unveiled. Nasser-ed-Din Shah stripped Zil-el-Sultan of all his power, and took away the rule of southern Persia. He left to the Zil only the rule of Esfahan, but even this was punishment: inside Esfahan the Zil was still governor. If he crossed the city's borders, he would be killed by his father.

Devastated, Zil-el-Sultan called his seers and asked for the cause of his downfall. They conferred for an entire day, extracted from the prince every promise of immunity for themselves and their families should he not be pleased with their answer. In the end they were unanimous: His Highness the Prince Shadow of the King, had recently distanced himself from a woman with a lucky face. Bring her back, and he would regain his luck.

Zil-el-Sultan called his Minister of Court.

"Release Taj-Banoo," he ordered. "Send my carriage to bring her back."

Hannah returned to the palace in full glory: she was twenty-five years old, a startling woman, strong and confident and aware of her own power now that Zil-el-Sultan believed she controlled his fate. She married him again, regained her title, her wealth in Esfahan, her power within the harem. He swore he would give her anything she wished. She asked that he forgive Tala, and let her leave Esfahan with Solomon the Man. It never occurred to her that she should protect Peacock: she had been sent to Zil-el-Sultan at the age of nine, left alone among strangers with only the mission to keep alive and protect herself. She had been told to deny her past, her family, her longings. Peacock, like Leyla and Joseph the Winemaker, was only a shadow Hannah saw in the dark and often did not recognize.

She sent Tala's nursemaid to Juyy Bar.

"Go to Tehran," the old woman relayed Hannah's message. "Nasser-ed-Din Shah is your father's enemy. He will take you into his court if only to spite the Zil."

The nursemaid came back with news from Juyy Bar. Tala was pregnant, she said, and from the shape of her stomach and the width of her steps when she walked, the nursemaid swore she would have a boy. Solomon the Man had divorced his Jewish wife, and was about to sell his house in Juyy Bar. He had forgotten his three children from Peacock. He had forgotten their mother. He was devoted to Tala and only to Tala, and he would take her to Tehran, he had promised, as soon as his child was born and Tala could travel.

 Joseph the Winemaker was desperate to keep Solomon from leaving. He had heard news of Tala's pregnancy, and of Solomon's plan to go to Tehran. He had gone to Solomon's house a dozen times after the day Tala threw him out. He had begged to see Solomon, asked that he stay in Juyy Bar, take Peacock back, save his children. Tala met him at the door every time, and refused to let him in.

"My lady of ladies." Joseph the Winemaker bowed to his grandchild, who did not know him. He saw Hannah in Tala's face, saw Leyla in her expressions. "My lady of ladies, you don't know our pain. Solomon the Man is the light of all our lives. When he came here, he brought rain. If he leaves, we will all be lost. My daughter will be shamed. Her children will starve. My lady of ladies, Solomon the Man has a heart of gold. He won't spare us his mercy."

But Tala was impossible. She had taken over Solomon's life, his mind, his heart. She had made him forget his every loyalty, made him bury even his love for his daughters. Joseph the Winemaker thought the situation through, and realized that Tala must have charmed Solomon with a sophisticated spell. He shared his theory with Raab Yahya, who laughed at Joseph's simplicity and offered a much easier one:

"The man wanted Love. He found Love."

Joseph the Winemaker cursed Raab Yahya and every other rabbi in the world. He went home and gathered his life's savings, then went to call on Malekshah the Devil Catcher.

Malekshah the Devil Catcher commanded powers greater than those of any other witch or sorcerer in Persia. He had spent his youth meditating in the ruins of the ancient city of Rei, capital of the old Persian Empire, seat of the throne of Cyrus the Great, home of Spirit-Princes and Jinn-Kings. As a result of his meditations, Malekshah the Devil Catcher had gained enormous spiritual powers, and once managed to capture the king of a tribe of jinns who inhabited the ruins of Rei. He had released the Jinn-King, but his very act of mercy had placed Malekshah in command of the entire tribe. Now he worked out of a shop overlooking the Shah's Square in Esfahan. For the price of a cow, or the head of a Jew, he ordered the jinns in his service to perform tasks impossible for mortal men. Joseph the Winemaker was terrified of Malekshah, and resentful of the price he exacted for his services. Nevertheless, he went to see him, painfully uttering his wish as he extended to the Devil Catcher a bag full of silver coins.

"My life's blood," he said as Malekshah's fingers closed around the neck of the bag. "You have here the money I put away to buy myself a shroud."

Malekshah the Devil Catcher weighed the bag in his hand and sniffed in disapproval.

"I can't guarantee results," he said casually. "There is only enough here to employ jinns of light. Jinns of darkness are more accurate, but also more expensive."

The jinns of darkness, Joseph knew, acted quickly and aimed for direct results. They inhabited the night, invisible but strong, and unless summoned to perform a task, they were largely harmless; they only strangled anyone who accidentally stepped on their tails, or walked over their children sleeping on open roads. The jinns of light, by contrast, were playful and mischievous—and therefore less reliable. They amused themselves by leading unsuspecting humans into traps from which escape was impossible. Along the way, they tended to lose sight of their original goal, and often left their tasks half-done.

Joseph the Winemaker dreaded the thought of having his wish distorted and changed. In his younger days he would have bargained with Malekshah, sworn poverty, pleaded mercy. Today he resigned himself to getting only what his money could buy.

"Return Solomon the Man to my daughter and my ghetto," he told Malekshah, and watched the bag of coins disappear into a chained coffer.

Solomon the Man dreamt of his children. He slept in Tala's arms the night of Joseph the Winemaker's meeting with the Devil Catcher, and all night long he saw Heshmat and Sabrina running toward him across a sun-bleached courtyard, with their arms outstretched and their feet bare. They were small and beautiful, their eyes golden, their hair light, their skin perfect. They rushed into his arms and when he picked them up, he felt the sun in his heart.

He woke up and told Tala he wanted his children back.

"Impossible," she bristled. "You must leave me first."

They fought for the first time in four months. Tala wanted Solomon for herself. She resented him for loving others, resented every day and hour he had ever lived without her, despised everyone he had ever loved besides her. She was not jealous of Peacock; Solomon never spoke of her. She was jealous of the children.

Now, as he stood in the alley outside Solomon's house every day, Joseph the Winemaker heard Tala scream at Solomon in frustration:

"For *you*," she said, "I had my mother go to jail. I broke my father's pride, left the Palace of Forty Pillars to live here among *Jews*. For *you* I gave up my home and my title."

Joseph the Winemaker thought his money was well spent with the Devil Catcher.

"Any day now," he announced to Peacock, "your husband will come back to you and his children."

 Solomon the Man walked toward his children one early dawn, and the sound of his footsteps awakened Peacock from her nightmares. She went to the door, opened it, and walked out into the cold air.

"Solomon," she whispered, and he emerged like a wish. She saw herself in his eyes.

"Solomon."

She stood unveiled, her hair, soft and dark and lustrous, long to her waist, her skin the color of the night, her eyes radiant. She raised her hands to him and he touched her, awed by her beauty, as if to prove she was real. She was crying, he realized, and he wanted to touch her face, but he was afraid.

"Forgive me."

She did not answer him. She had not understood.

She took his hand and led him into the basement. He saw his children uncovered on the ground, huddling close to each other for warmth, trembling in their sleep. He fell to his knees and cried.

Tala had agreed to take only one child: she wanted Arash, because he was a boy, she said, and carried his father's name—because, Solomon the Man knew, though he never dared admit it openly, Arash was the one Solomon had wanted least, the one he had barely known, the one in whom Peacock had placed her greatest hope. She would take Arash and only Arash, and if Solomon insisted on taking the girls, she would leave him and go back where he would never find her again.

He looked up at Peacock. She read his mind.

"No," her eyes flared.

Her voice shocked Solomon. He was terrified that his daughters would wake up to see him take Arash and leave them.

"I will send money for you," he begged Peacock. "I will come back and see you."

She knew she could not stop Solomon; a father owned his children even in death. She watched him take Arash. Then he walked out and left the girls. On the floor, Sabrina was dreaming of her father who would come—she was certain—to save her from Peacock.

 Joseph the Winemaker fell ill the day Solomon left Juyy Bar. He stayed in bed, heartsick and dismayed, and lost his appetite completely. Every day he became thinner and more disappointed. After a while he lost his sight, his voice, his hearing. His spine curved and his skin stretched so tightly over his body that he looked inhuman, and so, when he grew a layer of soft hair, like a new kitten, he knew he had come to the end.

"I have grown the Devil's hair," he mumbled to Peacock, who could not understand him. "I am going to die and go to hell."

Joseph the Winemaker died like a starved child—like his bride of half a century ago, Khatoun, who had been seven years old the night of her wedding. Peacock buried him in 1890, and lived for a while on the revenues from the sale of his winery. Just as she ran out of money, a messenger came from Tehran, bringing food and gold and greetings from Solomon the Man.

"From Solomon," he said as he unloaded the sacks of rice and flour in front of Mullah Mirza's basement. Sabrina and Heshmat were dancing around the messenger's horse, touching the bags of food and uttering their father's name as if it were holy. The messenger put down the last sack, then extended a pouch full of gold coins at Peacock.

"There will be more," he promised, pleased with himself and his mission. Peacock saw his smile and felt a storm of resentment erupt in her.

"Damn him!" she screamed, so loudly the girls froze in their place. She took the pouch from the messenger and threw it back at him.

"Damn him, and damn you if you ever come back."

She pushed the man with her fists, kicked his horse, screamed at her daughters that they were not allowed to touch the food. She opened the top of the coal stove in the yard and, before the terrified eyes of her children, threw one bag of flour after another into the fire.

"Tell Solomon the Man we don't want his charity."

Only later, when the rage had calmed and she could see through her pain into her children's faces, did Peacock realize the extent of devastation she had brought upon them. For days they sat by the stove, inconsolable, and pleaded to the flames for the food their mother had burned.

In vain, Peacock tried to explain.

"Solomon the Man," she told her daughters, "took my life, my youth, my son."

Sabrina never forgave her. Heshmat would not understand her until decades later, when she was old, and herself wounded by life.

"It's *your* fault," they told Peacock as they cried into the night for their father. "It's your fault he left us."

The next time Solomon's messenger came from Tehran, Peacock met him at the door with a butcher's knife. The man left without unloading the food. The neighbors did not interfere. Heshmat and Sabrina never even cried.

"I will find work myself," Peacock said to the audience

that stared at her silently outside Mullah Mirza's basement. "I will go to work and become rich, support my own children, buy my own house."

They lived from day to day, fighting the ghetto's derision, fighting each other. Sabrina had declared war on her mother and announced she would leave her soon—to become a whore, she said, or to marry a Muslim and shame Peacock for life. She went out all day hunting for food, sifting through the garbage outside the neighbors' homes, begging in Esfahan. She came back exhausted and afraid, faking indifference toward Peacock, insisting that Heshmat should go with her the next day. Peacock swallowed her anger and told herself she would soon end her ordeal—that she would find work, rent a room in a decent house, feed her daughters and keep them from the streets.

She went to all the shops in the ghetto and asked for work. Then she went to the bazaar in Esfahan, and at last to the homes of Solomon's wealthy Muslim friends. Everywhere she was refused. In the end she found a heap of worthless fabrics—bits and pieces too small or frayed to be used in a garment—thrown away outside a shop. She tied the fabrics into a bundle and came back to sell them in Juyy Bar. She went from house to house, calling all the women, insisting that they buy from her. Every morning she left the house, promising to return with sweetbread and halva. Every night, Heshmat waited for her in the alley outside the basement, and broke into tears when she saw Peacock empty-handed.

"Look at you," the neighbors told Peacock in contempt. "You were the wife of Solomon the Man, the envy of the world. Look at you now."

Heshmat had found a friend: Saba, who lived three streets away, in a house full of light and warmth. She was an only child, the seed of Ismael the Gutterman's marriage to a crippled orphan from Yazd. Ismael the Gutterman had been eighty-nine years old at the time of the wedding, and the grandfather of eleven children. He had spent his life shoveling human excrement from the bottom of open gutters on the street, and loading the waste in a wooden basket he carried on his back. He sold the bounty to farmers who used it for fertilizer, and he had made a good living for himself and his children, but his wife died and left him alone. Ismael the Gutterman decided a wife was cheaper than a maid, and sent for the lame girl from Yazd. But even the rabbi who married them swore that Ismael could never meet the demands of matrimony. Ismael the Gutterman had taken his challenge seriously. On the night of his wedding he had filled a bowl with three dozen raw egg yolks, added a jar of saffron and a quarter-kilo of crushed white cumin, then drunk the potion in one continuous gulp. Half an hour later, aching from the rush of diarrhea that would plague him for the rest of his days, he had run to his bride and entered her with a penis as hard as the day he first knew a woman. He had taken the lame girl's virginity, given her Saba, then retired to doze permanently in the corner of the house.

Still, the lame girl from Yazd was content and grateful for her life. She could have been an old maid, living in her father's house until she died. Instead she had a husband and a home of her own, and a daughter she adored more than God. She surrounded Saba with love and attention, sang her to sleep, cooked for her every day. She brought Saba's friends home and fed them generously, asked them to stay the day, to come back tomorrow. After the first time she went to her house, Heshmat played imaginary games in which she was Saba, and Peacock the lame girl from Yazd.

But once, when Heshmat went to call, she found Saba in bed, surrounded by her mother and her aunts. They were washing Saba's eyes with cold tea, giving her small doses of opium to smoke. They poured sugar water down her throat and restrained her when she screamed. Saba was in pain, the lame girl from Yazd told Heshmat. She had contracted trachoma.

"Be careful you don't touch her wounds," Saba's mother warned her. "You could catch this yourself."

Heshmat watched Saba that day and imagined that she, too, had become ill. She would stay in bed, with Peacock next to her, and even Solomon the Man would come back from Tehran to see his ailing daughter.

When no one was looking, Heshmat rubbed her finger into Saba's eyes, then into her own.

That night she felt as if there were salt in her eyes. She floated in and out of sleep and touched the small tumors—like bits of sand that grew harder every hour—that had emerged alongside the inner lining of her eyelids. By morning her face was throbbing and she saw everything through a thick, bloody fog.

She dragged herself out of bed and called Peacock.

"Mama. My eyes hurt."

There was no answer.

She felt for Peacock with her hands, then searched for Sabrina. The beds were empty, the house quiet.

"Mama. Sabrina. My eyes."

She crawled outside. The sun was warm on her face. It was the middle of morning, she realized. No one would be home until late at night.

"Mama," she cried, but no one could hear. "My eyes."

Heshmat's days stretched into hours, and the hours into minutes infinitely long and empty but for the pain and the burning in her eyes, and the fear of the darkness where she was left to suffer alone. Sabrina sat by her bed and washed her eyes, but Heshmat barely felt the water. Peacock held her head and cried with her in pain, but Heshmat never heard her screams. A week passed and the pain grew worse. Peacock rubbed fresh wheat into Heshmat's eyes to ease the pain. On Yom Kippur she fasted for forty-eight hours: "So that God will hear my scream," she explained to Raab Yahya, "and answer with mercy."

They had not eaten for days. Sabrina begged in Esfahan, and brought home a bowl of rancid meatballs and spoiled vegetable stew. Peacock knew the meat was not kosher. She accepted it nevertheless.

"Eat this." Sabrina put a spoon to Heshmat's mouth, but the pain was too strong.

Sabrina put the plate on the shelf above Heshmat's bed.

"Never mind," she said. "It will be here in the morning."

Near dawn, Heshmat woke up hungry, and remembered the meatballs. She felt her way in the dark, and found the shelf. She reached into the plate. The meatballs were moist and round. She put one in her mouth.

She screamed—her jaws open—and did not dare close her mouth. The meatball was alive. It had legs that moved.

Sabrina jumped awake and saw Heshmat gagging.

"Scorpion."

Without thinking, she reached into Heshmat's throat and grabbed the animal. It stung her palm. This time, Sabrina cried.

Peacock grabbed Sabrina's hand, opened it, and flung the scorpion to the ground. She emptied the kerosene from the oil lamp onto the scorpion and set it on fire. She put the burnt shell back over Sabrina's wound: a scorpion caught and killed was the best cure for its own venom.

Minutes passed. Sabrina's hand swelled and her face became gray. Realizing that the poison had entered Sabrina's blood, Peacock put her child on her back and ran to the house of the nearest doctor.

"A knife," the man called, but by then Sabrina's eyes were fading. He cut a hole around the bite and looked for the poison. It was too late. Sabrina was cold and still.

* * *

159

Peacock held Sabrina's corpse until the hardness of death had set in and the child's arms were petrified. At the burial she washed Sabrina, walked her into the grave, and covered her shroud with violets she had picked in the wild. Then she went home and nursed Heshmat's eyes.

"We should leave this town," she heard Heshmat whisper in the dark. "We should go where people don't die."

The next month they were gone.

 They set out for Tehran in the summer of 1892. They traveled for weeks in the vast and unyielding desert, and along the way, many in their caravan fell ill and died from the heat. One morning they looked into the horizon and saw a stunted city without domes or minarets, surrounded by a deep moat and, beyond it, a mud wall. This was the capital of the Qajars, the city they had chosen over Esfahan—over Shiraz and Kashan and Yazd—to house their throne.

The wall around Tehran was pierced by arched gates decorated with tiles. Through the gates, Peacock's caravan entered a long stretch of sand broken only by a few ruined houses where no one lived. Tehran was dry and dusty and unfertile. Not far to the north, along the shore of the Caspian Sea, the land was lush and green and generous. But Tehran was cut off from the Caspian by the mighty range of the Elburz Mountains—the peaks so high they stopped precipitation and humidity from reaching the desert on the southern side of the mountain. Riding through the wasteland outside the capital, Peacock could see the snow that covered the Elburz year-round. It was here, thousands of years ago on this frozen mountain, that Arash the Archer had thrown the arrow that saved Persia.

Their caravan stopped in Tekkyeh—Tehran's central square, where four large thoroughfares crossed. Here a horse-drawn trolley provided public transportation for Muslims. Herds of livestock blocked most of the square as they passed through the city. Dozens of mules, camels, and donkeys, flocks of hens and turkeys muddled through the crowd of pedestrians. Veiled women rode alone. White-turbaned mullahs sat on padded saddles. Beggar children stopped every rider.

Peacock and Heshmat left the caravan and advanced on foot toward the Jewish ghetto. Away from the Tekkyeh, streets narrowed into winding lanes between long stretches of mud walls. They were unpaved, dusty, covered with garbage from all the homes, plagued with dogs that fought the beggars for trash. The air, trapped under the arched roof of the alley, sizzled with heat and the smell of putrefaction. There were no trees here, no gardens in sight.

Peacock and Heshmat found themselves lost in the crowd of vendors and children, of mullahs in brown robes and green turbans, of half-naked dervishes covered only with loincloths. There were Arabs in white robes, blue-eyed foreigners in strange attires and riding in fancy coaches. A gentleman in expensive clothes rode an Arabian mare. Behind him, a dozen servants guarded his fool, the madman he kept on hand—such as all gentlemen owned—to amuse him with his lunacy.

Soldiers with torn uniforms and no weapons sold rotten fruit on the streetcorner. Palace guards loitered in the shade of a wall, smoking opium and chewing dates.

Outside mosques, government buildings, and the homes of the rich gathered masses of beggars—many among them blind, crippled, or mad. In every district, thieves, murderers, and pimps had formed their own union, with designated areas of operation and religiously observed rules of conduct.

They found the Jews' ghetto. It was smaller than the Juyy Bar in Esfahan, less crowded. Its streets—paved with up to a foot of mud and garbage—were covered with arched roofs that retained heat in the summer and humidity in winter. Its houses, made of raw, unbaked clay, were cracked and lopsided and forever threatening to collapse in one of Tehran's violent quakes. But the ghetto was positioned at the center of town, exposed to Muslim quarters through six gates that were open except in times of approaching pogroms; closer to the Shah, the mullahs were less powerful, and the Jews safer.

It was almost dusk when Peacock and Heshmat set out to find a room. They knocked on people's doors and asked if they could rent a room on credit, or sleep in a courtyard until they had found a home. They went to the ghetto's main synagogue, then the two smaller ones. Even the rabbis turned them away.

"Go to the Pit," everyone said. "You can sleep there on the street."

The Pit was the ghetto's square, its slaughterhouse and open-air garbage dump. It was never cleaned; every time the Jews tried, the mullahs stopped them. Enclosed on all sides with shops and houses, the garbage was piled higher in some places than the structures around it. Here the poorest of the ghetto's vendors sold rotten fruit, stewed lamb's entrails, and lentil soup. The doors of all the houses were broken, the windows sealed with patches of cloth, the rooms crammed with people and disease. Outside, the sun baked the blood of slaughtered animals as flies devoured what little the butchers threw away. Dogs fought hungry children for scraps. Lice crawled up the legs of pedestrians.

Peacock stood at the edge of the Pit and held Heshmat.

"We should never have come."

It was almost dark. They haggled with a vendor about the price of a bowl of lentils, split the food in half, and ate quietly. All around them on the street, others were preparing to sleep. When the food was finished, Peacock spread an old chador on the ground, used her bag of fabrics as a pillow for herself and Heshmat, and sat next to her daughter, waiting for night to fall. Slowly the moon rose and the sounds of the ghetto faded as men returned to their homes and women gathered their children into their beds and around their fires. Forsaken by the day, the Pit-dwellers sat around the edge of the square—the moon painting fear onto their faces, the night awakening their sense of desperation—and stared at the mountain of waste that was their home. One by one they stopped fighting their shame, lay down their heads, and prayed for sleep. The more recent arrivals, like Peacock, refused to lie down. She was sitting up with her back against a wall, Heshmat's head in her lap, and she had just closed her eyes when she heard a cry.

"You there!"

Peacock looked up.

"You, there. Don't sleep yet."

From the other side of the square, an impeccable white cloud moved toward her across the darkness.

It was a woman, dressed in layers of white, her hair, dry as corn leaves, unbraided and long around her shoulders. When she came closer, Peacock saw that the woman was old, her face covered with a cake of white powder, her lips painted amber. "I am told you sell fabrics."

She smiled with the charm of a three-year-old.

"My name is Zilfa." She extended a hand to Peacock, who did not know what to do with it. "I embroider handkerchiefs, and I'm looking for white silk."

 Zilfa the Rosewoman was her father's only child and the inheritor of all his money. She had been pretty—long ago, in the days of her youth, before age ate away at her strength. Her hair had been fiery red, her skin was white, and her eyes—she insisted until the day she died—took on an almost jade glow if she stood in the sun at the right angle in the right time of day.

She had had suitors from the time she was three—men lured at first by tales of her father's wealth and later by accounts of her own fair skin. Her father, Mirza Davood of

163

Tehran, had declared her engaged seven times before she reached the age of fifteen, but each time, Zilfa the Rosewoman had refused to marry the man he chose. She had let Mirza Davood sit through hours of negotiation and interview, allowed him to promise her hand, and then, days before the wedding, announced she was not pleased with the choice.

Mirza Davood was a respected man in his community. He was the wealthiest of all the merchants, more educated than all the rabbis together. He owned the larger of the two wells in the ghetto and, in times of drought, always gave water away for free. He knew he should force Zilfa to marry the man of his choice—the son of the moneylender, for example, with the blond mustache and the long overcoat that made him look like a Cossack, or the handsome son of Salman the Scent Seller, who always smelled of his father's perfumes and bowed before Mirza Davood every time he came into the house. But Mirza Davood respected Zilfa's wishes and allowed her a say in matters concerning her future. He was an enlightened man, he explained to his wife every time she cursed him for his softness. He had studied Hebrew and Arabic and even three years of medicine in Baghdad. He could plead and reason with Zilfa, but he could not force her to marry against her will. He held on to his liberal views until Zilfa ruined her life and brought shame upon her parents.

A man came to stay at Mirza Davood's house—a Muslim, with a tall black horse and eyes that had known no sorrow. His name was Sardar Ali Khan—heir to the throne of the defunct Zand dynasty in Shiraz. He lived on a three-hundred-acre estate famous across Persia for its gardens and architecture. In his house there were forty-seven bedrooms, three ballrooms, each larger than the ghetto square, and a polo field. The ceilings and the walls were all hand-painted with miniature figures of legendary heroes and fairies. The stables kept three hundred sixty-five horses—one for Ali Khan to ride on each day of the year. Zilfa the Rosewoman saw her father's guest the first night, and determined that he alone was the man worthy of her hand.

"It's Ali Khan," she declared to Mirza Davood, "or it's no one."

Mirza Davood was a good Jew, a prayer leader at every Sabbath service and a scholar in Talmudic law. That his daughter could even speak of marrying outside her religion brought despair to his heart and made him realize he had failed in raising her. He told Zilfa that Ali Khan was already married—to his niece, whom he had loved since childhood—and to a dozen other, younger women whom the niece had hand-picked and brought to the harem. Zilfa was undaunted by the news.

"He must leave them all," she concluded. "I will not share my man with another."

Mirza Davood hit Zilfa across the mouth, then locked himself in prayer to atone for the violence. His wife sat in the courtyard of their house and threw fistfuls of dirt onto her face and hair. Zilfa the Rosewoman, meanwhile, planned her meeting with Ali Khan.

She must be direct, she decided, but also subtle. She must leave a strong impression, command undivided attention. She was aware of the risk she was taking. She thought it worthwhile.

She took a length of white silk and sewed a handkerchief with lace edges, and white roses in each corner. She dabbed the roses with perfume she had received from the son of Salman the Scent Seller. One morning she woke up early to braid her hair and paint her eyes. Sardar Ali Khan stepped into the courtyard to saddle his horse. Zilfa the Rosewoman walked out of her room unveiled and called his name. She went up to him, her face glowing in the first light of day, and gave him the handkerchief.

"A token of admiration," she said, and Ali Khan was so charmed he took a bow of gratitude. But he rode away from Tehran and never came back.

* * *

165

Zilfa the Rosewoman had gambled with her life and lost. She remained unveiled, and was banned from her father's house. Mirza Davood sent her to live in the Pit, in a one-room rectangular house with no windows, and a tiny yard where nothing was expected to grow. Zilfa the Rosewoman came to her new home with joy and optimism. Ali Khan, she insisted, would send for her soon. In the meantime, it was her intention to make her house beautiful.

She would sleep in the only room, she decided, and use the basement as a place to "practice the arts." In the yard she would make a garden and plant roses. The neighbors laughed at her; nothing grew in the Pit but weeds and garbage, they said. Zilfa the Rosewoman planted seeds in the garden, and watched them bloom in full color.

With the allowance she received from Mirza Davood, she hired a voice tutor and a painting teacher. Samira the Seamstress came in once a month to make Zilfa dresses out of thin, clinging fabrics. Zilfa the Rosewoman insisted on transparent sleeves and refused to wear veils. She sent to the bazaar once a month for creams and perfumes from Salman's shop. She sat in her rose garden every morning and brushed her hair in the sun. She removed the hair from her legs with the flame of a candle, applied pastes made of vegetables and rose petals to her face, rubbed her hands with lard, and put snake oil on her lashes to make them long. And she waited for Ali Khan to come.

She waited five years, ten, fifteen. By the age of thirty she had become conscious of her age. Frightened by the deterioration of her skin, she soaked her face in goat's milk that she hid guiltily from the hungry children in the Pit. She worked less and slept more, and asked the women in the Armenian quarter—for she would never admit weakness to the Jews—for remedies against old age.

"Sheep's semen," they told her. "Apply it to your skin twice a week."

Zilfa the Rosewoman was disgusted and outraged by the suggestion. She would devise her own medicine, she decided, and came up with new herbal masks and mud potions. She practiced laughing with her lips close together—to keep lines from appearing around her eyes. She slept with her head lower than her body—to keep the glow in her cheeks. She wrapped herself from chin to toes in a tight sheet designed to keep the skin from sagging.

At forty she gave in and sent a messenger to Shiraz, to ask about Sardar Ali Khan's intentions toward her. The messenger returned too soon; Ali Khan had died in the Plague of 1866. His sons were all grown and married. His grandchildren had taken over the house.

Zilfa the Rosewoman threw the messenger out and cried for seven days. Then she came out and tended her flowers.

At fifty she sent word to all her old suitors and announced her readiness for marriage. She woke up later now, hoping to postpone the moment when she saw the world and realized she was still alone. Leaving her bed, she rushed to cover her face with powder, painted her lips and her eyes, then sat in the garden and embroidered white silk handkerchiefs with roses on each corner. She sewed two dozen handkerchiefs a day, stacked them in neat piles at the corner of her basement, and told her visitors she was saving them for her dowry. A year later she had filled every inch of her basement with white handkerchiefs and was still shopping for silk.

 "I will show you my samples first," Peacock lied to Zilfa the Rosewoman, as she fumbled in her sack for the best of her pieces. "I want you to get an idea of the kind of merchandise I offer."

She was conscious of the accent that marked her immediately as a stranger, trying to hide from Zilfa the faded scraps of fabric that dropped from the bag. She took out a green taffeta, part of a dress that had belonged to Mad Marushka.

"This is an antique," she told Zilfa the Rosewoman. "It belonged to royalty in Esfahan."

Zilfa the Rosewoman looked as if she had been insulted. She turned her head away from Peacock and forced a half-smile.

"Thank you." She was already walking away. "Perhaps another time."

"Wait," Peacock called her. "I have more. That was not my good piece."

She emptied the bag on the ground and began to sort through the rags. Reluctantly, Zilfa stopped. She knew she had come to the wrong peddler.

"White," she reminded Peacock. "I only need white."

Peacock extended a piece of brown silk at her.

"Yes." Zilfa looked for a way out. "But I need *white*."

Peacock showed her a yellow, stained piece.

Zilfa the Rosewoman was about to protest, but she saw Peacock all flushed and flustered, and realized the extent for her need. She straightened the row of pearls around her neck and summoned patience.

"Where do you come from?" she asked, ignoring the fabric extended to her.

"Esfahan." Peacock was relieved to have stopped Zilfa. She pointed to Heshmat. "This is my daughter."

"Pretty girl," Zilfa remarked honestly. "But where is your man?"

The question surprised Peacock. For the first time in her life, she was among people who did not know her past.

"I don't have a man."

"Is he dead?"

Peacock was at a loss to explain.

"He's not dead. I left him."

Zilfa the Rosewoman raised her chin in disbelief.

"What do you mean, you left him? Do you mean he *divorced* you?"

"I mean I *left* him." Peacock was irritated and embarrassed.

"You ran away." Zilfa tried again. "He abused you and you ran to save your life."

Peacock stuffed the yellow fabric back into her bundle. She had lost interest in the sale. She wanted only to distance herself from Solomon's memory.

"He married someone else," she said. "He fell in love with a thirteen-year-old girl and brought her into my house, so I took my children and left."

She motioned to Heshmat that they should leave. She straightened her chador on her head, tightened the cheap metal clasp that held together the corners of her veil behind her head, and was about to walk away when Zilfa stopped her. She reached over casually and lifted Peacock's veil.

"But you're beautiful," she exclaimed, embarrassing Peacock even more. "Why would he have left you?"

Peacock rearranged her veil and began to walk again.

"Wait," Zilfa commanded, so engrossed in the effort to solve Peacock's mystery that she had become oblivious of the rules of etiquette she so ardently observed in normal times. "Did you love him, then—this husband you say you left?"

Peacock would not answer.

"You must have loved him," Zilfa declared, thrilled to have discovered a love story. "You wouldn't have left unless you were jealous."

Heshmat liked Zilfa. She let go of Peacock's hand, and approached the old woman.

"My father is here in Tehran," she said. "He's married to Tala Khanum, the daughter of Zil-el-Sultan."

Zilfa the Rosewoman was pleased with the new revelation.

"So you came to get him back," she decided for Peacock. "You came to reclaim him from the Qajar."

It never occurred to her that the story was unlikely.

Peacock dragged Heshmat away.

"Wait, I said," Zilfa commanded, now impatient. She took Heshmat's hand. She cleared her throat, and made an announcement.

"This is against my policy," she said, "but you can stay with me for a while, till you get your husband back."

She took them to her house, and let them sleep in her garden. In the morning she announced breakfast.

Zilfa the Rosewoman ate in what she called a civilized manner: at a table, with chairs—she only had two—and white linen. She came to the table fully dressed, made up, and coiffed. Appalled by the Middle Eastern custom of sharing food from the same bowl, she designated plates for every guest, decorated the food with herbs and flowers, placed rose petals in everyone's tea. She demanded that her guests converse with her about "matters of interest to refined people"—about the state of opera in Europe, fashion in the Czar's court, art in the Shah's palace. Peacock and Heshmat looked at one another in confusion and opted for silence. Zilfa talked for everyone. Only when the meal was finished and they were clearing the table did she broach the subject of Peacock's fate.

"I think we should wait before calling on your husband," she suggested, scrutinizing Peacock closely. "It will do no good for him to see you in this state. You must gain some weight, have some decent clothes made, use proper makeup."

Peacock swallowed her tears.

"I'm not here for Solomon the Man," she said, wondering if it was true. "I'm here to find work."

Zilfa the Rosewoman winked at Heshmat conspiratorially, and decided to humor Peacock.

"What kind of work?"

"Anything."

Zilfa the Rosewoman said she knew a Muslim in the bazaar: a jeweler with an Esfahani accent, she recalled, who had come to Tehran with a chest full of stones.

"His name is Ezraeel." She chuckled. "I happen to know he's partial to Jewish women."

She brought her face close to Peacock and savored the

gossip. "He's married, but I am told he keeps a mistress right here in the Pit."

She straightened herself again, suddenly indignant, and assumed a proper distance from Peacock.

"Anyway, I am above this sort of talk. *I* know him because I bought these pearls from him." She showed Peacock her pearls. "He has the best stones in the city. I've told him that when I get married, I want his purest diamond."

 Zilfa the Rosewoman took Peacock to see Ezraeel. They walked from the ghetto to the Tekkyeh, then bribed a coachman who agreed to overlook the law barring Jews from riding through town, and who drove them to the bazaar. Peacock was terrified of getting caught, but Zilfa the Rosewoman insisted on the carriage ride; she would not walk to the bazaar like a pauper, or present herself to Ezraeel the Avenger in dusty clothes. She sat in the carriage looking defiant and unafraid, but the moment they started moving, she pulled the curtains shut and grabbed the yellow patch on her chador into her fist.

The carriage went past the Shrine of the Seven Daughters, crossed Emamzadeh Ismael—the city's oldest quarter—and stopped just outside the Tchar-Sou, the meeting place of Tehran's four greatest bazaars, and the home of the Imperial Prison. In ancient times, Zilfa the Rosewoman told Peacock as they dismounted the carriage, heroes had sat in the Tchar-Sou, on a balcony higher than all the other structures in Tehran, from which they had kept watch over the people. Now the balcony was occupied by the Dorougheh—the head of the city's guards. All day long, the Dorougheh sent his men to roam the city, looking for thieves and outlaws and, most of all, suspects against the crown. At night he sat on the Balcony of Justice, received the prisoners arrested that day, and pronounced sentence. He sent the men into the Imperial Prison just below his balcony.

"Look!" Zilfa the Rosewoman exclaimed in horror as they approached the Balcony of Justice. "That's the prison."

Peacock saw a trapdoor in the ground, fortified with iron bars. The Imperial Prison was an underground cave with no windows and no access to the outside except this door, through which prisoners entered. It was infested with rats and vermin, immersed in darkness, full of corpses. Prisoners whose families did not bring them food every day died of starvation. Those who were perceived as a threat to the monarchy were quickly executed. The rest lingered in darkness until they succumbed to disease or suffocated in large groups from lack of air. Few men had ever left the Imperial Prison alive.

"Quick!" Zilfa the Rosewoman trembled in disgust as she circled around the trapdoor to avoid the prison. "Don't go near there."

Peacock began to follow Zilfa, hesitated, then gave in to curiosity and moved closer to the prison door. She approached the trapdoor, leaned over, and looked through the iron bars into the darkness. Seeing nothing, she moved closer, put one knee on the ground, and peered in. A hand grabbed her. She screamed and struggled, but the hand was insistent. Through the bars of the trapdoor, a man with a black face and long hair was begging Peacock for money with which to bribe the guards and buy food.

He was covered with grime and smelled like a corpse, his eyes hollow, his mouth black and toothless. His ankles were chained to the ground, but he had pulled himself up with one hand, and he did not release Peacock until one of the Dorougheh's men came up and beat the prisoner's wrist with a club. He let go, fell to the ground, and began to sob.

"Get up!" Zilfa the Rosewoman stood above Peacock without attempting to help her. She was angry, embarrassed by the incident, ashamed to be associated with Peacock. "I told you not to go close. Now get up."

Away from the prison, the Tchar-Sou was crowded with vendors and shoppers and animals. Trains of mules and donkeys shouldered horses and sheep. Housewives bargained with peddlers. Vendors sold cows' intestines and sheeps' brains, lambs' testicles, chicken entrails, and fried grasshoppers.

The bazaar was a network of narrow, unpaved corridors covered with domed roofs. Every few meters a shaft of light fell through the openings in the tops of the domes, cutting the darkness and striking the people as they passed through it. In the weavers' court, vendors sat smoking their Kalyans next to piles of cotton goods imported from Manchester. In the booksellers' court, old men sold handwritten manuscripts painted on deerskin. In the metalworkers' gallery, half-naked youths—their bodies lighted by fire—bent over hot anvils. Zilfa the Rosewoman maneuvered herself through the crowd, and entered the jewelers' bazaar with regained confidence. She greeted a few shopowners who barely noticed her, then stopped half a meter outside the arched entrance of Ezraeel the Avenger's shop; Jews were not allowed inside believers' shops. Their very presence, their touch defiled the premises permanently. A young boy sat in the shop, ready to greet customers.

"Zilfa of Davood," the Rosewoman called out to the servant boy from her place in the corridor. "I have business with Ezraeel Khan."

The boy threw a disdainful glance at the visitors, then looked away. He did not get up to call his master. Ezraeel the Avenger, he knew, did not receive Jews.

Peacock looked at the servant, then at Zilfa, and wondered what the next move could be. Inside the shop, silk rugs decorated the floor and the walls; heavy velour drapery hung from the arches; a large, gold-plated samovar steamed next to a display of dates and sweets.

"Call your master," Zilfa asked politely when it became obvious that the boy was ignoring them. "Tell him it's the Rosewoman who bought the pearls."

The boy spat in her direction.

"Get lost, Jew."

Zilfa the Rosewoman grasped her pearls as if for balance. She was trembling, so pale her lips had become blue, so flustered Peacock could feel the tears in her voice. She had come in her best clothes, dressed up like a queen and made up with all her skill and art, and here, at the door, she was being shunned by a peasant in canvas shoes. A thousand pairs of eyes, she felt, were watching her.

"Call him," she tried to command, but she sounded as if she were pleading. At the back of the shop a curtain opened, and a man stepped out holding a whip. At his sight, Peacock felt weak, and trapped.

"You're impatient, Jew." Ezraeel the Avenger slapped the whip handle into the palm of his left hand as he approached Zilfa and Peacock. He came to the door of the shop and stopped. He was tall, forbidding, his face pale and hostile, his eyes the color of golden agates. His lips hardly moved when he spoke.

Zilfa the Rosewoman touched the edge of her face with her fingertips, as if to make certain she was not falling apart. She lifted the sides of her skirt, took a step forward in her satin shoes, and summoned her most confident voice.

"Greetings." Her hands trembled on the skirt. "It is nice of you to receive us."

Ezraeel the Avenger stared her down.

"I am Zilfa," she tried again. "I bought these pearls from you."

Ezraeel the Avenger had remembered Zilfa the moment he saw her. She had come to him with a bag full of small change, and said she wanted his best diamond. She had poured all her money on the rug in front of the store, and insisted she wanted to buy only from Ezraeel—"Nothing but the best for me." After much pleading, she had settled for the cheapest of his pearls.

"I told you not to come back," Ezraeel said. Zilfa the Rosewoman blushed the color of her lipstick.

"I have brought a friend to you." She pointed to Peacock,

suddenly anxious to remove herself from Ezraeel's attention. "She is from Esfahan—like yourself, I believe—and she has quite a reputation—among Jews, that is—for salesmanship. I thought she may be of help to you—somehow."

Ezraeel the Avenger looked at Zilfa, then slowly turned to Peacock. His eyes burned her. She stepped forward, next to Zilfa, and tried to look Ezraeel in the eye.

"I am a peddler," she said. "I can sell anything. Give me some gold—a chain or a bracelet. I will sell it on commission."

Ezraeel the Avenger looked as if he were suddenly stunned. He tried to peer through Peacock's veil. She realized she had gained his interest, and went on.

"I know you do well here," she insisted. "But you could do better. I will sell what none of your customers want."

He gazed at her, then motioned with his head that she should come inside the shop. Excited, Zilfa the Rosewoman also tried to enter.

"Not *you*," Ezraeel told her, and Zilfa almost dissolved on the spot.

Inside the shop, Peacock stood before Ezraeel and waited for him to speak. He stared at her. He stared for so long she felt drops of perspiration bead on her skin under the chador, then slide down her body.

"Open your veil."

Even the servant boy was shocked. He looked up at his master, uttered a prayer to guard against evil, and hurried to the back of the shop where he would not be seen. Peacock turned to Zilfa for help, and saw that she was gone—unable to bear Ezraeel's treatment of her.

Ezraeel the Avenger came closer to Peacock.

"Let me see your face," he commanded.

Peacock stepped backward, aiming for the door, but Ezraeel grabbed her by the arm, and yanked at her veil. The buckle snapped behind her head, the veil came away, and Ezraeel the Avenger saw a young woman with a face he would adore.

175

Ezraeel the Avenger had come to Tehran with a box of jewels, and the ruby that Muhammad the Jew had stolen from Honest the Antiquarian half a century before. In his heart, Ezraeel carried the image of his mother—Afagh, who had come from the mountains of Kurdistan to die in the house of Muhammad the Jew— and of his father, wrapped around the body of Sanam as they became engulfed by a single flame.

He rented the largest shop in the bazaar and established a jewel trade. He found himself a wife—a woman so pale and insipid he could never remember her name, and so called her, conveniently, "the Boys' Mother." He also found a mistress, a Jew from the Pit called Assal, with skin so white Ezraeel always ran his finger along the side of her cheek to search for powder. Assal had been married once, for seven weeks, and robbed of her virginity before her husband had succumbed to malaria. Now she slept with Ezraeel, hoping that in time he would fall in love and marry her. He was rich, and Assal did not mind that he was Muslim. He came to her once a week—on the eve of the Sabbath, as if to defile the holiness of the day—and in all the time she knew him, he never once gave her money or food.

Of the Boys' Mother, Ezraeel the Avenger would have five sons. Of Assal, only one—Besharat the Bastard, who was born in the third year of their relationship, and whose arrival marked the end of Ezraeel's interest in Assal. When he found out she was pregnant, Ezraeel married Assal. When her son was born, he left her and never looked back.

But even at home, surrounded by his children and his wife's relatives, Ezraeel the Avenger could not find peace. His sons came to him for love, and found only his anger. The Boys' Mother tried to please him, but instead aroused his contempt. It was not, as some believed, a question of understanding him, of recognizing his love beneath the anger, of responding to his moods. It was much simpler than that: Ezraeel the Avenger hated his offspring for no reason and with no reserve.

He was a young man, twenty-five years old and handsome, but his life had long since been marred by hatred and revenge. He had burned his father's house, stolen Marushka's jewels and then pursued and tortured her until slowly she had gone mad with fear, and then he had killed her—there in the desert, where he left her to rot.

The day Zilfa the Rosewoman brought him Peacock, Ezraeel the Avenger despised the woman as soon as he saw her. He would have turned Peacock away, slapped her face with his whip and kicked her out of the bazaar she had come to soil with her presence. It was true he slept with a Jew, but he did so more out of hatred than lust—to denounce Assal, he told himself, for the whore that she was. He hated Jews and hated Peacock's Esfahani accent, which reminded him of the past, but then she had spoken, and her voice had aroused in him desire he had never felt before. He tore off her veil and saw her—dark and stunning, black hair and green eyes and skin that was unctuous and strong and maddening. He reached for her, and ran his finger along the side of her cheek. Before him, Peacock had trembled like a trapped sparrow. Ezraeel the Avenger looked at her for a moment longer; then, softly, he turned away and gave her back her veil. He went to an alcove in the wall, and took out a chest full of gold. He gave Peacock a dozen gold bracelets.

She stood looking at the gold, afraid to touch it, unable to refuse. A long time later, she took the bracelets and ran out of the shop. Ezraeel the Avenger recognized her footsteps amid the thousand sounds of the bazaar.

Walking home that day, lost in the unfamiliar neighborhoods and the overwhelming crowds of Tehran's streets, Peacock thought about the Avenger and wondered if she would ever dare go back to him again. She showed Zilfa the bracelets, but said nothing more of the encounter.

That night, asleep in Zilfa the Rosewoman's basement,

Peacock dreamt she was a girl, running through a strange garden with dried trees and a mansion in the background, chased by a vengeful child who grabbed her—Peacock screamed and woke up—and forced her out into the barren world of her hunger.

 "Watch out for the dogs," Zilfa the Rosewoman cried behind Peacock as she saw her leave for the bazaar. Three weeks had passed since the meeting with Ezraeel. Peacock was still living with Zilfa, but she had sold all of the bracelets, and was eager to collect her commission. She was going to the bazaar to find the Avenger.

"It's almost closing time," Zilfa cried as Peacock faded down the alley. "Watch out for the dogs."

The bazaars of Tehran were guarded by a pack of wild dogs. During the day, the dogs roamed the bazaar's roofs. At night, four hours past sunset, a bugle sounded for the closing of all the shops and streets. Only the city's night-watchmen, and the privileged few who had access to the night's password, were allowed to remain outside. Then the dogs, as savage as wolves and trained to kill, were let loose in the bazaar to guard against thieves.

Peacock arrived just as the night bugle sounded. She thought about turning back, but she realized she would never reach home in time for the closing of the streets, and decided she was safer in the bazaar. She ran through the Tchar-Sou into the jewelers' bazaar. Outside Ezraeel's shop, she stopped and listened for the dogs. She went in. He recognized her instantly.

"I brought your money." She extended a pouch of coins at him. He saw her hand—small but strong, dark and chapped but fine. He could already guess, by the size of the pouch, that he had taken a loss—that Peacock had sold the bracelets for much below their cost. He reached for the bag, and then, without intending to, he closed his fist around her hand.

She did not tremble this time. She only eased her hand free, and remained before Ezraeel with her face still veiled. She was not afraid of him anymore; she had recognized the boy in her dream.

She unveiled herself. This time he saw the eyes of Muhammad the Jew.

"Your father," she said, "was my mother's brother."

Ezraeel the Avenger never overcame his longing for Peacock. He never touched her again in his life. He wanted her and despised her at once, and he never managed to conquer either emotion.

He let her sell more of his gold, and ignored the loss. He gave her a loan so she could rent a room on the Pit, buy a mattress and a comforter for herself and Heshmat. He taught her about stones—agates and turquoise at first, then rubies and diamonds and sapphire. He sent her to the homes of his rich clients with a letter of introduction and a pocketful of jewels. The Muslims received her only to oblige Ezraeel, then showed her the door and asked that she not return. Peacock went back, once a month, once a week, shunned by the servants who cursed her impurity, snubbed by the ladies who were outraged by her appearance, ignored by the men who complained openly to Ezraeel for having sent them such a nuisance. Slowly, through years of relentless effort, Peacock established herself.

"He's losing money on you," her clients told her every time she went to their house. "He could sell the same stones for twice as much out of the shop."

Peacock knew it was true; Ezraeel the Avenger had been kind to her. Just as he robbed his associates, destroyed entire families by making high-risk loans at outrageous interest, just as he had ruined Assal the Whore with his refusal to marry her, Ezraeel the Avenger watched over Peacock and showered her with benevolence.

Reza Khan the Maxim was born in the north, in the village of Alasht, six thousand feet above the sea, in a thatch-roofed mud shack that clung to the edge of a precipitous slope. The winters were cold in Alasht, the summers arid. Most of the village's children died in infancy. Most adults never even saw the world outside.

A year after his son was born, Reza Khan's father died. His mother, Nush Afarin Khanum, took Reza and moved to the house of her brother in Tehran. She found another husband, remarried, and left Reza to the care of his uncle. The uncle, in turn, gave Reza away to a friend—Amir Tuman Kazim Khan, who was a general in the largely nonexistent Persian Army. In this house, Reza met his first Jew.

Amir Tuman Kazim Khan was a wealthy man with high connections and friends in important posts. He wore expensive clothes, rode horses with red tails, boasted an impressive collection of fine rugs and jewels; he had the portrait of every Qajar king woven onto silk carpets hanging from the walls of his home. His family emblem was engraved onto a ruby that he wore as a ring. The names of Allah and the Prophet were etched into fine agates that he gave away as gifts to his friends. Every New Year, Kazim Khan ordered a bag of gold coins from Ezraeel the Avenger, and distributed them among the servants and well-wishers who called at the house. The year Reza came to live with Kazim Khan, Ezraeel the Avenger sent Peacock to deliver the coins.

She came in her faded chador with the cheap metal clip that held her veil up and that distinguished her immediately as being poor. She had brought the bag of coins, she said, and some chains and bracelets she thought Kazim Khan may be interested in. Reza was baffled by Peacock's accent, but Kazim Khan immediately recognized a Jew.

"What province do you come from?" he asked without enmity.

"From Esfahan." She fumbled in her pockets and

brought out a letter of introduction with Ezraeel the Avenger's insignia. "Read it for yourself," she said proudly. "You will see that I have good credentials."

Amir Tuman Kazim Khan glanced at the letter, then smiled. He waited for Peacock to arrange a row of gold chains on a piece of black velvet.

"Look here," she urged Kazim Khan. "I think you will like these."

Not until she had left did Kazim Khan tell Reza that Peacock was a Jew.

"But you let her in," the boy protested, suddenly terrified that he had become soiled and dishonored. "You touched her gold. That whole bag of coins was in her hand."

Amir Tuman Kazim Khan raised his hands before Reza and held them out for the boy to examine: Reza found no stain, no sign of disfiguration, no evidence of sudden impurity. Kazim Khan sat down, and told him of the Jews he had known: there was a singer, Solomon the Man, whose voice could arouse nature and awaken God's angels. There was a woman, once married to Zil-el-Sultan, who always denied her origins, and whose very absence had deprived the prince of his good fortune. There was a ghost, Esther the Soothsayer, who foretold the deaths of kings.

"Never underestimate the friendship of a Jew," Kazim Khan told Reza. From then on, every time Peacock came to the house to show jewels, Reza Khan the Maxim watched her as if she were a ghost.

He grew up in Kazim Khan's house, but he always remained a stranger. He had a room of his own, food to eat, a chance to study with Kazim Khan's children. But he was conscious of his humble status—an orphan boy, half-guest, half-servant, ill at ease among his benefactors, resentful of his fate. He was an intelligent boy, capable of great thoughts and deep understanding, but he grew up angry and introverted, with no friends and few acquaintances. For a while he tried to study with the tutors who came to the house. But he was older than Kazim Khan's children, and they laughed every time Reza made a mistake. Once, when she was in the house waiting for Kazim Khan, Peacock saw the children mock Reza's handwriting.

"He even writes like a peasant," they said, and Reza turned pale and cold and looked away. After the lesson, Peacock called him.

"Look at you," she said, "so tall and handsome. I saw you first when you were just a boy."

He was grateful that she had not mentioned the incident she had just witnessed. His eyes, dark and forbidding, suddenly filled with tears. Peacock took his hand.

"Doesn't matter what they say," she consoled Reza. "Doesn't matter that you were a peasant. You're going to be King someday."

Reza Khan the Maxim studied with the tutor long enough to be able to read, then quit his lessons. In 1893, when he was fifteen, he enrolled in the first group of the Cossack Cavalry Brigade at Tehran. Then he left Kazim Khan's care and went to live in the newly built House of Cossacks, next to the drill ground in Tehran.

He devoted himself entirely to his training, prayed he would find a home among the Cossacks. He had impeccable discipline, believed in loyalty and bravery and even heroism. Almost immediately he distinguished himself among the Cossacks, and earned quick promotions. The lower ranks feared and emulated him. His superiors commended his behavior and beliefs. Still, every day he stayed among the Cossacks, Reza Khan the Maxim became more convinced that he was serving an evil cause.

The Persian Cossack Brigade had been created in 1885, under the leadership of a Russian commander—Baron Moadel—and had the mission to protect the Shah and the foreign legations in Tehran. It had been established at the request of Nasser-ed-Din Shah, who had gone to Europe in

1878 and had been a guest of Czar Alexander II. Impressed by the Cossack regiment guarding the emperor, Nasser-ed-Din Shah had asked the Czar to create a Cossack unit in Tehran. He was proud of his Cossacks, aware that they were better trained and equipped than his own army. He knew the Cossacks were on active duty with the Czar, that their leaders told them they were there to serve *Russia's* interest in Persia. He knew Russia was his country's greatest enemy, that the Cossacks, though Persians, were allowed to speak only Russian and Turki—the language of Azerbaijan. He knew this, and yet Nasser-ed-Din Shah welcomed the Cossack regiment, and asked them to stay in Persia for at least forty years.

"This is wrong," Reza Khan the Maxim told Kazim Khan every time he was on leave from the mission. He had become tall over the years. He had dark hair, a thick mustache, merciless eyes. "The Shah has put himself and Persia at the Czar's mercy. He is training an army loyal to his enemy."

Offended by Reza's criticism, Kazim Khan would bite his lip and say a prayer to keep himself from getting angry. He would explain to Reza that Nasser-ed-Din Shah was a great man, that he had a great vision for Persia, that he had set out to modernize his country, bring it out of the past, shine the light of progress into its eyes. He told Reza that the Shah went abroad to represent his nation before the world, that he brought home with him the latest in progress; he had, after all, given Persia its first university and modern hospital. He had introduced art, theater, photography.

"It is true," he said, "that you serve the Czar. But without the Cossacks, we would have no army at all."

Reza Khan the Maxim came away more disturbed by each discussion. Nasser-ed-Din Shah, he argued, had brought progress, but at an intolerable cost: for every adviser and every loan taken from Europe, His Majesty had promised a part of Persian soil, a natural resource, or an alliance. In this way he had sold Persia's minerals, forests, and rivers.

He had allowed foreigners to rule for him, sign treaties for him, buy his country's raw products and sell them back to Persians at ten times the cost. His actions lent credibility to the mullahs who condemned every monarch as an imposter—a usurper of the position entrusted by God to the clergy.

"A king has a duty to protect his kingdom's integrity," he told Kazim Khan, who exploded at the suggestion that Nasser-ed-Din Shah was failing his nation.

"Without a king," he screamed as he walked away to mark the end of each visit, "this country will be destroyed by the mullahs."

Reza Khan the Maxim left early for the House of Cossacks, locked himself alone in the barracks, and wondered about an uncertain future destined for failure and doom.

Peacock wanted Ezraeel's greatest stone.

"I want a diamond fit for a queen," she told the Avenger in the spring of 1895. She had worked with him for three years, managed to sell to all of his clients. Now, she said, she wanted to sell to the queen.

Ezraeel the Avenger raised an eyebrow and smiled with kindness.

"Are there no bounds to your ambition?" he asked. "Do you imagine the queen receives anyone who knocks on the palace doors?"

Peacock became flushed and embarrassed. Her eyes— she no longer veiled her face before Ezraeel—filled with tears he could not explain.

"I have a son at the palace," she said quietly. "He is seven years old. He may still be living with the women."

Ezraeel the Avenger was stupefied. He saw Peacock look up at him, and across the distance that divided them, he thought he could feel the heat of her skin. He demanded no explanation.

"And if you find him?" he only asked. "What then?"

Peacock shook her head. She had known she would lose Arash the day he was born. She knew she could never reclaim him, now that he was tied to royalty.

"Just to see him again," she said.

On Friday, day of audiences and receptions, Ezraeel the Avenger sent his carriage to fetch Peacock at the ghetto. He waited for her outside his house at Sar Cheshmeh. He was dressed in formal clothes: a white linen shirt open at one side, fastened with a single button at the right shoulder; a quilted silk vest; a long silk robe tied at the waist and closed with a button made of knotted silk thread. He saw the carriage approach through the midmorning traffic, and went up to greet Peacock. The coachman stepped down and opened the door for him. Ezraeel the Avenger did not recognize the woman he found inside the carriage.

Peacock was dressed in regal clothes, made up and perfumed and so beautiful his eyes teared when he saw her. She wore an emerald-colored embroidered chador, a green silk blouse with long sleeves that opened lengthwise, a full skirt—the color of the blouse—that fell to her ankles. She wore white cotton stockings, green-and-gold slippers, an emerald veil. She smiled at Ezraeel.

"Zilfa the Rosewoman thought I should impress the Queen," she explained shyly. Lined with black antimony, her eyes seemed larger, more expressive, of a deeper green. Ezraeel the Avenger never stopped looking at her till they had reached the palace.

From Sar Cheshmeh, they rode to Gas Lamp Avenue— a wide thoroughfare, buried in garbage, down the center of which ran the tracks of a horse car. Half an hour later, fighting the traffic of vendors and pedestrians, of unbridled mules and camels and donkeys, they reached the Square of the Cannons, outside the Palace of Roses. The square was full of dust and dirt, its ground broken, bleached by the sun. In the center, surrounded by a fence constructed from a thousand broken rifles, was a huge basin filled with garbage. At each corner of the basin stood an old cannon, the spoils of a triumphant war—hundreds of years ago, when Persia had had an army—against the Portuguese Empire. The cannons stood on broken wheels, prevented from collapsing only by a pile of debris accumulated under them.

On one side of the square Peacock saw the Imperial Bank of Persia—established, directed, and controlled by the British. Behind a naked flagpole she saw the army compound, where half-nude, undernourished soldiers sat smoking opium.

The carriage went through the Square of the Cannons, and entered another avenue that led up to the arched entrance of the Palace of Roses. Here, in sharp contrast to the soldiers in the square, a group of officials, dressed in elaborate uniforms, stood waiting for Ezraeel behind the entrance gates.

Ezraeel the Avenger greeted Djouhar—the Queen's black eunuch—then introduced Peacock. The eunuch sized Peacock up, and appeared pleased. Still, when they began to walk into the palace grounds, he was careful to maintain a proper distance and avoid defiling himself by touching the Jewess.

They went into a large courtyard with high walls made of yellow and blue tile, in the middle of which was a marble pool full of goldfish. They climbed a large staircase, and entered a room reserved for the master of the eunuchs. It had stained-glass windows, walls painted with miniature figures, a picture of His Majesty Nasser-ed-Din Shah Qajar painted on canvas. Below the picture, against the wall, was a single high-backed chair that only the Shah was allowed to occupy.

Djouhar crossed the room, and led Ezraeel and Peacock through a wide corridor, into another court, at the end of which hung a heavy curtain of red velvet, closed, and guarded by four eunuchs. Djouhar gave the password, and the guards opened the curtain, revealing a third courtyard, this one paved with bricks and shaded with trees. Around the courtyard Peacock saw the wide-open windows of the maids' apartments.

"I will leave you here," Ezraeel the Avenger said. Having served as Peacock's introduction and escort, he now entrusted her to Djouhar's care, smiled in encouragement, and walked away.

Djouhar led Peacock up to another curtain.

"Inform the Chief Eunuch that Ezraeel's servant has arrived," he commanded one of the eunuchs guarding the curtain. The man disappeared behind the curtain, then returned with the Chief Eunuch. They asked Peacock's name and business, confirmed that she had been introduced by Ezraeel the Jeweler, then allowed her to enter.

"Hear ye, hear ye!" Djouhar screamed at the curtain. "Strangers are entering. Let there be no female in sight."

The curtain opened onto the main harem grounds.

There was a flowered stage—an endless courtyard spotted with dozens of pools, hundreds of fountains, thousands of birds singing in the branches of cypress trees. There were small green hills covered with narcissus and Persian hyacinth and, running across them, hundreds of women and children in colorful robes, rushing playfully in every direction as they escaped the eyes of the intruder who had just been announced. The women were all dressed in ballet skirts, the latest fashion in Nasser-ed-Din Shah's court. He had gone to Paris, attended the opera, and liked the ballerinas' skirts. Returning home, he had brought with him a dozen French seamstresses who sewed the new skirts for his wives and daughters.

Peacock watched the women escaping into their apartments around the field. Even after the court had emptied, she could hear their voices and feel their eyes staring at her through the etched-glass windows of their rooms. She followed the Chief Eunuch toward the Queen's chambers.

They went up a marble staircase onto a balcony with stained-glass doors, where Peacock was received by the Queen's Badji—mistress of the maids. The Badji was an old woman, vigorous and difficult and known for her cruelty. She had come to the harem as a beautiful girl of thirteen, discovered by Fath Ali Shah's eunuchs and brought to him on a year-long temporary contract of marriage. At the end of her contract, when she was discarded from the harem, the Badji had been employed by another wife as her maid. She had stayed on and learned the harem intrigue, protected her own position by destroying other maids, served her mistress by spying for her against the other wives, sneezing when the Shah called on a new find, poisoning enemies, rewarding friends. Three times, when the Shah's queens had borne him sons, the Badji had killed the children by placing in their beds the pillows used by other children infected with measles. She had killed two rival maids by giving them smallpox: she had brought in bathwater from the homes of people with the disease, and poured the water into the healthy maids' bath. In this way, the Badji had established her position within the harem and become more powerful than any wives she served. When Nasser-ed-Din Shah became King, she was assigned to the Queen Qamar-ol-Dowleh; the Queen had married the Shah against her will, under great pressure from the palace, and for years the talk around the harem was that she might try to escape.

"Follow me," the Badji commanded Peacock with open resentment. "Don't stay long."

They entered a room furnished with rugs and heavy drapery, with brocaded cushions and cashmere tablecloths. A huge candelabra of colored crystal hung from the hand-painted ceiling. Underneath it was a table of white and black mosaic, covered entirely with white narcissus.

At one end was a window with long, stained-glass portals. Next to it was a bed with long posts and white chiffon curtains.

The Badji left Peacock next to the table and disappeared

from the room. Peacock looked about her, waiting for the Queen.

"*Salam-ol-aleikom*," a voice greeted her from behind the curtains that surrounded the bed. "Come closer and let me see you."

Peacock moved toward the bed. A hand emerged through the layers of chiffon, pushing back the curtain to reveal Qamar-ol-Dowleh, Queen of Persia, Moon of the Empire.

 Queen Qamar-ol-Dowleh was one of Nasser-ed-Din Shah's four official wives. She was twenty years old, stunningly beautiful, her face untouched by rouge or antimony, her figure small and thin and still childish. Her father, a wealthy landowner and tribal khan, commanded great influence and enormous power in his own territory. He had received many offers of marriage for his daughter—then named Leila—since she was a child of six. He had refused a proposal by Nasser-ed-Din Shah's uncle, then governor of Shiraz. He had also rejected an offer by Persia's Grand Mullah—an old man who pledged earthly delights and heavenly salvation if only he could have Leila. The Khan was not swayed by wealth; he wanted his daughter to have a happy marriage.

But the time came when Nasser-ed-Din Shah, always seeking to expand his harem, heard of the Khan's beautiful daughter, and decided he must have the one no one else had been able to reach. He sent messengers to the Khan, asking for Leila's hand in marriage. The Khan refused. Nasser-ed-Din Shah made repeated requests, promised ever-increasing wealth, then lost patience. He wanted Leila, he said, or he would declare war on the Khan's tribe and massacre them.

"You choose," the Khan told Leila when she was sixteen. "If you decide against marriage, we will fight the Shah to the last man."

Leila married Nasser-ed-Din Shah, had her name changed to Qamar-ol-Dowleh, and came to her prison in the harem. She brought her nursemaid, the woman who had raised her since birth, but the Shah fired her and assigned Badji to wait on Qamar-ol-Dowleh instead. Soon after that, he found another wife—Ayeshah—and forgot the girl he had so ardently pursued. He gave Ayeshah the Palace of the Sun, five hundred feet away from the Palace of Roses, and he hardly ever called on Qamar-ol-Dowleh again.

"Welcome," the Queen said, and smiled at Peacock with infinite sadness. She sat reclining against large white pillows. "Our friend Ezraeel Khan promises you have brought Us great treasures."

Quickly, Peacock knelt before the bed and opened the velvet pouch in which she kept her stones. She laid them in small rows across the satin sheets: rubies and emeralds, green and yellow sapphires, cut diamonds the size of apricot seeds, enormous pearls—the best of Ezraeel the Avenger's collection.

The Queen glanced at the stones, then waved her hand.

"Put them away," she said. "No jewel in this world will help lessen the boredom of my life."

She noticed the yellow patch of cloth attached with a pin to Peacock's shirt. She sat up, suddenly interested, and asked Peacock to lift her veil.

"So you're a Jew, then," she said with childlike excitement. "I don't think I ever saw a Jew before."

She jumped down from her bed, barefoot, and circled around Peacock. She gaped into Peacock's face, touched her hair, the top of her forehead.

"But you have no horns," she said without malice. "I was told Jews have horns—small ones, you know, like the Devil." She began to search for a tail. Then suddenly she looked up, visibly scared, and went pale. The Badji had kept an invisible guard outside the room and was now upon the Queen with a threatening face and disapproving eyes.

190

"Your Majesty must not leave her bed," she said, taking Qamar-ol-Dowleh's hand and leading her back into the sheets. The Queen obeyed her resentfully, climbed into the bed, and waited for the Badji to leave again. She motioned to Peacock to come closer.

"That woman is always spying on me," she whispered, tears in her voice. "It seems I am pregnant, you see. My first one miscarried. This time Hakim Bashi—the Court's doctor—has confined me to bed."

She swallowed her sadness and forced a smile.

"You must come back," she whispered, hoping the Badji would not hear. "The eunuchs don't like for me to have a friend, but I will ask His Majesty's special permission. Now that I'm pregnant, he will grant my wish."

A thought clouded her eyes. She leaned closer to Peacock.

"Tell me," she asked, "is it true you drink the blood of Muslim children?"

Once a month after her first visit to the harem, Peacock was summoned by Qamar-ol-Dowleh to the Palace of Roses; she was admitted under the pretext of offering jewels to the Queen. She went at first to satisfy Qamar-ol-Dowleh's curiosity about Jews, but after a while she became her only friend. Most of the time she found the Queen alone in her bed, crying and homesick and trapped in her own rage.

"The hardest thing about my predicament," Qamar-ol-Dowleh confided in Peacock, "is knowing it will never change."

Peacock became a familiar sight at the harem. She was allowed to mingle with the other wives—always under the Badji's watchful eyes. She befriended the thousands of eunuchs and chamberlains and pages, the courtiers and spies, the door-listeners and detectives. She came to know the mullahs, professional confessors, and star-readers in permanent residence at the harem. She recognized the mascots and interpreters of dreams, the boys and girls with lucky faces, the sneezers and the food-tasters. Everywhere, Peacock looked for Arash.

She could not ask for him, for the Badji would have killed her if she knew Peacock had come to claim a royal child. She listened for his name in every conversation, but he was never mentioned. She wondered if Tala had changed his name. She learned that Tala lived with Solomon in a mansion in Shemiran, that she had many children of her own, that Solomon the Man had become Nasser-ed-Din Shah's close friend—so much so that the Shah had excused Solomon from having to bow before his own children: Tala's children were of royal blood; Solomon the Man was not. Every other husband in that situation would have had to go through life bowing before his own children from the time they were born.

In the end, Peacock asked Qamar-ol-Dowleh.

"It is hard to tell," the Queen sighed. She was moved by Peacock's tale, eager to help, but she had little power, and even less knowledge about the harem. "I see a thousand children inside these walls. I don't know any of their names."

She saw Peacock's disappointment. She reached over and held her friend's hand.

"But suppose you found him," she echoed Ezraeel the Avenger. "What would you do if ever you found him?"

 Nasser-ed-Din Shah was going to have the celebration of the century. He had been King for fifty years—by far the most powerful of the Qajar kings—and he planned to commemorate the half-century mark with national festivities. He scheduled a nationwide jubilee for the summer of 1896.

All of Persia began to prepare. Governors of every province were requested to come to Tehran in May. Every regiment of warriors and every nomadic cavalry were ordered to march in parade. In his own honor, the Shah exempted all peasants from two years of taxes. He sent home the few young men still enrolled in his army, and promised amnesty for all prisoners.

In Tehran, triumphal arches were erected on every street, shopowners decorated their stores, and the royal kitchen began to feed all the poor. The Shah's eunuchs gave away new clothes to children. Shrines and holy places declared they would house any and all pilgrims. Mullahs were offered cough medicine to clear their throats so they could chant louder in praise of the Shah. Sacred fountains were enlarged to hold greater quantities of holy water, as miracles were predicted to happen on the day of the jubilee. Nasser-ed-Din Shah himself, close to seventy years old, announced he would empty his harem of his thousand temporary wives, only to replace them with new ones.

Peacock went to the palace now on a daily basis. Qamar-ol-Dowleh wanted no part of the celebrations, but the Badji insisted that the Queen must appear at her husband's side on the day of the jubilee. She had called in weavers and seamstresses to prepare a special gown for the Queen, ordered the stables to build a new carriage for the Queen, and summoned Peacock to bring her the greatest stones in the city. In the midst of the frenzy, just when she had stopped looking for Arash, Peacock found her son.

She had left the palace one late afternoon, and was walking slowly through the gates of the Square of the Cannons. She was not in a rush to get home that night; in the spirit of the celebrations, Nasser-ed-Din Shah had lifted the restriction on walking after dark, and allowed anyone to roam the streets freely. At the entrance to the square, Peacock stepped back to allow passage to a regiment of the youth division of the Persian Cossack Brigade. She saw the young boys riding past her in a cloud of dust, and did not move until she thought they had all passed. She started to walk again, but she felt someone looking at her, and turned around. There was a boy, mounted on a horse and wearing a Cossack uniform, staring at the yellow patch on her chador.

In the twilight he appeared pallid and lost, but his eyes were dark and his features pleasing. She thought he was the same age as Arash. She smiled at him. Then suddenly she felt the fear of death tear through her heart. The boy, she realized, was a younger image of Solomon the Man.

She raised a hand and beckoned Arash. He came on his horse, one hand resting on the gun he had not yet learned to use.

"Take a bow," he ordered, and put the tip of his whip on Peacock's shoulder.

Peacock reached for him. Frightened, Arash pulled back.

"Unveil yourself," he commanded, as if to identify the enemy. "Unveil and introduce yourself."

Peacock opened her veil. Arash went limp. His eyes filled with tears. She raised a hand to touch him, there on his knee that trembled against the horse, but in the instant that she moved, he drew his gun and backed away.

"*Die!*" he screamed, cursing her for the years of longing and abandonment. "*You die!*"

 Arash the Rebel was one year old when he arrived at Nasser-ed-Din Shah's court in Tehran. He had come with Tala and Solomon the Man, exhausted by the protracted journey from Esfahan, trembling with fear and consternation in his white starched shirt and the padded silk jacket Tala had insisted he must wear. He was terrified of Tala, of her tempestuous moods and impossible demands, terrified also of Solomon the Man—this father he had rarely seen before, who had suddenly taken him away from Peacock. During the trip he had ridden alone, in a coach, with only a maid at his side. Then, as throughout the rest of her life, Tala the Qajar refused Solomon closeness with Peacock's son. Arash the Rebel had sat in the carriage with the maid, and watched the endless yellow desert— bands of nomads traveling in caravans with camels and

194

sheep and donkeys, the men dressed in loose white and gray clothes, the women in bright red and yellow skirts, or in black chadors. The journey had taken twice as long as expected: Tala refused to wake up in the dark, when the caravan was supposed to start each day. By the time she got ready to leave, the sun was up, and they had to wait in the tents for sunset. They reached Tehran with their animals sick, and their servants heat-stricken.

Arash the Rebel remembered standing in a strange courtyard on the day of their arrival and pulling at his starched shirt as if to release the heat he could not escape. He remembered lying in a cool, windowless room in the King's *andaroun*—a basement with brick walls, and in the middle, a pool of fresh water supplied by a well. He stayed there for days, perhaps weeks. He was running a high fever, and he refused to eat. Two maids watched him. Once a day, Solomon the Man came to see him.

But the fever had not stopped, and after two weeks the basement had taken on a foul smell—like things decaying before their time. The night maid swore she had seen a child, a boy like Arash but with icy skin and frosted hair, sitting in a corner of the basement, staring at the sickbed.

"It's Jebreel," announced the court doctor, Hakim Bashi. "It's the angel who watches over the deaths of children."

Hakim Bashi ruled that Arash was dying of heartache—for his mother, no doubt—and demanded that Peacock be brought to him immediately. He was told that Peacock was in Esfahan, that it would be weeks before she could be reached and brought to the capital.

"Well, then," Hakim Bashi, declared, "let the boy's father carry the burden of his death."

That night, Solomon the Man came to the cooling room, and showed Arash a picture of himself with Zil-el-Sultan and Peacock: there was Zil-el-Sultan, tall and wide-chested and dressed in a jewel-clad gown. Next to him stood Solomon, and then a girl, dark and thin and terrified, staring ahead of her as if to pierce the cardboard with her eyes.

"Your mother," Solomon the Man told Arash, wondering if he would understand.

Arash the Rebel gaped at the image in the cardboard rectangle, and for the first time in his young life, he spoke Peacock's name. Slowly the foul smell left the basement, the frosted angel stopped visiting, and Hakim Bashi declared a miracle.

Later, Arash remembered getting lost in Nasser-ed-Din Shah's palace—the expansive rooms and endless corridors that stretched before him like a treacherous maze, leading to bejeweled halls with mirrored ceilings, where walls made of miniature pieces of glass multiplied a single image into a thousand, and where hundreds of chandeliers cried infinite tears of cut crystal.

He lived in the Palace of Roses until he was five, then moved to the Palace of the Sun. He rarely saw his father or Tala; they lived in another mansion, and Tala had been pregnant every year since she came to Tehran.

In the Palace of the Sun, Arash was assigned his own quarters and servants: he had outgrown the *andaroun*, he was told. He was a man and could no longer live with females.

He slept alone in a vast room furnished with every luxury, in a bed so immense that Arash always thought it would swallow him in his sleep. He studied with a tutor every morning and afternoon, learned Persian, French, and Arabic, calligraphy, art, and mathematics, riding, polo, and marksmanship. Once a year he went hunting with the Royal Urdu.

It was the most exciting event of the year, the one time all of the Shah's family traveled together. They went north, to the jungles of Mazandaran, to chase boars. Arash the Rebel stayed in a tent with Solomon the Man. Tala was assigned to the women's camp, but she hunted with the men, and refused to sleep except with her husband. Arash the Rebel watched Tala ride away every dawn on her black horse. She galloped behind a dozen hound dogs, a rifle in her hand and a storm of golden hair on her shoulders, and returned tired but elated, her face scratched and bruised by the branches of trees, her skin glowing with the sweat of excitement as she dragged behind her the day's prize. She was always the last to return to camp. She stumbled off her horse, found Solomon the Man in his tent, and threw herself at him, making love—Arash knew as he stood outside the tent—with such urgency that she would tremble for hours after, and her legs would be unsteady, and every time Solomon the Man raised his eyes to smile at her, Tala the Qajar would blush with pleasure and lower her eyes to hide her love.

Slowly, through the years of his childhood, Arash the Rebel learned to overcome his longing for his mother. He made peace with his own surroundings, and accepted Solomon the Man as the distant relative who sometimes loved him. He kept the picture of Peacock hidden in his private chest, but looked at it less often, and her image began to fade from his mind. When he was seven years old, his tutors enrolled him in the youth division of the Persian Cossack Brigade. Arash the Rebel studied Turki and Russian, and received military training from an older youth named Reza Khan the Maxim. He still lived in the palace, but he spent all his days at the House of Cossacks next to the drill ground in Tehran, and for the first time in his young life he began to make friends and to feel at home in his surroundings. Away from the palace he could forget his life, lose himself in uniform anonymity, and escape the feeling of estrangement he suffered every time he saw Tala and her children with Solomon the Man. He worked hard, embraced the military discipline imposed fiercely by Reza, and at the end of the first year he earned the distinction of graduating first in his class. When the minister of court demanded a Cossack youth to serve as the Shah's escort during the anniversary jubilee, Arash the Rebel was awarded the honor. He was exulted, so proud he rode alone to Solomon the Man's house and shouted the news as he ran through the hallways. Even Tala was pleased. She lifted Arash in her arms and smiled at him with all her resplendence, and for the first time ever, Arash the Rebel thought he would forgive Tala, find his father in Solomon the Man, and let go of the cardboard woman with the green eyes that beckoned him every moment of his life.

 Four days before his fiftieth-anniversary jubilee, Nasser-ed-Din Shah made a pilgrimage to the holy Shrine of Shah Abdol-Azzim, near Tehran. It was to be a historic visit, the Shah had promised, for immediately after the pilgrimage he intended to renounce his prerogative as despot, and proclaim himself "the Majestic Authority of all the Persians." In that spirit he had allowed the city authority to relax its watch over the citizens, to stop keeping a record of the strangers who flocked into the caravansaries, and to allow everyone to participate in the pilgrimage with the Shah.

The pilgrimage was scheduled for one and a half hours past noon. Arash the Rebel, part of the royal escort, rode to Shah Abdol-Azzim ahead of the cavalcade. He was accompanied by his *Laleh*—Master of the Menservants—and his Master of the Bridles. All the way from Tehran to the shrine, the road was jammed with men and women, walking or riding mules and donkeys, who were traveling to Shah Abdol-Azzim just to see the Shah. The town itself was so crowded that Arash could not find a place to leave his horse. The shrine was packed with pilgrims who had wanted to visit the holy man before their King arrived.

Arash the Rebel left his horse with his Master of the Bridles, and went to join the welcoming party. A company of eunuchs, dressed in their most colorful and extravagant clothes, stood at formation in front of the shrine. Behind them was a regiment of the royal army, and then, closest to the shrine itself, a line of young Cossacks.

At exactly half past one, a horseman galloped toward

the shrine and announced to the Cossack leader that His Majesty's cavalcade was near. The Cossack leader sent Arash and another boy to clear the shrine of all pilgrims.

His mission accomplished, Arash returned to take his place in the welcoming line. He saw the Shah's cavalcade.

A dozen warriors rode in front, leading twelve eunuchs on Arabian chargers with painted saddles and gold and silver harnesses.

There was a single horseman on a white horse, who cried, "Stand back," as his charge danced in the air and reared. "Stand back and take heed."

There came a pair of white horses—covered with gold embroidery, wearing bejeweled harnesses with high aigrettes of red plumage. The horses advanced slowly, leading another pair, then a third. Behind them was the royal coach.

The Shah's coachmen were dressed in purple clothes, with gold strings hanging from their shoulders and wrists. The coach was gold, lined with purple velvet. The runners who walked alongside it wore purple crowns, white breeches, and red shoes.

Five hundred mounted men brought up the rear of the procession.

Outside the Shrine of Shah Abdol-Azzim, Nasser-ed-Din Shah's Prime Minister, Atabak Amin-al Sultan, ran forward to open the carriage door. Two high officials held His Majesty's hand and helped him alight. Arash the Rebel heard the crowd gasp and moan in excitement as they laid eyes on the Shah.

Nasser-ed-Din Shah was a big man with a round face, superior eyes, and a strong mustache. He wore a coat of gray and orange brocade, a Western collar, and a black tie over a white shirt. He had a purple shawl, a leather belt studded with enormous diamonds, black trousers, military boots. His lambskin hat, tilted to one side, was adorned with a single diamond as large as an egg. In the heat of summer, he wore a long coat lined with Russian sable.

He greeted his Prime Minister and acknowledged the officials, then turned toward the shrine.

"We shall proceed," he ordered, and quickly the Prime Minister led the way. They were accompanied only by a royal guard, Arash the Rebel, and another young Cossack.

Shah Abdol-Azzim was small and dark and full of echoes. There were narrow, airless corridors where the heat was trapped and dust rose with every step. There was a small room with a low ceiling where the holy man was buried. The Shah went through the shrine, came up to the mausoleum, and touched his forehead against the silver rail surrounding the grave. He was murmuring a prayer when Arash the Rebel looked around and saw a stranger approach.

It was a man—a pallid creature with an unshaking hand. He came up to Arash and held out a letter, indicating he wanted to give it to the Shah. Atabak Amin-al Sultan tried to interfere—to take the letter from the man and deliver it to His Majesty without letting the stranger come close. Nasser-ed-Din Shah waved him away; he was in a generous mood, and he wanted to receive his subject himself. The man came up to the Shah. Instead of the letter, he extended a gun. Arash the Rebel heard the world explode.

In the tumult and the panic that followed the shooting, Arash saw Nasser-ed-Din Shah spread on the ground, his Russian sable coat splattered with blood. The Cossack leader and the royal guards charged the attacker, took away his gun, and tied his hands. The man never resisted even for a moment.

Atabak Amin-al Sultan came up to the Shah, shaking violently, and pressed an ear to His Majesty's chest. All he heard was the sound of the crowd outside the mausoleum— the people, having heard the gunshot, bursting into a frenzy of cries and questions as they wondered about the monarch's fate. Atabak Amin-al Sultan decided that the Shah's death could not be revealed. He stood up above the corpse, his face crimson, and suddenly recognized the assassin: he was

Mirza Reza of Kerman, a man with close ties to the clergy, who had spent his life opposing Nasser-ed-Din Shah. For years he had been in jail, tortured and abused but always released under pressure from one mullah or another. He had complained of the Qajars' injustice—of Nasser-ed-Din Shah killing half a dozen men only because they had approached his caravan at a time when he did not wish to receive anyone; of the Shah's son performing scientific experiments on helpless peasants, ordering a gardener to put his face into a pot of boiling rosewater just to observe the effects of a severe burn on a man's eyes and lips. The last time he had been released from jail, Mirza Reza of Kerman had gone to see a mullah.

"The Shah is unjust," Mirza Reza had said.

"Then you must create your own justice," the mullah had advised.

Atabak Amin-al Sultan ordered the guards to keep Mirza Reza inside the shrine. He went out to face the crowd:

"Praise God," he announced with unwavering conviction, "His Majesty the King of Kings is alive and unharmed."

Inside the shrine again, he ordered that the assassin be taken away. Mirza Reza was placed in an open carriage, his hands still tied, but as he rode toward Tehran and death, he looked at the people and smiled with dignity.

Atabak Amin-al Sultan called for the royal chair. He picked up the Shah's corpse, and arranged it on the chair so it was sitting straight, the eyes still open. With Arash's help, he held the corpse in place and waited for it to harden. Arash stood in the shrine for hours, suffocating as sweat poured down his face and into his clothes and boots, wondering about a future without Nasser-ed-Din Shah. Then, at last, Atabak announced that it was time.

"Hold His Majesty's hand," he commanded. "Talk to him as you walk."

Through the crowd of spectators outside Shah Abdol-Azzim, and all during the ride back to Tehran, Arash the

Rebel spoke to the corpse of Nasser-ed-Din Shah. He had set out on the mission still a child. He returned a man.

At midnight the next day, Nasser-ed-Din Shah's heir, Muzaffar-ed-Din Khan Qajar, was sworn to the throne. Only then did Atabak allow news of the assassination to spread to the people. Soon afterward, Mirza Reza Kermani would be hanged before the entire city. Standing on the gallows, he would face his executioner and say:

"I have done what was right."

 Salman the Coal Seller had worked since he was three years old. He was always black—like the actors who performed on the streetcorners in Tehran, and who painted their faces and hands with coal— and he coughed so badly everyone knew him by the sound of his lungs. He wore a long, soot-covered coat, carried the coal in an enormous bag the size of his own body, and which he dragged across his shoulder. Even in his youth, before he had ever married, Salman the Coal Seller knew he would die of consumption.

He was born into a family of scholars, but he never learned how to read. His father, a Talmudic instructor, had escaped a massacre in a Russian ghetto only to find himself in Juyy Bar. He was young when he arrived, but he had come with great expectations, and the very shock of reality had made him weak and disappointed. He knew nothing of the Persian language, and seemed unable to learn. He could not teach, could find no other work, and above all, he could not accept Juyy Bar as his new home; he had risked his life and abandoned his ancestors' graves in order to escape oppression. In Juyy Bar he was victim not only to the mullahs, but also to the Jews, who treated him as an outsider and refused him kindness. His wife, the only educated woman of her time, was forced to work as a maid in the

Armenian quarter. She was beautiful but frail, and after a few years in Tehran she took ill and died in the cold of winter. On the anniversary of her death, Salman the Coal Seller's father ate poison and committed suicide in bed.

Salman the Coal Seller would have died that first year, but Taraneh the Tulip took him in and raised him as if he were her own. She sent Salman to work, taught him to buy the coal, scoop it up with his hands at every house where he stopped, count his change, and haggle for each penny. At night, when he came home, she bathed him and changed his clothes, put him in a clean bed with sheets that smelled of fresh bleach. Salman the Coal Seller loved Taraneh more than his life—loved her more than he would ever have loved his own blood. He grew up thinking of her as his mother, believing she would always be there, but then, all at once, she met the son of Esfahan's governor, and told Salman he must manage alone. When she left, Salman the Coal Seller abandoned himself to darkness.

He began to store the coal in his room, and did not mind when the walls turned black, the rug became spoiled, and the water tasted of soot. He ate bread and cheese every night, never washed or changed his clothes, slept on the bare rug, and used the bag of coal as his pillow. He lived in this way for many years, and almost died twice of pneumonia, but when he was twenty years old, Taraneh the Tulip came back. She dragged him out of his house and forced him to marry a lame girl.

"Have a child," she commanded. "Live again."

They had Blue-Eyed Lotfi, a boy with white skin and crystal eyes, whose arrival changed Salman's life again: he was born in 1882, and because of him, Salman the Coal Seller thought he was blessed.

He had six more sons after Lotfi, raised them all in a clean house, sent them to Raab Yahya's Torah class, and refused to let them touch the coal that was killing him in his youth. In 1898 he heard that a school had opened for Jews in the Tehran ghetto. Salman the Coal Seller abandoned his house, gave away his coal, and moved to Tehran with his sons.

A man had come to the Pit—Monsieur Jean, a Frenchman with a graying goatee and a three-piece suit that he wore in the blazing heat of summer, and that never seemed to wrinkle in spite of the heat. He came as a guest to the court of Muzaffar-ed-Din Shah. He was a messenger, he said, from the Jews of Europe.

In 1878, Nasser-ed-Din Shah had journeyed to London, and met with the heads of the Alliance Israélite Universelle. They had confronted him with reports of massacred Jews, of unequal treatment before the law and disproportionate poverty, of the mullahs commanding greater power than the Shah and releasing their vengeance upon the Jews.

"Lies!" Nasser-ed-Din Shah had exclaimed in fury. "All of my subjects are treated equally and with dignity."

The gentlemen from the Alliance inquired why Jews in Persia were not allowed to read and write the national language. Flustered, Nasser-ed-Din Shah and denied knowledge of the fact. They asked if His Majesty would allow the situation to be remedied—if he would permit a school to be opened for the Jews of Tehran.

"Of course!" Nasser-ed-Din Shah insisted. "We will even pay the teachers' salaries Ourself."

He had come back to Tehran and hoped to forget the entire incident. For two decades nothing was heard of the Alliance again. Shortly after Nasser-ed-Din Shah's assassination, Monsieur Jean arrived.

"Your Majesty," Monsieur Jean told Muzaffar-ed-Din Shah, "your father made a commitment to the people of Europe. It is upon you to honor his word."

Muzaffar-ed-Din Shah was trapped in an impasse: to refuse Monsieur Jean's wish would be to alienate Europe. To accept it would be to anger the mullahs of Persia. He weighed his choices and allowed the school.

"The Jews of Tehran," Monsieur Jean wrote in his first report to the Alliance in London, "have treated me as if I were a Messiah. 'Now that you have come,' they say, 'we can die in peace, and know that our children will be saved.'"

On opening day in the Pit, Monsieur Jean woke up in the dark and put on his suit, which he kept pressed under his mattress. He stepped into the courtyard to use the toilet, and suddenly thought himself under siege: hours before class time, the house was already filled with students—boys, mostly—standing with their shoes under their arms and their faces smeared with doubt, coming to him like a fallen tribe in search of salvation, as if waiting for the word that would break their spell and free them from their bondage.

Salman the Coal Seller walked up to Monsieur Jean. He had brought all seven of his sons.

Blue-Eyed Lotfi attended both sessions of Monsieur Jean's class: in the morning with the boys, at night with the girls and the adults. He completed every year with honors, and when he was eighteen, Monsieur Jean offered him the school's first scholarship to France.

Salman the Coal Seller was enthralled at news of Lotfi's success. He cried with his wife, boasted to all his friends, gave away a whole bag of coal in celebration. Then he found out that the boy had rejected the scholarship; he had fallen in love, Lotfi told his father without shame, and he intended to marry.

He knew a girl from school—Heshmat, daughter of Peacock the Esfahani, who peddled gold. She was two years older than Lotfi, but they had sat across from each other ever since the school first opened, and Blue-Eyed Lotfi had always known he would marry her as soon as he started to work and earned a living.

Against all of his parents' objections, Blue-Eyed Lotfi gave up his chance at Europe and married Heshmat instead. They held the wedding in Zilfa the Rosewoman's house, in her garden where she had planted only white for the season, on a day when the air sparkled and the world radiated color. They were so poor they lived in Salman's room and slept on a borrowed mattress for the first year. Then Blue-Eyed Lotfi accepted a job as assistant to Monsieur Jean, and became the school's first Jewish teacher. Salman the Coal Seller was so proud of his son's position that he forgave Lotfi. His other children grew up and went to Europe and became doctors, but among them all, Lotfi remained his father's favorite; he had been born in the darkest years of Salman's life, and the very light of his eyes had blazed a trail of hope through the Coal Seller's heart.

 Arash the Rebel was fifteen years old when he left the palace to live in the Cossack headquarters at Tehran. The year was 1903, and Muzaffar-ed-Din Shah had just acquired a handful of machine guns for his army. The guns were called Maxims, and they were placed in the care of a Cossack officer named Reza Khan. Himself trained by a group of European advisers, Reza Khan the Maxim in turn enlisted Arash and nine other Cossacks in the machine-gun division. Together they went through Persia—machine guns in tow—and trained other Cossacks in every town and province where they stopped. For the first time in his life, Arash the Rebel saw Persia as it really lived and suffered. Slowly, as he served Muzaffar-ed-Din Shah and Reza Khan, Arash understood that the Qajar dynasty was about to falter.

The year he became King, Muzaffar-ed-Din Shah had sold to Greece the exclusive right to exploit Persia's rich northern forests. A year and a half later he had bestowed upon the French the license to extract and own all of Persia's archaeological treasures. Then he decided that he needed a vacation—to Europe, of course, for he was the son of Nasser-ed-Din Shah and planned to keep alive his legacy. To raise money for the trip, he sold to Belgium all of Persia's customs revenues.

In Tehran, and especially around the bazaar, where the mullahs had the greatest influence, people spoke of limiting the Shah's powers. From Europe and Russia they had learned the idea of nationalism—of a people bound together not by religion or race, but by a common border; of the duty of kings to protect their country's soil and integrity. Secular-minded nationalists had joined forces with the clergy, and together they demanded the establishment of a parliament and the writing of a constitution. Each group had a distinct and opposing goal: the nationalists envisioned a law based upon modern secular thought; the mullahs planned a constitution drawn from the Qoran, one that placed the clergy above the Shah. Still, they joined forces against the Crown, each group believing it would overpower its ally once it had achieved victory.

Muzaffar-ed-Din Shah learned about the alliance of his opposition, but he was in no mood to address problems. He went to Europe and stayed for many months, returning only when he had spent the entire Belgian loan and run out of money. He came back sulking; it was not fair that he should be so limited, that money should be such an issue. He was entitled to greater extravagance than he was allowed. He should have been able to take more than the three hundred aides and wives who accompanied him on the last trip; he should have been able to stay longer, buy more toys for himself. He was, after all, the King.

He tried to console himself by building a palace—a magnificent structure high atop Hyssop Hill, just north of the capital. He would call it the Palace of Joy, make it a white, semicircular structure with tiers of open verandas, and around it he would build a royal menagerie in which to keep specimens of native lions, tigers, and leopards alongside imported fauna. To finance the venture, and to raise money for his next trip, he decided to secure more loans.

From Russia—his country's greatest enemy—he borrowed twenty-two and a half million rubles. In return, he promised never to build a railway in his own country. The British became jealous and wanted a concession as well. The Shah gave to D'Arcy exclusive license to extract and own all of Persia's oil.

In 1904 a plague came to Tehran. It was a small outbreak of short duration, and it took few victims, but in the atmosphere of anger and discontent that prevailed in Persia, it struck a special note of tragedy. Certain that they had once again become objects of God's vengeance, the people of Tehran screamed for help and ran to hide. They had no doctors, no place to take the sick, no one to administer guidelines for general hygiene. Annoyed by the vision of devastation he faced in his own capital, Muzaffar-ed-Din Shah took another loan, and went back to Europe.

Tehran's two greatest clerics, Seyyed Behbahani and Seyyed Tabataba'i, declared an alliance between themselves, and joined the nationalists: the Shah, they insisted, must allow the writing of a constitution based upon Shiite principles, the establishment of Islamic courts, and the appointment of Islamic judges who would wield ultimate authority even over the Crown.

Muzaffar-ed-Din Shah came back to Persia and listened to his Prime Minister report on the mullahs' demands. He found the entire matter too complicated for his attention. He was not about to strain his mind listening to rebels' requests, he said. But he did announce that he had just given another concession to the Russians: to build and operate a bank at the center of the Amir bazaar in Tehran. The site designated for the bank was a cemetery where victims of the recent plague had been buried.

The mullahs called for a Jihad. The Shah, they said, was selling the country to the enemy. Banks operated on the principle of usury—charging interest on borrowed money—which was in direct contradiction to Shiite law. To build their bank, the Russians would have to desecrate Muslims' graves, carry away believers' corpses, and bury them in unholy places and unmarked graves.

The day the Russians broke ground on the cemetery, the mullahs of Tehran ordered the Amir bazaar closed down in strike. Mobs walked the streets, wielding torches and demanding that the Shah expel the Russians. Believers occupied every mosque and listened to their clergy speak of the Qajars' treachery. Nationalists gathered in every district and joined the people on the street.

From his barracks in Tehran, where he had returned with Reza Khan the Maxim, Arash the Rebel watched the unrest and found himself rooting secretly for the resistance.

Muzaffar-ed-Din Shah was disgusted by the unrest in his capital. Wishing only to regain his peace of mind and return to his beloved Europe, he conceded immediately to the rebels' demands. He paid the Czar his damages, restored the cemetery in the Amir bazaar, and asked the mullahs if they would forget the entire incident.

It was too late, the mullahs responded. The rebellion had spread throughout the country. The Shah must agree to constitutional rule, or face war. One Friday, three thousand of Tehran's mullahs gathered in one place, and left the city. They went to Qom, staged a sit-in at a mosque, and swore they would not return unless the Shah conceded to their demands.

Tehran was paralyzed. The people were in a panic. The Shiite clergy were the believers' only link to God. To be abandoned by mullahs was to be damned by God. Even the dead could not be buried without a mullah's blessing. Once again, mobs returned to the streets, asking that the Shah bring back their holy men. Ein-al-Dulah, the Prime Minister, suggested sending Cossacks to bring back the mullahs by force. But Muzaffar-ed-Din Shah was afraid of confrontation.

"Send for them to Qom," he commanded Ein-al-Dulah. "Tell them they can have their damn parliament."

And so the mullahs returned triumphant, riding through Tehran in royal carriages sent by the palace, greeted by welcoming crowds. It was a spectacle of shame and mockery, the essence of what had always been the curse of Persia: the men with the turbans wishing to supplant the man with the crown.

 Zilfa the Rosewoman decided to learn French. She had embroidered a roomful of white handkerchiefs, reviewed all of her singing and painting lessons, stretched the time it took to apply her makeup beyond endurance, and still she found herself with long hours in which she did nothing but contemplate the ravages of time on her skin. She went to enroll in the adult section of the Alliance school.

"I have come to learn," she told Monsieur Jean with such confidence he had no choice but to overlook her age and accept her. "Assign me to your most difficult class. I will be your brightest pupil."

She went to class religiously, pored over her notes and asked questions long after the other students had gone home. She spent all her free time studying, even stopped painting and embroidering so as to devote more hours to her French. Every day she wore a new dress to school, and took special care painting her face. She bought new jewelry. After a while she denied her age and claimed she was not a day over forty. Then she invited Monsieur Jean to her house for lunch.

"Come." She smiled at him like a girl. "We will have a civilized afternoon."

At the end of the year, when the Alliance recognized its best students, Zilfa the Rosewoman was awarded third place in her class. She stood before a small crowd of pupils, blushing, and when Monsieur Jean approached to hang the bronze-colored medal around her neck, she bent her head without lowering her eyes, so that their gazes locked and he had to look away, startled by the intensity of her soul. That night, sitting alone in the empty school, he received a message from Zilfa: he was invited to her house, to have dinner this time, and to converse with her in the language of poets and lovers.

They spent the summer meeting regularly at Zilfa's house. They appeared together on the street, Monsieur Jean in his pressed suit and his walking stick and hat, Zilfa always unveiled, dressed in white, her sleeves transparent. He lent her his arm and walked to her left, helped her around every pothole, and carried her over every ditch. They engaged in heated conversations about poetry and art and music. Monsieur Jean was always serious and pensive, Zilfa argumentative but deferring to his judgment. At night they returned to her house for a glass of wine and a piece of bread and cheese.

On opening day in the fall, Zilfa the Rosewoman went to school with a crown of roses on her head, and announced her engagement to the principal.

She bought a diamond ring for herself, and a gold watch for Monsieur Jean. She invited her friends to the wedding. It would be a Western-style reception, she advised everyone, lest they be offended: the bride and groom would be married first by a Catholic priest and then by a rabbi. They would sit together, and their guests, men and women, would share the same room.

For a week Zilfa the Rosewoman had her house painted and prepared. She put new plaster on the walls, cleaned the rugs. She pruned the roses, ordered a small gazebo made of wood, which she then covered with white gauze. On the day of her wedding she awoke in the dark and put on her painter's gown and hat. She took a brush and painted blue stars all over her house.

And it was in this way—as they saw her from their roofs that early morning before she married Monsieur Jean—that the people of the Pit would remember Zilfa the Rosewoman.

She stood in her garden before a wall, a clean brush in her hand, and felt neither the cold nor the morning wind as she tried to capture the deep blue of dawn, the radiance of the stars in the moment before they faded. She wanted to bring the light into her house and free herself of the darkness where she had lived alone and ostracized, counting her hours and her days, waiting for the man who would arrive, she had always known, to make her queen of her dreams and give her children that she would dress in white, with roses in their hair and pockets full of candy. She wanted to salvage the sun and inhale the breath of waking angels and keep the light in her eyes through the long, endless journey of hope.

 In October 1906 the first session of Parliament convened in Tehran. Composed of clergymen and nationalists, it set about the task of writing a constitution. It immediately broke down into an internal war over the nature of the new law.

The nationalists prevailed. Persia's first constitution bypassed God and his disciples. Based on the Belgian model of 1830, it granted all citizens equal rights before the law. It pledged specifically to defend the life, property, and integrity of all Persians, regardless of religion or race. It even went so far as to outlaw the existence of ghettos—the forced exile of any person to a particular place or neighborhood, the refusal of residence to anyone based on religion.

No sooner had the constitution been ratified than the mullahs declared it null and void. They had joined the nationalists only to advance their own cause, planning to dismiss them once the Shah had agreed to their demands. Instead, they found themselves written out of the country's new laws. They called upon the believers to avenge them.

On the eve of Passover the mullahs ordered the annihilation of the Kermanshah ghetto.

It was spring in Persia, but Kermanshah was always

frozen. The mob killed thousands of Jews, burned the entire ghetto into dust, left the wounded to freeze on the streets. The mullahs issued a *fatwah*—holy order—barring all believers from selling food or clothing to Jews. Without food or fire, dozens starved and froze in the streets every night.

The nationalists in Tehran learned of the massacre, and appealed to the Shah for help. They were refused. The mullahs held on to their *fatwah*, and the Jews kept dying.

But then a caravan of food arrived in the Kermanshah ghetto. It was sent by a Muslim, a leader of the Kermanshah community, a man of undeniable religious faith and an unwavering belief in Islam. He had bought all the food in the bazaars of Kermanshah, called his most loyal servants, and sent them to the ghetto to feed the survivors of the massacre. The next day he sent clothes and blankets and coal, milk for the children and medication for the injured.

He sent help every day, ignoring his friends' warnings, insisting that Islam was a compassionate religion, that the prophet Muhammad had preached humanity and benevolence, that the Qoran, correctly interpreted, taught peace and progress. For weeks he fed and housed the Jews until, faced with his unshaking resolve, the mullahs of Kermanshah backed down. The ban was lifted, and merchants were allowed to end the boycott.

It was this, Zilfa the Rosewoman told Peacock in the days after the Kermanshah massacre—the change the constitution had brought: it had given force to the cries of human compassion that the mullahs had choked in their own flock. It had conveyed to the believers the true meaning of Islam, and celebrated the greatness of a religion that at the height of its glory built a civilization larger and more merciful than any other of its time.

Two months after the creation of the first Parliament, Muzaffar-ed-Din Shah died. His heir, Muhammad Ali Shah, took the throne swearing to crush the Constitutional Revolution. He gave his prime minister the specific task of infiltrating Parliament, widening the rift between the mullahs and the nationalists, and conquering both groups. Then he made a deal with the Russians and the British: in return for their help against the rebels, Muhammad Ali Shah allowed the signing of the Tripartite Agreement of 1907, in which he gave the northern half of Persia to the Russians, and let their forces occupy her soil. He gave the south to the British, and kept the center as a neutral buffer. In 1908, encouraged by the rebels' infighting and confident of Russian support, the Shah made his final move.

He called to the palace General Lyakhov, the Cossack commander, and ordered that he surround the house of Parliament on a day when it was in full session and the members were all gathered inside. When the cannons were in place and the Cossacks at their guns, Muhammad Ali Shah ordered that they bombard Parliament.

In the massacre that followed, hundreds of unarmed men lay throbbing in their own blood, begging for mercy and receiving none until Parliament was destroyed and the Cossacks had run out of lead. Pleased with his accomplishment, Muhammad Ali Shah placed Tehran under martial law, appointed Lyakhov military commander, and dared his opposition to respond.

Tehran died. The rebels surrendered without a word. That night, Arash the Rebel deserted the Cossacks.

It was an early evening in June 1908, and Solomon the Man sat in his mansion at Saltanatabad. He was reviewing his accounts on an abacus when he looked up and saw his son.

"I have come to say farewell."

Solomon the Man felt his hand tremble on the abacus. He had known, he had always known, that Arash would leave. Now he saw him in the half-darkness of the room, pale and afraid but determined, and he understood.

"Where will you go?" Solomon asked.

"To Tabriz." Arash saw the devastation in Solomon's eyes. "To join Sattar Khan."

Solomon the Man realized that Arash was a man, that Solomon had never seen him grow, that he had lost the child he brought from Esfahan and would never know the man who was leaving him. All at once he wished he could undo the years of his life.

"The Cossacks," he sighed, "execute deserters."

They stood facing each other in the silence. Solomon the Man remembered the day, long ago in Juyy Bar, when Arash had been born in their house—the midwife running to Solomon with her face flushed and her hands full of blood, grabbing for the gold Solomon gave anyone who brought good news.

"A boy," she had cried. "You have a son."

Arash the Rebel kissed his father's ring.

"Forgive me," he asked. Solomon grasped his son's hands.

"It is you," he said, "who must forgive."

He saw Arash leave, and never saw him again.

 In the city of Tabriz, home of Qamar the Gypsy, where the Great Massacre of 1830 had come to pass, Sattar Khan went to war. News of the shelling of Parliament had reached every major province in Persia, and caused rebels to surrender. In Tabriz, it ignited a fire that would burn the monarchy to its roots.

For many years now Sattar Khan had been leading the rebel forces of the north and the northwest. They called themselves Mujaheds—fighters for the cause—but they never knew the exact nature of their war. They had been rebels all their lives—bandits and horsemen and mountain riders, raised in the harsh environment of Azerbaijan, with the wind on their backs and shadows all around them. Removed from the influence of the mullahs by the physical contours of their homeland, they were known for their courage and independence.

Sattar Khan had been raised on horseback, a rifle in his hand since he was a child. As a youth he had been famous in Tabriz for his marksmanship and his unfearing heart. He had been drafted by the Royal Guard into Muzaffar-ed-Din Shah's army, and he had served proudly until the Shah killed his brother. Accused of stealing food from the royal kitchen, Sattar's brother had in vain sworn innocence. He had been executed by direct orders from the Shah.

"Avenge my son," Sattar's father called to him when they received news of the death. "Avenge your blood and my name."

Sattar Khan escaped the Royal Guard and gathered a band of friends. They rode from town to town, looking for trouble that would end in a confrontation with the Shah's forces. They stole from the rich and gave to the poor, attacked soldiers everywhere they found them. There was no war they sought to win, only a cry of anger they wanted the Shah to hear.

Many times in those years, Sattar Khan was caught and imprisoned. He was tortured and beaten and starved, interrogated and locked in solitary confinement until he had forgotten how to speak. But his name had become famous across Azerbaijan, and the Shah did not wish to make a martyr of him. Sattar emerged from prison emaciated and pale, and for a while resigned himself to an ordinary life. He worked as an appraiser of horses, or served as a guide on hunting expeditions. Then again he sought his friends, and rode through the open country in search of a fight. At the turn of the century, Sattar Khan heard of the constitutional movement and found his cause.

And so, the day Muhammad Ali Shah bombed Parliament in Tehran, Sattar Khan's forces moved to occupy Azerbaijan. By the time Arash the Rebel joined him in Tabriz, Sattar Khan was fighting not only the Shah's soldiers but also Russian troops; Muhammad Ali Shah wanted Tabriz back; the Czar, fearing that a revolution in Persia would feed the flames of discontent in his own falling empire, had sent troops to aid the Shah.

Arash the Rebel enlisted on the side of Sattar Khan, and fought against his own Cossack friends. Fresh troops arrived from Russia and Tehran. Tabriz was surrounded and placed under siege. The rebels were cut off, and all lines of supply severed.

For weeks in the winter of 1908, Arash the Rebel watched his new allies die of famine and disease as they resisted the Shah's drive. The cold paralyzed everyone. Defeat seemed inevitable. Faced with the end, Arash the Rebel asked himself why he had joined the battle, and never found an answer. Was he fighting for Persia, he wondered, or against Tala? Was he inspired by a sense of justice—like the man, Mirza Reza of Kerman, who had given his life to take Nasser-ed-Din Shah's—or was he prompted only by vengeance?

"*Your* son," he imagined Tala screaming at Solomon the Man through the halls of the Palace of Joy, where they gathered to follow news of the war. "*Your* son has betrayed my blood."

The siege broke in Tabriz. Sattar Khan had sacrificed almost all of his men, but he emerged victorious, and led his forces toward the capital. Throughout Persia his triumph inspired rebels to take up the fight once again. In the south, Samsam the Bakhtiari united his forces, took Esfahan, and rode north to join Sattar. Suddenly, Muhammad Ali Shah wanted a truce.

Sattar Khan joined Samsam the Bakhtiari, and together they rode on the capital. Running to save his life, Muhammad Ali Shah abandoned his palace and took refuge in the house of the Russian ambassador in Tehran.

"Your son," Tala sobbed before Solomon the Man. *"Your* son destroyed us all."

She packed her bags and joined the Shah at the Russian embassy. Solomon the Man did not go with her. He was a Persian, he said, and he would not seek help from the enemy.

It was early morning, July 1908, and a kingdom had been lost.

 Arash the Rebel was appointed by the National Council to negotiate the terms of Muhammad Ali Shah's departure from Persia. He went to the Russian embassy, where the Qajars had taken refuge, and found the Queen sobbing amid her suitcases and servants. She did not recognize Arash; she was too busy cursing the British. They had promised the Shah their support against the rebels, tricked him in this way only to secure the Tripartite Agreement of 1907. Now that they owned a third of Persia, they had abandoned Muhammad Ali Shah and caused his demise.

Muhammad Ali Shah was pale and confused, dressed entirely in black—like a woman in mourning—and walked around with the dejected air of a houseboy punished by his master. He did not receive Arash; he would not negotiate with traitors. They communicated through an intermediary.

Running from the palace on the sixteenth of July, Muhammad Ali Shah had taken his own family treasures, enormous cash reserves, and what he could carry of Persia's crown jewels. Among the crown jewels was the famous Darya-ye-Nur—Sea of Light—a one-hundred-eighty-two-carat diamond, which the Shah claimed was his. He had also incurred exorbitant debts to the Russian and British governments, as collateral for which he had pledged hundreds of acres of Persian territory in the north.

Arash the Rebel demanded that the Shah return the crown jewels, sign over to Persia ownership of the territories in pawn to Russia and Britain, and leave his Crown Prince, Ahmad—who was twelve years old and crying in his mother's lap—as a hostage in Tehran. In return, he said, the National Council would grant the Shah safety in exile, a palace at Crimea, and five thousand pounds sterling a year.

Muhammad Ali Shah refused the offer. Five thousand pounds, he said, was a slave's salary. Crimea was not a suitable destination for a king. Crown Prince Ahmad was too young to rule, and must accompany his father to exile. The crown jewels belonged to him and should not be returned.

Weeks passed and the negotiations failed. By September the National Council had raised the Shah's salary to 16,666 pounds sterling a year, and changed the location of his palace from Crimea to Odessa. It was agreed that Ahmad would be left in Tehran—to serve as a figurehead monarch for the new constitutional government, and ensure that his father would never stage a return coup against the rebels. But Muhammad Ali Shah would not surrender the crown jewels. Feeling that the Russian ambassador had sided with the rebels against him, he telegraphed the Czar and asked that his rights be protected. The Czar answered promptly: Muhammad Ali Shah, he said, should accept an immediate settlement.

Two days after receiving the telegram, Muhammad Ali Shah left Tehran for Odessa. He took along his Minister of War, five hundred loyal soldiers, and Solomon the Man's wife.

Arash the Rebel watched Tala board the carriage that would take her out of Tehran. She was flanked by her children—all eleven of them—and as she sat in the carriage and pulled the drapes closed, she did not even turn to look in the direction of Arash. He wondered how she would live without Solomon the Man. He wondered if he had really wanted to destroy his father's life.

On the morning of Ahmad Shah's coronation, Arash the Rebel rode to the Russian embassy to escort the new Shah to his palace.

He was told by the embassy guards that he should wait outside for the crown prince. An hour went by. Then another. Then at last the embassy gates swung open:

Far in the distance, up the cobblestoned pathway that led through the garden, Arash the Rebel saw a parade of molten light move toward him.

It was a child, a boy with black hair and a round face, dressed in a thick military uniform and a Turkish fez. His jacket was covered with diamonds cut in different shapes and each as big as a walnut. His eyes were swollen and red from tears.

He had been crying for days—ever since his father was driven from the throne and Ahmad was chosen King. He was twelve years old, and all he wanted in the world was to be at home with his mother.

Arash the Rebel was stunned at the sight of the child. He had known Ahmad all his life. He had known, all the time he negotiated with Muhammad Ali Shah, that Ahmad was only a boy. Still, he saw him walk out toward the gates, recognized the glimmer of tears in his eyes, and suddenly remembered himself—small and feverish, lying in a basement and staring at his mother's picture as he sobbed into his pillow.

In Saltanatabad—the Palace of Kings—a deputation of the National Council greeted Ahmad Shah.

"We pray, under God's shadow, that Your Majesty will serve his nation with justice and honor," the head of the delegation announced to the new King.

"Please God," Ahmad Shah replied bravely, but his chin trembled and he fought to keep his voice, "I will."

Tehran was in chaos. The government that had replaced the monarchy had no clear leadership and no plan of action. Having reached Tehran victorious, Sattar Khan and his army of rebels now found themselves without a war to fight. Parliament asked that they surrender their weapons, but they refused. Weeks of stalemate ensued. Yesterday's allies became enemies. In the end, the National Council dispatched troops to bring Sattar's forces under siege and confiscate their weapons. The rebels fought back. In the battle that followed, Sattar Khan—hero of the revolution and the man who had saved Persia from the Qajars—was shot and severely wounded. He died soon after—of injuries, and a broken heart.

But even with Sattar Khan dead, the new government faced grave threats: the mullahs were fighting the nationalists, and the British government was undermining Parliament. There was no army, no police, no one to restore calm. In the palace, Ahmad Shah cried day and night for his parents. Once, when he could no longer stand the pain of separation, Ahmad Shah would steal a horse from his own stables, and ride in the dark toward the northern gates of his capital. Alerted by spies, the Shah's Russian house-tutor would send Arash to bring Ahmad back. He had been headed for the border, the Shah would confess to Arash, toward Odessa, where his father lived with his ten wives.

Arash the Rebel cried with the Shah that night. He realized that to avenge himself, he had repeated Solomon and Tala's crime. He knew his revolution had failed. In 1910 he left his post at the National Council and disappeared from Persia forever. Fearing that they had been betrayed by their young ally, the Council searched Tehran and every other province, but came up empty-handed. They whispered tales of intrigue and treason, of mortal death and ghostly departure, but in the end, they never managed to solve the mystery of Arash the Rebel: that he had given all to battle, and realized he wanted none of the spoils.

In Saltanataband, Ahmad Shah wrote every day to his

father—loving pages full of sorrow, in which he confessed his most private thoughts. He entrusted the letters to his closest friend. He waited for an answer. He waited years for an answer. The letters, he would later learn, were taken to the Russian embassy, where they were opened, scrutinized, and left to become matters of public record.

 Reza Khan the Maxim watched the revolution of 1908, then he watched it fail. He saw the destruction of the old system, saw it replaced by anarchy, and wondered if Persia would survive.

The Tripartite Agreement of 1907 had resulted in a virtual occupation of Persia by foreign powers. They ruled each province through their own embassies, and refused to cooperate with Tehran. Twice in two years, Parliament appointed prime ministers only to see them abdicate in the all-pervasive atmosphere of confusion and impotence. Everywhere, bandits and highway robbers held the population in terror. Self-proclaimed governors defied orders from Tehran. Persia needed an army—a single, unified force to battle the enemies outside and within, to restore calm and allow Parliament to rule. Under the Qajars, her security had been entrusted to independent police detachments: the Russian Cossack brigade, the Swedish-led gendarmerie, the British-organized South Persia Rifles—each of which took orders from a foreign government. Now, without money or leadership, she was farther than ever from creating an efficient fighting force.

In 1914 the First World War broke in Europe. British and Russian forces, already occupying Persia, closed Parliament and took over the rule of the country. Soon thereafter, Germany found its way into Persia. Seeking to weaken the British stronghold, the legendary German spy Wassmus crept into the south and enlisted ethnic tribes seeking independence. He hired them to fight the British, creating civil war in a country already destroyed by occupation, disorder, and poverty.

Reza Khan the Maxim was thirty-six years old. His first wife, Hamdam, had been a woman of low origin who did not understand his ambition, and who had given him only a girl. He had abandoned Hamdam and their daughter and married again—this time to a wife of higher birth. He had no friends, not even among the Cossacks, but all his life he had cherished his acquaintance with Peacock. In the days of Persia's greatest tumult, when he felt himself standing on the brink of disaster, Reza Khan the Maxim went back and found the Jew from Esfahan.

"You said once I could be King," he told her in her windowless room in the Pit. He had been struck by those words, had felt his insides boil with excitement every time he remembered that encounter. Amir Tuman Kazim Khan had told him of a Jew who foresaw the death of kings. Reza Khan wondered if Peacock had the same powers.

"You must tell me what you know," he insisted. "Tell me my future."

Peacock smiled. All through her childhood, in times of hardship and disappointment, her mother had whispered to her Esther the Soothsayer's prophecy made on the day Peacock was born. Now Peacock repeated the words for Reza Khan:

"A man shall come, riding from the north, with blood on his hands, and the wrath of God in his eyes.

"He shall sit on the Throne of the Sun, and with a sweep of his hand he shall reach across this empire to free our people."

Reza Khan the Maxim felt the veins in his temples about to burst.

"How do you know I am that man?" he asked.

Peacock put her fingertips to his forehead.

"It says so right here—where Cain bore his mark."

It was the winter of 1914. Leaving Peacock's house, Reza Khan inhaled the stench of rot rising from the Pit, and watched the children running barefoot in the snow. He went home. He had found his destiny.

He climbed in the ranks of the Cossacks, and inspired great loyalty among the troops. He was conscious of his lowly status in society, aware that nothing in his past and lineage fit the mold of the traditional nobleman-turned-savior. He could not yet alter his dead father's rank in history, but he knew he could improve his station through marriage.

In 1915, he took a third wife—the daughter of an army commander—and at last felt he had achieved a suitable status in society. He gave his wife a title, Taj-Malek, the Crown Lady, and told her she would soon be Queen.

 Solomon the Man was fifty-three years old when Tala left Persia. He let her go and tried to salvage his own life, to start over in a country now hostile and unwelcoming to the vestiges of the Qajars. He tried to forget Tala; she had left as easily as she came to him, blamed Solomon the Man for Arash's treason, and abandoned him without a word of explanation. Still, every time he remembered Tala's smile, Solomon the Man trembled with desire. He sent a letter to Odessa:

"Come back, my passion," he told her. "You have been away too long."

He wrote another note, this time entrusted to a messenger with clear orders to bring back an answer. He suspected that Tala was ill, or imprisoned in the castle at Odessa. He imagined Tala crying through the night into her pillow, calling Solomon's name, digging her nails into the walls of the room she could not leave—how else could she have stayed away so long?—and praying that Solomon would arrive, at dawn when the sky was new, to save her in his arms. Before the messenger had come back—bringing, Solomon felt in his heart, no word of Tala—he left Tehran and embarked for Russia.

In Odessa he rented a room, unfurnished and cold, and sent word to Muhammad Ali Shah's castle.

He waited for Tala through days and nights of agony, never leaving the room for fear that she might come while he was gone, tortured at the thought that she would not arrive. He imagined her running to him in the dark, her breath cold and anxious, tearing at her clothes as she fell into his arms and he took her back into the farthest corner of his room, there against a stone wall, and loved her with his hands and his eyes, taking her into his bed and spreading her pale body onto the sheets—surprised, as always, at the contrast in the color of their skin—touching her so gently that her eyes never moved, and when at last it was over she would stay in his bed, her face radiating their passion, and say she forgave him Arash's betrayal.

She never came.

Solomon the Man stayed in Odessa—alone, without work or money or a goal. When his money ran out, he tried to sing at cabarets and teahouses, and found that his music was unknown and unpopular. He sought love from strange women, paid prostitutes just to come and sit with him for a night, but in the end he felt he had disappointed everyone. He went to the palace of Muhammad Ali Shah and came back dejected and ashamed. He drank and drank, and by the time he realized he could not stop, he was old and sick and could find no reason to save himself.

He developed an illness, a gnawing ache that spread from his stomach into his chest and arms. He became weak and yellow, unable to eat, haunted by insomnia. He lay on the floor of his rented room, barely surviving on the money he made by singing in tearooms, and thought about the life he had left in Persia.

He thought of the women he had loved, the children,

all grown, that he had abandoned or lost. He thought of the strangers he had befriended, the voice that had come to him like a gift from the angels, but which he could no longer command. In the end, when he began to vomit blood, he thought of Peacock.

He remembered the child he had married—dark and shy and cold as the sparrows in winter. He remembered her magnificent eyes on the night of their wedding, when he had hoped, until the moment he lifted Peacock's veil, that he would find in her Zil-el-Sultan's Hannah. He remembered his daughters. He knew Sabrina had died.

Solomon the Man sat up in bed, surrounded by shadows and the sound of his neighbors' poverty, and for the first time in six years he understood the cause of his fall: he had lost his luck, abandoned his daughters, and sinned against his wife. He had destroyed Peacock and taken away her son. For this, Solomon the Man was certain, he had been cursed.

He summoned all his strength, and counted his money; he would go back to Persia, he decided, to Juyy Bar, where Sabrina was buried. He would find his daughter's grave, throw himself on her corpse, and demand forgiveness before he died.

 From Russia, Solomon the Man went to Turkey, then down into Azerbaijan. After two months of traveling, he arrived at Sari—a town in the Persian province of Mazandaran on the Caspian shore. Before the Revolution, Solomon the Man had always heard the Shahs speak of their "unbeatable" army in Sari—the one they all claimed was capable of retrieving every province lost to Russia in the last century. Now, as he walked through the town, Solomon the Man looked for the army and found nothing. Instead, he saw hundreds of blind people—old and young and even children, more than he had ever seen in any town or province he had traveled: during the early days of the Constitutional Revolution, the governor of Sari, a staunch monarchist, had blinded everyone suspected of harboring revolutionary sentiments.

The fabulous army, Solomon the Man soon learned, was composed of two dozen soldiers—half-naked and addicted to opium—who earned their living by toiling in the fields. Their arsenal—that legendary arsenal so vaunted by the Qajars—was composed of two cannons. The first one was used only once a year, in the month of Ramadan, when the soldiers fired it to inform the public it was time to break their fast. It had broken wheels, and rested on a pile of bricks. Every time it was fired, it raced backward, and the soldiers would have to pull it forward again, lift it with great difficulty, and place it on a newly built pile of bricks.

The other cannon was used for churning milk to make butter.

Solomon the Man decided to find the Qajar palace, and ask for a night's stay. The palace was an ancient structure, built by Shah Abbas the Great in the seventeenth century. Inherited by the Qajars, it had been neglected from the start, and after the Revolution it had fallen into ruin. Still, Solomon the Man knocked at the gates and hoped for an answer.

"Get lost!" a voice thundered at him through the thick cluster of trees inside the palace grounds. "We're closed."

Solomon the Man knocked again.

"*Get lost*, I said!" the voice raged again, but Solomon was desperate and he knocked a third time.

The voice approached ferociously:

"Who is it, I say, that dares my anger?"

It was a Negro—seven feet tall, naked to the waist, with inhuman muscles and enormous hands. He charged through the palace grounds and attacked the gate with his chest, forcing the metal open and emerging like a demon.

"*Get lost!*" he said, but then suddenly he looked into

Solomon's face and stopped himself. He pulled back, eyes lowered to the ground, and fell to his knees like a slave. He took Solomon's hand and brought it to his eyes.

"My life your sacrifice," he said. "Solomon Khan! My master! Forgive my impudence."

It was Rubi the Executioner, guardian of the Qajar palace, holder of the governor's Sword of Justice.

"My life your sacrifice," he was crying on Solomon's hand. "I would have paved this earth with my own eyes had I known you were going to step on it."

Rubi the Executioner had been born in Constantinople, and sold as a child to a rug merchant who had raised him as a slave. By the time he reached adolescence, Rubi's enormous figure and bulging muscles had made him the strongest of all slaves. A wealthy pasha bought him from the rug merchant for an unprecedented price. But while in the pasha's service, Rubi fell in love with one of the master's wives—a white Turk with flesh as soft as the inside of a dream—and one night he forced his way into the harem and attacked her. He was caught and condemned to death.

"Tie a rope around his ankles and throw him in the Bosporus," the pasha had ordered his servants, but there wasn't a man in all of Constantinople who dared tackle Rubi. For months the pasha kept Rubi in prison and waited to find an executioner who would kill the slave. At last he was approached by a friend.

"Sell me the Negro," the friend had asked. "I can use him to kill my enemies."

For years, Rubi the Executioner murdered people he did not know. When his master had rid himself of every possible foe, he sold Rubi to a Greek slave merchant who took him to Tehran and put him on auction.

Rubi the Executioner was only twenty-five years old at the time. He knew his age because slaves, like horses and cows, were issued birth certificates when no one else kept a record of their children's births. He was at the peak of his physical strength, but the years of killing and captivity had worn on his soul, and he had become as sensitive and vulnerable as a child. The day of the auction, he stepped on the platform before the bidders, but instead of flexing the muscles of his naked body, he looked at the audience and burst into tears.

It was a shocking performance, so contrary to the expectation of the bidders that the Greek merchant canceled the auction and, taking advantage of Rubi's weak moral state, beat him for the first time since he was a child. He did not bother to schedule another auction. He knew no one would buy a mad giant they could not control. He was about to leave Tehran with Rubi when Solomon the Man approached him and bought the slave. Then Solomon freed Rubi.

In 1892, Rubi took a bag of gold, his ownership papers, and his birth certificate from Solomon the Man. He went north, to Mazandaran, and found a job with the governor of Sari. He was entrusted the Sword of Justice, and appointed head of the palace guards. In ten years his name became dreaded throughout Persia. He killed his victims by strangulation, using only his thumb and little finger. He beheaded the corpses, stuffed the heads with straw, and used them to decorate his house.

When the Revolution displaced Sari's governor, Rubi the Executioner lost his Sword of Justice and his post as head of the palace guards. Stripped of his purpose and rendered without importance, he nevertheless kept on guarding the palace long after he had stopped receiving a salary. He became bored and depressed, suddenly haunted by visions of those he had killed over the years, disturbed by the sight of all the women and children he had blinded at the governor's orders. He became a recluse, smoked opium until he was addicted and destroyed, and when Solomon the Man arrived, he had not spoken to a soul in three years.

"May I be thy sacrifice," he told Solomon as he wiped his tears. "You can't stay in the palace—the rats will eat you alive."

He laughed to hide his embarrassment, revealing sharp, uneven teeth blackened from constant use of *shireh*.

"A man of your stature deserves the greatest of mansions, and I am ashamed to offer you less. But all I have is my own home, and I can only pray that you will forgive my poverty."

He took Solomon to a dark alley near the palace. He stopped in front of a door, so low even a child could not pass through it upright, and pushed it open with his hand. Rubi the Executioner never locked his door; he knew no one dared enter his house without permission.

There was one room, damp and bare, with no light except through a tiny window with iron bars. A dirty carpet was spread on the floor. A bundle of sheets and blankets were tucked in a corner. On the walls, Solomon the Man realized in horror, Rubi the Executioner had displayed rows of human parts.

There were hundreds of legs and arms, hands and ears. There were thirty heads, cured and stuffed and arranged in one neat row: Turkoman chiefs, Rubi explained to Solomon, who had rebeled against the Shah, been captured, and brought to justice by the Executioner.

"Take my bed," Rubi insisted. "You have but to spend the night here. Tomorrow I will take you to Tehran myself."

 In Tehran, occupying Russian troops were fighting enemy Turkish soldiers on the streets. Persia had become a battleground of the First World War. British troops shot all day at German battalions, and everywhere, neutral Persians were caught in the crossfire and sacrificed. Rubi the Executioner took Solomon to the safest place he could find—the caravansary in Tekkyeh—and from there he set off to find a coach that would take them to Esfahan. He soon learned that the roads were closed—occupied by foreign troops that used them to transport weapons and food to their bases. No one dared travel out of Tehran for fear of being shot by hostile soldiers.

Rubi the Executioner did not give up his search. He went out every day, looking to buy a carriage he would drive himself, and everywhere he spread word of Solomon the Man's return. Crowds of people came to the caravansary to find Solomon. The great-grandson of Old Man Gholi knelt before him and kissed his feet. The Grand Keeper of Tehran's whores wept on his hands and offered him his youngest virgin. Ahmad Shah the Qajar sent his people to ask Solomon for news of his family in Odessa. Then a stranger came.

It was a woman, dressed in a black chador, trembling as she approached the entrance to the caravansary. Solomon the Man saw her but paid no mind; he had been vomiting blood all afternoon, and he felt as if he would faint any moment. The woman came closer and stopped before him. He thought she was a beggar, or that she had mistaken him for another. He wanted to look away, but she would not release him from her stare.

"Can I help?" he asked.

She remained still. Then she opened her veil.

Solomon the Man looked at the face before him and longed to remember. He smiled at her uncertainly, his lips barely parting, and tried to imagine who she could be: a whore, perhaps, that he had once loved; a servant he had left behind; a beggar he had once fed. She touched his arm. His memory, like a dormant plague, began to stir.

Peacock.

He waved her away, rubbed his hand over his eyes, and prayed that she would be gone when he looked again. He felt his vision become blurred. He tasted blood in his throat. Then his legs gave out and he slipped into a spell of unconsciousness deep and everlasting as death.

She took him home and called a doctor. The man came a day and a half later; he was dressed in a European suit, smelled of cologne, and revealed no sign of compassion for his patient. Peacock despised him.

The doctor took Solomon's pulse, listened to his heart and to his stomach. He shook his head. The patient, he announced coolly, would die before the end of the week.

Peacock walked the man out, and slammed the door behind him. That night she called Heshmat to come and watch her father. She was leaving, she said, on a pilgrimage to the tomb of Sara Beth Asher in the Zagros Mountains. God owed her a favor, and it was time He paid.

 She rode in a carriage for eleven days, then trekked on foot through dry desert and dusty plains to reach the tomb. She arrived at sunset, and found a group of pilgrims already camped at the base of the mountain. It would be dark soon. Peacock had to wait for morning.

The next day, she was the first to climb. The others followed, each man or woman carrying a small child on his or her back. The tomb of Sara Beth Asher was a long and narrow cave—so narrow that only small children could crawl through it safely. Bigger persons risked being caught in a passage without air, far enough from the mouth of the cave that their screams would not be heard and they would suffocate before anyone could reach them.

But Peacock had come alone; she had to face God herself. She had to demand the miracle He had never before rendered.

She reached the cave at midmorning, and prepared to enter. A thousand years ago, Sara, daughter of Asher, had been pursued through the desert by hostile soldiers. She had come to the Zagros Mountains and tried to hide in the cave. The soldiers had followed her inside. She had pushed forward, crawling through the sinuous passage, praying for her life. In response, God had created an opening through which

232

she had slipped into the gates of the Promised Land. Behind her, He had sealed the passage with a stone so heavy no man had been able to move it since. But He had made Sara His messenger, and her tomb a place of pilgrimage. As proof of His presence, He had arranged that air would seep through the stone and keep pilgrims from suffocating in the cave.

At the mouth of the cave, Peacock took off her chador and shoes, tied the corners of her skirt together, and pulled her single braid of hair into a bun behind her head. She lit a candle and held it in her teeth. Then she lay on her stomach, took a breath as deep as her lungs, and pushed into the cave.

She crawled through the darkness, feeling the air become thinner, keeping her eyes ahead and hoping to remember which way she had come. The cave, she knew, had many arms. On the way back, disoriented by her claustrophobia and the darkness, she risked slipping into the wrong arm and losing her way in an airless chamber.

Three minutes into the cave, Peacock felt the lack of air and realized that her candle was about to be extinguished.

She pressed forward, her arms tight at her sides, and propelled her body by the movement of her feet. Dirt filled her mouth and nostrils. Wax from the candle melted between her teeth and on her tongue. The flame sputtered, then died. She stopped. She had taken a wrong turn.

Panicked, she pressed her hands under her stomach and retreated. She felt the heat, the weight of her head, the slowing of her blood. She had gone back one body-length when her feet touched a stone wall. She was trapped, buried.

She closed her eyes. Sweat dripped from her lashes. She was going to die here and Solomon the Man would never know—never be saved. She put her head to the ground and lay there. Then suddenly she looked up: The candle's wick, she realized, was still red from the dying flame. She must be close to a channel of air.

She dug her teeth deeper into the wax and pushed herself forward in the only direction possible. She felt a breath—

Sara's breath—on her face. The candle erupted once again into flame. Weeping with relief, Peacock put her head to Sara's gravestone and whispered her prayer:

"Please, God," she asked, "save my husband."

In Peacock's house, laughter bloomed again. Doors were opened and light poured in. Sheets smelled of rosewater and bleach, floors were strewn with mint and lime leaves. Solomon the Man had been given new life and was about to recover.

Returning from Sara Beth Asher's tomb, Peacock found Heshmat waiting at the door.

"It worked," Heshmat cried. "He is awake."

Peacock rushed inside and found Solomon sitting in his bed. He had aged. His face was no longer startling, his eyes were almost extinguished. Yet before him Peacock felt belittled and awed; he was Solomon the Man, and the sky wept and the earth blossomed into a thousand fields of violets every time he smiled.

Solomon the Man began to eat, and his vision cleared of the spots that had blinded him. He sat in bed every morning and told Peacock stories of Russia. They were all happy tales, but he cried when he recounted them. Later, without Peacock asking, he told her of Tala, of his other children. Then, at last, one day he dared utter Arash's name.

"You would have loved him," he said to Peacock. "I loved him."

Peacock looked away from Solomon the Man, and waited for the pain to cut through her. She felt nothing—only a numbness where her heart had once been torn. Too many years had passed.

She stayed at home and refused to answer Ezraeel the Avenger's calls. In the years since she had first befriended Qamar-ol-Dowleh, Peacock had made a name for herself and established an ever-growing clientele. She catered to the richest and most respected of Muslims, commanded their trust, their confidence, and, in time, their friendship. But she never opened a shop of her own—Jews were barred from operating business in the bazaar—and she never left her partnership with Ezraeel. He loved her, everyone knew, and though he never demanded more than her friendship, he would not have allowed her to leave. Now he called for her every day, and Peacock did not respond.

She bought Solomon new clothes, cotton shirts and silk trousers and fur hats. She took him to the bath twice a week and paid a professional washer to help him. When he returned, she greeted him with cherry nectar and grated apples dipped in sweetened rosewater. She bought new clothes for herself. She dyed her hair with henna, wore perfume, put on white embroidered dresses that made her look like a bride. She was an old woman—close to fifty, she imagined, though she did not like to count—and suddenly she wanted to live.

People in the ghetto began to speak of Peacock with pity and derision.

"A grandmother already," they said, "and she thinks she's a new bride."

When she brought home fabric for new gowns, her neighbors snickered and raised their eyebrows and asked her if she were planning to get married again. Peacock the Jew never answered them, but their words made her ache.

Solomon the Man saw her excitement and realized he could not disappoint Peacock a second time.

"Don't think I have recovered," he told her one day in his softest tone. "I am only having a remission. I have had them before. The next time I get sick, I know I will die."

Peacock laughed at him and tried not to believe. She went out that day, aiming for the bazaar, but on the street she forgot her destination. She knew Ezraeel awaited her, that he had sent for her and suffered when she did not come, that he wanted her now as he had wanted her in the past, wanted her and despised her every day and hour since he had first torn off her veil and seen the eyes of his father. Ezraeel the Avenger wanted her, but she did not go to him that day.

She walked aimlessly, through alleys full of children and dogs and the smell of burning coal, past houses bursting with the sound of their inhabitants' lives, into run-down shops that remained open after dark, the owners hoping to sell what no one had bought all day. Then at last she went home and called Solomon:

"I must know why you came."

Solomon the Man stared at his child bride with the terrified eyes, and reached across the room to calm her. In the light of the oil lamp, her face was as beautiful as he had ever seen it. He lied:

"I came for *you*."

He lived for another two months. By the time he died, Peacock felt she had never known bitterness at all.

 Solomon the Man died in the last days of the Great War, in a time of famine and despair and hopelessness, but the day she buried him, Peacock swore that a novel era would begin. He had appeared in 1875, at the height of the Great Famine, and the moment he had arrived, the earth had become gentle. Now that he was dead, God would bring pity on the world and grant relief to the living.

In Persia, occupying Allied forces had destroyed ten thousand farming villages, stolen millions of cattle, and swept away every trace of law and order. A hundred thousand Persians had already starved to death before the government announced a famine. Epidemics swept the country, crime was rampant, and, even in the capital, no one dared step out at night. The rich stayed home and survived on hoarded supplies. The poor stole, or killed, or died.

In Tehran the treasury was so empty the government struck coins from old cannons left behind by the Russians, and which had been melted down for the purpose. In Gilan, on the Caspian Coast, Russian Bolshevik forces had organized a rebellion aimed at converting Persia to communism. In Azerbaijan, Kurdistan, and Khorasan, the population had risen against the monarchy and demanded self-rule.

In 1920, Reza Khan the Maxim was promoted to general and placed in command of all the Cossacks in Qazvin, near Tehran. He went to the British, to the mullahs, to his troops. He told them all he was about to stage a coup d'etat. He did not intend to dethrone the Shah, he said; he was only interested in saving the country from ruin. He gained everyone's support. On February 22, 1921, he descended upon the capital, and took Tehran without resistance.

He left Ahmad Shah in his palace, declared loyalty to the Crown, and appointed himself Minister of War. Quickly he reorganized the scattered troops of the Persian Cossack Brigade, and formed an army that he led against the separatist movements across Persia. When he left Tehran, he was just another soldier vying for power. When he returned, he was a hero.

The mullahs were displeased with Reza Khan's popularity. To make a show of force and assert their dominance, they called for a massacre in the ghetto: it was the "Mullah's Mule Incident," the most famous of all the pogroms in Tehran.

A group of children were crossing the street outside the Alliance school in the ghetto. A man intercepted them, riding a mule. He was dressed in servants' clothes, and he forced the mule into the crowd of children without regard for anyone's safety. The Alliance teacher, Blue-Eyed Lotfi, had been raised in times of relative safety in the ghetto, and so did not know the proper rules of conduct. He, of course, would never have stopped a gentleman riding through the ghetto, but he did stop the servant, and asked him—lest they be trampled by the mule—to allow the children right of passage.

The servant was outraged, his mule incensed. They were no ordinary servant and mule. They were in the service of a clergyman—a grand mullah, a holy person. Blue-Eyed Lotfi had insulted a mullah's mule by asking that it yield to infidel children. He would not go unpunished, the servant promised. The entire ghetto would be made to repent.

An hour after the incident, the mullahs of Tehran called for a massacre. Blue-Eyed Lotfi, they said, had insulted a mule belonging to a grand mullah. His offense, by extension, was directed at the institution of Islam. As always, all Jews would be held responsible for the acts of one.

On Monday, September 4, 1922, mobs surrounded the Tehran ghetto. The Jews hid in their homes and barricaded their doors. That night, and through the next day, the siege continued. Since the entire massacre was for the benefit of Reza Khan, the mullahs were waiting to gather bigger and more impressive crowds. On Wednesday they ordered attack.

Someone screamed a prayer in Arabic, and thousands of men moved at once. They went through the gates of the ghetto, into the streets. They attacked the first homes, set fire to the first temple. Suddenly they stopped, shocked by the sound of gunfire from behind them. Everyone turned to look.

Reza Khan the Maxim had come with his Cossacks and surrounded the mob around the ghetto. He had ordered his men to draw their rifles and fire a warning salvo, then aim at the center of the crowd.

"Disperse!" Reza Khan bellowed. He had no special love for the Jews. But he would not allow the mullahs' lawlessness.

"Disperse now, or I will open fire."

The world stopped. No one made a sound. Reza Khan the Maxim was prepared to kill believers in defense of infidels. All that remained to be seen, now, was whether his troops would remain loyal.

In every other instance in history, when a Shah had sent soldiers to stop a massacre, the men had deserted their service and joined their brethren in holy war. It was the natural order, the reason why the Shahs could never exert force against the mullahs. Now, as the mob waited, Reza Khan faced the greatest challenge yet to his authority.

The soldiers did not move. Their rifles never wavered.

"Disperse!"

Through the graveyard streets of the ghetto, where even ghosts were afraid to walk, Peacock the Jew heard the echo of Reza Khan's voice, and shook with the ripple of Esther the Soothsayer's laughter.

In October 1923, Ahmad Shah the Qajar left permanently for Europe. Reza Khan the Maxim, the orphan child from Alasht, became prime minister and ruler of Persia.

He began with new names: Persia had been the old empire; Iran would be the new kingdom. He also invented a surname for himself—Pahlavi—constructed a noble background for his dead father, and chose a birthday: March 16, 1878. From there he set out to conquer the clergy.

He removed the mullahs from positions of administrative authority. Divorce and marriage, the registration of documents and property, the collection of taxes for the national treasury—were placed within the realm of authority of the central government. Penal and civil codes were reviewed to accommodate secular, modern ideas. Hands were no longer cut off as punishment for theft. Polygamy was still legal—Reza Khan himself had taken three wives—but girls could no longer be forced into marriage against their will. Then he freed the Jews.

He abolished the rules of impurity, opened the ghettos, and allowed Jews into the mainstream of life. He let their children into Muslim schools, gave them jobs in lower echelons of government, granted them permission to live anywhere in the city. He became the mullahs' greatest enemy, and every Jew's champion.

"Look at me," he told Peacock on the eve of his coronation. "I have fulfilled your soothsayer's prophecy."

239

Peacock went to see Ezraeel the Avenger. She rode the horse-trolley through the center of town, and walked the rest of the way into the bazaar. She found half of the shops closed, the merchants absent, the counters empty. In the alleys, no porters ran about, no donkeys pushed at crowds of pedestrians. Ezraeel the Avenger's neighbor saw her approach, and came to greet her.

"You are late," he said. "Ezraeel died last night."

Ezraeel the Avenger had died in bed, in his sleep, where every night for half a century he had dreamt of Afagh screaming under Marushka's hands. Many years ago he had written a will, signed before the bazaar's most respected elders, and entrusted to Tehran's greatest scribe. Afterward he had summoned his children to the house, and warned them to expect the worst:

"So there will be no contesting it after my death," he had told them before witnesses, "I have left nothing of my wealth to my family."

They did not believe him. At his funeral, the Boys' Mother cried herself blind. Ezraeel the Avenger had asked to be buried alone, in a grave enclosed by a wire fence. His sons, he had ordered, must be buried elsewhere, far away from him who had not loved them in life and whose memory he despised. On the day of the reading of his will, the family gathered in his house in Tehran—greed in their eyes and worry in their smiles. They sat together on the floor and waited for the scribe to open the will.

The scribe chewed on his mustache, spat out the strands of tobacco stuck between his teeth, and began to read in a slow monotone. The men craned their necks and moved closer to listen. Halfway through the reading, they thought they had heard him wrongly, and asked that he start again. Once more they interrupted him. With every reading the audience became more agitated and the objections and cries of disbelief became louder until everyone had grabbed the will, examined its authenticity, and seen with his eyes what his ears had refused to believe: Ezraeel the Avenger had left nothing to his wife and five sons. He had willed everything to a stranger, a Jew by the name of Besharat, son of Assal, who lived in the Pit.

 Reza Khan called Peacock to the Palace of Roses in Tehran. She had not seen him for many years, since that day in the winter of 1910 when he came to ask her his future. He was older now—close to fifty— and his hair had begun to turn gray. His eyes were as hard as ever—as hard as in the days of his childhood, when he was alone and unprotected and helpless in the home of strangers. But through the decades of war and victory, Peacock realized, Reza Khan had become vain and haughty and intolerant of human weakness. He was not yet King, but he lived in a palace, and he planned a coronation for April of 1926. Peacock, he told her, was to help with the building of a crown, the mending of the Throne of the Sun, which had been tarnished and damaged during the years of Qajar rule, and with the choosing of tiaras for the Queen and her daughters.

"You will work at night," the Minister of Court explained to Peacock after the Shah had dismissed her. "You must observe total secrecy, and apply yourself with unfailing diligence. Reza Khan demands perfection. He forgives no failure."

The next evening, Peacock returned to the Palace of Roses and waited at the gates for her escort. Two guards in army uniforms led her through the garden, and into the inner chambers of the palace. She was met by six men : Reza Khan's Attorney General, the ministers of Court and War, the Master of Ceremonies, and the acting Treasurer General—an American who had come to Iran as part of the famous Millspaugh Mission. They led her to a vaulted room. The door was locked, sprinkled with wax seals. Only when all six men were present could any of them open the seals.

The door opened onto an enormous hall—empty and quiet and lit only by streams of moonlight that poured in through narrow windows around the room. The walls were painted with miniature figures of legendary Persian heroes. The floor was paved with a gem-studded carpet. On shelves and in glass cases, upon tables and inside open chests, Peacock saw the crown jewels of Persia.

She saw crowns of diamonds, swords sheathed with rubies, scepters of emerald. She saw chests full of gold, warriors' helmets ablaze with precious stones, shields that dazzled the eye. She saw coffers full of loose stones, rows of unstrung pearls, enormous cupboards packed with priceless enamels. She saw a world globe, supported by a solid column of diamonds, with seas made of flat emeralds and continents of rubies.

The American in the group sighed faintly, and knelt next to a chest of unset stones.

"Such treasure!" he exclaimed as he thrust his arms shoulder-deep into the jewels. "My God, such treasures!"

Peacock worked continuously for two months. Every night she was escorted to the vault door by the delegation of ministers. Once inside the vault, she was left alone to work till dawn. Only the American, the acting Treasurer General, insisted on his right to stay. All night long he roamed the halls, dressed up in the regalia of kings, trying on various shields and daggers, and bearing different crowns. On the night of April 24, 1926, Peacock finished her work. The next day she attended Reza Shah's coronation.

In the Audience Hall of the Palace of Roses, Peacock stood among a host of dignitaries invited by Reza Shah, and waited for the ceremonies to begin. The guests were lined up on either side of a long corridor: at one end was the door through which the Shah would emerge. At the other was the Peacock Throne. In deference to the clergy, who believed music unholy, Reza Shah would conduct his coronation in complete silence.

The door opened at the end of the aisle. It revealed a child—the crown prince Muhammad Reza—seven years old and dressed in military uniform. As he walked past the guests, he locked his eyes onto the Peacock Throne and never looked to his sides until he had reached his destination.

The Prime Minister followed the Crown Prince. He held a jewel-studded cushion bearing the famous Kiyan Crown. Behind him was the Minister of Court, with the Pahlavi Crown, then the Minister of War, with the "World-Conquering" sword of Nadir Shah the Great.

Sardar Asad the Bakhtiari walked in with the Pearl Crown.

The Minister of Justice carried a gem-studded staff.

The Minister of Public Works displayed the 186-carat "Sea of Light" diamond.

There was a pause, then a string of lesser ministers and generals each bearing the treasures of other dynasties: the sword of Shah Abbas, the bow of Nadir Shah, the coat of mail of Shah Ismael.

The procession stopped. Everyone turned to the door. Reza Shah the Great entered the Audience Hall.

He wore a royal cloak encrusted entirely with pearls. He had on a cap adorned with the diamond aigrette of Nadir Shah. He walked the length of the aisle and sat upon the Peacock Throne. He removed his cap, and placed on his head the new Pahlavi Crown. Trumpets sounded. Chandeliers glared. In the eyes of Reza Shah, Peacock saw the triumph of a man, come from nowhere, who had become King.

An hour later, still in full regalia, Reza Shah sat in a gilded coach drawn by six white horses, and rode through the decorated streets of his capital. His guests rode behind him, also in gilded coaches.

There followed a procession of three hundred fifty

mounted warriors from the nomadic tribes, each dressed in their local costumes, then a parade of Reza Shah's new army.

At the Palace of Joy, his new residence of choice, Reza Shah was greeted by the greatest of Iran's clergymen. In traditional religious ceremony, the clergyman presented to the Shah a sacrificial ram. Reza Shah grasped the ram's horn, brought the animal to the ground, and slit its throat with a single stroke of a knifeblade. Peacock watched him as he killed the ram. His face never moved. But his hands, drenched in blood, shivered in disgust and pulled away.

A man shall come, riding from the north, with blood on his hands. . . .

 Besharat the Bastard was in Paris on scholarship from the Alliance. He was studying architecture and living above a barbershop when he received news of his father's death.

"Ezraeel the Avenger has died, God curse his soul, and left you all his money," Assal had dictated to the scribe who wrote the letter. "He must have hated you less than his other sons."

Besharat the Bastard abandoned school and scholarship and sailed back to Persia.

He took over the shop, the moneylending business, the house where Ezraeel the Avenger's wife and sons had lived all their lives. He dismissed all the old employees and hired new ones, raised salaries, paid all of Ezraeel's outstanding debts. And he built himself a house.

It was three stories tall, with glass windows and brick walls, and a garden three square kilometers wide, where life-size sculptures of men and animals lurked in the shadows of giant trees and enameled columns. It had seven tiled pools, filled once a month with water from the garden's own wells. In the center of each pool were winged cherubs—replicas of those Besharat had seen at a museum in Paris. All day long the sun reflected against the large glass windows of the house and glared in the eyes of passersby. At night, servants placed torches in every corner of the garden, so that even on the hills outside Tehran, peasants and travelers could see the lights on the Avenue of the Tulips, and know that Besharat the Bastard had arrived.

He was caught in the fever of being modern, the sudden longing for foreign ways and new thoughts, which appeared at the turn of the century among the upper classes. Among the Muslims, it led to a condemnation of religious fanaticism and a sudden adoption of European customs. Among the Jews, who had barely stepped out of the ghetto, it forced a realization that to be accepted in the new world they must first shed the vestiges of their past. They changed their accents, improved their appearance, abandoned the strict practice of their religion. Besharat the Bastard ordered chairs to sit on and forks to eat with, spoke French to his friends, and cut all ties with the ghetto. Still, when it came time to marry, he was unable to go against tradition. For two thousand years, his mother told him, marriages had been arranged. Girls were chosen by matchmakers and mothers. Matrimony was a decision best left to the wisdom of elders. Besharat the Bastard would have liked to marry a girl he knew—whose face he had seen, whose voice he had heard. His mother put an end to that thought.

"Marry a girl who lets you see her face before the wedding," she warned Besharat, "and you have married yourself a whore."

He let Assal work with matchmakers and interview prospective brides. In 1928 she announced she had found the girl. Besharat the Bastard got married.

They had brought him Naiima, the only daughter of Jacob the Rug Merchant, who had fathered eighteen sons before God gave him a girl. There was a traditional wedding, with the bride and groom taking separate vows of marriage. Later, Besharat the Bastard stepped into the bridal chamber to meet his wife for the first time. He lifted the veil off Naiima's face and prayed he would find in her something he could love.

She was fair-skinned and plump, her hair thick and healthy, her teeth perfect. She had brown eyes, thin lips that hardly moved when she spoke, and a way of walking, even with shoes on, that allowed her to go through stone corridors and up marble steps without ever making a sound or arousing attention. She was a shadow, Besharat thought even before he had touched her, a ghost come to lie in his bed at night, to steal his secrets and never share with him her own.

"Give me a son," he asked her. "I will demand nothing else of you."

Naiima of Jacob tried desperately to please Besharat. She realized he did not love her, felt his disappointment every time they were alone together. But she had come to his house determined to stay, and she knew how to *win*; growing up with eighteen boys, she had learned to fight, to be patient, to persist longer than her opponent. Her first goal was to give Besharat the son he wanted.

She went to Besharat's bedroom after every purity bath, ate every foreskin smuggled out of the circumcisions she attended. She made secret trips to see old midwives in whose powers she had come to believe, offered generous gifts to rabbis so they would include her in their prayers. She wanted a boy, she told them, not just a child, but an heir for Besharat Khan.

Two years after they were married, Naiima was still not pregnant.

"Take me to a doctor," she asked Besharat. "They know things midwives don't."

Besharat the Bastard resisted the idea at first. He did not like to take his troubles to strangers. He was not about to discuss his wife's fertility with other men. But another year passed, and all of Tehran began to talk of Besharat's childless marriage. Terrified he would be accused of impotence, Besharat conceded to Naiima's incessant pleas and took her to see a doctor.

At the hospital he explained the problem, then asked for a cure. The doctor wanted to examine Naiima—to put his hand, gloved, he assured Besharat, who could not see a difference—up through her crotch and into her uterus. Mindful of Besharat's outrage, the doctor nevertheless carried the insult further, asking that "the husband" present a sample of his sperm—produced on the spot, and placed into a sterilized container—for examination. Besharat the Bastard took his wife home and never called on a doctor again.

He turned to other cures instead, age-old recipes that had never violated a man's honor.

"We have been cursed by the evil eye of the jealous," Assal convinced him, and set out to break the spell. She called doctors and old women expert in the art of exorcising the evil eye. She burned wild rue seeds twice a day, and filled Besharat's bedroom with the thick white smoke until his skin smelled of wild rue and his eyes teared. She planted sharp objects—skewers and knives and nails—in every corner of the house and the garden, filled a large bowl with salt water and soaked Besharat and Naiima's undershirts in it for twenty-four hours at a time. She repeated special phrases before visitors so as to guard against their jealousy. She bought live sheep, chickens, and lambs, slaughtered them in Besharat's garden, then wiped their blood on the soles of Besharat's shoes. Still, Naiima's womb remained dry and as quiet as a graveyard.

Five years after he had married Naiima, Besharat the Bastard realized she would never give him a child. He knew his alternatives: to divorce Naiima, or to take a second wife—provided he would treat both women with equal care and dignity, sleep in both their beds until they were old, and force the natural mother to share her children with the infertile wife.

Besharat the Bastard thought he could never manage

two wives at once. He told Naiima he was going to divorce her.

She fell to her knees.

"Marry another if you want," she begged. "Marry a dozen women, but don't send me away."

Besharat the Bastard was moved by Naiima's desperation. But he persisted in his decision until she produced a real weapon:

"Well, then," she threatened, "divorce me and I will sleep with other men. I will become a whore, tell everyone they have lain where once only *you* were master."

Besharat the Bastard hit Naiima—she knew he would—but after that he never contemplated divorce again.

In 1933, just as he was about to set off on a journey for France, Besharat the Bastard announced his intention to find a second wife. He left in the spring, when the weather was calm and the long trip aboard ships and trains would be tolerable. Seven months later, he came back with a woman.

 Her name was Yasmine. She had purple eyes and copper-colored hair. She painted her lips amber, painted her fingernails the color of her lips. The first time Besharat saw her, she was wearing a dark blue dress so tight at the waist she could not lean back in her chair. Before she had ever spoken to him, he found himself wondering if Yasmine's children would have her eyes.

She was a secretary at the cigarette factory Besharat had come to visit. She was the boss's secretary, she always pointed out, the second most important person in the entire business, more capable than the men who occupied higher positions than she did. And she was difficult.

She never smiled at the nervous young men who brought her silk scarves and boxes of chocolate that had consumed their week's salary, never befriended the other secretaries. She read books all the time, novels and travelogues and historical texts about the Orient and Russia and Africa. She smoked cigarettes in spite of her father's objections, spent hours studying maps of faraway places, learned the names of rivers and seas, retraced borders, memorized facts.

He told her he was a rich businessman come to trade with the company, that he had a mansion in Tehran, servants and cooks and even a car—one of the seven in the entire city. He told her about Persia, land of poets and warriors, where the air was pearl-white and soft, the sky forever paved with stars, and the earth fertile with the blood of those come to conquer, who had in turn been vanquished. He spoke the French he had learned in the Alliance school in the ghetto. His accent was thick and heavy, his vocabulary limited. Since the tobacco concession of 1891, he explained to Yasmine, more and more Persians had given up the habit of chewing tobacco and turned instead to the Western way of smoking cigarettes. Realizing that the market was vast and uncluttered, Besharat the Bastard sought to import French cigarettes into Persia.

He came back to the factory every day, stopping at her desk before he went in to see the boss, bragging about his wealth and his contacts in the East, asking Yasmine to join him for dinner—in his hotel, he boasted, as if the very fact that he had rented a hotel room and not a studio in someone's house should impress her. For the first three days of his courtship, Yasmine did not speak to him. On the fourth day she looked up from her desk and smiled.

She wanted to go to the cinema—a dark, crowded room, she explained, where men and women sat together and watched images bouncing off a white screen. Besharat the Bastard was afraid of the idea. He felt he was about to commit blasphemy. But he was eager to please Yasmine, and so he agreed to take her.

At the cinema he became convinced that watching those

ghosts without bodies—human shapes that disappeared at the flick of a light—was tantamount to devil worship. Halfway through the show, he walked out.

He waited for Yasmine on the sidewalk outside the theater. She appeared moments later, looking concerned and almost amused.

"My eyes hurt in the dark," he lied to her.

They never went back to the cinema again.

On Sunday they took a carriage ride through the woods outside Paris. Yasmine sat opposite Besharat, holding her gloves in her hand. She spoke to him for the first time of herself.

She was an only child, she said, the daughter of parents who had started a family late and were already old by the time she was born. She had been eight years old when the Great War broke out. Her father was drafted, her mother forced to work in an ammunition factory thirty kilometers away from home. They had no other relatives, no one to care for Yasmine. She had stayed alone in her parents' apartment in the middle of Paris. Every Sunday her mother had come back to see her.

"I walked to school with the neighbors' children," Yasmine told Besharat. "At night I stood in bread lines. Every night someone dropped in the line, starved or exhausted. Two men would step out and move the body to the side of the alley, then come back and take their places in line. Once a day, soldiers set fire to the corpses to prevent the spread of disease."

Besharat the Bastard watched Yasmine in the dark. Her face was impassive as she spoke, but her lips quivered, and her cheeks grew as pale as her dress. He realized he had never had a conversation with a woman before.

"The worst thing was the rats." Her voice jolted him. "When the sirens went off and we knew the bombs were coming, we had to rush down into the basement. It was crowded and airless, so dark all you could see were the whites of other people's teeth. There were rats everywhere—each one as big as a cat. When they bit, they took a piece of your flesh. They bit me twice, so after that I stayed in my room and watched the bombs explode."

Besharat the Bastard proposed to Yasmine the third time they met. She did not accept. He told her he would not let her go until she did.

He remained in Paris for no reason but to be close to her. He took her to work every morning and spent all day in a café outside the factory, drinking tea and smoking Persian tobacco that he rolled into cigarettes himself. In the afternoon he met Yasmine again and spent the evening with her. Her parents were alarmed. Her boss warned her against the stranger with the dark lips. Yasmine was fascinated with Besharat.

"I may go with you," she told him one night in the third month of their courtship. They sat in a crowded dance hall full of smoke and laughter. "I think I may marry you."

Besharat the Bastard looked as if he had been stabbed in the heart. His eyes filled with pity. He took Yasmine's hand and walked out of the dance hall.

On the street, a middle-aged woman with grotesquely painted lips sold roses. Besharat bought them all.

They walked in silence, Yasmine holding the roses to her chest. Near her apartment, Besharat suddenly spoke.

"I have a wife in Iran."

Yasmine opened her arms, stunned, and let the flowers—pink roses so pale they appeared silver in the moonlight—fall into a jagged line on the sidewalk.

Yasmine made up her mind to go with him. She knew that Iran was backward and undeveloped. She had read accounts of the country's poverty. But she felt another war approaching in Europe, and she thought she could hide from it in Iran. She would go there, she decided, and chase away Besharat's other wife, overpower Naiima with her confidence and beauty. As mistress of Besharat's house, she would live like the wives of colonialists in Africa, hiding from the ugliness of life outside, in the comfort of a small community of foreigners where the ways of the West had been faithfully reproduced. It would be the adventure of a lifetime, a chance to live the tales she had read about all her life.

She helped Besharat obtain a forged passport on which Naiima's name was not recorded. They were married at the end of winter. On the way back from the courthouse, Yasmine stopped at her parents' apartment to say good-bye. Her mother cried. Her father did not speak to her at all.

They sailed on a steamship from the southern shore of France to the Turkish border, then embarked on a long train ride toward Iran. From Rezaiyeh, they rode the Trans-Iranian Railway to Tehran. Besharat's car awaited them at the central station.

"Put this on." Besharat held out a black scarf to his new bride. "You shouldn't be seen with your head bare."

Tehran was gray and dusty, its streets crowded, its gutters filled with garbage. All the way from the train station to the Avenue of the Tulips, children chased the car, banging on its windows, pushing their scarred faces against the glass, climbing the bumpers and slamming their fists on the roof every time the car came to a stop. Yasmine looked at Besharat. He felt her question and did not reply.

She recognized the house from Besharat's accounts. Her heart dropped. She would be swallowed by this house, she thought, forgotten among its walls and never again heard from.

Three men stood urinating against the garden gates. The driver honked, and they ran away, penises in hand and laughing. Inside the garden, Besharat the Bastard reached over and opened Yasmine's door. She stepped out of the car, and found herself surrounded.

There were four women, unveiled and disheveled, smelling of sweat. They pulled at Yasmine's scarf and examined her. She looked for Naiima among them. The first three were old, the fourth one too young.

"Go with them," Besharat told Yasmine. "They will show you what you need."

The women took Yasmine through the yard and into the house, up the black stone staircase and into Besharat's bedroom on the second floor. The room was dark with shadows, crowded with furniture. There were chairs with armrests in the shape of lions' heads, thick velvet drapes printed with blood-red flowers. The floor was paved with stone and covered with Persian rugs.

Assal grabbed Yasmine's arm to feel her flesh.

"Too thin."

Another woman, blinded by cataracts, also felt Yasmine's arm. The young girl—a maid, Yasmine imagined—pulled her hair.

"Let go!" Yasmine protested. The blind aunt loosened her grip. The maid pulled harder, then released.

"The hair is real, all right," she announced to the others. "But it looks like someone shaved her head for adultery."

Assal grabbed Yasmine's breasts.

"No tits."

Panicked, Yasmine shoved her aside and went to the door.

"Besharat!" she summoned her husband at the top of the stairs. Her voice echoed down the staircase. It brought no answers.

"Besharat!"

Assal came up behind her.

"Shut your trap," she said in Persian.

Yasmine ignored her.

"Besharat! Come!"

A hand slammed against Yasmine's mouth. It was Assal, hitting her new daughter-in-law for the first time. Yasmine was startled. Trembling, she waited to regain her balance, then attacked Assal.

Long after dark, Yasmine heard Besharat's voice in the corridor. He came into the room and closed the door. His face was pale, his eyes dark. She wanted to run to him, but he would not look at her.

"You can't hit my mother," he said without preamble. "You are the new bride in the house. You must obey everyone else. Even old servants take priority over a new bride."

Yasmine sat up in her chair, and stared at the man who had brought her roses in Paris. He undressed in the dark, his back turned to her, and slipped into bed. She wanted to ask him about Naiima.

"I need a bath," she said instead. "I couldn't find the bath."

Besharat the Bastard was thinking of the neighbors, wondering if they knew that Yasmine had hit Assal.

"I need a bath," she said again.

Besharat the Bastard sighed.

"My mother will take you to the well on the fifteenth of your cycle," he answered.

Yasmine did not understand.

"I need a bath *now*," she answered. "I need to wash myself."

Besharat the Bastard closed his eyes.

"You can take a bath twice a month," he explained, "before and after you menstruate. You can't go any other time, and you can't ever go alone."

They lay next to each other, awake but silent, overcome by the realization that they had made a mistake. Hours later, barely asleep, Yasmine felt a light in her eyes and opened them. A woman stood above her. She had a round face, a thick braid down to her hips. She wore a heavy white gown, her breasts rising against it as she breathed. She brought the light closer to Yasmine and stared at her: it was Naiima, come to examine the enemy and gauge the size of the battle.

Naiima followed Yasmine, silent and intangible, eavesdropping—though she could not understand French—on her conversations with Besharat. She was always there, like a vision summoned by the breath of a witch, creeping past closed doors and beyond stone walls, appearing in Yasmine's bedroom late in the evening, watching her through the keyhole early in the morning, searching her clothes, examining her sheets. She even took Yasmine to the well.

She entered the water first and held on to the side of the well. The water was cold, but Naiima did not wince. She watched Yasmine undress.

"Come in," she signaled.

Yasmine closed her eyes and submerged herself. When she pushed up for air, a hand pressed down on her. She struggled. Naiima held on for a moment too long, then released. Yasmine tried to escape. Naiima grabbed her arm.

"Six more times."

Every morning the women invaded Yasmine's room at dawn and forced her out. In the kitchen, Assal demanded of her the most menial of household chores. Yasmine refused to work. When they hit her, she hit back.

"Throw her out," Assal commanded Besharat twice each day. "Kick her out, or I swear I will do it myself."

Besharat the Bastard was embarrassed and enraged at Yasmine's behavior. When he asked her to change her ways, she screamed at him. When he ignored her, she came after him, burst into the first-floor living room where he received guests, and complained of the treatment she had received. When he hit her, she fought back.

"Lock her up," Naiima advised as she hovered around Besharat, serving his meals. "Put her into a room and keep her there till she learns obedience." She did not wish for Besharat to divorce Yasmine. She, too, wanted children with foreign blood and purple eyes.

The fighting stopped. Yasmine was sent into the second-floor bedroom, and forbidden to wander. Twice a day she was served her meals. She asked for a divorce and a ticket back to Paris. Besharat the Bastard refused. She threatened to escape. Besharat the Bastard locked away her passport and refused to give her money. She tried to calm herself, to regain perspective. She stayed in her room and read. Besharat the Bastard burned her books.

Yasmine wrote to her parents—lies, fairy-tale accounts of the life and the country she had come to Persia to seek, love stories where Besharat was the unfailing hero. Her mother wrote back at first:

"Your father refuses to utter your name," she complained to Yasmine. "I can't sleep nights for the anger in his breath, and the burning in my stomach."

The burning in her stomach became a tumor. The letters stopped coming. Yasmine's were returned unopened, marked "Addressee deceased"; she recognized her father's handwriting on the last batch of mail that came back from Paris.

She let Besharat sleep in her bed even as she burned with resentment. It was her only weapon, she thought, the one chance she had of beating Naiima and gaining Besharat's confidence until she had found a way to leave.

"My God," he whispered in the dark as he emptied his seed into Yasmine and exhaled the breath of exhaustion, rolling back with a prayer that inside her, life would grow. "You have the skin of an angel."

But one morning in the third month of her stay in Tehran, Yasmine woke up to find that her sheets were stained with blood. Besharat the Bastard jumped from the bed, furious, and called Naiima.

"She's impure," he told her. "Take her away."

Yasmine was led into the impurity room on the third floor. She was placed under watch, allowed to touch nothing but her own plate, to sit nowhere but on the two cushions designated for impure women. That night, when she tried to leave the room, the maid stopped her.

Yasmine did not fight the girl. She waited until the house was quiet. Then she crept out and made her way down to the second floor.

She opened the door of Besharat's room, she saw Naiima in bed, her head on Yasmine's pillow, making love to Besharat as she stared at the shadow in the hallway.

 Blue-Eyed Lotfi had lost his job. When Reza Shah opened the ghettos, Jews were allowed into Muslim schools, and the Alliance felt that its mission in Iran was accomplished. Slowly it began to lessen its presence inside the country, and by 1936 it had closed the school in Tehran's ghetto.

Blue-Eyed Lotfi had a wife and seven children to support. He had moved from the Pit, and was renting two rooms in a house on Sar Cheshmeh, just outside the ghetto. He had some small savings—money that Heshmat had put away every year since their marriage—but their rent was high, and he knew he must find work immediately. He kept talking about starting a trade—importing goods from Europe and selling them in Iran—but all his friends told him he was mad. "Things haven't changed *that* much yet," they said, "no one believes a Jew has anything worth selling."

Blue-Eyed Lotfi stopped talking to his friends, but did not give up on his plans. When he saw an advertisement in the newspaper—the Ministry of the Interior looking for individuals fluent in the French language—Blue-Eyed Lotfi seized the chance and headed immediately for the Ministry.

He was dressed in the European clothes Reza Shah had imposed on Iranian men only two years earlier. He had on a hat with a brim, a shirt with a collar and buttons up front, a jacket and pants. Blue-Eyed Lotfi did not like to admit it, but after two years he still felt trapped and uncomfortable inside the new clothes. As he walked the street he saw the other men, also dressed in the new fashion, looking embarrassed and almost pathetic as they tried to find a comfortable corner within the confines of their padded jackets and starched shirts.

When Reza Shah had first announced the imposition of the dress code, the country had sighed in unanimous protest: they could not understand the advantage of wearing these angular suits over their own silk and cashmere, woven by hand, in exquisite colors. The suits were made of cotton—a poor man's fabric—that was grown in Iran, stolen by the British, woven in Manchester, and sold back to Iranians at unconscionable profits. The hats required an exact fit, stained easily, and could not be washed. They blew away in the slightest wind, or else squeezed a man's temples and left a white circle around his head where the blood had been drained.

But ever since he had first introduced the law about the new dress code, Reza Shah had exacted obedience from all the men of Persia. Blue-Eyed Lotfi smiled at the recollection of an incident that had amused even the Shah: On one of his many inspection tours around the country, Reza Shah had scheduled a stop in a village near his hometown of Alasht. The village had gone into bedlam at the news; as always, they knew, Reza Shah expected to meet the heads of each community he stopped to visit. He had already warned that they were to appear in European suits.

But no one in the village owned a suit, and no one had

ever seen a hat of the kind they were required to wear. Nevertheless, the village decided it must try to fulfill the Shah's wishes. Someone was sent to a nearby town to buy fabric. Photographs were obtained of European men in suits and hats. After that, every able-bodied woman in the village abandoned home and family, and set about the task of duplicating the image in the pictures.

The work was slow and excruciating; no one was used to cutting shoulders and collars. There were no sewing machines, and at night the women could only work by the light of a lantern. Still, by the eve of His Majesty's visit, they had managed to improvise a suit to fit each man in the receiving line.

"What about *hats*?" the village chief screamed when he saw the men try on their suits for the following afternoon. "What are we going to do about *hats*?"

There was no time or fabric left to sew hats. In desperation, the men turned to the village "inventor"—the thirty-six-year-old son of a farmer who was too lazy to sweat all day in the fields, and so applied himself to the task of "conceiving brilliant ideas meant to advance the future of mankind" while his wife and parents worked longer hours to compensate for his absence. The "inventor" mulled over the picture of the hat they were supposed to make, then came up with an idea. He ordered the men to gather up all the pieces of tin can in the village. He took the cans to the village tinsmith, who beat them flat, cut them in the shape of top hats, and welded the seams together. They painted the tin black. By the time Reza Shah arrived that afternoon, every man in the receiving line wore a European-style dinner hat.

The Shah walked past the receiving line, pleased at the men's appearance, and stopped to commend the village chief for keeping his people in line with Iran's progress. Just then a hailstorm broke out. Balls of ice crashed against the metal hats with a noise similar to that of gunfire. Reza Shah drew his pistol and turned to find cover. Then he looked up, through the blinding sheet of ice that separated him from the village men, and saw black paint running down the faces of the men, who stood immobile and mortified.

At the Ministry of the Interior, Blue-Eyed Lotfi presented himself to the guard at the door, and asked to see a person in charge.

"I speak French and English and Hebrew," he said. "I can read and write in four languages. I have come to seek a job."

He was taken from one room to another, questioned and interviewed and mostly left to wait. Then he was asked to go home. No one but the Minister of the Interior was allowed to hire help. The minister himself had to ask permission from Reza Shah.

Three weeks passed without news. Then one day a messenger came to the house at Sar Cheshmeh: Reza Shah had reviewed Lotfi's application, and given him a job. He was to go to Paris, on a trade delegation, and purchase five hundred thousand rials' worth of ladies' ready-to-wear apparel.

"I *knew* it," Blue-Eyed Lotfi screamed with delight as soon as the men had left the house. "Reza Shah is going to ban the veil."

He went to France, and took with him all of Heshmat's savings.

"You will lose it," she warned in protest. "You will spend it on junk no one will buy back from you."

She had lost faith in him ever since he had first spoken of the banning of the veil.

"Such absurdity!" She had bit her lip in shame. "The neighbors will hear you and think you've lost your mind."

Blue-Eyed Lotfi had to fight for the money, but in the end he used his prerogative as the man of the house, and overcame Heshmat's resistance. In Paris he bought the ladies' clothing, then set out to find a cosmetics factory, where he spent Heshmat's money on a trunkload of powder and rouge and lipstick, which he brought back to Sar Cheshmeh with a treasure-hunter's pride.

"God help us." Heshmat went faint at the sight of the products. She leaned against the wall, waiting to regain her balance, and did not even look at her husband's disappointed face.

"I must hide this trash before the neighbors come in and see it," she concluded. "Later, when it's dark, we can put it in bags and throw it into the Karaj River."

Blue-Eyed Lotfi had no intention of throwing his future into the Karaj River. Reza Shah—he explained to Heshmat with the same obstinacy with which he had defended his conduct leading to the Mullah's Mule Incident years earlier—was about to ban the veil. Why else would he spend his money on half a million rials' worth of ladies' clothing? He knew that their dependence on the veil had forced the women of the lower classes of Iran into a habit of wearing old and unseemly dresses both inside and out of the house. That was why he wanted the French outfits: to offer them as a substitute for the chador.

"Hush up," Heshmat begged Lotfi as she ran to close the door. "People are going to think you want to run prostitutes from this house. You will bring a massacre right here in Sar Cheshmeh."

Once freed of the veil—Lotfi described his vision to Heshmat—women would feel the need to appear attractive on the street. The days of antimony and rouge made of crushed insect wings were over.

"Look at this!" He took out individual boxes of powder and rouge for Heshmat to see. "Look how beautiful this package is. Smell the perfume in it. What woman wants insect wings when she can have French perfume?"

And so the chest remained in Blue-Eyed Lotfi's house—hidden, in the interest of appeasing Heshmat's fears, behind a stack of pillows and comforters used only in winter—and slowly permeated the air with the scent of powder and perfume. Terrified of her neighbors' reaction—"You are only confirming their suspicion of Jews," she told Lotfi—Heshmat burned every incense and used the room for storing dried herbs, which emitted a strong scent of their own. Nevertheless, as summer approached and the heat became entrapped inside the house, the chest of cosmetics from France took on an essence of its own and emitted such distinct and overpowering smells that everyone sniffed their way up to Blue-Eyed Lotfi's room and demanded the right to inspect its contents.

"Prostitutes' tools," one woman accused when she discovered the chest. "The smell of the Devil," someone else affirmed.

Heshmat pleaded with Lotfi, but in vain.

"Any day now," she sobbed, "a mob is going to attack us right here outside the ghetto."

He told her he would fight the mob.

"What about your children?" she argued another day. "You have *daughters*, Lotfi, *daughters*! What man is going to marry a girl raised with 'prostitutes' tools'?"

But then one morning they heard footsteps in the courtyard, and saw the door to their bedroom burst open in the dark. Blue-Eyed Lotfi sat up with a jolt and reached for the butcher's knife he kept hidden under his pillow. Then, in the midst of his terror, he recognized Peacock's voice.

"Leave that and come outside," she said. "Reza Shah has banned the veil."

The mullahs of Persia threatened war. The men swore to kill. Women cried that they had been robbed of their honor; only whores and adulterous wives went unveiled. For the first time since the Mullah's Mule Incident, all of Tehran stood against Reza Shah. To protest his orders, it was decided, women must continue to wear their chadors.

Reza Shah posted soldiers on the street, with orders to arrest every woman in a veil. The soldiers tore the chadors off the women's heads, ripped them to shreds, burned the veils, and, in return, offered a dress and a hat—purchased in Paris by Blue-Eyed Lotfi.

Suddenly, all the women stayed home.

The war over the veil augured a bigger confrontation between Reza Shah and the mullahs. For centuries, Shahs in Persia had observed the Islamic Feast of Sacrifice. Every year on the day of the feast, a mullah would slaughter a camel in Tehran's Square of the Cannons. A crowd of believers would then attack the camel, grabbing at pieces of raw flesh, and from there they would run to the Palace of Roses, where the Shah would be awaiting them on the Terrace of the Marble Throne. The first person to present to His Majesty a piece of the sacrificial camel's flesh would receive a royal reward.

The year after he had banned the veil, Reza Shah called the practice of slaughtering the camel barbaric, and canceled the celebrations of the feast. From there he went on to deliver another blow to the mullahs: he inaugurated the University of Tehran, took away from the mullahs the power to influence the minds of the young, and entrusted it instead to secular professors trained in the West. Shortly thereafter, the university opened its Faculty of Medicine where, in direct violation of clerical teaching, human corpses were dissected and studied: Life and death, Reza Shah had commanded, were no longer the domain of God and his agents.

The mullahs rebelled. Seeking to end Reza Shah's reign, they used the same method that had brought down the Qajars: they all left Tehran, and staged a sit-in at Iran's holiest shrine.

It was a fail-proof device, the mullahs knew. Faced with the prospect of losing a king or losing their mullahs, the people would opt to overthrow the Shah. Reza Shah, on his part, could not force the mullahs back into the city without storming the shrine—an act of which they did not believe even *he* was capable.

Reza Shah responded by sending armored troops to encircle the shrine.

"Come out," the military commander warned. "Or I have His Majesty's orders to bomb the shrine."

Their rebellion crushed, the mullahs came back to Tehran. The university's Faculty of Medicine continued to dissect corpses. But the matter of the veil remained unresolved: the chador had disappeared, but was not abandoned. Reza Shah could prevent the women from walking on the street with their veils, but he could not force them out of their homes. In Blue-Eyed Lotfi's room the perfume was becoming rancid, and the rouge had melted inside the decorative cases. Heshmat ordered her children to keep out of the way of the neighbors.

So it was until that morning in the spring of 1937 when Reza Shah rode through Gas Lamp Avenue in his newly purchased Rolls-Royce and saw an old woman, small but invincible, beaming as she paraded without a veil. She wore a beaded skirt and a rhinestoned shirt, a green scarf, white stockings, and satin shoes. She had pearls around her neck, gold on her wrists, jewels on her hands. She had red and yellow ribbons in her hair, rhinestones on the frames of her glasses. As she walked, men stopped, stupefied, and glared at her insolence. Women came to their doors, unveiled, lurked in the doorway, looked around for a reaction, then stepped out into the street.

Reza Shah Pahlavi stopped the car next to the woman in the rhinestones. He pulled down his window and recognized Peacock.

He smiled for the first time in anyone's memory.

 Peacock the Jew was seventy years old and a spectacle to behold. She lived in a house on Shah Reza Street, and worked longer and with more intensity than anyone younger than herself. She catered to Tehran's richest and most famous—to Reza Shah's daughters, the wives of his ministers, the brides of the ministers'

sons. She walked from house to house, dressed always in the most colorful clothes—in layers of red and green and blue chiffon, sequined shirts and satin shoes and rhinestones on everything. She had shrunk with age, but her back was always straight, and her eyes still magnificent. Her hair was a stark silver, her skin almost black.

She carried the stones in her pockets—wrapped in pieces of cloth or old newspapers she collected everywhere. She sat in the bedrooms of the ladies of court, or in the offices of influential men, and stuck her hands in her pockets and took out fistfuls of jewels that she spread before the client.

"Touch them," she would say. "Hold them in your hand and see eternity."

Still, at the end of the day, when the work was done and there was no place to go but home, Peacock was alone. Heshmat lived close by, but now that the veil was slowly being abandoned, Blue-Eyed Lotfi was running a thriving business out of the basement of his house. He had even talked about renting a shop on the Avenue of the Tulips, and moving his house from Sar Cheshmeh to Simorgh Street.

"Come live with us," Heshmat asked, but Peacock refused. She sat in her bedroom at night, still in the day's clothes, and reviewed her accounts on an abacus. She took out the jewels from her pockets, set them in neat rows across the table, and opened the newspapers from around each one. She did not look at the stones when she was alone; she stared at the words in the newspaper, and wished she could read.

The newspapers reported important events, Peacock knew, events that affected everyone's fate. She learned about them only from the conversations of people she met during the day—the bazaar merchants, the peddlers, her clients. Most of them were illiterate like Peacock, and the news they had was barely more than a recounting of rumors they had heard from others. They spoke of places unknown to themselves except through tales of peoples past—of Russia and America and Europe—of Reza Shah's dealing with foreign countries, and of a game he played: setting one enemy against the other to maximize his own advantage, trying to shake loose from the dominance of the British.

"Imagine that," the merchants exclaimed, "biting the hand that fed him. Without the support of the British, Reza Shah would never have been King. He negotiated with them, got their permission to make a coup against Ahmad Shah. Now he sides with the Germans to get rid of the English."

It was a mad idea, Peacock recognized—the assumption that Reza Shah could become independent of the English. Ever since the reign of Nasser-ed-Din Shah, everyone knew, nothing happened in Iran without direct involvement on the part of His or Her Majesty's spies. Peacock did not place much stock in the stories she heard. She did not believe the rumors about Germany introducing laws against its Jewish population.

The merchants claimed that Reza Shah was allying himself with Hitler against Britain. Reza Shah had *freed* the Jews, Peacock reminded everyone. He would not side with a country that persecuted them.

But the rumors persisted, and because of them, Peacock wished more and more she could read. The papers, she thought, held the key to the truth.

In 1937, electricity came to Peacock's street. One night, Blue-Eyed Lotfi came to her house and screwed a glass bulb into the ceiling of her room. Lotfi pulled at a string. Light burst into Peacock's eyes and blinded her.

She was so excited by the new invention that she could barely sleep at night. She walked into her room after dark, pulled at the string, and stood smiling at her surroundings as if she had discovered them for the first time.

266

"Things look different at night," she confided shyly in Heshmat. "I like watching them when that light shines."

It was all Reza Shah's doing, Peacock thought gratefully: the electricity that lit her nights, the water that flew in the pipes of Heshmat's new house on Simorgh Street, the hospital where Heshmat's daughter went to give birth.

"On *sheets*!" Peacock had rejoiced when she saw the girl rolled out of the delivery room. "My God, you delivered on *sheets*!"

Reza Shah was her hero—the boy she had recognized as chosen and who had gone on to fulfill her ancestor's prophecy. Peacock could never believe that he would betray the Jews.

Blue-Eyed Lotfi went to France to buy stock for his new shop, and came back with a gift for Peacock. It was a radio—a large piece of furniture made of wood and glass that lit up with the turn of a knob, and that Lotfi claimed could talk. "That's heresy," Peacock laughed, but Lotfi attached a cord to the outlet in the wall and turned a knob.

A man spoke at Peacock. His voice was deep and husky, and he used the formal language one used to address important people. He was about to tell the news, he announced as if he were blessed with knowledge unknown to others. He was going to relay everything that had happened in the world that day.

"In the Name of God," he began, "His Majesty Reza Shah Pahlavi, King of Kings, today signed a treaty of friendship with Germany."

He went on to explain about the treaty. He spoke of Germany's leader—a man called Hitler who believed in the superiority of the Aryan race. Iranians, except the Jews among them, were also Aryans. There would be a war soon, the announcer promised, a war greater than the First World War, but this time Iran would not be occupied. Her economy would not be destroyed, her people would not starve. This

267

time, thanks to Reza Shah, Iran had taken the side of the mighty and would be rewarded for her foresight. Germany would defeat the English and the Russians. As a token of appreciation, Hitler had promised to give back to Iran provinces stolen from her by the imperialist Czars.

Blue-Eyed Lotfi would always cry when he remembered Peacock's face that night before the radio.

 Peacock demanded an audience with Reza Shah. She went to his office in the Palace of Joy, and found him screaming at his Prime Minister: Reza Shah always screamed at his servants. The man stood before him, head bent and eyes on his boots, and never once made a sound until he was dismissed.

"Go," His Majesty yelled at last. "You are not a man of action. You are not a man at all."

The Prime Minister walked past Peacock with his lips pale and his face chalk white. His hands trembled as he left the room.

Reza Shah paced up and down his office in the military boots he still shined as in the days of his service with the Cossacks. He did not greet Peacock; he never acknowledged that he had known her before. She was a reminder of the days of his humility, and the very sight of her made the Shah feel as if he were still no more than the orphan boy from Alasht. But he did grant her an immediate audience when thousands of others waited a lifetime for a chance to see the Shah, and were never received.

"Make it quick," he said as he stopped behind his desk and faced Peacock.

"Your Majesty—" Peacock stepped forward. She had spent agonizing days trying to solve the riddle of Reza Shah's alliance with Hitler. She would not waste time with her question: "What if there is a war? What if the Germans win the war?"

Reza Shah pretended he had not understood.

"What of the Jews you saved?" Peacock insisted.

Then his eyes softened. He looked at Peacock, and for an instant she saw a man trapped and embittered by the harshness of choices he was forced to make.

"I will renounce the Jews," he said. "I will renounce anyone to save Iran from her enemies."

 Reza Shah had saved Iran from disintegration. He had conquered the mullahs, built an army to defend the borders and a police to overcome the internal chaos of the last three centuries. He had kept the Russians at bay and the British at arm's length. He had built the first trans-Iranian railway, brought schools and hospitals and vaccines. Tehran's water supply was still contaminated by the sewage that poured into the river and seeped into the wells, but malaria and trachoma and intestinal disease, always endemic, had begun to diminish. Ten years after he had become King, Peacock thought, he looked at his accomplishments and believed himself infallible.

He was an infantryman from a nonexistent army, and overnight he had become King. He was a soldier trained under foreign occupation, and he had become independent. He was a poor boy, born in a hovel at the end of a village dirt road, who now lived in a palace with halls of mirror and rooms full of treasure. He had become vain and intolerant and corrupt.

He lived simply, in a bare room in the Palace of Joy, with his mattress on the floor and no luxuries. But he went around confiscating the best of Iran's lands—the most populous villages, the greenest valleys, the lushest forests—to register them in the names of his children. He had a son— the Crown Prince Muhammad Reza, who was so shy he never dared speak in his father's presence. Peacock had seen Muhammad Reza as a boy, riding his Arabian mare around the Square of the Cannons, raising a storm of dust that almost hid him from view. Even then, Peacock remembered, the boy's eyes were languid, and his voice as he commanded the mare, shook with indecision. He was not—he could not have been—the son Reza Shah had wanted.

Reza Shah had sent the boy to Europe, to a Swiss boarding school designed to educate young aristocracy. Muhammad Reza learned to ski, fly airplanes, drive fast cars. In 1938, at the age of nineteen, he returned to Iran to take his place next to his father.

He found Reza Shah beleaguered and preoccupied: nothing worked fast enough in Iran, the Shah complained; no one was dedicated enough. The Minister of Finance, Davar, had recently failed to come up with funds necessary for a public works project. Victim to Reza Shah's wrath, Davar had worked late into the night at his office, then killed himself. He had left a note:

"I am committing suicide," he had written, "because I am exhausted."

Reza Shah had no time for failure. He did not attend Davar's funeral.

But there was a bigger problem: a man by the name of Mossadeq—a rich landowner turned nationalist who had been Reza Shah's enemy for decades. Reza Shah had imprisoned Mossadeq, but the man was old, and doctors had warned His Majesty that Mossadeq would die in jail.

"Release him, then," the Crown Prince advised his father. "If he dies, he will become a martyr, and we will never escape his legacy."

Reza Shah was tired and frustrated and dismayed. For the first time ever, he did as Muhammad Reza suggested.

Then he told the boy that he had arranged a wife for him—Princess Foziyeh, daughter of Egypt's King Farouk and Queen Nazli. Muhammad Reza had never seen Foziyeh, but his older sister, Shams, assured him that he would be pleased with the find. In 1939 he went to Cairo to fetch the bride for the wedding.

*   *   *

It was going to be the affair of the century, a gala like no other in the East, so sumptuous it would dazzle the royal family of Egypt and prove to all of Iran's neighbors the great progress Reza Shah had brought to Iran.

At the palace, Reza Shah hired an enormous staff just to see to the details of every arrangement. He assigned Peacock to a team of jewelers—young men dispatched to Europe earlier that year for a crash course in gemology and jewelry design, and entrusted to them the job of preparing stones for each female member of the family.

The bride and groom, it was decided, would sail from Egypt to the port of Khorramshahr, on the Persian Gulf, then travel to Tehran aboard a special train built especially for the wedding, and equipped with every conceivable luxury. In Tehran they would first attend a gala reception, European style, hosted by Reza Shah to welcome Queen Nazli. The wedding would take place the following evening.

Suddenly, Peacock heard that a great disaster had taken place: the bride and groom, Reza Shah had been told by a trembling Director of the Railroads, were indeed aboard the special train. They were accompanied by her mother, a suite of personal maids and nannies, half a dozen ladies-in-waiting. But they were in the middle of the Great Persian Desert—in a place where no man or beast could survive—and their train had stopped: it had run out of food, and water, and electricity.

Reza Shah imprisoned his Director of the Railroads, and fired every other man in charge of his son's journey. He sent for the travelers on another train, and received them personally when they arrived at the palace. Muhammad Reza was still mortified by the fiasco. Foziyeh was crying to her mother that she wanted to go home. Queen Nazli told Reza Shah that his country was uncivilized.

They spent the day bickering over Foziyeh's income and inheritance. Since she was to be married to the Crown Prince of Iran, Reza Shah insisted, all of Foziyeh's income from the

271

court of Egypt should automatically be sent to Iran. Queen Nazli refused categorically, and would not negotiate. By the time the arguments ended, the marriage had already been poisoned.

That night, at the European-style gala, seating arrangements were mixed up, and guests began to bicker with one another over their places at dinner. Reza Shah fired his Grand Master of Ceremonies and the Grand Master of the Court on the spot. But Queen Nazli was not satisfied. She told Reza Shah she was disappointed with the welcoming ceremony. The Shah ordered the palace maids to pack Nazli's bags without her knowledge. The morning after the wedding, he would ship her out of Iran along with all of Foziyeh's ladies-in-waiting.

He sat back that night, and watched the religious ceremony without emotion. Halfway through the prayer that would bind his son to the princess of Egypt, Reza Shah looked up and saw Peacock next to him. He shook his head. The look in his eyes augured disaster.

"Things," he said, "are not as they should be."

In 1939 the Second World War began in Europe. Officially, Iran declared her neutrality in the war. In fact, Reza Shah harbored German agents on Iranian soil, and later refused to allow the British access through Iran to Russia. The German Minister, Dr. Schacht, visited the country, and asserted once again that Iranians were "pure Aryans, exempt from the provisions of the Nuremberg race laws."

"It's the end of you all," the merchants in the bazaar told Peacock, without bothering to hide their excitement. "Hitler's taking over the world, and the Jews are as good as dead."

They were all her friends. They would have mourned her, even, but all their lives they had heard their mullahs speak against infidels, and now they could not help but succumb to joy at the prospect of seeing Jews eliminated once and for all.

272

* * *

In 1941, Germany invaded the Soviet Union. Needing a route through which he could dispatch much-needed supplies to the Russians, Churchill looked once again toward Iran. He asked Reza Shah to expel the Germans from Iran, and to provide free access to Allied troops and transport trucks.

Reza Shah refused; he never imagined that Hitler might lose the war. Churchill threatened an invasion. Reza Shah ignored him. By the time he realized the scope of the danger he was courting, Allied troops were already descending on Iran.

On August 24, 1941, Indian forces under British command entered Iran through the south. The next day, Peacock watched Allied planes fly over Tehran, dropping leaflets: Iran, they said, was an occupied country. Reza Shah had been deposed, whisked from the throne and shipped away to exile in South Africa. His son, Muhammad Reza, was placed on the throne by the Allies, then locked up in his palace.

Peacock had come to believe the voice on the radio.

"In close concert with our Russian ally," the announcer interpreted Churchill's speech before the House of Commons, "we have rooted out the malignant elements in Tehran."

 A woman came to Besharat the Bastard's house, in the days of the Allied occupation when the farms could not produce and the factories had stopped working, when imports had disappeared and the poor starved, when the Russians diverted the rice and wheat of the northern provinces for their own use, and American soldiers spent their dollars buying whores and whiskey. The roads were occupied by Allied troops transporting military supplies—endless lines of military vehicles loaded with food

273

and guns and medicine, traveling painfully through the un-paved roads of Reza Shah's fallen kingdom—while Iranian peasants, their lives bundled on the backs of mules and don-keys as they escaped their ravaged farms in search of food they would not find in the city, waited all day for the right of passage. The Allies required each Iranian to obtain a visa in order to travel within his own country. At inspection points, the peasants arrived exhausted and half-starved, chil-dren strapped onto their backs or asleep in women's arms, faces covered with thick dust that made one indistinguishable from the other. They held out their visas and spoke too loudly to the soldiers, who did not understand their language: "Looking for work," they said, smiling optimistically.

In the cities, the new immigrants joined the thousands of unemployed men and women who lined up outside bak-eries and grocery shops, loitered at the doors of the rich, or begged the foreign soldiers for food and money. Their daugh-ters walked the streets at night or gathered in nightclubs where they sold themselves in return for a full meal. Their sons searched for a way to vent their anger, and in the end joined one or another of the political organizations—among them the Communist Tudeh, set up by the Soviet Union—that promised to return Iran to independence.

The woman who came to Besharat's house was bone-thin and dark, with sunken eyes and the hands of a crow. She appeared once every few weeks, always dressed in wid-ow's black, carrying a shopping bag under her chador: Reza Shah was gone, his son imprisoned in the Marble Palace. No one enforced the ban against the veil anymore.

From her window on the second floor of Besharat the Bastard's house, Yasmine saw the woman approach the gates, and watched her cross the garden. She seemed smaller the closer she came to the house. When she reached the front door, she knocked so lightly no one heard her. Still, the woman would stand there, a shadow behind the dusty etched glass inset of the front door, and did not dare knock again. In time, someone would see her.

274

"It's *her* again," Yasmine heard Naiima cry to Assal in the kitchen. "It's the Boys' Mother."

Then the Boys' Mother would call to Naiima, and plead to be let in.

"Just for a moment," she said. "Just to see Besharat Khan one last time." No one answered her. Naiima and Assal went about their business as if the Boys' Mother did not exist. She would plead for a while, turn her face up toward Yasmine's window, and even beg her for help: Ezraeel the Avenger, she repeated the same litany every time, had left her penniless. Her sons had all married bad women who refused to support her now that everyone was hungry. It was not fair— not even possible—that she should be reduced to such a state as this. She was, after all—she *had been*—the wife of Tehran's greatest jeweler.

The Boys' Mother sat on the ground, hugging her plastic shopping bag, and unleashed a storm of tears.

"Let her in," Assal would order Naiima toward the end of the afternoon. "People will hear her on the street and think we're uncivilized."

Naiima opened the door.

"Into the kitchen," she commanded, and the Boys' Mother ran.

She sat there, on the broken stool reserved for beggars who came to eat three-day-old leftovers, and watched Assal prepare her son's dinner. Assal's clothes were covered with dust, her face blackened as if by soot. The Boys' Mother asked her for a drink of water, or a piece of bread.

"Go eat at your own house," Assal would say without bothering to look at her. Purposely she would gather all the food left in the pantry from the day before, and throw it away where the Boys' Mother could see.

During the war years, Besharat the Bastard more than tripled the wealth Ezraeel had left him. Before the occupation, as soon as he heard news of Germany's invasion of the

Soviet Union, he bought out all the sugar in Tehran and Qazvin and Yazd. Later, during the famine, he sold each ounce for ten times its real price. In his kitchen—this Jew-boy who had run barefoot in the Pit all through his childhood, this bastard son of Assal the Whore who now treated the Boys' Mother worse than a dog—in *his* kitchen, Besharat the Bastard threw away leftover meat that the Boys' Mother would have given her life to eat.

So the Boys' Mother watched the food and swallowed her hunger. Right before the start of the evening curfew, Besharat the Bastard came home and had his dinner, then his tea. He talked with his mother, reviewed his accounts, smoked a few cigarettes. Near midnight, he finally agreed to see the Boys' Mother.

She walked into his room clutching her shopping bag close to her chest. She marched up to him as if toward death, then stopped at the oak table that separated Besharat from the world. She never looked up.

"I have no money for you," Besharat the Bastard would say, blowing the dust off his desk. The Boys' Mother did not speak. On the floor under her feet, a silk carpet depicted rose-cheeked maidens pouring wine for their lovers after a day's hunt. Besharat the Bastard waited for a moment, then decided that the issue had been resolved.

"Go home," he said, and busied himself with his papers again.

Suddenly the Boys' Mother would explode. She would let go of her chador, lunge across Besharat's table, and beg.

"Look at you," she would say. "Look at you, all clean and comfortable in my husband's chair, spending my children's inheritance, getting fat off my blood. You have to give me something, enough to eat, enough to live. I was his wife for thirty years, married him when I was fifteen and never once disobeyed his word. I gave him sons! *Sons!* I deserve something."

The words gushed out of her in a single breath, always

276

ending with a final gesture of humiliation: she unlocked her fingers from around the shopping bag, and released a small avalanche of putrid chicken claws and feet—purchased that day after hours of waiting in line, with coupons, issued by the Allies, that she had to beg for, or buy on the black market. Besharat the Bastard always winced at the sight of the claws.

"This is it," the Boys' Mother sobbed, digging her hands into the mass of raw skin and bones, and raising it to Besharat's face. "This is all I eat."

There was no cause for pity, Besharat the Bastard always responded. When Ezraeel the Avenger was alive, back when the Boys' Mother was the wife of Tehran's greatest jeweler, Assal the Whore had often taken her son begging at their kitchen. The Boys' Mother had refused Besharat even her garbage.

"Go eat at your own house," she had said.

 Besharat the Bastard moved from the Avenue of the Tulips north to Palace Street. He lived across from the mansion of the famous Dr. Mossadeq, in a four-story home where Assal—beleaguered by old age and overwhelmed by new wealth—lost her way in the thirty-seven rooms with connecting doors, the three sets of stairways each leading to a different part of the house, the four-car garage and the three levels of underground storage where Besharat kept his precious new merchandise—rubber that was used to make tires for Allied trucks, and for which he was paid in British pounds and American dollars.

Inside the house, water flowed from pipes that opened with the turn of a knob, the maids spent hours watching their own reflection in porcelain bowls called toilets, and every night, Naiima walked from room to room—like a muse with a holy touch—and pulled at a string connected to a small glass bulb that suddenly bathed the room with light.

But even here, Yasmine was captive. She had been married to Besharat for nine years, and they remained childless. Every day she asked him for divorce.

"Let me go," she demanded, her voice throbbing with hatred. Besharat the Bastard no longer spoke French to her. She had been forced to learn Persian.

"Send me home, and tell your friends I have died."

He kept her under constant watch, did not allow her to leave the house, never gave her money. She lived in a room on the third floor, overlooking Palace Street and Dr. Mossadeq's house, and he had told her she could never leave: he wanted children, wanted *her* children, and as long as she denied him, he would keep her prisoner in his home.

"No womb that has been dry for me," he said, "will carry another man's seeds."

Assal told Besharat he must give up. He had tried first with Naiima, then Yasmine, then with a host of other women—whores he slept with, not taking off their chadors to see their faces, only to try his luck at making them pregnant. He had taken every opportunity and tried every old remedy, and in the end the world had begun to believe that it was he—Besharat the Bastard—who was sterile, and not his wives.

"Give it up," Assal told him. She was blinded by age, suddenly more accepting of life's cruelties. "Accept that you will die without an heir. Find someone who will bury you, and be done with it."

Besharat the Bastard never stopped believing in his own virility: Naiima, he insisted, was infertile. The whores he had slept with all took potions to kill his seed. Yasmine denied him on purpose.

"It's her way of avenging herself," he told Assal with untamed conviction. "She sleeps with me and keeps herself from getting pregnant just to prove I'm not a man."

So he went back to her, for two weeks every month,

making love without passion or even desire, and immediately afterward he left her bed and shut the door behind him.

Alone in her room, Yasmine would open her window, lie still in bed, and listen to the darkness. The streets, under martial law, would be quiet but for the sound of night patrols and the laughter of drunken foreign soldiers heading back from the brothels. Near ten o'clock, Yasmine would hear the cars that carried—with special permission from the Allied military government in Tehran—friends and relatives of the young Shah to the Marble Palace, where he received them with his Egyptian wife. The guests would play cards with His Majesty, watch movies, go for midnight swims in one of the palace's many pools. The next morning they would return in the midst of the day's rush, looking absurd in their evening jackets and long, beaded gowns, the men aching from the night's whiskey, the women wearing dark sunglasses and bouffant hairstyles, looking pale under the makeup they bought from Blue-Eyed Lotfi. They would rush home and sleep till dusk, but as soon as they awoke, the street would come alive again. The maids who worked in the houses eavesdropped on their ladies' conversations about the night before, and related to each other every bit of palace gossip they could find. Foziyeh, it was said, was discontent. She was bored with her life, tired of the daily games of tennis, the midday rides on palace grounds, the venomous intrigue between the Shah's older sister, Shams, and his twin, Ashraf. Years ago, when his daughters were of marrying age, Reza Shah had designated two young men—one the son of a Prime Minister, the other a descendant of a powerful family in Shiraz—as his sons-in-law. He had brought the men to the palace to introduce them to his daughters. Both girls had both liked the son of the Prime Minister; he was better looking, taller, more gallant. Faced with a conflict, Reza Shah had let Shams, the older sister, marry the Prime Minister's son. Ashraf had cried for a week, then married the boy from Shiraz and hated him and Shams all her life. Because Shams had championed Muhammad Reza Shah's marriage to Foziyeh, Ashraf tried to undermine her in every way.

Every night, Yasmine listened to the cars heading toward the palace. When they were all gone, there would be silence, but still Yasmine could not sleep. She was plagued with prisoner's insomnia, the state of permanent frustration that exhausted her without allowing rest. At midnight she would crawl out of bed, her mouth dry from the dust that lingered on her pillow and invaded her lungs and her nose, and lie facedown on the balcony floor. Across the street, Dr. Mossadeq sat up in his living room and listened to his radio blasting the midnight news.

Yasmine listened to the speaker and tried to understand all the words in Persian. She wanted news of the war, of France under German occupation, of Americans marching into Paris. She lay in the dark, her stomach cold against the balcony floor, and tried to imagine Paris after the bombings.

"It's destroyed," she told herself. "It's all destroyed."

She wanted to see Paris and understand that it had changed, that she could not go back—that there was nothing to go back to. She wanted to convince herself that she must stay in Tehran and accept her fate, make peace with Besharat and his wife.

One night in the autumn of 1943, the radio shut down halfway through the broadcast. The next morning, Tehran's telegraph office closed down, the city's borders were blocked, and the streets were jammed with occupying soldiers in trucks and armored vehicles. Naiima came home from the butcher's shop to announce that the Shah had been arrested. An hour later, Besharat the Bastard brought different news: "It's Reza Shah," he announced, his voice choked with excitement. "They say he has come to make a coup."

The evening paper confirmed rumors of Reza Shah's triumphant return from exile. The next morning, however, speculation began that it was not Reza Shah, but indeed Hitler himself, who had landed troops in Iran. The Allies, it was said, had closed off Tehran to save the capital. Terror choked the Jews. Besharat the Bastard closed off his house and waited for the outcome of the war on Iranian soil. That night he came to Yasmine's bed, trembling with fear, and made love to her without resentment. Afterward, he stayed in her bed and listened for Mossadeq's radio, which refused to come to life.

For three days, the shutdown continued. Then, suddenly, the borders were reopened and the radio resumed its nightly broadcast. Tehran, it was revealed, had been the seat of a conference by the heads of the world's greatest powers; they had charted the end of the war, and determined the course of Iran's future.

Besharat the Bastard sat up in the dark that night, and stared at Yasmine: beneath her cold surface and her furious skin, he felt life about to stir.

 All of Tehran received news of Yasmine's pregnancy. Besharat the Bastard was so grateful for the miracle, they said, he had decided to please God in return: he called the Boys' Mother, and gave her enough money to live on for the rest of her life. She told him she wanted to go to Israel, where many Jews had already emigrated from Iran. Besharat the Bastard bought her a one-way ticket, and even wrote to a friend, asking that he help the woman settle in the new country. In return, he asked only that the Boys' Mother bless his child.

"It's not for me to bless anyone," the Boys' Mother said. "You have done wrong by the child's mother. No one conceived in bitterness will ever be blessed."

Besharat the Bastard spat behind the Boys' Mother and wished aloud that her ship would sink on the way to Jerusalem. He brought Yasmine out of her prison and surrounded her with every luxury his wealth could provide. He turned the first-floor living room into a bedroom for Yasmine, hired two maids just to wait on her, brought in a cook just to prepare healthy meals. He allowed the holy sisters of the Jean D'Arc Mission in Tehran to visit Yasmine, let them bring her books and speak with her in French. He called Peacock to the house, and ordered a set of diamonds—a pair of earrings, a ring, a necklace, and a bracelet—that he would present to Yasmine, he said, on the occasion of his son's circumcision. Peacock came in her glittering circus clothes and measured Yasmine's neck, her wrist, her finger that had not swollen in spite of the pregnancy.

"You will have a beautiful child," she told Yasmine. "Take care that it does not inherit your sadness."

Yasmine looked at her, this old woman who had kept nothing of her youth's beauty, who touched Yasmine with the tip of her dried fingers and spoke to her as if to an old friend. She would not trust Peacock. She would not hear her words. From the moment she found she was pregnant to the hour of her child's birth, Yasmine closed herself to the world and allowed no emotions.

It was her only defense, she told herself, the one chance she might have to save herself: once she had given him his child, Besharat the Bastard might agree to let her go. She could leave Iran, go back to Paris. But to do so, she would have to leave her child for Besharat. She must, therefore, keep herself from wanting it.

So she carried the infant without thinking about its existence, and concentrated instead on the single goal of regaining her freedom. From the room she had moved to, it was impossible to hear the sound of Mossadeq's radio, but Yasmine never stopped thinking of Paris. She saw her mother—alive in spite of what her father had written on the envelopes—standing in the cramped living room of their apartment, where Yasmine had last seen her. Her mother wore the olive silk dress, now faded and loose, which she had bought when Yasmine was a child. In those days she had been taller and fleshier, and she had worn the dress only on special occasions when she went dancing with her husband. She had left Yasmine alone with her dinner, and returned home at dawn—the child waking up to the sound of a key turning in the door, watching her mother walk in with a smile, smelling of perfume and humming the tunes she had danced to all night.

The day Yasmine left the apartment to go to Iran with Besharat, her mother had worn the olive silk dress and cried in the living room. Her father had stood at the window, his back turned to Yasmine, and never said a word in response to her pleas of forgiveness and her promises that she would come back, soon, to see them for a whole summer. In the end, Yasmine had left with her suitcase, descending the steps with quivering knees. At the top of the staircase her mother had cried, "My child, I will never see you again."

Outside, the sun had glared in Yasmine's eyes, blinding her temporarily so that when she looked for Besharat, she saw only a white spot where he had been standing, and for an instant she had felt relief—thank God he has vanished—till her eyes adjusted to the light and she saw him waving at her from the opposite sidewalk.

In the last month of Yasmine's pregnancy, Besharat the Bastard hired a doctor from the Russian hospital to assist with the birth, and brought in two midwives in case the doctor failed. When the labor began, he called Naiima and Assal, and allowed twenty-three other women—relatives and elders—to preside over the birth. They sat around Yasmine's room, watching her writhe in pain, questioning the doctors' methods, and insisting that the midwives should take charge of the delivery. As soon as the doctor had pulled the steaming infant out of Yasmine, Naiima ran forward and grabbed the baby before the doctor had even cut the cord.

"A son," she cried triumphantly, raising the boy for all to see. "We have a *son*."

Cyrus the Magnificent wanted to be American. He wore American clothes, drove an American car. He read American novels, spoke English even to people who did not understand him. He memorized the map of the United States, the Preamble to the Constitution, the American national anthem. Cyrus the Magnificent had never stepped outside the borders of Iran, but he lived in dreams of Hollywood.

He was a handsome man—"American looking," he liked to describe himself to people who had never seen an American. He was tall, with fair skin and light hair. He had a straight nose, a perfect face. He spoke Persian with a foreign accent, used big words and grand gestures, tried to project his voice as if he were performing alone onstage.

Born in Tehran, the youngest son of Heshmat and Blue-Eyed Lotfi, he had spent his childhood listening to Lotfi talk about Europe.

"In Europe," Blue-Eyed Lotfi had always said, "men are civilized, and Jews are human."

Cyrus the Magnificent decided early on that he wanted to study in Europe. At school in Tehran, he studied French and English, and asked his father every year to enroll him at a university in Paris. He worked as an errand boy at the British embassy in Tehran, and saved all his money for the trip to France. But the year he turned twelve, with his plans made and his English money sewn to the inside of his pants pocket, Cyrus the Magnificent woke up one morning to find his dreams shattered: war had broken out in Europe, and the Germans were killing Jews.

Cyrus the Magnificent stayed in Tehran and watched the occupying soldiers on the streets. He saw the Americans, tall and handsome and confident, spending their dollars, buying women and food and the resentment of the mullahs. He saw them gathered in empty grocery shops, where they drank homemade arrack. They would stand in groups of three or four, and invariably one of them would take out a book of postcards, folded like an accordion, that he flipped open on the counter. There, Cyrus the Magnificent saw real-life *houris*—ghosts of beautiful women with painted eyes and revealing clothes, chests heaving and lips puckered as if in invitation to love. Cyrus the Magnificent would have paid with his life to meet one of those women.

He approached the soldiers, and impressed them with his English. He offered a deal: he would give them silk stockings and perfume stolen from his father's shop, in return for the postcards. By the end of the occupation, he would boast to his friends that he owned a picture of every woman in Hollywood.

He was in tenth grade and struggling through his math and physics courses when he learned that Franklin Delano Roosevelt, President of the United States of America, had been in Tehran for a conference with Churchill and Stalin. Cyrus the Magnificent was so enraptured by the news that he forgot to go to school for his semiannual science exams. Instead he went to the bazaar—always the source of the quickest and most complete news about the happenings in the city—and listened to the merchants talk about the Tehran Conference. The Allies, it was said, recognized that Iran's economy had been destroyed by the occupation, and had promised to help her as much as possible. More important, however, was that they also recognized her desire for independence, and had pledged to withdraw their forces from Iranian soil within six months after the war had officially ended.

"It's the Americans," the merchants all agreed among themselves. "The Americans are forcing Russia out. The British would stay, but they can't afford to."

By the time Heshmat discovered her son in the bazaar, the fall term had ended, and Cyrus the Magnificent had officially failed all the exams. Seething, Heshmat banned her son from the bazaar, and swore she would keep him at home till he had forgotten all his dreams of America. She was a strong woman, severe with her children, and she would have carried out her threat, but Cyrus managed to disarm her as always:

"I can't think about tiny molecules and petty multiplications, when right before my eyes the world is in the making."

Two days later, he was back in the bazaar and chattering with the merchants.

In the aftermath of the Tehran Conference, the United States and England withdrew their forces from Iran. The Soviet Union refused to leave. Throughout the war years, it had built a Communist Party—the Tudeh—inside Iran, and now planned to use it as an arm to gain access to the country's government. The year Cyrus the Magnificent graduated from high school, the Soviet Red Army established puppet governments in Kurdistan and Azerbaijan, and proclaimed their independence from the rest of the country. In his first act of leadership since he had been declared king four years earlier, Muhammad Reza Shah dispatched forces to recapture Azerbaijan from Stalin. The troops had only traveled a hundred and fifty kilometers from Tehran when they were confronted and stopped by Russian tanks.

"Reza Shah was right," Blue-Eyed Lotfi said as he paced the house in the days and weeks following the defeat in Azerbaijan. "He knew that if Hitler didn't win the war, Stalin would swallow Iran and act as if we never existed at all."

For a year the Tudeh reigned in Iran. Cyrus the Magnificent again lost sight of the demands of ordinary life, and spent his time following the news. It was the beginning of the Cold War. The Americans could not afford to lose Iran to Stalin. In 1946 the Shah asked the United Nations for protection against the Soviets. In response, the United States confronted Stalin, and at last forced the Red Army out of Iran.

It was only a partial victory. The Soviets took their tanks, but left in their stead a Communist Party that was the single most powerful political force in Iran—and the only organized party. Nevertheless, Cyrus the Magnificent hailed the outcome, and fell in love with America all over again.

He would have gone to America then, but Heshmat stopped him; he was to attend the University of Tehran, she dictated. He was to become a doctor, save lives, make his parents proud. Cyrus the Magnificent flunked out of his first semester at the university, and refused to go back. He was not willing to suffer the rigors of higher education. He was too concerned with the drama of life, he explained, too enamored of the world's greater pleasures, too much—he admitted with unrestrained pride—like Solomon the Man.

He left the university, and went into business instead. With money he had borrowed from Peacock—Blue-Eyed Lotfi had not forgiven Cyrus his failure in college, and so refused to trust him with money—he bought a piece of land and built the first two-story apartment building in Tehran. He moved into the top floor, and rented the other apartments. He walked around town dressed in a beige tweed jacket with leather elbow patches, a brown ascot, and brown leather gloves with holes in them, "like race-car drivers in Hollywood," he explained to his friends, who were baffled by the appearance of the gloves. He was waiting for Heshmat to forgive him, for Blue-Eyed Lotfi to offer his blessing, and then, he said, he would go to America.

The year after he had built the apartments, Cyrus the Magnificent met Laa-Laa. It was winter, and Cyrus was lying in bed, taking an afternoon nap, when he heard the first knocks on the door. He thought of answering, then decided against it. The hallways were cold. The building had no vacancies.

But ten minutes later the pounding had not stopped, and Cyrus went to the door. It was snowing again. The wind screeched through the hallway.

Laa-Laa walked in with a burst of cold air and a rush of snowflakes.

She was young, so beautiful that Cyrus thought she would vanish if he dared bat an eyelid. She had on a thin summer dress—yellow and pink chiffon, tight at the top and flared around the knees. She wore white shoes, a large summer hat. She put down her cardboard suitcase and leaned against the wall to catch her breath. Her eyes radiated warmth. Her skin was covered with moisture.

She had left home on a warm summer day, Cyrus thought, and on the street she had found winter.

She took off her hat. Her hair was the color of burnt sugar.

"I need a room," she said in her best Persian.

Cyrus the Magnificent did not understand her.

"I need a room," she repeated in Russian.

Cyrus the Magnificent recognized the language and cursed his own bad luck.

"Damn!" he exclaimed in Farsi. "She's the enemy."

"I have no vacancies," he told her in Persian, and turned around to leave. She took his hand.

"I have no vacancies," he said in French, then again in English.

She put his hand between her legs, where she was warm and bare, and then she kissed him till he thought he would melt from the heat of her skin. He tore off her top, lifted her with her legs hugging his waist, and by the time he noticed the neighbor gawking at them, Cyrus the Magnificent was deep in love and lost to Laa-Laa's magic.

He never married her—he could not marry his enemy— but they lived together for three years, and every month she threatened to leave. Cyrus the Magnificent was so infatuated with Laa-Laa that he did not sleep nights for fear she might not be there when he opened his eyes in the morning. To prove his love, he signed over to her ownership of his building. Soon after that, Laa-Laa found another lover.

She brought the man to live with her in Cyrus the Magnificent's apartment, and changed all the locks. It was winter

again, and Cyrus the Magnificent banged his fists on the
door till he was bruised and exhausted.

He had on his beige tweed jacket and his racing-car
gloves. He crouched against the wind, and walked the streets
till the pain of Laa-Laa's betrayal had sunk from his chest
down into his stomach. He could not face his parents. He
turned up at Peacock's door instead. He was pale, and he
laughed too loud.

"Damn Russians!" he said as he walked in. "They get
you *every* time."

 Yasmine closed her eyes, weak from the effort of
the birth, and let the dread of Naiima's voice run
through her like poison:

"We have a son," she had cried, as if she were
the child's mother, and yet Yasmine told herself she must
let it be.

"Call the nursemaid," Naiima ordered a cousin present
at the birth. "Tell her to rush over and feed Besharat Khan's
heir."

She had arranged for the nursemaid long before the
birth, interviewed a dozen pregnant women due to give birth
around the same time as Yasmine. She wanted a healthy
woman, one with no prior children who had drained her
strength, one who would agree to conspire with Naiima and
keep the child from its natural mother. She had not told
Besharat about the nursemaid; she was afraid he would op-
pose her, insist that Yasmine should feed her own child.

"But it's impossible," she now argued with him before
all the witnesses. "This woman is *foreign*. If your son drinks
her milk, he will become a stranger to you. He will be a
Christ-worshiper, a Jew-hater. She will fill him with her poison and he will grow up to hate you and yours."

Feigning sleep, Yasmine heard Naiima and this time
prayed she would convince Besharat. Then, all at once, she

felt a warmth on her chest; Besharat the Bastard had taken the boy from Naiima, and placed him at her breast.

He kept Yasmine in the room on the first floor and called on her every morning, noon, and nighttime, and though he did not sleep with her anymore—a breast-feeding woman could not become pregnant—he treated her gently and with kindness. He only forbade her to speak French to the boy; she might poison the child's mind against his father, Naiima had suggested, and Besharat agreed. Yasmine was asked to speak only Persian, so that Naiima could understand her when she eavesdropped. At night she was allowed to keep the infant in her own bed.

Slowly, as she watched the child grow bigger and felt her heart overwhelmed with love, Yasmine found herself less preoccupied with the thought of leaving Iran. After a decade of isolation, she was at last becoming part of the household, and could no longer stand the thought of living alone. She spoke to the maids, the cook, the vendors who came to the door with their merchandise stacked on the backs of lame donkeys, the peddler women who carried their junk on their backs. Most of all, she spoke to Peacock—who was called to the house regularly, always instructed to bring identical pieces for Besharat the Bastard's two wives. Slowly, Yasmine stopped listening for the evening news. At night, instead of waiting for Mossadeq's radio to start, she would close the windows, watch her son in his sleep, and wish she could see his dreams.

She breast-fed the boy till he was two years old. The summer after the Russians left Azerbaijan, she became pregnant again.

"Give me the boy," Naiima begged her husband with tear-filled eyes. "You have given that stranger two children. You owe me at least one."

Besharat the Bastard recalled the pledge he had made long ago to Naiima and her God: as the husband of an infertile wife, he could marry twice, provided he gave equally to both women, slept with both of them till they were old, and forced the natural mother to share the children with the other wife. He took his son away from Yasmine, and gave him to Naiima.

Yasmine fought Besharat for the child. She fought Naiima and Assal and all of their relatives, but in the end, everyone knew she would lose. Naiima moved the boy out of Yasmine's room and into her own. She hovered around him all day long, objected to the slightest contact between mother and child. At night, when the boy cried for Yasmine, Naiima stood in the doorway and refused her entry.

So Yasmine attacked her, with her words and her hands and her anguish, and the two women rolled on the ground fighting like stray dogs until they were both wounded and bleeding and the maids separated them.

"Watch out," Naiima told the child every time Yasmine approached him. "That woman is violent."

Besharat the Bastard observed the battle between his two wives and refused to interfere. In a few months, he told himself, Yasmine would have another child, busy herself with the new infant, and make peace with Naiima again.

"You are committing an unforgivable crime," Peacock warned Besharat every time she came to the house and witnessed the fighting. "You are buying a curse that will never release you or your children."

Yasmine had a girl—dark, like Besharat, but with purple eyes. Besharat the Bastard rejoiced at her birth and promised Naiima would never touch the girl. Two years later, when the child was weaned from the breast, he reneged on his word.

"Suit yourself," Naiima had told him with a cool head. "Let that stranger raise your daughter, but remember, no one will marry a girl trained by a Christ-worshiper."

Besharat the Bastard made Yasmine pregnant for a third time, then gave her daughter to Naiima.

Peacock rushed to see her the moment she heard the news. "Madame Yasmine," she said, "you must not give in so easily to Naiima. You must fight her, fight Besharat." Yasmine was cold, pale, hard. She had fought her best battle and lost. Now she was thinking of escape.

 "You must help me," Yasmine told Peacock the day she came to warn her against surrendering to Naiima. Yasmine stood up and went to the door, looked through the crack, then opened it to check for spies. She found no one. Not even Naiima dared eavesdrop on Peacock.

Yasmine came back and sat close to Peacock. Her lips were pale, her eyes drained of color.

"I must leave this country," she said, shocked at the greatness of the confidence she entrusted in Peacock. She looked down at her stomach. She was three months pregnant. "When this child is born, I must flee."

She waited for a reaction. She thought Peacock would be astonished or frightened or outraged. Instead, she found her unmoved—as if listening to a story she had heard many times before.

"I need money," Yasmine went on, trying to keep her resolve intact. She raised her wedding ring to Peacock.

"Bring me cash," she asked, "in return for this ring. I can't take it off as long as I'm here, but I will leave it for you, I swear, before I go."

Peacock shook her head in sympathy. For years she had known—everyone had known—that Yasmine was contemplating escape. It was the natural response, and Besharat the Bastard had prepared against it.

"You could never leave," Peacock told Yasmine. "Even if you had money and a passport, you couldn't get across the border. Every Iranian woman needs written consent from her husband or father to leave the country."

Yasmine knew about the required consent form; she had heard about it on Mossadeq's radio.

"All I need from you," she told Peacock, "is enough cash to get me back home to Paris."

"Madame Yasmine," Peacock insisted, "don't give up your children. Don't give up your man. They will haunt you till the end of your life, leave a hollow space, the size of a baby's hand, that you could never fill inside your heart."

Yasmine drew her hand away from Peacock, and immediately she was closed and hard and out of reach again.

Peacock felt old and exhausted. She stood up and left Yasmine without another word. Behind her, Yasmine heard the door close, but did not turn to look. She had forgotten Peacock. In her mind she was retracing the maps she had so often studied as a young girl in Europe, watching herself, free and unharmed, walk out of Besharat's home and across Iran's borders, wearing her winter coat and her high-heeled shoes.

In 1947, Princess Foziyeh left the Shah; just as the Soviets were leaving Iran, the Queen took her only daughter and moved back to "civilized Egypt." Soon after that, Muhammad Reza Shah's twin sister, Ashraf, found him another wife: Sorraya, daughter of a Kurdish tribal chief, and the most startling beauty Iran would ever remember. She was sixteen years old, innocent and ravishing. She had white skin, high cheekbones, black hair and emerald eyes, and a queen's manners. She liked crocodiles; people said she kept them as house pets in the palace.

So the Shah married Sorraya, stepped out of his palace to reign, and discovered that his country was in famine. In 1945, Iran had no food and no income. By 1950 she had even run out of bread.

But the poverty, Muhammad Reza Shah knew, was largely artificial. Iran had oil—oil that was pumped and refined and controlled by the English, oil that had been given away by the Qajars in a concession to the English, who took eighty percent of the profits from the sale of Iran's oil. Now that she was starving, they said she was a bad risk, and refused to lend her money.

The Shah went to them—politely—and asked to share the oil money on a more equitable basis. He offered a fifty-fifty formula. The British laughed at him. The Anglo-Iranian Oil Company, they said, pumped Iran's oil, refined it, and sold it. Without English technology, Iran would have to let her oil stay in the ground, give up even her twenty-percent share.

The Shah came home empty-handed and braced himself for famine. He had done his best, he told the people. There was nothing else to do.

But inside Parliament, Reza Shah's old enemy, Dr. Mossadeq, went to war. In 1944, Mossadeq had initiated a law that forbade the government of Iran to negotiate any oil agreement with a foreign power without the prior consent of Parliament. Now, faced with the Shah's reluctance to confront the British, he stood up before the nation and cried the words that shook the world:

"Nationalize oil!"

Yasmine had another girl—also dark—but this time, when they brought her the child to feed, she refused. She put her two hands over her breasts, closed her eyes, and bit down on her lip as the infant cried in her lap and begged for food. Besharat the Bastard came in and ordered her to act like a mother, but Yasmine would not move. He tried to force her, but in vain. Even after they had dragged Yasmine's hands away from her breasts, she fought so hard that she frightened the child, and it could not eat. For two days they struggled. Then Besharat the Bastard gave in and hired a nursemaid.

"You're not a mother," he told Yasmine, "you're a witch."

Yasmine gave up her children, and moved back into her old room on the third floor. She found it small and melancholy and buried in dust. It did not matter, she told herself. She would not stay long.

Inside Parliament, Mossadeq had won the representatives' support for his plan to nationalize oil. He stepped forth and asked the Shah to declare himself on the issue.

Muhammad Reza Shah came out opposed.

Nationalization, he said, was illegal and would anger the British. It was also unwise, for without foreign expertise, Iran would be deprived of what little income she was allowed.

"Traitor!" Yasmine now heard Mossadeq's voice broadcast on the same radio he had listened to every night for a decade. He was accusing the Shah of being a coward, of serving the British at the expense of his own people. Oil, he said, was more than a source of revenue for Iran; it was a matter of pride, of national integrity, of human dignity.

"Let us starve!" he cried in the course of violent and spectacular speeches in which he became agitated and angry and so inspired by his own vision that he would fall to the ground unconscious and be carried out by his aides.

"Let us *all* starve. Let the English leave and take with them their engineers. Let one generation of Iranians sacrifice itself and regain our national resource."

Afterward, he received journalists and photographers in his home. Yasmine watched them file into the house, heard Mossadeq scream at them the terms of his nationalism. He would appear in his pajamas, sitting cross-legged on his bed, and he spoke so fervently that Yasmine could feel the street come alive with his words. It mattered little, he said, that two or three generations of Iranians would suffer from poverty. It mattered even less that the English would not be there to pump the oil from the ground. Let the oil stay in the earth. A time would come when Iran could train her own experts, and make her own children masters of the land.

He spoke sincerely, his bald, cone-shaped head shaking with excitement and his face flushed with passion as he captured, in one session, the sympathy of his harshest critics. He had already taken control of Parliament. Now he took the people.

In March 1952, Mossadeq called on the workers of the Abadan refinery to strike. In Tehran, he forced five consecutive prime ministers out of office, and took the job himself. Eager to succeed, he allied himself with the only organized political force inside Iran: the Communist Tudeh, which shared Mossadeq's enmity toward the British. It was a desperate move—a clear alliance with the Soviet Union—but in the heat of the battle, Mossadeq had lost sight of his nationalist dreams, and wanted most of all to win. He expropriated the Anglo-Iranian Oil Company, and sent the English engineers home.

Suddenly, the British wanted to talk. Mossadeq refused. He was ruling the country, and he did away with all pretense. He locked the Shah in his palace, and surrounded him with troops loyal to himself. He sent members of the royal family—among them Ashraf—into exile in Europe and America. Afraid that he would be assassinated, he planted soldiers all the way up and down Palace Street and all around his own house.

"There is going to be a war soon," Besharat the Bastard warned his guests on the first floor of the house. All through that year, the house had been filled with neighbors and friends and curious relatives who came to watch the happenings in Mossadeq's house. Besharat the Bastard was so confident of his vision that he had already taken steps to protect his household against the Tudeh and the invading British army: he had drawn barbed-wire fences all along the top of the brick wall that surrounded the house. He had built shutters for every window, bought locks and wooden poles for every door. He had even filled his basement with food and supplies to last the family three months.

"Mossadeq has antagonized the British," he warned his guests, "and now there is going to be war."

Upstairs in her room, Yasmine used her hand to wipe the dust off the window glass. Through the opening she created, she watched the soldiers standing guard around Mossadeq's house, and thought about the time they would draw their guns. She, too, was counting on a war—on a day when Iran would plunge into chaos, the police and the army would become engulfed in battle and lose count of their citizens. Then Yasmine would run, in her high heels and her winter coat through the streets of Tehran and across the city's borders and all the way north to Russia, where, years ago, she had arrived on a ship from France.

 Besharat the Bastard returned home only an hour after he had left for the office. He jumped out of the car, and dismissed the chauffeur:

"I won't need you for a few days."

He grabbed the keys from the man and stuffed a handful of bills, much more than a week's salary, into his fist. He pushed the chauffeur toward the door, then locked the gates.

He walked into the house, screaming for Naiima.

"Send the maids home!" he commanded, rushing toward the kitchen and the backyard where the servants worked. Naiima ran behind him and watched as he ordered the maids and the cook to leave the house immediately. He paid them all—ransom money, Naiima thought, meant to curb their resentment of their masters and perhaps even induce a sense of loyalty. When they had all left the house, Besharat the Bastard locked all the doors, and barricaded them with long wooden poles. He nailed all the shutters closed, and ordered his children again to keep away from the cracks in the doors and windows; members of the Tudeh, it was known, were ruthless fighters who spared no innocents. For weeks they had been walking the streets, intimidating the citizens in order to gain support. Outside every house, they stopped and shoved the blades of their butcher's knives through the cracks in the doors and windows, stabbing unsuspecting inhabitants.

Besharat the Bastard emptied the safe in his room, and hid the contents inside the sacks of flour stored in his basement. He rolled up the more expensive rugs on the floors and the walls, and dragged them up three stories to a storage room beneath the roof. Then at last he called the household and, trembling, broke the news:

"The Shah has fled the country," he said. "There's going to be a bloodbath."

In the summer of 1953 the Shah's twin sister, Ashraf, had been in exile in Europe when she was approached by members of the American CIA. They asked her to return to Iran, smuggle herself into the palace where the Shah was surrounded by Mossadeq's soldiers, and deliver a word to His Majesty. Always the braver and more ruthless of the twins, Ashraf agreed. She returned to Iran with the aid of friends, reached Queen Sorraya, and handed her a letter, the contents of which have never been fully discovered. Two weeks later the Shah and Sorraya boarded a small plane and left Iran in the dark of night. They flew to Baghdad, and from there to Rome. Behind them, the CIA moved in to fight the Russians.

They did not bring troops; they hired an army in Iran. They paid starving, unemployed Iranians, and asked them to stage demonstrations in support of the fleeing Shah. They enlisted the help of Shaaban the Brainless, leader of a workers' union in Tehran. Shaaban carried around piles of banknotes that he distributed to anyone who would declare himself a lover of the Crown. They spent so much money and stirred such force that Mossadeq became terrified:

"The CIA has come to kill *me*," he cried.

No longer the bold man with the unfearing heart, he ran

to his home—this veteran of Reza Shah's jails, who had been willing to sacrifice three generations of Iranians for the sake of pride—and surrounded himself with armed soldiers. On the streets, fighting had broken out between the Tudeh and the Shah's new supporters.

In the house of Besharat the Bastard, Yasmine had not slept for three nights. She remained at the window, dressed in her street clothes and her shoes, and watched every event on the street. She had no money; she had never seen Peacock after the day she came to warn Yasmine against leaving. But she told herself that she would sell the ring elsewhere, and raise enough to buy food for a few weeks and a ticket out of Iran.

Above all, she kept herself from seeing her children.

On the morning of August 19, 1952, Yasmine saw American tanks rolling down Palace Street toward Mossadeq's house.

"My God, it's happened!" Naiima screamed downstairs, running in circles like a blind mouse.

Gunfire erupted on the street. From her window Yasmine saw Mossadeq climb onto the roof of his house, and run away like a thief in the night. She saw Tudeh soldiers fleeing before American tanks. Seeking shelter, they scaled the walls of Besharat the Bastard's home, crawled through the barbed wire, and landed in his garden with bloody clothes and pieces of torn flesh hanging from their hands and faces. They ran through the dusty, dry rose gardens, and broke down the door to the house. Yasmine was ready. She grabbed her coat and ran.

Downstairs she heard the sound of her children crying. In a blur, she saw Besharat the Bastard, his son and older daughter in his arms, looking for refuge from the invading Tudeh mob.

"Yasmine!" he called her, his voice—she was startled at this—ringing with the same urgency with which he had spoken to her in Paris. "Yasmine!"

She went out the door.

On the street, she forced her way through the mob, blinded by fear and dust, deafened by the sound of gunshots and the roar of the tanks rolling toward her.

"Stand back!" someone screamed at her, but she kept running. "Stand back!"

The tank fired. The force of the explosion hurled Yasmine off her feet and carried her a few yards till she crashed against the side of the gutter. Daylight burst into flames. Yasmine heard the sound of the wounded screaming, and felt the heat of the fires around her. Mossadeq's house was half-crumbled. The Tudeh was on the run.

Lying there on the ground, Yasmine watched the battlefield on Palace Street and, for the first time since she had left Paris, understood she could not go back: "It's like *this*," she told herself. "It's all destroyed."

She saw the streets leading nowhere, the buildings inhabited by rats, the monuments wrecked and obsolete. She saw the invalids who still felt pain in limbs they no longer owned, women shivering in food lines, dropping dead. She saw her parents' apartment, full of cobwebs and her mother's moth-eaten clothes.

It was too late.

She tottered back to the house of Besharat the Bastard and accepted her prison.

 Cyrus the Magnificent lived with Peacock for a year—until Laa-Laa sold to Heshmat the apartment building she had stolen from Cyrus. Cyrus the Magnificent rented his old flat back from his mother, but everywhere, he saw reminders of Laa-Laa. He hated her and missed her at the same time. He would have taken her back— even married her, he knew, to keep her from leaving again— but she did not come, and Cyrus grew resentful. Instead of Laa-Laa, he directed his anger at the Russians. In the months after Mossadeq's failed coup, when the Americans brought the Shah home and once again made him King, Cyrus the Magnificent watched the crackdown on the Tudeh and other communist sympathizers with inordinate pleasure. He told himself the Shah was avenging *him*.

The Shah had returned to Iran determined not to lose control of his throne again. He captured Mossadeq, placed him under house arrest—he was afraid to create a martyr by killing him—and set out to purge the country of all opposition. In the armed forces he apprehended a thousand officers on charges of conspiracy and sedition. In the cities he appointed military governors to search every house for communists. Day after day, suspects were rounded up and taken away to prison. Trials were short, sentences predetermined. Defense attorneys sympathetic to their clients ran the risk of coming under suspicion. Judges who failed to hand down severe sentences were investigated and abused.

Throughout the crackdown and the purges, Cyrus the Magnificent felt his anger subside and his wound begin to heal. He still despised Russia, but he forgot Laa-Laa's betrayal and went back to look for her in the house she had bought with money from the sale of the building. She lived there with her new lover, and she had told the servants to beat Cyrus if he ever came calling for her.

Cyrus the Magnificent never did recover from the humiliation of being confronted by Laa-Laa's maids. Nevertheless, he stayed in Iran, and told himself he would never leave. He still loved America, but he could not bear the thought of being so far away from Laa-Laa.

He found himself drawn to the increasing numbers of Americans who came to Iran after 1953. They were technical and military advisers, and they brought their families and lived in exclusive enclaves built in the most prestigious parts of the city. They brought their music, their schools, their films. When the first movie house opened in Tehran, featuring an American Western, Cyrus the Magnificent felt he was about to be reborn.

He had seen the film seven times already, sitting amid a handful of adventurous youths who brought their own chairs—the theater did not provide a seat except on the floor—when someone's mother walked in and dragged her son out of the hall. Within minutes the theater was invaded by frantic parents trying to save their children from the evils of cinema: the local mullah, Cyrus soon learned, had declared movies unholy.

"The images on the screen," the mullah had declared that day in the course of his afternoon sermon, "come to life by extracting the souls of the people in the audience."

There was no point in questioning the issue; the mullah in question had confirmed the ruling with a superior, who had in turn asked God in his sleep.

"It stands to reason," the superior mullah had argued in defense of the theory. "How else could these American actors suddenly learn to speak in Persian?"

So the theater shut down, and it would have remained closed except that many young men from more educated backgrounds protested, and at last the owner gave in to his greed and reopened with a different film. This time the room filled up. Driven by curiosity, anyone with the slightest taste for danger had come to find out if souls were indeed extracted from among the living.

On the day of the first screening, Cyrus the Magnificent stood up for the national anthem, sat through the newsreel, and watched the entire movie without incident. When the lights went on, everyone gathered their chairs and their picnic dinners and filed out into the street, where a crowd of their friends waited for the results of the encounter. They were still talking in the alley when the theater owner appeared, looking as if he had been bitten by a scorpion.

"God help me," he whispered to Cyrus the Magnificent. "There is a corpse sitting in that hall."

* * *

302

So the theater shut down indefinitely, and Cyrus the Magnificent felt a void in his life he could not fill. In 1960, looking to duplicate the thrill of the movies, he went to the American Community School in Tehran and asked for a course in theater and acting. The school, he was told, offered no such course. The closest they came was history lessons. Cyrus the Magnificent enrolled in a class, and met "Miss Jansen from Hollywood."

She was the school's history teacher, serving a three-year term in Tehran. She was not beautiful or glamorous or rapacious, like Laa-Laa. She had a flat bust, skinny legs, dull blond hair.

Cyrus the Magnificent knew she was not pretty, but he found himself drawn to her nevertheless: she was American—Laa-Laa's political opposite—and he thought if he married her, he could forget Laa-Laa and find the courage to leave Iran.

He invited her to his house and showed her the postcards he had collected during the war. She brought her gramophone and played for him her American records. They made love. She told him he was magnificent: "Better," Cyrus boasted later to his friends, "than American men." He knew she was flattering him, that she had been a virgin until she slept with Cyrus, and had no way of comparing him to anyone else. He liked her kindness.

"Miss Jansen from Hollywood," he introduced her to his friends, "land of moguls and movie stars."

He went to see his mother, and announced he was marrying Miss Jansen.

"But she's a *Christian*," Heshmat cried. "Jews don't marry Christians." Cyrus the Magnificent married "Miss Jansen from Hollywood," and told her he would go back with her to America. The year was 1964, and the world, as Cyrus liked to say, was again about to be remade.

Ruhollah the Soul of God was born at home, in a small mud-brick shack in the rural town of Khomein. His father, a mullah of the Musavi clan, was poor but powerful. He claimed to be a direct descendant of the prophet Muhammad. He wore a black turban; lesser clerics wore white.

Ruhollah the Soul of God spent his childhood amid the tumult of the Constitutional Revolution. In 1921 he moved from Khomein to Qom, where he studied theology and learned to preach. There he heard of a Cossack soldier—Reza Khan the Maxim—who had risen to the top of Persia's government. Ruhollah the Soul of God had never liked the Cossacks or the government. He knew he would despise Reza Khan.

He stayed in Qom and continued his studies. He watched Reza Shah pave streets through mosques and bazaars, close down religious schools, conscript the youth of Iran—the mullahs' soldiers—into his own army. At the mosque, and inside religious circles, Ruhollah began to preach against Reza Shah. At thirty he married Batoul, the thirteen-year-old daughter of a powerful mullah in Tehran. Later he earned the title of Ayatollah—Image of God. When Reza Khan implemented a law demanding that every citizen choose a surname, Ruhollah the Soul of God called himself Khomeini.

He watched Reza Shah undo himself by opposing the Russians. Ruhollah the Soul of God told himself he could do better: Reza Shah had commanded only an army; Ruhollah the Soul of God would command heaven and hell.

In 1941 he published a book—*Secrets Exposed*—in which he attacked the monarchy and its servants. Over the next decade he professed a vigorous application of Islam to the everyday life of all citizens, preached that the clergy must direct itself at politics as well as social issues. He preached for ten years, but in the 1950s he found his voice drowned by the clamor of Mossadeq's rebellion. Ruhollah the Soul of

God was growing restless and impatient. He would have made a bid for control of Iran, but the Americans brought back the Shah.

In the ten years after Mossadeq's coup, Iran became rich from oil. The Shah did not insist on national control; he shared the profits equally with a consortium of British, European, and American companies. Nevertheless, Iran's share of profits rose from $34 million a year to $437 million. With the money, the Shah rebuilt the armed forces destroyed by the occupation, established schools and hospitals, constructed roads and dams. He brought jobs, education, a system of public sanitation and health. Seven hundred years after the Shiite invasion, he said, Iran was once again on the road to progress.

But the people's expectations grew faster than the Shah could fulfill them. The most fortunate ones moved out of their hovels and away from their poverty. Overnight, a class of millionaires was created who lived in mansions, drove American cars, and took shopping trips to Paris and Rome every summer. They stopped practicing their religion. They never went to the mosque. They celebrated Christmas: they liked the tree, and the lights, and the amusing old man in the red suit.

In the provinces, peasants and shepherds and small-town merchants heard of the new wealth, strapped their lives onto their backs, and came to the cities. They saw the mansions, but when they searched for a place to live, they were forced into shantytowns made of tin cans and cardboard, into the old Jewish ghetto now abandoned by Jews, into hovels dug underground, or into wooden crates.

"Look around you," Ruhollah the Soul of God screamed in the mosque. "The Shah has given Muslims nothing but pain and shame and moral degeneration. He has allied himself with infidels, made himself rich at others' expense."

The royal family—with its sixty-three princes, princesses, and cousins—was Iran's wealthiest. The Pahlavi

Foundation, headed by Princess Ashraf, owned shares in all of the most profitable companies, and allowed access only to those it favored. The Shah's relatives were in charge of every aspect of financial life in Iran. They acted arbitrarily, took anything they wanted without even bothering to write a law to that effect. They went hunting in the northern forests, and discovered a beautiful new region upon which to build a villa. They did not buy the land. They confiscated hundreds of acres—to assure privacy.

"Look around you."

In 1958 the Shah had divorced Sorraya after a childless marriage, taken his third wife—Farah—and fathered a son. Confident of his power, he had moved with greater strength against the clergy, taking away their lands to give to the peasants. He had formed a closer relationship with the United States, and gave women the right to vote.

In 1964, Ruhollah the Soul of God called for demonstrations against the Shah. Overnight, the streets filled with his disciples. Khomeini addressed the crowd and let his rage erupt:

"I beseech you," he warned the Shah, "*respect* the religious authorities."

The Shah quelled Khomeini and sent him to exile in Turkey. But Khomeini went to Iraq and, from there, reestablished contact with his disciples in Iran. Throughout the sixties and the seventies, they would spread his message inside the country. They worked through a network of mosques and religious meetings, and later began to distribute the Imam's sermons recorded on cassette tape. The Shah, Khomeini insisted, must be overthrown.

"Sooner or later," Cyrus the Magnificent warned his relatives in the privacy of a quiet room away from the ears of the Shah's spies, "sooner or later, the mullahs will defeat the Shah. It has always been that way, and when it happens, God help the Jews."

He told his wife they were leaving for America, and bought two tickets for Hollywood. They were all packed and ready to leave when Laa-Laa returned.

It was winter 1965, and Miss Jansen from Hollywood had spent the day shopping for souvenirs to take back to America. She came home and smelled a light perfume. She went through the corridor feeling a heavy silence, sensing she had walked uninvited into a stranger's home. The door to the living room was made of carved oak, with a large inset of etched glass. Through it, Miss Jansen from Hollywood saw the end of her life.

Cyrus the Magnificent stood pale and immobile, facing a woman in a summer dress, with intoxicating eyes and scarlet lips. Miss Jansen from Hollywood had never seen Laa-Laa. She saw the terror in her husband's face, and recognized the enemy.

She remained petrified in the hallway. She felt a strange heat—as if the air had suddenly run out, as if she were standing next to a flaming stove in the dead of summer. Sweat ran from her scalp onto her face and down her chin. She took off her lambskin coat, but her dress was stuck to her, and her shoes had become small tubs of water.

Cyrus the Magnificent went up to Laa-Laa and stood so close to her that their foreheads almost touched. He raised a hand to touch her. She closed her eyes. He was about to kiss them, but then he stopped.

Abruptly, he left the room. He did not even see Miss Jansen as he walked by her. Behind him, Laa-Laa remained immobile, shocked from the rejection she never thought possible, and when at last she had gathered her strength enough to leave, her face had lost its beauty. She marched slowly past Miss Jansen, opened the door, and stepped out. It was cold. Laa-Laa shivered in her summer dress.

* * *

In the days and weeks that followed the encounter with Laa-Laa, Cyrus the Magnificent became ill and impatient. He stayed in the house all the time, as if afraid to step out and find Laa-Laa on the street, as if certain he would not have the power to resist her a second time. The morning of his scheduled departure for America, he sent for his family to come to the house and say farewell. He hugged his brothers and sisters, everyone's children. He cried on Peacock's shoulder. Then he sat in a taxi next to his American wife, rode away to the airport, and never even looked down to see his home and his country fade under the wings of the airplane. The year was 1965—the beginning of Iran's decade of glory— but Cyrus the Magnificent knew he would never come back.

 Besharat the Bastard became rich in the oil boom— so rich he hired six accountants just to keep track of his income. He had started by selling imported cigarettes, but after Mossadeq, he expanded into household electronics, automobiles, and industrial machinery. For everything he sold, the market in Iran was vast and voracious. Besharat the Bastard occupied a twelve-story building as his headquarters, kept three hundred families on his payroll, bribed countless officials, and reserved an entire dock at Iran's southern customs just for his products. Still, every night when he left the office, sitting in the back of his chauffeur-driven Mercedes with the tigerskin rugs, Besharat the Bastard prayed aloud he would die that night in his sleep.

In 1953, Yasmine had returned home and begun to fight once again with Naiima. She never won, but she managed to poison the house with her anger, and in the end she deprived Besharat of any pleasure his children may have brought to him. They grew up in an atmosphere of enmity and intrigue—objects of everyone's rivalries, witnesses to everyone's cruelty. The girls married as soon as they could. The boys stayed—Naiima made them stay—but they drew away from the two women, cut themselves off from their father, and bore his name in shame. Yasmine watched them, clenched her jaws in anger, and, one by one, lost her teeth—so that by the age of forty—this woman who had embarrassed men with her beauty was toothless and old.

Naiima, on her part, swallowed her hatred and became fat—so bloated she could no longer climb up and down the steps of the house on Palace Street. She served Besharat with everlasting devotion, obeyed his every wish, accepted his every insult. She observed the rites of purity as religiously as in the past, lay in his bed even as he belittled her. Up to the time of her menopause she tried to become pregnant—drinking potions and buying spells, even visiting the Russian hospital without asking permission from Besharat the Bastard.

Yasmine found out about the visits to the hospital. She tried to betray Naiima, told Besharat she had heard Naiima talking on the phone with doctors, had seen her leave early in the morning just after her husband stepped out of the house, and come back in the afternoon, drained and pale and full of tears. Besharat the Bastard believed Yasmine, but he did not become angry. He felt pity for Naiima, and called her to his room that night and told her it was over, that he had accepted her as she was: a woman, though she could not have children; a friend, though she lied to him; a wife, though she had destroyed his passion for Yasmine. They had grown old together. She was his lover and his warden.

But of all the tragedies of his life, Besharat the Bastard suffered most from the dust: it had begun to attack him first in the house on the Avenue of the Tulips, and every year it had become thicker and more pervasive. It lingered in every corner and on every shelf, in the fringes of all the rugs, in the folds of the drapery, between the sheets. The maids cleaned morning and night, but the house was always dirty. They left the furniture perfectly arranged, and came back to find it in disarray. They swept the floors, and saw grime return as soon as they put away their brooms. Naiima yelled at the maids, and Besharat screamed at his mother, but no one could chase away the dust. Yasmine washed herself four times a day—standing naked in her bathroom, where she rubbed her skin with a wet sponge—but the moment she stepped out, she tasted grit between her teeth again.

"It's from the street," Naiima declared. The Avenue of the Tulips had become crowded with heavy pedestrian traffic, vendors and beggars, and increasing numbers of cars. Tehran had grown northward, and the houses in Besharat's neighborhood were replaced by stores and garages and cabarets. In Besharat's house, flowers refused to bloom, trees never grew, and the statues he had once commissioned with such pride were pitted and crumbling. The pools were filled with moss, and all the poison in the world would not kill the frogs. Besharat the Bastard moved, but the dust followed him.

On Palace Street, his neighbors lived in immaculate rooms and bathed in sparkling pools, but every time Besharat opened a faucet, water poured out gray. In Vanak, Blue-Eyed Lotfi raised orchids and exotic plants in his garden, while Besharat the Bastard fired one gardener after another, and never managed to grow a twig. Even as he moved to the very north of Tehran, to Zafaraniyeh, he found the windows so clouded by dust that the house was in permanent darkness.

Terrified of the entropy he could not stop, lost in the bitterness he could not overcome, Besharat the Bastard retired in 1965, and never came out in public again. He closed the doors of his house on visitors, shut the windows on the dust, and sat alone at the table where, years ago, the Boys' Mother had come begging for food.

Nargess the Washing-Woman had come to Tehran in the early years of the 1960s. She had come with her husband, who was a bricklayer, and with their three young sons. In Tehran she gave birth to a fourth and last boy that she named Mehr-Allah—God's love—because she had been close to forty when he was conceived, and she believed he was a miracle.

Nargess the Washing-Woman had set out for Tehran with great expectations. She would put her husband to work, and send her sons to clerical school. She would buy a house, become rich, hire maids to wash *her* clothes for a change. She would stop working, sit in the sun every day and bask in the world's envy. Instead, Nargess the Washing-Woman was forced to live in the Pit, in an abandoned hovel that had once belonged to a Jew. From the moment she arrived until she left the Pit twenty years later, Nargess the Washing-Woman was convinced she would burn in hell for the crime of living in a house once inhabited by infidels. The walls, she believed, were infected with the odor of Jews. The floor was soiled no matter how often it was scrubbed. The air was cursed, and it was all the Shah's fault.

She blamed the Shah for not making her rich enough to live elsewhere, blamed his father for letting Jews out of the ghetto and allowing Muslims to replace them. It was true that her life had improved in Tehran. But there were others from her background who had become rich beyond reason: there was a shepherd who now owned factories, a truck-driver who was head of Iran's television. There were Jews—Jews—who lived in the hills of Shemiran, in homes with cast-iron gates and seven-car garages, while God-fearing Muslims worked for them and remained invisible.

Nargess the Washing-Woman was convinced that the Shah had set out to destroy the institution of Islam. It was not only what he did for the Jews—allowing them to become rich, send money made in Iran, by the sweat of Iranians, abroad to Israel where it supported the Zionist empire that was bent on destroying Islam. It was not his offensive treatment of the clergy, or simply the fact that he lived a corrupt and unholy life—gambling in foreign casinos or in his palace, sleeping with infidel women when he went on skiing vacations to France. It was not just the shameful manner in which he allowed his sister, Ashraf, to conduct herself—changing husbands like underwear, whoring around with every young boy she could get her hands on, and later rewarding the good ones with American Corvettes, taking over every profitable business in the country, and all the while boasting of her "humanitarian efforts on behalf of the poor and the downtrodden." It was not even that he allowed the importation of washing machines—pieces of metal, Nargess had been told by her sons, that replaced people in the task of cleaning clothes. She had not seen the machines, and she could not imagine they were real. The Shah, Nargess believed, had transgressed much further and more irreversibly than that: he had allowed television.

Nargess the Washing-Woman had seen television when she first came to Tehran—before she learned that it was unholy—and she had been so intrigued by the invention, she had actually stood and watched the man who sat inside the box talking at her. Then all of a sudden she had realized she was unveiled—there in the middle of the living room of the house where she had been washing clothes—that her hair was exposed and her sleeves were rolled up, showing the flesh of her arms, and then she had screamed and run away and wept the whole night for her tarnished honor.

Her husband had forbidden her to work in the house with the television set, but everywhere else, Nargess would soon discover, the same problem persisted. The other maids confirmed her suspicions:

"The man in the box," they said, "looks at you like a dog in heat."

Nargess the Washing-Woman never laid eyes on another television set again, but she did learn later on, when even believing Muslims had been charmed into allowing evil-eyed strangers into their privacy, that the Shah had put unveiled women into television boxes and in everyone's home.

In almost every house she worked, Nargess the Washing-Woman ran into Peacock. She had noticed Peacock first at the Pit—this old, old woman with the crumpled skin and the hardened joints, dressed in all the colors of the devil, as she had stood one early dawn in the street outside Nargess's house. Nargess the Washing-Woman had not known many Jews in her life, but she recognized them all by their smell.

"Get lost, you old bitch," she had screamed at Peacock through the half-open door of the courtyard where she sat to have tea with her sons. Later that morning, washing clothes in a house at Shemiran, she had looked up and seen Peacock walk past her in the yard.

"God help me," she had exclaimed. "That thing is a ghost."

She saw Peacock in other homes, on the street, back in the Pit. She asked the other maids. They confirmed that Peacock was a Jew, that she worked for the Shah and his relatives, that she owned enormous wealth.

"In her house at Niavaran," they told Nargess, "she has a trunkful of jewels she doesn't even lock."

Nargess the Washing-Woman became fascinated with Peacock. She could not help thinking of the jewels in the open trunk, serving no purpose, stolen—Nargess assumed—from helpless believers like herself. She could not help her anger every time she saw Peacock in the Pit, walking around in her masquerade clothes with the glaring colors and the rows of gold, smiling at the Muslims who knew her from the street, who went to her—this Jew whose life, some mullahs still claimed, was worth less than a dog's—asking her to use her influence in their favor, speak to her friend, the wife of the Minister of Housing, to help place their name on a waiting list for apartments, or to call the Minister of the Interior and try to get him to issue a telephone after the applicants had waited four years.

313

The next time Peacock came to the Pit, Nargess the Washing-Woman stopped her.

"What do you want here?" she asked Peacock outside her house. "Why do you come here?"

"I used to live in this house." Peacock smiled with her toothless gums. "I lived in the same room you live in. I come back so I won't forget."

Nargess the Washing-Woman was a good Muslim and an honest maid. But in the face of all the riches she saw, she could no longer accept her own poverty or justify another's wealth. One morning she followed Peacock out of the Pit, and all the way up to her house in Niavaran. She waited outside till Peacock had had her tea and left for work. Then she forced the lock on the door and went inside.

The house was small, built in a European style, without a courtyard. There was a garden in front, where Peacock grew mint and jasmine, a long and narrow hallway covered with a Persian rug, a small kitchen empty but for a gas stove and a refrigerator. There were two bedrooms—one bare, the other decorated only with a bed and a radio. Next to the bed, there was a wooden chest without a lock.

"There!" Nargess the Washing-Woman felt her heart about to burst. She grabbed the top of the chest, and flung it open.

She stared at the contents. She reached inside, felt with her hands what her eyes did not believe. She picked up a fistful, held it to the light, then grabbed more. She emptied the trunk, but still she remained baffled.

There were clothes, tattered and worthless and old—men's trousers and shirts and coats, a dozen hats, a few handkerchiefs. There was a bottle of perfume never opened, silk scarves that came apart at the touch, sheer stockings still wrapped, a white linen gown. There were combs with blue enameled handles, a small vinyl record with the picture of a gigantic white dome in the center, bottles of nail polish, powder, and a yellow wind-up bird that sang in a cage. There were old schoolbooks and pictures of women in outdated clothes, lace veils and silver brushes, music boxes that whispered soft, foreign tunes, china dolls with long painted lashes, and mirrors so beautiful they could lie.

Nargess the Washing-Woman stared at the junk before her and, for the first time in her life, was ashamed of her own hatred.

 Tehran's days were long and noisy and filled with the sounds of traffic. There was no dawn, no moment of beauty and peace when darkness faded and the sun came up and the air, as in Esfahan, emitted the scent of blossoming jasmine. In Tehran the sun was brutal and impatient and without grace. Night erupted into daylight, and then there was no refuge from the noise and the crowds and the mad rush of lives in hot pursuit. Hours passed and still the day was young. The crowd thickened on the streets, and cars were ensnared in the never-ending congestion. The shops did not close until midnight. Phone lines were always jammed. Peddlers harassed every household. Beggars pulled on the sleeves of pedestrians, only to curse them if the offering was small. Children climbed onto the windshields of cars and begged to sell American cigarettes. Then at last it was dark, but the streets still buzzed, and the traffic remained knotted. People slept from exhaustion only to awaken with a start, and realize it was day again.

Cyrus the Magnificent wrote urgent letters from Hollywood:

"You must leave Iran," he pleaded with Heshmat and Peacock. "Sooner or later the Shah is going to fall. You must leave before the mullahs take over."

He had never forgotten the incident with the movies: one mullah's ban against films having led to a city-wide opposition that would take years to undo. It was then, Cyrus the Magnificent would later realize, that he had come to understand the awesome power of the clergy in Iran: one mullah's claim that watching movies would lead to death— baseless as it seemed to all the graduates of Tehran University's Faculty of Medicine—had indeed come true before the eyes of the skeptics gathered that afternoon at the theater on the Avenue of the Tulips. Cyrus the Magnificent remembered standing there that afternoon in the alley, caught in the uproar that erupted as soon as word of the death had spread among the crowd, and the moment someone called, "Dead man! Dead man in the theater!" the entire southern part of Tehran had boiled to life. A mob had attacked the theater, raised the corpse—already stiff in the chair—above their heads, and walked the length of the Avenue of the Tulips, screaming, "Dead man in the theater!"

After that, it was as if an ill wind had begun to blow inside Cyrus's head, nudging him at first, making him hot and ill at ease and always seeking respite. The air in Tehran had begun to feel heavy in his lungs. The night had lost its glory. The streets, painted with familiar scenes, had begun to seem overcrowded and ugly. Cyrus the Magnificent was no longer the child he had been when he first dreamed of living in the "Civilized West." Laa-Laa had destroyed his innocence and made him bitter. Hollywood was no longer a child's dream. It had become a safe haven for escape.

It was because of the wind that he had married Miss Jansen from Hollywood—though she was not pretty, or Jewish, and he had no passion for her. It was the wind that had helped him resist Laa-Laa when she came back promising eternal faithfulness. He had left Iran, but even now, as he heard news of the country's astonishing progress and unprecedented accomplishments, Cyrus the Magnificent felt the wind, and could not shake the nauseating smell of corpses in theater chairs.

In 1971 the Shah celebrated twenty-five hundred years of continuous monarchy in Iran. He invited heads of state from sixty-nine nations, received them in royal style at Persepolis, and spent $200 million in one week. Meanwhile, in the province of Fars where the celebrations were held, and in neighboring Sistan and Baluchistan, famine took scores of Iranian lives.

From Iraq, Ayatollah Khomeini issued a message in response to the celebrations:

"Anyone who studies the manner in which the Prophet established the government of Islam will realize that Islam came in order to destroy these palaces of tyranny.... Are millions of the people's wealth to be spent on these absurd celebrations?"

The message, reproduced by dissident Iranian students in the United States, had also been distributed among believers inside Iran.

In 1973 the Shah led the OPEC oil cartel in a demand for higher prices from the West. He spoke of building a petrochemical plant in Iran, becoming independent of the West, producing finished petroleum products in Iran instead of buying them abroad.

At home, he cut off Savak's "donations" to the clergy that kept them from speaking out against the Shah, denounced the mullahs as "medieval black reactionaries," and welcomed Jews, Christians, and Baha'is into ever-higher echelons of public life. He talked of uprooting the bazaars, building highways through the old city centers, eradicating "worm-ridden shops" to replace them with supermarkets. He even replaced Iran's Islamic calendar with a new Persian one. He was the Light of the Aryan Race, Iran's political as well as spiritual leader.

Cyrus the Magnificent read a quote from His Majesty in *The Guardian*: "It is true hegemony that We have in Our country. Everyone is behind their monarch, with their souls, and their hearts."

Afterward, Peacock would remember, everyone said that the Shah should have acted differently. He should have known the ills of his nation and responded before it was too late. He should have taken the threats against his regime more seriously, and eliminated the opposition before it had gained momentum. He should have been more fair, less corrupt, more democratic, less eager to westernize Iran. Afterward, everyone looked back and saw the footprints of doom, but up to the days and weeks before the fall of the Pahlavi dynasty, few Iranians believed its demise possible.

In 1977, Jimmy Carter was elected to the United States presidency on a ticket of democracy and human rights. He reviewed Iran's human-rights record and found reports of repression and torture. The repression had been done with the direct consent and clear support of the United States and the West. The torture had been institutionalized under the aegis of the American CIA. Now, suddenly, Carter asked the Shah to loosen his grip upon his nation and restore his subjects' human rights.

Muhammad Reza Shah had never liked Carter. He did not believe the man capable of understanding the principles of government in the Third World. He explained to Carter that he faced a grave danger from the mullahs. He told him about the Russian desire to take over Iran, about the threat of war from Iraq's Saddam Hussein.

"My people," he said, "do not *want* democracy. They do not *understand* democracy."

The most vital issue, he said, was to modernize as fast as possible. The only way to do so, he maintained, was through dictatorial rule. Later, when Iran had achieved universal literacy and people had gained the tools with which to inform themselves about politics, then the Shah would give them the right to choose.

Carter brought more pressure, and placed the Shah in an impasse: the Shah had ruled Iran singlehandedly for twenty-five years, and knew he could not change the system

318

overnight. But he did not wish to alienate the United States, and he thought—in those mad, feverish years of the late seventies when anything seemed possible—that his throne might withstand the force of opposition, that his people loved him and would fight for him, that his army was loyal. Suddenly, to the horror of his closest friends, the Shah dismantled the barriers to speech and action.

He released a number of political prisoners from jail. He let them publish and tell accounts of the horrors they had suffered, let the press print criticism of his regime and even of the Shah himself. He let the Red Cross into his prisons, and dismissed Hoveyda—his Prime Minister of twelve years and one of his fiercest allies—to replace him with a more liberal-minded man. Through the summer of 1977 he let political organizations form and operate in the open. The nationalists joined the Communists, who joined the Islamic Marxists, all in the quest to overthrow the Shah. Aware of the power of religion, they agreed to use a clergyman as a symbol to unite the people: Ayatollah Khomeini was the obvious choice. Everyone lent support to his name, and let him walk in the forefront of the struggle.

And so the ill wind blew and blew and at last culminated in the tragedy that Cyrus the Magnificent had always expected. In 1977, just when the Shah had begun to discover the true scope of the opposition to his regime, a movie theater filled above capacity burned in Abadan. In it, trapped behind doors that had been locked from outside sometime after the start of the film, were four hundred men and women whose souls were spirited away by the images on the screen. Unaware, the authorities put out the fire and opened the locked doors—releasing into the world hundreds of painted effigies now granted eternal life and given the mission to restore to Iran its long-exiled Prophet.

In January of 1978, Khomeini ordered the bazaars closed down, and sent theology students to march down the streets of Tehran, demanding his return. All through that year, demonstrations continued. Khomeini, it was common knowledge, had become Imam, had achieved sainthood. His profile was etched into the moon, a lock of his hair had been found among the pages of the Qoran.

"It's time to go," Peacock echoed Cyrus the Magnificent the next time she went to see Heshmat. "It's too late for me, but *you* must leave while you still can."

They spoke in private, away from the ears of the servants, who mostly supported the upheaval.

"Pack what you can, and don't ever think you will come back."

The next day the women of Iran—women who had been freed of the veil, given permission to divorce their husbands, granted protection from their fathers, even allowed to vote— these women donned black chadors and marched by the tens of thousands to demand the return of the veil.

"It's the Americans," Heshmat's oldest son fumed as he abandoned home and business for what he insisted would be only a temporary exile. "The Americans want to see the Shah go. He's become too independent, too cocky, and they never like that. *They're* putting the mullahs up to this."

Perhaps, Peacock thought. But all across Iran there were women marching who had *opted* to wear their chadors, who held on to the corners of their veils and chanted Khomeini's name.

The demonstrations grew larger and more violent. The police began to shoot. To mourn the dead, Khomeini called for more demonstrations, and every time, the casualties rose. The Shah's generals were begging for action; the time to stop Khomeini, they said, was now.

But the Shah could not decide.

Drawn and gaunt and already defeated, he called the American and British ambassadors to his palace almost every day. He asked them for directives.

"What am I to do?" he pleaded. "What do your governments want me to do?"

The ambassadors gave him conflicting and unclear advice. The Shah realized that both governments had already dismissed him as a viable leader for Iran, and were searching for allies among the opposition. His generals knelt before him, swore allegiance, and promised they could save the Pahlavi throne in spite of the Americans; all that was needed was to eliminate a few thousand men in charge of the revolution. It was a sacrifice well worth making. Without the Shah, the mullahs or the Communists would kill millions. Iran's enemy, Saddam Hussein, would invade and show no mercy.

The Shah called the ambassadors back to the palace.

"How many deaths," he asked, "would Jimmy Carter tolerate in order to save an invaluable ally?"

The generals realized that the Shah was ill, and had lost the will to fight—that he was brokenhearted to see the extent of the hatred against his rule, that he was under pressure from the United States to give in, that he had lost support at home and abroad and knew he would not gain it back again. They suspected that he was undergoing cancer treatment that clouded his judgment and made him vacillate between one position and another—that he was depressed and had lost touch with reality, even refused to read the press, which no longer referred to him as the "King of Kings" and the "Light of the Aryan Race," but simply as "the Shah." They knew that he was betrayed by his most trusted friends, his army, his guards. But as the Shah watched the fall of his throne, he became concerned above all with his name in history, and decided once and for all he would not kill his own people.

For a while he tried to appease the mobs by making more and more concessions. He pretended that he had not known of their ills. He turned against his most loyal friends, blamed them for the corruption and the cruelty of his own government, dismissed them from their posts, and sent them to jail or to exile. He appeared on television, looking drawn and ill and stricken with grief, and for the first time in two decades he tried to speak to his people as if they understood. He did not refer to himself with the royal We, did not call himself King of Kings. He asked for patience, compromise, faith. He warned against the division and chaos that caused weakness. "Don't give in to the plans of foreigners," he warned. "Don't let Iran be consumed by the Russians. Don't let war destroy the Middle East."

In Paris, where he had moved his headquarters, Khomeini responded that the time for compromise had passed. The Shah must go, he said, no matter what the cost to the lives of the believers. He was not afraid to sacrifice people for victory; every dead man became a martyr and inspired others to die for the cause.

On Friday, September 8, 1978, the mullahs called for a sit-in at the Jaleh Square in the slums of Tehran. Wavering once again from his position, the Shah allowed the use of force. His army opened fire, and found itself forever drowned in a sea of blood.

Peacock looked out the window of her house in Niavaran. It was early morning, January 1, 1979. Snow had fallen the night before, and the street was quiet. A man, dressed in his pajamas, opened his front door. He was grabbed by three others with machine guns. They shot him, set fire to his corpse, then left.

All across Niavaran, people heard the gunshot and saw the flames. No one came out of their house. These were the last days of the Shah's rule, and the reign of terror had begun.

In the three months prior to the Shah's departure for Egypt, more than a hundred thousand Iranians had escaped to the West. Among them were Peacock's daughter and grandchildren—gone to join Cyrus the Magnificent in Hollywood—all of her Jewish friends, and most of the Muslims. Heshmat had begged Peacock to go with them.

"I was *born* here," Peacock had said in response. "My daughter is buried here."

She had lived through a century of war and upheaval. She would see the end.

The Shah left on January 16, 1979. Two weeks later, Khomeini returned. Almost immediately, the leaders of the revolution confiscated the wealth and properties of the rich. Peacock lost everything but the house she lived in.

Nevertheless, she stayed in Tehran—alone but for Naiima, who came calling once every few weeks. They had known each other for years, ever since Peacock had first brought the diamond necklace that Besharat gave Yasmine on the occasion of her son's birth. Naiima had always disliked Peacock, but now that they were alone and trapped in war, she came to seek her company. Besharat the Bastard, she told Peacock, refused to leave his house. He had already warned Naiima that the revolution was going to destroy him. One by one, Naiima's servants had quit their jobs, then returned to the house—the women in chadors, the men wearing beards—to warn Naiima of her day of reckoning.

"I can't make Besharat leave, you see," Naiima cried to Peacock, who offered no response. "It breaks my heart to see him so resigned, so unwilling to protect himself. This man was a lion, you know. In his days of glory, no one in the world could have matched his courage or his vision."

On the streets, armed bands of Komitehs—revolutionary councils—and Pasdars—revolutionary guards—conducted massive roundups and on-the-spot executions. Suspects were arrested in their homes, or dragged into parked vans in every neighborhood, where they were summarily tried and sentenced.

323

"There is no room in revolutionary courts for defense lawyers," the leaders of the revolution had declared. "They keep quoting laws to play for time, and this tries the patience of the people."

On February 15, Khomeini carried out his first formal executions. The victims were four of the Shah's top aides, betrayed by him and handed over—in a last attempt to save his crown—to the opposition. Among them was Nassiri, an army general who had served the Shah since the beginning of his reign, and gone to war for him against Mossadeq in the 1950s. Nassiri was taken onto the roof of the former girls' school in Tehran, and shot in the head. His picture, along with that of Prime Minister Hoveyda, appeared on the front page of the evening paper.

Thousands of executions followed. Khomeini gave his people a mission to defend the revolution of God against its enemies, to end the corruption of the rich and the infidel, to stop the influence of the Shah's former agents. Scores of unemployed youth enlisted in the Revolutionary Guard Corps. They were given plain green uniforms with yellow-and-blue badges encased in plastic and attached to their breast pockets. They were given arms—weapons confiscated when the armed forces joined the revolution—and sent out to gather suspects. But they were not trained in the use of the weaponry at their disposal, and they did not understand the awesome power of their tools. Every day a dozen children died accidentally as they played with hand grenades and machine guns. Scores of unsuspecting adults were hit by gunfire from weapons in the hands of playful youths. They were called martyrs—heroes of the revolution.

In Tehran's Behesht Zahra Cemetery, the line to bury the dead was half a kilometer long. Mourners carried the corpses up to the gates of the cemetery, then stood in line for an entire day waiting for undertakers to wash and bury the dead. By nightfall, many were still waiting. They left the corpses in the open air, there outside the gates of "Zahra's

Heaven," and went home to sleep. The next day the waiting would continue, but at the end, many returned disappointed. Undertakers refused burial to anyone who had been killed by the revolution. Enemies of Islam, they said, did not deserve a Muslim burial.

 Naiima could hear the jeeps rolling in her sleep. There were thirty Guards—eight jeeps—and they all had their machine guns aimed to fire. They broke down the gates of Besharat the Bastard's house in Zafaraniyeh, and drove through the desolate garden with the dried flower beds full of dust, where for years nothing had grown. They charged through the front door, blasting it off the hinges in an explosion of dust that mushroomed around them till they were blind. Naiima heard the explosion and sat up in her bed.

"Oh, God," she whispered. "It's happened."

She called for the maid to come and drag her out of bed. She could hear the Guards running through the house, tearing at every room and calling out for Besharat the Bastard. Naiima screamed for the maid again, then suddenly remembered the woman was gone—quit, like all the other servants. Only Mirza Muhammad, the Cook, had stayed with Besharat, but he was a religious man, and he would never enter a woman's bedroom.

Naiima struggled, and at last descended from the bed. As she stepped onto the ground, the weight of her body raised a cloud of dust from the floor. Her nightgown was made of two large white sheets sewn together at the top. Her hair was long and white, hanging around her gigantic face, which dripped with the sweat of fear and exhaustion. She took her crutches and lumbered out of her room on the first floor. Her feet, round and fleshy, left prints in the dust.

A dozen Guards were running up the marble staircase

to the second floor. The rest were scattered through the house, searching the living room and the kitchen, the yard, the bathrooms. They were stabbing the walls, emptying closets and drawers, tearing the covers off the furniture, ripping through the drapery and the rugs, poking holes into the air vents and the ceiling as they looked for incriminating evidence: money stashed away; a bottle of whiskey left over from the days of corruption, or bought on the black market for eighty times its original value; pictures of the Shah or his family, once required in every household to prove loyalty to the Crown, now evidence of opposition to the Imam. They went through the rooms no one had used in twenty years—where dust lay in a blanket three centimeters thick, undisturbed and sovereign in the house of Besharat the Bastard.

"Stand back!" a Guard screamed as he saw Naiima appear at her door. She recognized Mustafa the Orchid—the gardener Besharat had employed in their house on the Avenue of the Tulips. Naiima froze. The Guards were running up the stairs to the second floor. They found Besharat the Bastard's room, and kicked it open.

"Rise! Rise! You're under arrest!"

Besharat the Bastard stood dressed in a three-piece suit, his heavy leather shoes polished to perfection, his face shaved, his hair—thin and gray—combed back with precision. He stood next to the carved wooden table with the screaming lions' heads—the fingers of his right hand gripping the surface of the wood—and he did not move as the guards invaded his room. They put a machine gun to his chest.

"Are you Besharat the Jew, son of Assal of the Pit?"

Besharat the Bastard lowered his head in assent.

"You're under arrest for the crimes of Zionism and corruption."

A Guard pushed him from behind, and Besharat the Bastard started to walk. He moved with difficulty, his joints having atrophied from disuse, the suit he had not worn for years hanging loose from his frame. He came to the top of the stairs and saw Naiima, her face white, covered with a film of sweat and dust, her hands, like red balloons, clutching the corners of her chador under her chin.

"Besharat!" she implored as their eyes met. "My Besharat!"

She watched him descend the stairs. He was thin, old, helpless. In his eyes she saw a world of sorrow.

"Move!" The Guards' leader poked Besharat with the barrel of his gun.

At the bottom of the stairs, Mirza Muhammad the Cook knelt before him and kissed Besharat's hand.

"Agha," he sobbed, "I told them they are wrong. Yesterday the Komiteh stopped me to ask about you, and I told them you never bothered a soul. Agha, these men are non-Muslims, the enemies of Islam. Agha, they are worse than the Shah, worse than the Savak."

Mustafa the Orchid put his gun at the back of Mirza Muhammad's neck, and shot him.

"Let's go," he said, and shoved Besharat again.

At the door, Naiima wailing behind him, Besharat the Bastard stopped for a moment, looked at the explosion of blood and flesh that had been Mirza Muhammad, then turned his head and searched above the stairs. He saw no one.

He crossed the gravel pathway that led through the garden. A jeep waited for him. Trailed by the dust and the sound of Naiima's shrill screams, Besharat the Bastard greeted the Guards quietly. Just as he was about to board the car, he looked up at the house, and caught Yasmine watching him from her window.

They remained frozen, staring at each other. Besharat the Bastard raised a hand and waved at Yasmine, asking for absolution.

*　*　*

Yasmine saw a tall stranger, handsome and arrogant and unsure at the same time, standing outside her parents' apartment in Paris, waving at her one glorious morning as she stepped out in the white and lavender dress she had worn to her wedding. Her mother was wailing behind her.

"My child," she said, "I will never see you again."

 "The Forces of Revolution execute Zionist Criminal." Peacock stared at the headline in the evening newspaper, and felt her stomach burst with fear. She went to Besharat the Bastard's house.

"Ya-Allah! Ya-Allah!" she cried through the dust-filled corridor, but there was no answer. Naiima was not home. Peacock found Yasmine in her room.

"Ya-Allah, Madame Yasmine," she said as she entered uninvited. Yasmine turned away from the window. Her face was streaked with tears.

"I learned the bad news. I have come to offer my condolences, to see if I may lend a hand, to help with the burial and the wake."

Yasmine's eyes were like glass. Her face, wrinkled and deformed for lack of teeth, revealed nothing of the beauty she had once boasted. She made Peacock feel small and incoherent and expendable.

"I thought we could go to Evin and claim the body," Peacock persisted. "We may be able to arrange for a plot in the old Jewish cemetery."

Yasmine turned her back to Peacock, and stared out the window.

"Do what you like," she said. "He had it coming."

Hours later, Naiima came home. She trudged through the garden and into the house, panting from the weight of her body, and the moment she saw Peacock, she burst into tears.

"Peacock, Peacock," she sobbed as she struggled to walk faster. "They *killed* him. They *killed* my Besharat."

She grabbed Peacock's hand in her own wet palms.

"I was there, you know," she started again when her tears had subsided. "I was at the prison when it happened, begging for his life and promising dollars, and all of a sudden a Guard walks in to say he's just been shot."

She broke out sobbing again. She went to the bottom of the steps, and howled for Yasmine.

"Come down," she said. "We're both widows now."

She sat down on the floor. Her face was a deep purple. Her breath was about to shut out.

"And now that he's dead," she told Peacock. "Now, Peacock, that he's dead, there isn't even a son to bury him. He gave his all to have a child, and they all get up and leave the country so that in the end there's no one left to bury him. That was always his biggest fear, you know, that he wouldn't have a son to bury him. I can't even get ten men together in this town to pray for his soul."

She called up to Yasmine again.

"Come on down, Yasmine," she bellowed. "It's all over. We don't have to be enemies anymore."

She turned to Peacock.

"The thing is, you see, he never gave a penny to Israel. That's the thing. He wasn't a Zionist. He didn't give a damn about Israel. Now they kill him, they say, because he was a Zionist. It's like the old days, you know, when they said Jews weren't Iranians. They figure we're all Israeli spies, living here just to make money and send it off to Moshe Dayan."

She was about to call Yasmine for a third time, but she hesitated. She had stopped crying. She looked at Peacock with lucid eyes. She had a thought, a question that had gnawed at her heart ever since the first time she realized she was infertile, when she understood that Besharat the Bastard would take another wife and have her children.

329

"Do you suppose" she asked,—at the end, when nothing else mattered—do you suppose that he thought of her?"

In the kitchen, Peacock found a bag of dried cowslip leaves and made a heavy tea that she forced Naiima to drink. It made Naiima sleepy, and after a while she lay down on the ground and rested her head on Peacock's lap.

Night fell. The house was quiet. Naiima was dreaming of her husband.

He was tall and pallid, terrified as he stood handcuffed in his winter suit. The Guards forced him against a wall. A firing squad aimed at him. Someone screamed. Guns fired.

Besharat the Bastard accepted his death standing up, but just as he was about to fall, he turned to Naiima, and she saw the dark of his pupils before they lost their reflectiveness forever. In them, a young woman with white skin and copper hair raised her purple eyes at Naiima and offered an amber smile.

 It was summer, and the air smelled of tar and wood and gunpowder. By six in the morning the sun was already brutal. By seven, when Peacock woke up, her dress clung to her skin and her stomach turned with the heat.

She had wanted to spend the night on the roof, to escape her bedroom, where the walls perspired heat. Before Khomeini's victory, most people in Tehran had slept on the roof during the summer. Now no one dared stay outside.

Peacock washed her face. She thought she should eat, but it was too hot. She turned on the radio: "revolutionary news" from the front. Taking advantage of the chaos that pervaded Iran's military after the fall of the Shah, Saddam Hussein had invaded Iran in 1980. The war would last eight years and claim hundreds of thousands of lives. Every day, each side claimed complete and unconditional victory over the other.

Peacock left the radio on and went outside. She walked aimlessly past the charred buildings and the skeletons of homes, across mounds of shattered glass, around Revolutionary Guard stations where armed men strip-searched and interrogated pedestrians at random. She saw the shrines— bridal shrines erected on every streetcorner in the name of young boys who had died in the war. It was Khomeini's offering of gratitude to families who lost their sons in the fight against Saddam Hussein: a bridal shrine for the dead son, and a bag of rice for his parents.

Three streets away from her house, Peacock heard children singing a riddle and clapping hands. She turned a corner and came upon a bombed house. She looked inside.

She saw four boys, three teenagers and a child. They were naked, feet chained together and hands tied behind their backs. Around them a dozen girls danced in a circle. They had come to celebrate; they were about to watch an execution.

The boys, Peacock learned, were accused of treason, of conspiracy of thought if not of action, of aiming to bring harm to the revolution of Islam. One had spoken insultingly about the Imam. Two had joined the ranks of the Mujahedin. The last one, barely ten years old, had escaped from the war front and run home to his mother.

"Mama," he pleaded now to his sobbing mother, who begged three Revolutionary Guards for her son's life. "Tell them I will stay this time."

He was so terrified he had lost control of his intestines and dirtied himself. The other boys trembled so hard that the chain connecting all their ankles together clanked as loudly as the girls' singing.

The Guards' leader cried an order. The girls stopped singing. The Guard came forward, gun in hand, and recited a prayer in Arabic.

"Long live the Imam!" he cried.

"Long live the Imam!" his friends repeated the slogan.

The young boy stretched his arms toward his mother and began to run. He managed one step, then tripped over the chain and fell.

Machine guns fired. Peacock watched the blood of children spatter the dirty yellow sky, saw their bodies fall in spasms. She saw their faces in the moment they heard the shots—before the bullets tore them. She heard their parents cry as they watched their sons beg—a last breath, a last prayer.

The boy to the far right landed on his back, his stomach wide open and three holes in his face. The little one drew his limbs inward, and lay still.

"My people," the Shah had said, "do not want democracy."

The Guards' leader put away his machine gun.

"Long live the Imam."

"Long live the Imam."

"Death to America."

"Death to America."

"Death to the agents of Zion."

And there was a moment of calm, an instant when Peacock's eyes locked into the Guard's and she found herself purged of fear, understood that she must act, speak out, if only once, before she died. She stepped into the execution yard—removed and rational—picked up the machine gun with an unwavering hand, and placed the barrel on the man's chest. She did not fire.

"Death to you, you bastard, and your son-of-a-bitch brothers."

Epilogue
1982

In the women's prison where the Guards had taken Peacock, the mullahs ordered an execution. Peacock had been close to the Shah. She had helped the royal family rob the people of Iran by selling them jewels. No doubt she had spied for Savak. No doubt she was a Zionist. Her children were in America and her friends had all been accused of corruption and she herself had threatened a Guard and cried her betrayal in public. The mullahs sent Mehr-Allah the Guard to take Peacock outside the prison and kill her where the body would not be accounted for.

"So how old *were* you?" Mehr-Allah the Guard asked, and Peacock knew her fate. She walked away from her cell, trailed by her cellmate's laughter, and as she felt the hard ground under her feet, she prayed to God for escape.

They went down one gray cement corridor and into another. To their right was a bare wall; to their left, situated at great distances from one another, were the cells. They came up to a vault door. Mehr-Allah the Guard banged the butt of his gun against the metal and cried his name. The door opened. Peacock inhaled her first breath of air in three weeks.

It was night, and the moon smiled at her.

They crossed an empty yard. Someone drove up in a Peykan—Iran's brand of automobile—and Mehr-Allah opened the door for Peacock. He dismissed the driver. There was no need for a second man; Peacock was too frail to pose a threat.

Driving out of the prison grounds, Mehr-Allah looked in the rearview mirror. Peacock was crying.

"Are you afraid?" he asked.

She would not answer.

He drove downtown, and stopped the car just outside the old Jewish ghetto. The streets were deserted under martial law, but there were Guards everywhere. Twice they came up to the car and checked Mehr-Allah's identity.

"I'm putting her out," he told them of Peacock.

He sat in the car, its windows closed, and smoked an entire cigarette. He opened the window only to throw out the butt.

"My son died," he said suddenly. "He walked on a mine—in front of a tank."

Startled, Peacock searched for Mehr-Allah in the rearview mirror. She saw only his eyes.

"Why did you send him?"

There was a long pause. Mehr-Allah sighed.

"Because I *believe*."

He took out his gun and left it on the passenger seat next to him. He came around and opened Peacock's door.

She stepped out.

He opened her handcuffs.

"Don't go home," he told her. He was letting her go. "Don't go anywhere you are known."

Mehr-Allah the Guard had killed many for the cause. He knew he would kill more. But on this day of mourning for his child, he despised his anger, and he could not stand an old woman's tears.

Peacock placed a hand on Mehr-Allah's chest.

"Bless you," she said.

Mehr-Allah the Guard saw his enemy become his friend.

"And you," he answered.

Peacock walked under the indigo sky of dawn, through the ghetto and into the Pit, where she immediately recognized Zilfa the Rosewoman's house: it stood intact, between two structures leveled by Iraqi bombs. Peacock went closer. The door was unlocked, the yard full of garbage. But inside, the house was painted with blue stars.

In the bedroom, Peacock found the alcove where Zilfa

the Rosewoman had once spread her wedding bed with Monsieur Jean. Peacock sat down, reclined against the wall, and slept with the stars.

She was young, barely a woman, and her eyes were the color of rice fields at dawn. She stood before a sparkling mirror in the sun, dressed in a white gown with a shimmering veil. Her body was tall and lean and sculptured. Her hair was thick, her skin smooth and radiant.

She felt a shadow behind her, and turned. It was Solomon the Man, twenty years old, and come to see his bride. He lifted the veil off Peacock's face.

"You *are* beautiful," he said, and this time Peacock believed him.

Solomon the Man raised the veil above their heads— creating a canopy of light and shadow under which they would be married. The sun, filtered through the veil, was almost white.

He touched Peacock's hand.

"I came back for *you*."

A breeze pulled at the veil.

"Don't let go," Peacock warned. Without a canopy, they could not be married.

The breeze snatched the veil out of Solomon's hand.

"Look!" Solomon the Man laughed. The wind carried the veil across the wall of Zilfa the Rosewoman's house, over the roofs of neighboring homes, up into the glittering sky, where it became a small white cloud, and vanished.

Acknowledgments

In our house on Shah Reza Street, the rooms were filled with echoes. The hallways were long and dim and haunted by shadows. The garden—so vast I never thought I could find the end alone—hid the ghosts of strangers who came alive in the moonlight and spoke to me till dawn.

In our house on Shah Reza Street, my grandfather, Khanbaba Barkhordar—known to everyone as Agha (Sire)—walked around with his cane, dressed always in a suit, and commanded the servants as if to demand their soul. He was a tall man with great authority and boundless ambition. Among the first generation of Jews liberated from the ghetto, he had prospered under Reza Shah and spoke his name with the reverence due a god. He had an only son—my father—whom he cherished most in the world and who was to produce, Agha was adamant, many heirs of his own: My father was seventeen years old when he walked with Agha through the doors of my mother's home on Simorgh Street. He was a gorgeous boy, blond and dashing and dressed in a European suit with his hair greased back in the style of the time.

"But she's only fourteen," my mother's parents protested to Agha when he asked for her hand in marriage. Peeking through the living room curtains, I am told, my mother saw her suitor and declared that it would be he, or no one.

There was a fairy-tale wedding in the officers' club in Tehran. Agha invited a thousand guests, showered the bride with jewels, brought the newlyweds to live with him in the house on Shah Reza Street. My parents had three girls. Agha would have no heirs.

* * *

339

In our house on Shah Reza Street, Agha became old and ill and embittered by life's disloyalty. He stopped going out—his health failing so rapidly he hardly ever moved from his office on the first floor—and instead received his callers at home. I remember the men and women who crowded our house in that era and waited their turn to meet Agha. I remember sitting next to him in the big room with the stone floor and the large French doors that opened onto the rose garden, watching everyone and listening to their tales. There was a gray-haired gentleman, an uncle to the Shah, who came to the house every year and spoke to Agha of the memories of a youth they both mourned. There was a servant, a shivering old opium addict who had lost his ability to work and came once a week only to collect his pension. There was a woman—"The Lady of Light," Agha called her sarcastically—who had married twice and buried each husband when he drank, "accidentally," a glass of poisoned tea. Even as a child, watching those strangers and listening to their tales, I knew their voices would haunt me for life.

Agha tired of his callers, and slowly denied audience to most everyone. In his youth he had accepted no limitations. In his old age he refused to compromise with fate. He remained in the house, barely walking at all, and raged against God as if demanding war. My sisters and I, girls though we were, became his only source of happiness. He insisted that we attend the greatest schools, that we receive the best education, that we be sent abroad—to Europe, where women became ladies—and make him proud. He died when we were still schoolchildren, but my parents shared his dream. At a time and in a world where girls were at best expected to "marry well," my parents told my sisters and me that we must work. To them, and to Agha, I owe my first thanks.

I owe no less to my husband, Hamid, who came to

meet me for the first time on the grounds of the UCLA campus in the fall of 1980, and told me that I must give new life to the voices of all the men and women I had carried with me from the house on Shah Reza Street. He was young and handsome and brilliant. Like my mother peeking through the curtain on the day of her courtship, I saw Hamid and thought it was he or no one. From the moment I wrote the first word till the day I stopped working, he alone has made me endure. Among his many contributions to the book is its title.

I am also grateful to my teacher, John Rechy, who first saw the book in outline form, and has since worked with me on every line. He demanded structure where there was chaos, refinement where there was mediocrity, patience where there was despair. "In writing, as in life," he said, "you must try to achieve if only a moment of greatness."

I wish also to recognize the invaluable contribution of the late Dr. Habib Levy, Iran's foremost Jewish historian, whose life's work, *History of the Jews in Iran*, has served as a source for much of the actual history recorded in *Peacock*.

But above all, my thanks go to the people, whose lives have become the stories in this book. I began with my own memories, and then asked questions. I spoke to hundreds of Iranians, Jews and Muslims, old and young. Through years of interviews and volumes of books, I became familiar with a history—albeit recent—that had been buried by the last of the "ghetto generation" as if to wipe away three thousand years of suffering. I learned that Iran is a nation of paradoxes and contradictions, that its people—Jew and Muslim alike—are victims most of all to the violence of nature, the cruelties of their gods, and the ruse of their own ignorance. But above all, I learned that the children of Iran are brave and strong—capable, each of them, of achieving "if only a moment of greatness."

In this, I believe, she will find her salvation.